I thought I was done having strange delusions. How many years does it take for their fracking drugs to wear off?" I looked down at the small band they'd given me in the clear cube. "Should have known the second I *came to* in that room that this was all inside my head." With a vibrating hand, I pulled off what I'd thought was some sort of monitor, or lie detector, I had thought that briefly too. "Of course it's not." I dropped it on the floor. Then put my hand over my forehead. "You're just having a complete psychotic episode, you silly ignoramus, Kara." I laughed. "Porting and mages waving their hands and chanting spells." I snorted. "Most entertaining delusion yet." I walked past the giant men my mind had created. Well, at least I made them interesting, if not a little larger than life.

My illusionary Chase stepped in front of me, a concerned look on his face. I laughed. "Twin kings—*woo*, my mind worked overtime this round." I shook my head and patted him on the chest. "It all seemed so unreal but still very real." I gave him a sad look. "Only the craziest ever think of a place called Alterealm. I guess I've finally caved in." I shook my head. "So many wanting to get back to Alterealm." I wanted to cry suddenly. "Guess I made it before they did."

"What's happened?"

I spun around and looked at Rafael standing in the door looking very stern again. "Son of a bucket!" I rushed toward him. "That's why your walking around like nothing happened. When you should be lying in bed cursing the wound on your backside." I stopped at the step and looked up at him. From two steps below he looked twelve feet tall. Apparently, my mind felt the need to create giants. I grinned up at him. "Because you're not real and I didn't shoot your tush!" I put my hand over my mouth for a second. "I've been doubting my own accuracy since I saw you walking around like I hadn't shot you." I blew out a breath "I do feel better knowing that, really." I looked around. "A palace." My next thought had me slumping my shoulders forward. "Please don't let me come to in some dumpster. I really, really don't want reality to come crashing down like that." I said quietly.

The Telepath

Alterealm Series

Book 7

By J. Risk

Family tree at the end of The Chronos

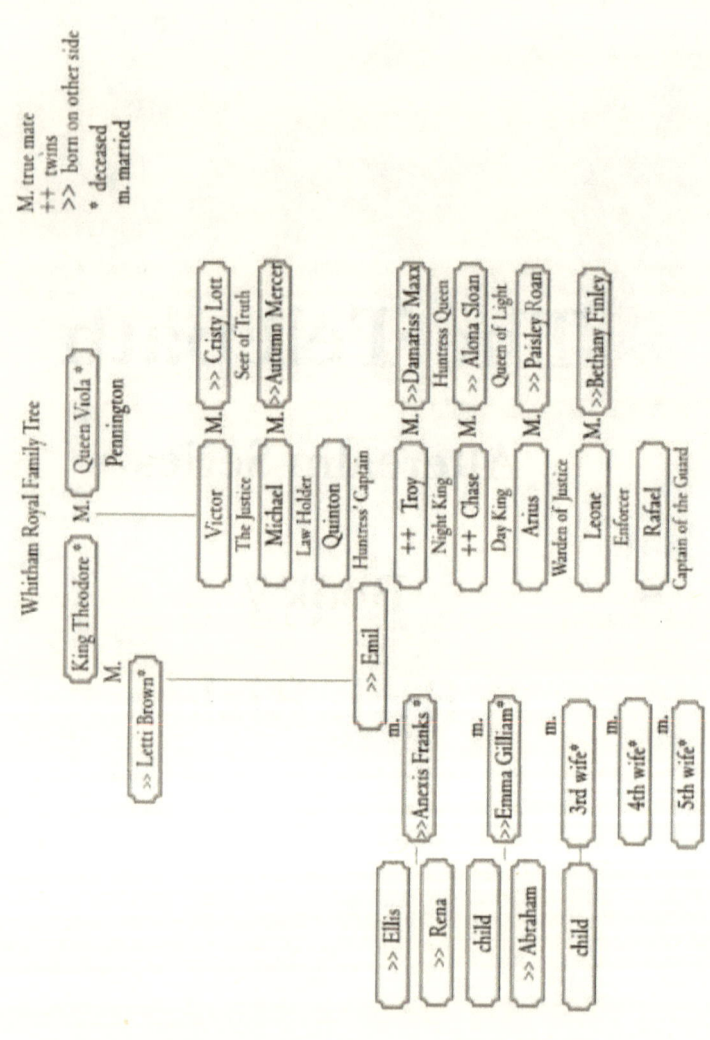

M. true mate
++ twins
>> born on other side
* deceased
m. married

Whitham Royal Family Tree

King Theodore *
M.

>> Letti Brown*

M. Queen Viola *
Pennington

Victor
The Justice

M. >> Cristy Lott
Seer of Truth

Michael
Law Holder

M. >>Autumn Mercer

Quinton
Huntress' Captain

>> Emil

m.

++ Troy
Night King

M. >>Damariss Maxx
Huntress Queen

++ Chase
Day King

M. >> Alona Sloan
Queen of Light

Artus
Warden of Justice

M. >> Paisley Roan

Leone
Enforcer

M. >>Bethany Finley

Rafael
Captain of the Guard

>>Anexis Franks *

>>Emma Gilliam*

3rd wife*

4th wife*

5th wife*

m.

m.

m.

m.

m.

>> Ellis

>> Rena

child

Abraham

>> Abraham

child

Published by FRP
Copyright © 2020 Roxane Kerr
Edited by Gaele L. Hince
Cover art by: Off the Wall Creations

ISBN: (Digital) 978-1-7774682-2-4
ISBN: (Print) 978-1-7774682-3-1

DEDICATION

For Lori — While I was writing this one and finding the next character that fit into the Alterealm family, I thought of you and how much you just *fit* in our family. So glad you are part of it.

xox

Prologue

I held my breath and went back around the corner, there were too many. *He* was here and others with him. I couldn't use myself as bait against eight men that size. I also couldn't be that close and not have all their thoughts slam inside my brain. I looked around and spotted the fire escape, it had a few missing sections, but as long as I stayed below that section, I should be okay. I'd watch from above and see how this played out.

Climbing it was scary, it wasn't in the best condition even up to the parts hanging half off the building. To distract myself from thinking about plummeting to the ground I ran through the past months in my head. What was going on? Had there been some sort of solar flare or meteorological event that had caused so many strange things to take place? I didn't know but things were getting really wacked and I was ready to go find some off the grid cave to live in. I hadn't survived the epic bull crap I'd had the misfortune to live through to be stuck in some insane area where weird things were happening, and women kept going missing and no one—NO one noticed.

By the time I reached the half way point, I decided this was a far enough distance. Perching in the hidden corner of the platform, I looked out between the bars. There were four women, near to my age hanging out back of the old supermarket building. Were they intellectually challenged? It was the only reason I could think of why someone would be that stupid to hang out there in this neighborhood, without large numbers or large friends to keep them company and safe.

Safe. Why didn't anyone think about that anymore?

I looked back to where the guys had been, I couldn't see them. I looked to the other end of the alley. Where did they go? I studied the darkened areas trying to see if they were sneaking up on them. Eight men against four women. It was disgusting. I could say that without a doubt because one of their thoughts had almost made me scream when they'd popped into my head.

Standing up, I leaned over and looked further down the forgotten space. I still didn't see them. I was just about to climb down and go tell those girls to get their butts home and stay there until they grew a brain when a guy came running out of the back of a building and headed toward them.

Big and blond was all I could think. Where were his buddies though? They had to be somewhere. Maybe they sent the pretty face in to distract the women. I'd seen that happen way too much. He was heading straight for them, holding his hand over his ear. Ugh. Just ugh. They were coordinating this abduction. What a slag.

Shaking my head, I'd had enough. I was so done with this city. Pulling my bag off my shoulders, I set it by my feet. As soon as I saved these clueless females, I was out of here. I'd rather live in a forest and take my chances with wild creatures then with human beings. They were disgusting.

Opening it I pulled out the two pieces of my bow. Quickly, while keeping an eye on the blond slag below, I locked the socket together and secured the string on the upper and lower limb. I tightened the riser, so I had good tension and flipped the sight slide out. Opening the quiver case, I hovered over which arrow to choose. Did I want to slow him down or stop him? I looked at him again as he moved closer, trying to appear like he wasn't rushing toward them, he was looking all around him probably making sure no one was around. I was glad he couldn't see me.

Nodding my head, I decided I wanted to stop him. I pulled out one of my bodkin point arrows. It wasn't a blunt point, it was more of a nasty metal pike that stopped very thoroughly. It also wasn't one of my cheap ones but stopping another woman from being taken was worth it.

I nocked the arrow and stood up, making sure my arms and bow cleared everything. Drawing back on it, I got him in the sight and then moved it down, I didn't want to kill anyone, that I couldn't live with, but leaving a mark on his backside I could do. Too bad it was a nice-looking backside was the last thought before I released it.

He went down, then mayhem happened. Four other guys came out of nowhere and a few women as well. These were not the pieces of dross I'd inadvertently heard in my head. The women went rushing toward those clueless females just 'hanging out' and a couple of the men went to my target.

Two dropped down where he lay—with my arrow sticking up in the air. One male with the brown hair was looking at the arrow sticking out of that nice butt and shaking his head. I think he was smiling.

Then I noticed the other two men, looking quite unhappy, as they looked all around them. I squatted back down. Probably a good time to get gone. I quickly disassembled my bow and put it back in my bag. I was just about to get up and climb to the top of the building when a tiny woman jumped down onto the landing with me.

She pulled the cable from her waist and turned to glare at me. "You shot my Rafael."

At least twenty voices flooded into my head out of nowhere. I grimaced, I'd thought the building was abandoned. I focused to block them, then turned my attention back to her.

I was just about to defend my actions when a large, very scary redheaded man dropped down behind her. His icy pale eyes moved over me with loathsomeness. He reached toward me. I put my arm up to block his hand and then my head felt like it exploded into a thousand pieces.

I dropped to my knees and threw up. That's when I noticed I was no longer on the fire escape.

Chapter One

Where the frack was I?

I pushed myself up on my knees, wiping my mouth while trying to figure out how I'd gotten from a fire escape into a tiny clear cubicle. I looked behind me, no, make that a box. Looking up, I blew out a breath, wrong again, a cube.

I jolted up to look all around me. My gear was gone. Getting to my feet, I paused to notice my boots are gone too. Still shaking from throwing up, I stepped around the puddle of spew and went to the wall, running my hands along it, feeling for a door or seam.

A noise startled me and I froze as I watched a red light travel down the side of the wall. It went to the floor, then moved back up, slowly. I wasn't sure, but I think I was just scanned. For what, I didn't know, but I was now at an eight on my freak out scale—or FOS as I liked to refer to it. If I reached ten, it wasn't going to be pretty.

I went closer to the wall and cupped my hands around my eyes, pressing my face against it. I was hoping it was a two-way mirror or—something. I couldn't see anything. Okay, I could do this. I huffed out a few fast breaths, it was clear, no bars, no cement walls, I may not be able to see out, but it gave the illusion of space.

My heart started beating out a staccato rhythm. Maybe that big scary guy was one of the abductors. If so, why did he have a girl with him, and why did the girl get so mad because I shot her Rafael? Rafael, really? Who named their kid that? A few hundred years ago, maybe. Didn't his mother like him?

I realized I was breathing like I had just run a mile and knew I had to slow down or my behavior would change without my noticing. I took a deep breath and closed my eyes. Don't freak out until you know the facts. *You are not locked up. You are not there again. You will never be there again.* Reassured, I turned and put my back against the wall and slid down. I'd just sit here and focus on my breathing for a few minutes.

Grabbing my shins, I pulled my legs tight into me, then froze. I ran my hands down my legs to my ankles. Pish! My knives were gone. How? Did I pass out? Is that how I got here?

The reflection on the far wall changed and suddenly there was someone standing on the other side. He had long black hair and didn't look friendly. From my vantage point on the floor, he looked like a giant.

I stood up slowly, then realized he was just as big as he appeared when I was sitting. His eyes were grey, not green or blue, but grey, and right now they were assessing me, very thoroughly. Crossing his arms over his large chest, he turned his head and spoke to someone. I couldn't see anyone else. I also couldn't hear him.

Turning, I looked all around. Actually, I couldn't hear any thoughts either. I put my hands against the sides of my head. Complete silence. That was rare. I wonder what these walls were made of, and if I could get some of it and make my own bigger cube—*if* I ever got out of here.

Taking a deep breath, I dropped my hands and blew it out slowly. When I turned around the man looked concerned. I stepped over to be right in front of him. Did I want to try reason? Other than abnormally large and scary looking, he appeared fairly intelligent.

"Hello?" I said quietly.

His grey eyes connected with mine.

"Good. You can hear me." I motioned around me. "I'm not sure where I am, but I believe there has been some sort of error, mostly on my part." He didn't move a muscle. "I *may* have shot the wrong man by mistake." I rolled my eyes, "okay, I meant to hit him, I never miss my target—" I realized that babbling wasn't going to buy me any favors. "I-I thought he was someone else that intended harm," I waved my hand around, "or to abduct these clueless twits that probably didn't have a whole brain cell among them."

I took a deep breath and tried to tone down the hostility. I smiled, not sure what else to say. "So-so if I could have my gear," I looked down, "and my boots back, I'll get gone." I nodded. "I was on my way out of this insane city before I spotted those disgusting men scoping out the aforementioned idiots." I took a quick breath, "I was just trying to stop more women from vanishing." I shrugged, not sure what else I could add to plead my case. He hadn't moved, his expression hadn't changed. "You should play poker," I blurted out before I could stop my mouth, "you have the face for it."

He turned to look at something, then shook his head. A woman, the same size as me, came into view. She had short black hair and there was something familiar about her. The giant looked unhappy as she walked by him to the wall and did something there.

"What's your name?" She asked.

I looked all around for the speaker but didn't see anything. "Kara." I gave her a weak smile.

"Cara…"

I shook my head. "Kar-a, like a car."

She gave me a patient look. "Kara, where are you from?"

I frowned, that was not a question I expected. "Planet earth?" I huffed out a breath. "The same city I was trying to leave. Okay, I'm not originally from there—actually I don't know where I'm from originally, but I've been in that decaying city for the last few years." I needed to shut up. I didn't spend a lot of time around people, for obvious reasons and tended to ramble when I was. That, and I was really trying not to freak out from being contained in a clear cube.

She nodded, then turned to the man and said something I couldn't hear. They both turned to look at something out of my view.

Another man came into view. He had pale blond hair and a goatee. He was also as large as all the other men I'd seen. The one with the black hair moved out of view, then that red light was moving down the wall again.

I watched it for a second, then turned to see him come back in. The three of them were looking at a tablet.

"Did I pass?" I asked sarcastically, then regretted it. My mouth and brain needed to work together if I was ever going to get out of here.

The woman moved to the corner again. "We're just making sure it's safe to move you out of there, Kara."

I frowned. "Why wouldn't it be safe?" I moved up to a nine on my FOS. "What's wrong? What did your scan say?" Had all the experimental drugs and therapy they'd tried done permanent damage? My heart felt like it had moved into my throat.

Reaching for the button, she nodded to the men. "Nothing bad. You're fine. You're completely human though, so that's a concern."

I stood there for a second, not even sure if I heard her correctly. I looked from her to the men, then back. "Whew," I pretended to wipe my brow, "and here I was worried I wasn't completely *human.*"

The blond smirked and looked at the dark-haired man for a moment before moving over to the button. "How many men?" He asked.

"How many men what?" I looked to the others like they could tell me. "How many men does it take to screw in a light bulb?" No one moved. "I don't know what you're asking." I reached into my pocket and they all gave me a hard look. "Relax." I pulled out the hair tie with two fingers and held it up for them to see, "just pulling my hair back." I motioned to the floor behind me where I had thrown up. "Feeling a little soiled at the moment." I made fast work of a loose bun and then crossed my arms over my chest.

"How many *disgusting* men did you see stalking those women?" The blond asked in a calm tone.

"Oh." I glared at him, why hadn't he just said that? "Eight."

"How did you know they were after those women?" He raised one eyebrow at me.

"Because I..." I almost said heard their thoughts, which never ended well when you told people *that*. "I overheard them." I had to play it cool. If I could fool doctors that stared at me for hours on end, for years I could fool some complete strangers into thinking I was perfectly normal.

"So why didn't you yell or call the police?" He crossed his arms over his chest.

I moved just my eyes from him to the other two and then back again. "Clearly you're not from the city. Call the cops and say what?" I snorted, "you think they give a pish? Nothing would have happened." I motioned up and down my body, "Do I look big to you? Yelling would have just added me to their to-do list."

The woman gave me an understanding look. I still couldn't figure out why she looked familiar.

I lifted my hands. "Look, I'm sorry I shot Rafael. He just appeared at the wrong time and was running right for those girls."

"How do you know my brother's name?"

Ugh. His brother. Just great.

He looked almost as scary as the dark haired one now.

"Uh, the girl that dropped down onto the fire escape with the big scary dude said *you shot my Rafael*." I tried to look concerned, but honestly, I was at a nine point eight right now and it wasn't looking like I was going to go back down on my FOS anytime soon. "I'm sorry. Is he all right? I aimed for his tush, lots of meaty tissue, nothing important to worry about—"

He looked like he wanted to grin but cocked his head to the side instead. He turned and started talking to the other two, waving a hand around. The woman was nodding, so I really hoped this talk was in favor of releasing me. She turned and walked out of my view.

I sighed and crossed my arms over my stomach, tying to think calming thoughts, which all things considered was never going to help, but I didn't want to start ranting like a lunatic. I turned to pace and saw the spew in the middle of the very tiny space. "Um, I really hate to put you out, but could I at least get housekeeping in here?" I looked behind me to see the blond man was paying attention. "Or, bring me a mop and pail, maybe some air freshener?"

The woman came back and handed the blond man something. He went back to the corner. There was a noise and his hand appeared through a small window. "Put this on."

I looked at it. It looked like a Fitbit monitor. I glanced at the woman to see as she raised her arm and was wearing one that was similar. Hesitantly, I stepped over and took it out of his hand. If it got me out of here, I'd dance a jig, however pretty that wouldn't be.

He pulled his hand back and the small window was gone. I couldn't even tell where it had been. Looking at the device, I turned it over, then put it around my wrist. Why I needed to wear a Fitbit, I didn't know. Maybe they wanted to monitor my vitals. Vitals that would sound like a heavy metal band right now. I did it up, then wanted to undo it when the thought of it being some sort of lie detector thing crossed my mind. I don't normally lie, I just don't always share all the facts. I held up my arm to show it was on.

"Step out from your door and through the door across from it." The blond said.

There was a whoosh noise and a door opened in the wall I'd been leaning on. I went over and stepped out. Two large men were on either side. Running was out of the question. I did as instructed, and the door whooshed closed behind me. I was now in a slightly larger, by that I mean maybe a foot larger than the last cube. This one had a bed and in a little cubby hole in the corner a toilet. "Oh, this is *much* better." I said, not even attempting to hide the sarcasm in my voice.

I turned to see them looking through a wall at me. "So I guess leaving has been taken off the table?"

The blond gave me a quick look. "That's up to Rafael and Victor."

Oh good. The man I'd shot in the butt had some say in whether I got out. "Victor?" I was hoping he was a reasonable person.

He nodded. "I believe you met him on the fire escape."

I was going to be living in a cube for the rest of my life.

Chapter Two

I had no idea how long I'd been in my silent cube. My heart was still beating at an insane rate. I sat on the bed for a bit, trying to stay calm, or as calm as possible in my current situation. If they were monitoring my vitals with their little bracelet, I had to be setting off bells and buzzers by now. I knew there was no way I'd get out of here if I freaked out, so I forced myself to lay on the bed, which I checked and was clean. I closed my eyes and willed my body to look relaxed.

The silence was nice. I could count, on one hand, the number of times in my life I'd had complete and absolute quiet inside my head. The years I'd been locked up were an abyss of misery and torture, being in such close proximity to many truly ill people whose minds weren't stable— It was a horrible nightmare that quite often resulted in me shattering and looking like a total lunatic alongside them. Faking the silence in my head had taken a carefully honed blank expression and three years of my life to learn. It could have been longer; I have no way of really knowing how long I had been locked up. The only way to tell how much time had passed was when celebrated Christmas was celebrated but I think I missed a few of those while I was trying to survive the never-ending screaming, crying and ranting inside my head.

A feeling prickled my skin. I opened my eyes and turned to see a very upset, however good-looking, blond man standing there looking at me. I was about ninety percent sure it was Rafael, but I was only going by the fact he was holding a bodkin point arrow in his large, white knuckled hand.

I moved slowly but his blue eyes didn't falter. When my socks were on the cool floor, I stood up. Judging by his glare, I would not be shown mercy or be allowed out of here. I took a deep breath and tried to keep my level of panic from rising any higher.

Clasping my hands in front of me, I tried to think of something to say. How's your butt didn't seem like a good option. Before I could come up with some spectacular opening, someone else entered. He turned to talk to them and I couldn't stop myself from looking where I'd shot him. He didn't look injured at all, if the way he moved meant anything.

I glanced to see who he was talking to. It was the man with the brown hair that had been there when I shot him, and he still looked amused. Maybe he was my way out of here. He didn't come off as brusque and as scary as the rest. Rafael turned back to me and reclaimed his glower. "So," I stepped closer, "you must have buns of steel." I motioned to him, "you're not even favoring that side." I realized after it came out, that it sounded less flippant in my head.

The man behind him covered his mouth, his shoulders shaking. I'm pretty sure he was laughing.

Rafael didn't move.

"Is the speaker on?" I knew it was by the reaction of the man behind him, but was trying for humor, even though I really had no idea how to be funny. "Um, Rafael—" I shrugged, "sorry about your name by the way, but it could be worse, you could have a handle like Eugene or Herman..." He didn't look impressed. I looked to see the other blond man was standing beside the brown haired one now, they both looked entertained.

I took a deep breath and exhaled. "Okay, so I'm really sorry I hit you in the tush—I honestly mistook you for one those disgusting slags that were after those idiot girls, figured they were sending the pretty face in to distract them…" He didn't move. The one with the brown hair behind him however, was bent over his knees laughing.

Rafael turned around and looked at them. His arm was waving around. I didn't know body language that well, but I assumed what he was saying to them wasn't pleasant. He stopped and stood there looking off into somewhere I couldn't see. I flicked my eyes to the other two, they were focused in the same direction.

I watched a clone of the man with the goatee come in, only he had no goatee. He paused and looked at me. The man with the long black hair was back. I don't know what he said to Rafael, but Rafael looked angrier than he did a few moments ago.

The twins and man with black hair walked out. Rafael turned and crossed his arms over his rather large chest and stared at me. My arrow was still clutched in his hand.

A whooshing sound had me spin around. The opposite side, where I'd come in opened. I backed away from the door, not because I was afraid of the three men coming in, okay, not just because I was afraid, but because I knew the silence in my head was going to end.

They stepped in and the glass door closed. I regulated my breathing, waiting for the onslaught of nasty thoughts. There was only one…

…*she's not part of it. We're wasting time here.*

I looked quickly at each of them trying to see which one I was hearing. None of their faces gave away anything.

The blond man without the goatee stepped closer. "Kara…"

He said my name in a way that made it sound, fancier, regal, I suppose was the word. I nodded and hugged my waist.

"No one is going to hurt you…"

14

I rolled my eyes at him. "Yeah because I believe three complete strange men when they say that."

The one with the goatee grinned.

Sarcasm wasn't going to get me out of here, I reminded my mouth. "I'm-I'm really sorry I shot your brother." I looked from one twin to the other.

He inclined his head and motioned to the other men. "Our brother."

I looked at the dark haired one. "He's your brother too?"

He nodded slightly.

That was bad for me. "I don't suppose I could speak to someone not related to Rafael?"

The one with the goatee shook his head, then jerked his chin to the wall they'd been on the other side of. "Only relatives here." He looked amused.

I turned to see where Rafael and one man had been standing was now filled with more bodies. Several large men and several concerned looking women. I immediately spotted the scary redheaded man that had done whatever he had to send me here. Standing beside him was the woman who had jumped down onto the fire escape. She was nodding to someone and looking at me, or above me.

With just my eyes I looked up briefly. A sound beside me made me turn back to the men in the cube with me. "That's a lot of family." I said quietly.

"Indeed." The one closest to me said.

I felt a pressure inside my head. Rubbing my forehead, I silently prayed I wasn't going to have a rush of intruding thoughts, because coming apart in front of these guys wouldn't end well. I had to convince them I was sorry. "I..." The pressure increased. I squeezed my eyes shut and pushed on my temples for a second. Opening them, I tried to breathe it away. It left just as suddenly as it started. Talk fast I prompted my mouth, in case it comes back.

...oh that's intriguing. Troy can't get in...

I ignored the thought that wasn't mine. "I—overheard those slags stalking those girls, who by the way shouldn't be hanging out there *alone*," I shook my head, "so I went up the fire escape to see how it played out... then this guy, your brother, comes slinking along in the shadows heading their way—" I lifted my arms out, "what would you think?"

"Troy?" The dark haired one said.

The one without the goatee turned to look at him and shook his head.

So, that's Troy. What can't he get into? I looked at the dark-haired man to see if it had been his thought. He was looking at me with an odd look on his face. I glanced over to the man with the goatee leaning against the wall with his hazel eyes locked on me.

...Kara...

My eyes went wide.

He grinned and looked at the floor for a moment. "Brother." He straightened up, he looked at his twin. "I believe her."

I tried not to look anxious. "I'm not in the habit of shooting people. Rafael was the..." I grimaced, remembering the Fitbit. "Okay, there was one other time I shot this freaky guy with glow in the dark eyes..." All three men looked at me all at once. "Pish," I hissed, "tell me you don't have a brother with glow in the dark eyes." My luck was at an all-time low today.

"What color were they?" The one with goatee asked, "the eyes."

"Purple." I said quietly.

"She can see mages." He said to his twin.

"I heard her, Chase." He said still looking at me.

Someone knocked on the wall. All of us turned.

The scary redhead motioned with his head for the men to come out.

The dark-haired one and Troy left. Chase inclined his head to me, a slight smirk on his face.

When the door whooshed closed, my head snapped to look at the people on the other side of the wall. I didn't know what was happening, but all of them were listening carefully to what the woman that had been mad I shot her Rafael was saying.

Chase moved closer to the wall, once again leaning on it. He said something and all heads in the room turned to him, then they looked at me.

My gaze darted around the group, from one to the next and next trying to find an ally. Someone had to feel pity toward the messed-up woman behind glass.

The woman that had asked me my name stepped to the wall. She gave me a curious look, then turned and said something to the black-haired man. He gave her a soft look, the kind of look only a man in love would have. Both turned and looked at Rafael.

I followed their movement and also looked at Rafael.

He didn't look impressed by whatever they were saying. Dragging his gaze from me he looked at the scary redheaded man. With a brief nod, the scary one walked out of my view. Rafael turned to follow but was stopped when Chase put his hand out in front of him. With a jerky movement Rafael handed him my arrow.

The whoosh of the door startled me again. I turned. The scary man stepped in and crossed his arms over his chest, looking down at me. Rafael stood in the open door.

"I've been asked to hold judgement against you for the time being..." The scary one said with perfectly formed words.

...like to see one of them get shot in the ass and see how forgiving they feel...

I glanced to Rafael, then bit my lip and tried to focus on what the other one was saying.

"...should you step out of line, even in the slightest I will..."

...this is ridiculous. Embarrassing...

"I'm sorry, Rafael." I said quietly. Honestly feeling it this time. "I can't even fathom how humiliated you must be feeling right now."

Rafael scowled at me.

"I was so—" I decided to tell a small fib, "afraid that those women would be taken. I acted too quickly without assessing the situation fully."

The scary one turned and looked at Rafael.

Rafael's expression was that of a stone statue. He looked away from me after a long glare to the other man and jerked his head. Spinning on his heel he walked out of my view.

"As I was saying…"

I turned my attention back to him, having no idea what he said.

"We need to ask you about some details. You told my brother Arius and his mate, Paisley, you were trying to stop more women from vanishing."

I nodded.

"You've witnessed this happening?"

I opened my mouth, then shrugged, "kind of, but I don't know how much help I'll be. I don't stick around when strange things start happening."

He nodded slowly, considering what I said. "We'll be able to ascertain if you have any useful information after you tell us more." He unfolded his arms and started to turn, then paused. "Are you able to hear what I'm thinking?"

I shook my head. "No." It was the truth, but I was worried what would happen if I said yes.

"You don't need to fear if you can." He titled his head to the side. "You are not the only person we've known with an ability of sorts."

I stood there, then realized he was asking me again if I could. "I can't hear what you're thinking."

"But you could hear what Chase thought?"

I looked to the wall that Chase was on the other side of. "Not much. Odd things here and there."

He inclined his head to me. "Very well." He motioned to the door.

I looked down at my feet. "Can I have my boots back?"

"We'll stop and get them."

I gave him a hopeful look. "And my gear."

He gave his head a quick shake. "Not at this time."

"I figured." Taking a deep breath, I walked through the open door and stopped outside it. I realized he intended to follow me and went a few more feet until I could see the space all those people had been in. Only Chase and the dark-haired man stood there. Chase motioned for me to come through. I did with hesitant steps.

"We always knew someday a woman would bring Raf down," Chase said with a slight grin, "we never imagined it would be with an arrow."

I chanced a glance at the dark-haired man on the other side of me, he looked like he was smirking. "You're Arius?"

His grey eyes locked on my face.

I pointed behind us at the scary one, "he said I told Arius about women vanishing."

His posture relaxed, slightly. "Yes, I'm Arius." He looked straight ahead again. "And that is Victor."

I nodded and kept walking. We were going through halls of glass rooms, either they were all empty or I couldn't see into them. I kept control of my breathing so I wouldn't panic. I glanced to Chase, he didn't seem as tense as his brother.

We stopped by a door and Arius went in it. Before I could figure out what was going on, he came out and handed me my boots.

I took them and bent down to put them on, not wanting to annoy any of these large men that would make them put me back in that cube.

...*relax, cupid, I've got your back*...

I looked up to Chase. He raised one eyebrow quickly at me, acknowledging I'd heard what he was thinking. I took a deep breath and turned my attention back to getting my other boot on.

"Your majesty."

I glanced up to see a man standing there with his head bowed.

"What is it?" Chase asked.

Majesty?

The man handed him a tablet, then bowed and backed away.

Chase put the arrow under his arm and took the tablet, tapping the screen a few times. He looked bored. Holding the tablet out to the man, he nodded. "If this is what was requested, then make it happen." He lifted his hand like he'd dismissed him.

The man bowed his head once more and walked back down the hall and out the doors.

Chase shook his head and glanced to Arius. "The move of the furniture."

Arius took a deep breath. "At least Paize controlled what she wanted."

Chase chuckled, "my beloved did as well, or the entirety of the both sides of the chambers would be redone."

I stood up.

Chase motioned to the doors. "Shall we?"

I started walking.

"You're not complaining about furniture Victor, did Cutie not find anything?"

"Bookshelves," he replied. "An entire wall of bookshelves."

Chase smirked. "At least you won't have piles of books to step over now."

We just kept walking, through miles of halls. I kept quiet, fitting pieces together while keeping an eye out for a window to see where we were. I knew most of the city, so if I could see outside, I might know where I was.

If Chase was a majesty, I guess that made him a king? At least I had a king on my side, that was something. I frowned at the carpeting. Rafael was his brother. I stopped walking abruptly. "I shot a prince in the tush." With huge eyes I looked up at Chase.

He smirked. "Yes, you did."

With my mouth open I looked at Arius, he also looked amused. "I-I..." I turned to look at Victor, he didn't look entertained by the idea, but he wasn't giving me that death-to-you look. I put my hand over my mouth then dropped it. "I didn't know we had a royal family…I mean, yeah I know there's royal families, but-but…" I looked back to Chase.

He gave his head a slight shake. "Let's continue, we'll cover who is who later."

I took a shaky breath and started walking, then stopped again. "Should I bow? Curtsy?" I frowned. "Do people still curtsy?"

Chase chuckled, "many do attempt to, and shouldn't." He put his hand on my shoulder. "Let's not get hung up on things like that right now, all right?"

I nodded again. "Okay. Yes. Pish. I can't believe I shot a prince." I put my hand on my forehead and started walking. Leave it up to me to shoot an arrow into the butt of a prince.

Chapter Three

Leaning on the table, I looked around. They had told me to sit, then gone back out into the hallway. It was an office, the desk being my main clue. I turned and looked at the large map again. I had no idea where it was for. I'd never seen a map of the city or the surrounding areas, so it may be what I was looking at. When you beg for change to buy a bus ticket while looking over your shoulder, you don't stop to look at maps and rationally select a destination.

I glanced at my arrow sitting on the table, wondering if they'd let me have it back. There was blood on the neck near the head. I grimaced, probably not getting it back. I had no idea how Rafael was walking like he was. Maybe I'd missed him? I doubted that, I saw the arrow sticking up when he landed on the ground. Could I have just nicked him, or it was caught in his pants?

I looked around the room, still no windows. Did these people not like seeing outside? Maybe the lack of windows was for the king's safety. Which made sense, even if running around the city without escorts didn't. I frowned, I might be projecting a bit there, but a prince sneaking around filthy alleys could be part of the reason he'd wound up with an arrow sticking out of his butt.

I fidgeted with my finger guard under the table. The leather was fraying at the edges of my three-fingered glove. I knew the worn spots from memory without looking at it.

I heard new voices in the hall, the nervous energy made me sit up straight. I wasn't being slammed with thoughts, which was really a rare thing, but I'd take it. Not freaking out in front of a king would be great.

A man with short, dark hair glanced in the door and turned to talk quietly with Chase and his brothers. It didn't take a big leap to figure out he was another brother. The black hair matched Arius' and the blue eyes were close to Rafael's. Another prince. Guess their parents didn't believe in birth control.

I could hear a woman's voice and tried to listen to see if it was Paisley. Why was that name so familiar? I mean, it wasn't a common name. But it wasn't her in the hall, the tone wasn't as gentle.

Chase came back in. "We're waiting on a few of the others."

I glanced up at him. I wasn't sure, but it seemed he was able to control if I could hear his thoughts or not. He just tucked his hands in the pocket of his jeans and stood there looking at me.

That was another thing, who would believe royalty wandered around dressed in jeans and t-shirts? Except Victor, he looked like some sort of leather covered warrior. Then again if you had the scary vibe he did, you could dress however you pleased.

Victor came in. "We'll use the group call for this." It wasn't a question and he didn't look to Chase for his approval, which meant he had a high rank in this family. What was higher than a king though?

Chase inclined his head. "Alona will be on the phone."

Arius came in, the other man and woman followed him.

Chase motioned to them. "This is my brother Michael and his mate Autumn."

I glanced to him briefly. "How many brothers do you have?"

Autumn snorted. "A whole collection." She sat down at the table across from me, her look hard as she studied me. "Ever hang on the southside?"

Michael turned and looked at her.

I gave a non-committal shrug. "Not when I could help it."

She smirked, or I think she did.

I looked at her. Really looked at her. "You teach," I didn't know the name of it, "some kind of fighting at the parks."

She nodded. "Self-defense. I don't think you ever participated." Her brows furrowed as she looked at me without moving.

Shaking my head, I willed myself to keep looking at her and not look away. I wasn't hearing her thoughts either. "No. Fighting just isn't my *thing*."

She made a point of looking at the arrow sitting on the table. "Yeah, got that."

I couldn't hear her thoughts. Something told me if I could hear what she was thinking, it wouldn't be any different that the words she spoke. "It's good," she looked back at me, "what you do. Help others." I shrugged, "most don't care and keep going." I nodded. "You care though and teach them how to stand up for themselves." Everyone was looking at me. "The real bullies would never admit they weren't perfect and take your instruction…"

Autumn nodded. "Yeah. I've had a few, they show their true colors fast enough though."

"You two know each other?" Arius asked in a quiet tone.

Autumn shook her head, then shrugged. "We've seen each other around." She looked over at Michael. "She's never been on the wrong side of anything I've witnessed."

He gave her gentle look and nodded briefly.

It was a long shot, but I was desperate to get out of here and get on with my life of hiding from the realities I couldn't change. I looked at Arius. "Your," I couldn't remember what

Victor had called her, "the woman that was with you earlier, I've seen her before, just can't remember where."

The only indication he gave that he heard me was his eyes briefly acknowledged me, otherwise he was a statue standing there. "She's a DJ."

That was it. I pointed at him, then dropped my hand back under the table. "Yes. I've seen some the events she's done...from a distance." I sat back, then glanced to Chase. "That's been driving me mad, trying to place her."

Chase smirked, "I'm sure she'll love to know you've seen her work."

The man with the brown hair from earlier came in. "Leone and Beth are busy helping Alona, but Troy and Daxx are on the way. Emil," He pointed to the hall. "is talking to Rena."

Chase nodded then motioned to him, "this is…"

"Let me guess, your brother?" I looked from the man back to Chase.

With a smile he nodded. "Yes, my brother Quinton."

I looked back at Quinton, he gave me an amused look. "Kara." I said quietly.

"I've been told not to thank you for shooting Raf in the ass," he shrugged, "but, I say it's about time."

I clamped my mouth shut before I blurted out a response.

Quinton sat down at the end of the table and crossed his arms.

Before I could decide if I should say anything a man came in from the hallway. I couldn't be sure, but he looked like Arius' twin, but there was something around his eyes that made him look older.

He stopped and gave me a quick once over, then incline his head. "I'm Emil," he motioned around the room.

"Everyone's brother?" I said sarcastically.

Autumn laughed and then cleared her throat and nodded her head while looking at Michael.

Emil smiled. "Yes." He paused for a moment. "I am intrigued with your choice of archery. I thought it an extinct method."

... a noble and worthy form of combat...

I hesitated, not sure if that had been his thought. Its pattern seemed to sound like the way he spoke, but that wasn't a sure thing. People often thought differently then they spoke. My brain prodded me, he was still waiting for me to say something. "I didn't choose it. It chose me."

He nodded his head for a moment, then looked to Chase.

...it's going to be a shit storm. She likes her, Crissy cleared her. The women are going to take her into their little gang and I'll be stuck dealing with a pouting, irate baby brother...

Trying not to be obvious I looked around at the men. The thought hadn't come from Quinton. Turning I looked at Michael, who only had eyes for Autumn. It was him. His eyes flicked to me as if he knew I'd just pinpointed what he was thinking. His look hardened and he moved over to perch on the edge of the desk.

Autumn turned her head and gave him a curious look. He glanced to me for a split second then shook his head. With a shrug, she turned around and continued typing on her phone.

I sat there silently, my hand moving around the edge of my glove. Irate baby brother. Because it couldn't be bad enough, me shooting a prince in the butt, I was pretty sure I shot the youngest in a large hoard of brothers. I let out a long sigh as quietly as I could.

"You need anything?"

I looked up to see Autumn looking at me.

"You want a tea, water, or something?" She nodded like I'd responded. "I'll get Daxx to grab some tea from Mitz. Between the porting and tossing your cookies, you're probably feeling like you were dragged through the sewers." She looked back to her phone and typed.

I glanced to Chase, he looked amused. Michael closed his eyes for a second. "Yes. Thank you." I didn't know if I wanted tea, or what porting was, but getting rid of the taste in my mouth would be good.

"Where is Raf?" Chase asked.

Quinton made some sort of noise. "Probably hiding at the temple, getting his ego stroked."

"Ah," he glanced to Victor, "we'll add him into the call."

"It might be best." Victor looked at me when he said it.

Several long moments of tense silence passed. I waited to hear thoughts from those in the room. There weren't any. These people were not normal. I almost laughed at my own thoughts, because yeah, I was *so* normal.

Troy came in with a blonde woman close to my size. She set a cup on the table in front of me, then backed up and put her hands on her hips and stared.

I looked to the cup, then back to her. I was sure they wouldn't drug me, but life had told me to not take chances. I knew that if they wanted me dead, most could just pick me up and snap me in two.

Autumn leaned over the table and picked up the cup, took a small sip and put it down. Leaning back, she lifted one eyebrow at me like most people would shrug.

I turned the cup, so where her lips had touched was not near where mine would. I picked up the cup and smelled it. It did smell good, kind of minty. I took a small sip and put the cup down. "Thank you." I gave Autumn a quick look, then my gaze moved to the blonde.

With a shrug she sat down beside Autumn. "I'm Daxx. I'd say nice to meet you, but then Raf would think I was happy you shot him." She looked at Autumn and smirked, then back to me. "You had me worried. I was afraid Hubert's bozos were using bows and arrows now."

I looked from her to Autumn then. "Who's Herbert?"

Autumn snorted. "Hu-bert. And he's a class *A* jerk that needs to be in a cage for the rest of," she waved her hand, "forever."

Nodding slowly, I met Chase's look for a second. "Okay." I didn't know what else I was supposed to say to any of that.

"Let's make the call and get this started." Daxx motioned to me. "If she knows locations, I'm all for kicking some ass today."

Troy's mouth quirked as he gave her an affectionate look.

I sat there looking around at these people, while sipping the tea. Which was really good. Many of them had tattoos down the length of their arm. I wondered if it had some sort of significance in the hierarchy of the royal family. I then noticed the two women had them as well. I couldn't be one hundred percent certain, but I thought Paisley may have had one too.

Chase set his phone in the middle of the table.

"You're live with the furnishing crew, we'll be coming at you from within the Palace walls."

I knew right then it was Paisley on the other end.

"So glad you drew the short straw." Daxx said.

"She is a god send," A woman with a soft voice said, "points and the men just follow her orders without question."

"That may be because they know her mate, beloved." Chase said glancing to Arius.

"Mine is a king, should they not fear me?" She asked.

"Only if you have your chucks in your hand." Autumn said grinning at Chase.

"Perhaps we could save this for a later time." Victor said abruptly. "Cristy?"

"I'm here." A woman answered.

"Where is here?" Daxx asked.

"My roof." Cristy answered.

Daxx glanced to Victor, a questioning look on her face. He gave his head a gentle shake. "Why are you back there?"

"Because I need to see why I couldn't see her." She made a strange noise, "I should have seen her, Daxx. Why didn't I see her?"

"You would have had to be standing and looking down the side of the building to see her go up the fire escape." Quinton explained. "Were you looking down?"

"No. No. To do that I'd have to stand on the ledge, and I can't do that here," she was talking so fast, "the bars broke off the ladder up here, so I can't use my strap and Victor gets upset if I do things without it." She blew into the mic, "I don't like it when he's upset."

I looked at Victor, the big scary man wasn't looking so intimidating right now as he listened to her.

"I should have seen her. If I did, she wouldn't have shot Rafael." She sounded frantic now.

Someone sighed. "I'm all right, little sis, don't stress yourself out over it." His voice was deep, but easy going.

That was Rafael? That voice did not match the man that had glared at me.

"I know you are *now*," she made a sound of exasperation, "but I don't want Vic to judge her. I've seen him *judge* before and it's not good," she mumbled something that sounded like blood, "I see the good all around her, I just need to figure this out. She's important…" She kept talking, but I couldn't understand any of it.

Everyone turned to look at Victor.

He closed his eyes and exhaled. "Cristy, heart, come down off the roof. It's going to be fine."

"But, Vic, you're the justice and I don't…" more mumbling.

Victor looked at me, his expression wasn't as cold as before. "Just come down off the roof. I don't believe my judgement will be required."

"Are you sure? I can stay up here and figure it out." She sounded winded.

"I am sure, heart. Why don't you go lend a hand with the furniture?" He suggested softly.

"Okay. I can do that." Cristy answered, sounding less frantic.

"The more help the better." A woman said in a soft tone.

"Okay Beth, uh," there was a pause, "I don't know if I can get there. Every time I picture there, I see *that* roof and I don't want to go there…"

"I'll meet you at the landing room, Crissy and bring you here." A male said.

"Meet Leone there, heart." Victor said with steady patience.

"Okay."

"I'll reconnect in a few minutes." Leone told everyone.

Daxx turned to Autumn. "How *did* you get out of helping with that?"

Autumn smirked. "What do I know about decorating? I lived in the back of a gym before here."

Daxx laughed.

"Yes, Autumn graciously referred to my knowledge for the placement of everything." Chase's *beloved* said.

Michael gave Autumn an inquisitive look. She shrugged at him.

"Once again…"

"Yes, yes." Chase cut off Victor, "we'll get on with the fact hunt post haste."

Troy looked amused.

I frowned and wondered how one of the twins wound up being king. Usually it was the oldest, that I knew, but that was a bit harsh when you're talking a few minutes apart—at least I always figured that's how more than one baby was born. Not that I'd ever personally be doing any birthing of any kind.

…cupid…

I came back to reality to see everyone in the room looking at me. My gaze paused on Chase, he raised an eyebrow in question. I nodded quickly and looked around. "I don't know what you need me to tell you."

"I, for one," Chase straightened up, "would love to hear more about you shooting the freak with the glow in the dark *purple* eyes."

Quinton sat up and leaned on the table. "You shot a mage? Tell me it was in the ass."

I opened my mouth to say something about shooting people in the butt, then remembered Rafael was on the other end of the phone. I shook my head. "I actually, uh," I glanced quickly to Chase then back to Quinton, "shot him through the hand."

"Ha." Chase nodded, "more than a few of us would like to do that from time to time."

"Or every day." Quinton said with a sneer.

"Why his hand?" Victor asked.

I took a deep breath, trying to coach my mouth to remember it was talking in a room with royal people. "I could hear..." they knew, so it was okay to say it...

"We're back." Leone said.

"Very good." Troy looked at me. "Kara was just going to explain how she came to shoot a mage in the hand."

"I'm all ears." Leone said.

Daxx motioned to me, so I'd talk again.

"I could hear his thoughts." I bit my lip and waited for the judgmental looks and accusing stares. There were none. Okay, that was new. "I didn't shoot him because of his eyes, that," I looked at Autumn, "I figured, each to their own, however weird it was." She nodded. "Then I heard what he planned on doing and it involved hurting someone," I looked around, still no disapproving looks. "I don't know who..." I leaned closer to the table, "then he starts rambling this bizarre stuff—and with the wind of," I waved my hand, "I don't remember exactly, but it kind of freaked me out." I gave Chase a wide-eyed look, "like I was hitting an eight on my FOS," his expression changed, "my-my freak out scale," I felt dumb saying it out loud, no one said anything, "so-so I shot an arrow through his hand as he was waving it around." I sat back. "He howled and cussed, but he stopped doing whatever he was doing." I ended quietly. "I didn't even care that it wasn't a cheap arrow."

No one said anything, in the room or on the phone.

Daxx turned and looked at Troy, he inclined his head like he knew what she was thinking. "Well, I for one..."

Michael shook his head. "There are too many unknown..."

"If you say variables, I'm going to throw something at you." Daxx said. She pointed to me. "She can *hear* a mage while they are," she looked at Quinton, then Michael, "casting or whatever it is they do."

"Oh," Crissy said, "she can help find the traitor that I haven't been able to find."

Autumn looked at Michael, "Eunice. She can see what she's really thinking. See if this sudden confusion is real."

I looked from one to the other, then to Chase.

Troy moved to stand by the table. "Are you able hear when you want?"

"You mean on purpose?" I scrunched up my nose like I'd just smelled something awful. "Why would I want that in my head? I try to not hear it."

"Mmm," he glanced to Arius.

I couldn't believe they were talking about this. Never, and I mean *never* in my life had anyone believed I could hear what a person was thinking. Second, why would I want to do it? I took a deep breath, trying to stay calm. My heart kicked up to super speed. My FOS was spiking close to a ten now and I couldn't stay calm, I couldn't just sit here and do this.

I jumped up from the table, the chair tipped over and I didn't even care. Royalty or not, they had no idea what they were talking about. I paced toward the wall, then stopped and held my head between my hands. No. No.

I spun around and ignored the wide-eyed looks. "I can't. Can't. No." I shook my head and waved my hand around like a lunatic. "I can't do it." With a jerky movement I looked at Chase. "You-you want me to *try* on purpose to hear what people are thinking?" I didn't wait for any sort of response. "I barely escaped. Barely." I mumbled more to myself then them. "If I ever get put back in there I-I'll…" I took a deep breath, "I won't survive. I j-just won't."

"What the hell is going on?" Rafael asked.

I whipped my head around to look at the phone. Reality came crashing through my panicked thoughts. I pointed to the phone and looked at a few of the men. "I shot your brother in the tush, a huge error on my part, and for that I'll," I shook my head, "do penance or whatever, but I can't go back." My hands started shaking, I looked at Chase, hoping he understood. "I just can't. They'll drug me again and-and…" I closed my mouth and stood there shaking, hugging my arms around my waist. There was no way I could describe what I'd been through and have complete strangers understand.

"What the hell is going on?"

I jolted and turned to see Rafael standing in the door.

…*I don't understand…*

I took a deep breath. Not now.

…*shit…*

"Chase? Is everything all right?" His wife asked on the phone.

…*Kara…*

I looked at Chase and shook my head. I was trying to not have a complete breakdown. The room suddenly started to close in on me. I need to look outside. "I need to look outside." I whispered.

"Troy." Daxx stood up.

Autumn stood up as well, then Quinton did.

"What's happening?" I think Paisley asked.

…*someone needs to help her…*

The more that stood up, the smaller the room seemed. I blew out a loud breath. "I need a window." I gave Chase a panicked look. Rafael stepped into the room. I shook my head.

…*what the hell did they do?…*

I pressed my hand against my forehead, trying to stop them.

The girl from the fire escape came running into the room, she didn't stop just came at me and grabbed me without a word.

My head filled with white noise, then my stomach lurched. I squeezed my eyes tight, this was a new reaction, I'd never had that reaction before. I swore there was a breeze, and opened my eyes. We weren't in that room. "What the pish just happened?" I glared at Crissy where she stood a few feet away. We were on a roof.

Chapter Four

"I'm sorry. I should have asked you first. I'm Crissy." She motioned around us. "I heard you say you needed a window and thought you wanted some air." She looked left then right. "There's lots of air here."

I backed away from her.

We were on a roof. A roof! Holy mother of pearl! I gaped at her. She was how I got from the fire escape to that cube. "It was you." I put my hand over my mouth. "You put me in that clear cube."

She frowned at me, then her eyes went wide. "No. No, that was Victor with his port box." She nodded.

...I wonder how those work...

...she doesn't look happy to have fresh air...

...maybe the library has a book...

...Victor is going to be upset I did that...

...grey hair and black eyes...

...has to be more pieces...

The voices just kept coming, or it was one voice, several thoughts at the same time. I put my hands up to my temples and backed up a few more feet. The word pattern...these were Crissy's thoughts. All of them.

Music started playing. Crissy looked at her phone and then tapped the screen.

"Cristy?" There was no mistaking Victor.

"I'm here. We're on my roof. I thought Kara wanted some air." She looked at me and bit her lip. "I don't think I helped her."

"Kara?" It was Daxx.

"Yes." I was having to focus hard to keep all of the thoughts out of my head. I wouldn't be able to block for long without another meltdown.

"Are you all right?" She asked.

I grimaced. "Not really." I looked around. "We're on a roof." I looked back to Crissy. "How the *pish* did we get on the roof?"

"That's complicated." Daxx said slowly.

I stared at the phone in Crissy's hand. "Can I get off the roof now?"

"Do you want me to…"

"I'll be there in a moment." Victor said before Crissy could finish.

She bit her lip. "He's not happy with me."

I could only shrug. He could get in line.

Victor was suddenly standing beside her.

He. Just. Appeared.

I hope they were watching what things like that did to me on their Fitbit. Or, I had suffered a complete mental breakdown and this whole day was in my head. It had been ten years since that last happened.

Giving her a quick once over to make sure she was all right, Victor turned to me. "I have a better location if you require fresh air."

"On the ground?" I glanced around. "I'm not normally afraid of heights, but I'm feeling…" I waved my hand in front of my face. "A little shaky right now."

He inclined his head and looked at Crissy's phone. "I'll take her to the courtyard."

"We'll meet you there." Chase answered.

Victor held out his hand to Crissy, she took it without question. When he held his other one out to me, I looked at it. "Take my hand, take a deep breath and then close your eyes."

I looked at his hand as I walked toward him. He closed his hand around mine, then looked at me. I nodded, took a deep breath and closed my eyes.

My head was filled with white noise again. Not as bad as before, but it still wasn't pleasant. I opened my eyes to see grass and stone. I let go and stumbled back several feet. Looking around I spotted a stone bench and quickly went to sit down.

Victor and Crissy didn't follow me.

"Everyone all right?"

I turned to see a woman with long black hair leaning over a railing on the top floor. A redheaded woman appeared beside her.

"Crissy you can't just vanish like that without a word." She scolded.

"Sorry, Beth. I could hear how upset Kara was getting and wanted to help." Crissy called up to her.

"We'll be down in a moment." The dark-haired woman said.

I was trying to decide if this was inside my mind or really happening. Looking down, I moved my feet over the grass. At least I wasn't on a roof now. I gave Victor and Crissy a cautious glance, they were keeping their distance. There was no way my imagination was creative enough to invent people like this.

Their body language told me he was expressing his displeasure that she'd vanished us to that roof.

This was really happening.

I looked around to see aged stone walls and pillars covered in vines. An archway in the wall held a large closed gate. I inhaled slowly, trying to steady my nerves. The air was clean, with a sweet floral scent. Nowhere in the city smelled like this. I inhaled again.

"It's the lavender."

A dark-haired woman was walking toward me. She stopped, leaving at least ten feet between us. Her smile was sincere. She pointed to a garden in the center. "I love the smell of lavender."

I looked over at the small purple flowers. "I've never smelled it before."

Her look showed no surprise. "I'm Alona. Chase's mate."

I frowned. "You're a queen. Should I be calling him king Chase?"

She smirked. "If you like," she shrugged, "or your majesty."

I nodded, feeling lucky I hadn't already upset him.

"You really shouldn't." Chase walked over and put his arm around Alona. He looked at me, "call me either of those." He waved his hand around, "I hear *my king* so much in a day, it really means little to me now." He watched me closely. "What we need to do is figure out what is the best distance is to stay back, so you aren't picking up too many thoughts at once."

I glanced at Crissy.

"Ah, yes, Cutie may be someone you'll have problems with."

I gave him a blank look.

"I can relate to what you're going through." Alona smiled sweetly at me.

I bit my tongue before something sarcastic flew out of my mouth.

"I'm an empath." She made an annoyed face, "I pick up on the emotions of others, whether I want to or not."

Wanting to understand, before I offended her, I tilted my head and studied her for a moment. I'd never met anyone who could possibly understand what I was going through. "So, walking down a busy street…"

She put her hand against her throat. "Is a nightmare. Sometimes to the point of being debilitating."

I nodded but couldn't think of anything to say. Someone who knew—really knew the fear of being around others was standing in front of me. Could it be true?

"Just so I understand," she gave me a gentle look, "you obviously have some sort of telepathy."

"If it has a name, I guess that's as close as I can get."

Alona nodded her head slowly. "Now, can you project thoughts to others or just perceive theirs?"

I blew out a breath, "if I could project, I'd be in a lot more trouble than I am right now."

She smiled. Chase chuckled.

Alona motioned to the bench. "May I?"

I gave her a skeptical look. "You might not want to get too close." I tapped my head. "It's a ticking time bomb up there."

She touched Chase's arm. "Oh, I think I'll be all right. Chase and I have a—" With a gentle look, she let go of his arm, "connection, he helps me control emotions, so they don't overwhelm me."

I couldn't keep the surprise off my face. "That's—" I shook my head, "Nope, I don't have a word to describe that."

"Oh, I understand that feeling well enough." Alona came over and sat on the bench, watching me for a moment. There was no judgment on her face. "I suspect those of us with greater focus won't affect you adversely." She smirked, "I had to learn how to erect mental barriers to protect myself."

"And it works?" I sighed. "I try, but it rarely works."

Alona gave me a slight shrug. "Most of the time, unless strong emotions are involved and then it becomes overpowering."

"I understand that."

Michael and Autumn appeared—out of thin air – to stand beside Victor and Crissy.

I startled, looking to Alona and back to them.

She gave Chase a sweet smile. "Perhaps having the others use the door would be better than just appearing?" She motioned to the glass doors leading from the building.

He nodded and touched his ear as he was walking over to Michael.

I realized they still had their group call happening. I just wanted my gear so I could get gone. I looked at Alona for a moment. "I'll answer questions and try to help, but I'd really like to get my gear and go before dark," I looked around as more people were coming out of the doors toward us, "if that's okay."

She gave me an understanding smile. "I will see what can be arranged." She stood up and walked toward Chase.

I inhaled deep and blew it out slowly. Just stay calm and get through this. Crumbs! Arius and Paisley were walking toward me. I looked the other way, so were Chase and Autumn. Just keep it together, answer the questions and you'll be fine, I told my brain...and mouth. I didn't need any more moments like in the office.

Paisley stopped, leaving a good distance between us. "Hi again." She smiled. "I'm Paisley."

I nodded. "I've seen some of your shows that you did by the old bridge."

She smiled. "Arius told me." She frowned, "you must have had to stand across the bridge to not pick up all the thoughts."

I shrugged, "I go higher up most of the time."

Arius turned and looked at Crissy. "That's not surprising."

Paisley waved her hand around. "I had an idea," she gave me a hesitant look, "to help you today, not permanently." She nodded and looked at Autumn, "Then you can be near us without your head exploding."

I jumped up and scooted around the bench. "I'm not taking any drugs."

She lifted her hands, "oh, no, no. I don't mean drugs." Paisley glanced at Autumn.

Autumn shrugged, "we're feeling a," she gave Paisley a hesitant look, "kinship to you." She shrugged, "we want to help."

"Kinship?" Chase stepped between us. "How do you mean?" He leaned down and looked at Paisley and then Autumn before his head snapped around and he studied me. His eyes looked wild.

"Chase. They don't mean that way." Arius said and then sighed.

Chase straightened back up and looked from one to the other again. "That's really disappointing. I'm looking forward to the next conversation we have with Elder Roan."

Paisley smirked, "just don't start running down halls."

He gave her a look, seeming as if he was offended. "That was one time." He whispered.

Arius cleared his throat. "Finish explaining, babe, before we have to muzzle a king." He grinned down at her.

Paisley nodded and put out her hand, Arius put a wide red bracelet in it. It looked like it was made of rubber. She held it up. "This is an inhibitor cuff. It blocks abilities and skills."

I raised one eyebrow and looked at it, then to her. "Skills?" I shook my head. "I wouldn't say what happens to me is a *skill*." I looked from one to the next and so on, until I was back looking at Paisley.

She offered a gentle smile. "Many of us have abilities here, Kara."

"Show her." Autumn said, crossing her arms over her chest.

Paisley handed her the red bracelet, then she glanced to Arius and nodded. Arius reached behind him and pulled out a knife.

I backed up a few feet.

Arius tossed the knife into the air, then it just stopped. Didn't fall.

I looked from the knife to him, wondering how he did that. He shook his head slowly and motioned with his chin to Paisley. I glanced to see she held her hand up facing the knife and was just standing there. "She's doing that?" I looked from Arius to Chase.

Chase nodded. "Yes, we have our own musical Chronos."

The knife fell and Arius caught it.

I know I'd just seen that, but my brain was struggling to accept what had just happened.

Paisley looked at Chase. "Musical Chronos?"

He winked at her before turning to me. "The cuff will help you, whether you continue to wear it is entirely up to you."

"Can I look at it?" I motioned to the bracelet.

Autumn stepped closer and handed it to me.

It was a hard, rubbery-feeling substance. I turned it over yet couldn't see how it closed nor were there any wires, it was just a red piece of rubber. I looked up when the redheaded woman came over with another big man. He had short red hair and compassionate brown eyes.

"I'm Beth," she motioned to the man, "this is Leone."

I nodded. "Another brother."

Beth grinned. "Yes." Her expression grew serious. "Being in one of the cells is unpleasant, I should know…"

I gave her a startled look.

"She highjacked Leone's mind and held him for ransom." Autumn said while smiling at Leone.

I thought she was joking. I glanced from her to Leone, then to Beth. No one was smiling. Highjacked Leone's mind? Ransom? For what?

Beth sighed, "that's behind us," she motioned to the bracelet, "we'd all like to talk to you, see if you have any pieces that will help us find Hubert and his men that are taking women." She looked at Arius, "we'll let you hold the device that takes it off. You can remove it whenever you want."

I bit my lip. I had serious doubts. "This," I held up the piece of rubber, "will stop me from hearing thoughts?" She nodded, "and you think I'll *want* to take it off again?"

She gave me an understanding look. "It's entirely up to you."

I nodded slowly and looked at it. "Well, fuzz. Can this day get any more messed up?" I hadn't meant to say it out loud. I glanced to see Chase smirking. "Sorry, sometimes I blurt things out and think I've said them in my head."

He smirked, "it must get a little busy up there," he motioned to my head.

"You have no idea." I took a deep breath, then nodded and looked at Paisley. "Okay. Let's do it." I held the piece of rubber out to her.

Turning, she held out her hand to Arius. He handed a hand-held scanner the size of a little phone. She took the piece of rubber and held out the scanner to me.

I took it and looked at it.

"Give me your arm." She said, moving closer.

I held out the arm that didn't have the Fitbit on it, questioning if I should even be considering this. Hadn't I been fooled before by the asylum staff telling me 'this was it', *the* thing that would help me. My arm was shaking.

"It's okay." She said softly and placed it around my wrist, pushing it together.

It wrapped around my wrist like a cuff and stayed there. I looked up at her, unable to hide the fear in my eyes.

"Just hold the scanner over the inside of your wrist."

I turned my arm over and put the scanner against it. The cuff fell off and landed in the grass. I looked down at it. "That is going to stop me from hearing thoughts?

Paisley nodded.

Bending down, I picked it up, still not believing a rubber bracelet could do that.

"Give it a try." Chase suggested glancing to Arius, "they've always worked, correct?"

Arius nodded. "Always."

...come on, cupid, what have you got to lose...

My gaze flicked up to the king. "Why do you keep calling me cupid?"

Paisley looked at him. "That's the best you could come up with? Cupid?"

Chase shrugged. "I know, Sarg, I'm off my game lately."

Rolling her eyes, she glanced back to me. "Awful nickname aside, you should give it a try."

My mind was really working to process all of this. "I'd just like my gear back, so I can go." I took a deep breath, "but if I can do something before I go, to stop women—even the intellectually damaged ones that are mentally incompetent enough to stand around and advertise they should be—"

Paisley smirked.

"Sorry." I touched my finger to my forehead, "I'm not used to conversing with people."

"Do you have family you'd like to call? Let them know you're okay?" Autumn asked.

I shook my head. "Whatever family I had, I haven't seen since they admitted me to the psychiatric facility when I was ten." None of them looked surprised by this.

"Should we check out where she's staying?" Beth came over. "Make sure they don't have cameras at her place?"

"They?" I sent Chase a curious look before turning back to Beth.

Beth sighed. "Those men you saw stalking the women are part of a much larger, organized group."

"I don't know anything about that. All I know is a lot of strange things have been happening the past few months." I looked at the bracelet in one hand and the scanner in the other. The sooner I told them whatever it was they thought I knew, the faster I could leave. I tried to wrap it back around my wrist.

Paisley reached over and held the one side for me while I wrapped the other to meet it. It sealed without a visible seam. I glanced to Beth. "I don't have a place. I've been on the move for the last month. Ever since this large, sweaty, bald man kept following me."

Chase raised an eyebrow and looked at Arius. "I'm sure if we show her a picture of Lou, he'll be that man."

"You know him?" My heartbeat increased.

"Not personally." Chase's expression was very serious now. "He was working with that large organization and is now a current resident with lifelong tenancy is our cells."

I closed my eyes, feeling relief. "I knew I did the right thing packing up and ditching that guy..."

Chase stood there staring at me, then he smirked. "You didn't hear what I was thinking."

I shook my head slowly, focusing on it now. "No." My breath caught in my throat as I looked at the cuff. "You were trying?"

He grinned. "Yes."

I hugged my wrist against my chest. It was too good to be true. I gave each person near me a brief assessment. Expert poker players, each one of them. Their expressions told me nothing. Out of the corner of my eye I saw Crissy sit down on the grass. I'd been near her twice and both times the speed of her thoughts almost brought me to my knees. I gave Paisley a cautious look, then walked slowly in Crissy's direction.

Victor watched, a hard look in his eyes as I approached her. Gripping the red bracelet, I stopped, leaving five feet between us. She glanced up from the notebook in her lap and smiled at me briefly, then looked back down. I wasn't hearing anything. Taking a deep breath, I stepped a bit closer and waited. Exhaling slowly, I waited. Her head was moving, she was mumbling quietly, but inside my head was absolute silence.

Was it possible? That the little red cuff could do that? I turned and looked around me. So many people and yet there was no noise or static inside my head. Alona smiled at me when I looked at her. I clearly did not have my poker face on. My expression probably showed the shock and amazement I was feeling.

Chase came over and stood there with his hands tucked in his pockets. "From the look on your face, the cuff is giving you something you've never had before."

I touched my head. "It's so quiet. Only my own thoughts, which aren't amounting to much right now."

He smirked. "I have a few brothers with the same issue."

Rafael appeared a few feet away. In his hand was my bag. His cold blue eyes moved over me slowly, then he paused on the cuff I was still hugging to my chest.

"I guess you didn't get the memo to walk through a door?" Chase said quietly to him.

Rafael shrugged. "I got it." He turned and went over to Victor.

Chase watched him for a moment, then turned back to me. "I'm told snacks and refreshments are being served in the solarium," he shrugged, "which, it seems, will be filled with plants to make it an actual solarium at a later date."

I had no idea what he was talking about.

He motioned to the windows on the other side of the yard. "It has a clear view of the outside, and we can leave the door open if you'd prefer."

Hugging my arms around my waist, I turned to walk toward it. There was only one thing I wanted more than leaving, something to eat. I couldn't even remember the last time I had eaten.

Chapter Five

I sat at the table near the corner. Some habits were hard to break. In the asylum, sitting in the corner allowed you to observe the rest of the room and not have to worry about someone coming up behind you. And, if there was a problem, everyone would rush for the door to escape, no one ran to a corner with no exit.

Gold and glass tables were scattered throughout the room, with a long one between the two doors. I was fighting the urge to pull my legs up and hug them, but didn't want to get the white cushioned chair dirty.

I held onto the rubber bracelet around my wrist, so far there were fifteen people in the room, sixteen if the small redheaded lady running in and out were to be counted. I wasn't picking up a single thought. Not one. I looked down at the cuff. I didn't know what was so special about this thing, and I didn't care. It was stopping other people's thoughts from invading my mind.

Rafael, still holding my bag, was talking to Crissy. He had a soft look of adoration on his face as he smiled down at her. She was either upset, worried or angry. Knowing what I did about her thought patterns, I may have been all three. The expression of loathing when he looked at me was gone, he looked cheerful. Maybe not actually cheerful, but at least nice.

Chase came over with a plate of food in his hand, Alona was beside him. He was nodding as she talked quietly to him. I didn't need to hear their thoughts or words to know that she was excited about the room and he was just happy she was happy.

He sat down in one of the other chairs at the table I was at. "You can go get something to eat." He motioned to the long table the red headed lady kept putting trays on.

I looked at his plate, then the table. "I can-I can take whatever I want?"

Chase smiled. "Yes. I suggest you do it now before my brothers get there."

I got up and slowly went to the table. I knew, without looking where everyone else in the room was. I couldn't help thinking, again, that all of this might be in my head. My eyes went wide when I saw the amount of food on the table. One more thing to make me think this was a dream. Never had I seen that much food—not from the same side of a window, that I was allowed to help myself to. Reaching the table, I picked up a plate. If it was in my head, at least I'd have a full stomach while stuck in this episode.

I hovered over the plate of sandwiches. He'd said whatever I wanted. I took one and put it quickly on the plate. Next were some sort of pastries. I didn't know if they were dessert or appetizers, but I took three. There were vegetables all lined up neatly beside a bowl of dip. I added some of those to the plate. I didn't need dip, eating fresh, not borderline spoiled vegetables would be good alone. There was fruit. I had no idea what the fruits were other than a few of the berries, but I filled the edge of my plate with those.

I looked at the full plate in my hand, wondering if they'd allow me to take any leftovers when I left. Of course, if I snapped out of it and hadn't really been here, I'd be hungry and there would be no leftovers. Turning, I went quickly back to the table and sat down. Neither Chase nor Alona said a word about the amount of food I'd taken.

As I raised the sandwich to my mouth the redheaded lady rushed toward me. I froze. Was this the part where I came to?

She held out a glass. "Here you are, love. Chocolate milk."

I lowered the sandwich slowly and took the glass. I looked into it. It looked like chocolate milk. "Th-thank you."

She smiled. "I'm Mitz. If you need anything let me know."

Nodding, I didn't know what to say.

She smiled again and moved out of the room seeming in a hurry.

I looked at the glass again and then took a sip. It was chocolate milk and was richer than any I'd ever tasted before. I set it down before I drank it all. "How did she know?" I glanced to the door she'd gone out.

Chase chuckled. "We have no idea. Mitz just *knows*."

Alona smiled, then nodded. "Eat something now, while their," she motioned to the others, "mouths are full."

She didn't need to tell me again. I took a bite of the sandwich. I had no idea what it was, but even the bread tasted better then bread ever had. This had to be in my head, which was too bad, I was looking forward to finding out how they'd put me that cube earlier and how they appeared out of nowhere.

I glanced up when Quinton, I think his name was, sat down.

He winked at me and took a much larger bite of a sandwich.

"This is nice." Alona said, turning her head and looking to the wall with the long table. "no reaching across tables and standing to pass things."

Quinton paused before he took a bite. "No brothers stealing off your plate."

Chase grinned.

"I don't think I've witnessed that." Alona said with a smirk.

"It happens." Quinton ate the rest of the sandwich in one bite.

"It is refreshing, beloved, and now you can redecorate the dining room and we'll still have somewhere to eat." Chase gave her a soft look.

Her face lit up. "Oh, that's a wonderful idea."

Lifting her hand, he kissed it.

"Keep the mushy crap down, don't make me go sit with Raf." Quinton mumbled before he devoured another sandwich.

Taking a taste of one of the pastries, I glanced around. Rafael was sitting with Leone and Bethany. My bag was beside him on the floor. I chewed slowly. I didn't know what it was, not a dessert, but it didn't have a definite flavor that I could identify. I took another bite. Whatever it was, it was good.

"While we're all in one place, perhaps we could…"

Alona shook her head and looked at Victor. "At least let her finish a sandwich before grilling her for details."

I looked from her to Victor.

He inclined his head. "Very well." He picked up his glass and took a drink.

I moved just my eyes and looked at Alona. She was much braver than I was. "Thanks." I said softly.

She gave me an understanding look. "Not a single one of them have ever been lacking mounds of food, they don't understand what it's like to be hungry for days."

My eyebrows went up. She didn't look like someone that knew hunger and struggle. I picked up a piece of the fruit, then realized I should have probably grabbed a fork or spoon.

Alona picked up a berry with her fingers and popped it into her mouth, then gave me a daring smile.

Grinning I put the fruit in my mouth. I chewed it slowly, trying not to drool the juice out of my mouth. Swallowing, I picked up my glass. "I don't know what that was, but it was amazing." I took a drink of the milk.

"I have to ask." Chase waved his finger in a circle. "Why chocolate milk?"

I set the glass down after a small sip. "I was twenty-four when I tasted it for the first time." I rolled my eyes, a little embarrassed at the admission. "I guess serving it in the institution didn't allow for calm emotions."

He grinned. "No, I'm sure the sugar rush wouldn't be of help."

I nodded and looked at my plate. I didn't know what to eat next.

"Brother, more than a few of us are going to fall asleep where we sit." Troy said looking at Chase.

Chase gave Alona a soft look, then turned to Troy. "Fair enough, brother king, I forget you night people aren't as skilled in sleep deprivation as I am."

Whatever I'd been chewing lost it flavor. Brother king? There were two kings? I'd never heard of that, not that I was knowledgeable in royal hierarchy, but still, two?

I ate another pastry slowly, while looking around. No one was looking anywhere but at me. Did they expect me to speak first? That never ended well. I didn't know what they wanted me to tell them.

"I have a few questions." Autumn turned in her chair and leaned onto her knees.

I leaned back in the chair, hoping that whatever she was going to ask I was able to keep my mouth from saying what I really thought. Automatically I started tracing around the edge of the guard still on my hand.

"You said your family dumped you off at a psych hospital?"

I held her look and nodded.

"When you were ten?" She glanced at Michael briefly.

"Yes." I traced it slowly, wondering why she was asking me this.

"Do you know your family? Their names?" She watched me, a strange look on her face.

I shook my head.

"Did they ever visit you?" Bethany asked.

"Not that I know of." For a half a second, I almost wished I could hear what they were thinking, so I could figure out why they were asking me this. How was this supposed to help them find the people taking women?

"Do you know your last name?" Chase asked.

Ignoring the annoyed look Alona gave him, I nodded slowly. "Yes, the one attendant always called me Miss Coffey."

Chase was quiet for a moment. "Doesn't ring a bell." He glanced at Michael. "Check the archives."

Michael gave him an abrupt nod.

"How long were you there?" Paisley asked me, an understanding expression on her face.

"Twelve years." I looked from her to Alona. "I think. I may have lost some time when I was in the solitary cells." I shrugged.

"Were you released?" Arius asked with a serious expression on his face.

I took a deep breath and let it out slowly. I'd already shot his brother in the tush, what could be worse than that? "No. I walked out the front door with a group of new interns that were touring the facility."

He turned and gave Victor a quick look. I couldn't tell what it meant.

"Perhaps we could save the personal history discussions for another time?" Troy suggested. "If Kara has any information that can help, the sooner we know, we can act on it."

I bit my lip before I blurted out that I just wanted my gear so I could leave. Under the table I touched the rubber around my wrist, wondering if I was allowed to leave, could I keep their miracle band.

"Have you witnessed any women being taken?" Troy stood up with his cup and went to the long table.

"Not grabbed kind of taken, although with how intellectually handicapped some of them are—" I stopped when his lips twitched. Stick to the facts I reminded my wandering mind. "I've seen them lured away under various different guises."

"How do you mean?" Victor asked.

"There's one slag—man, that is almost always involved, that's how I figured it out. He was there today."

Victor looked to Troy. "Perhaps he has an ability that allows him to do this with ease?"

"Seems likely." Troy mused quietly.

I wasn't sure what kind of ability that would be, just hoped I never found out first hand. "After," Troy looked back to me, "after I put that together, I'd go up on a roof or high location and check the neighborhood for women stupidly leaving themselves in a bad spot. Any time I spotted him, he always went for the girls. None came back."

"Did you ever follow to see where they went?" Michael asked.

I nodded. "Yeah, well, mostly. They went down into old tunnels and I," I glanced down at the leather I was tracing. It shouldn't make a difference to them if I admit it. I lifted my chin and held Michaels' look. "I can't go underground. I was put in a small windowless room whenever I," I shrugged, "whenever I *acted out*."

No one spoke for a few moments.

"Could you show us where?" Chase asked softly. "On a map."

I gnawed on my lip for a second. "I don't know if I could find it on a map, but I could take you there." Maybe if I did, they'd give me my gear and let me go.

"Perhaps tomorrow we could arrange it." Troy gave me a slight nod.

That meant I was here for at least the night. I glanced at the food in front of me. I supposed one night with food like this wouldn't be too hard to cope with. I nodded back to Troy. "Okay."

"Was it just the tunnel you followed them to?" Rafael spoke directly to me. I met his look, he wasn't glaring now, so that was progress.

"No. No, there's two other places. The one is a building *with* security doors, so I couldn't follow. The other time I followed them to the harbor."

Rafael turned in his chair and looked at Leone.

Leone nodded. "The Island is warded now. That building is a priority."

I frowned. "You're going there? To-to find the women?"

"They might still be there." Paisley said giving me a serious look.

"We've found many." Bethany sighed. "I thought they would have given up by now, after we found their data…"

"I don't think they're being as selective now." Daxx stood up and went over to stand beside the glass window overlooking the yard. "There's no way they're all *diluted* relatives from here. One here and there, sure, but groups of women just hanging out." She looked to Troy and shook her head. "I think they're beyond desperate now."

Troy turned to Quinton. "How are the team searches going?"

Quinton sat back and crossed his arms over his chest. "We're finding fewer at the locations from the data sheets."

"They've regrouped." Troy turned to Chase, a look passing between them briefly before he looked back to me. "Would you be willing to look at some photos to see if this man you've just mentioned is one of the ones we got when you…" He glanced to Rafael while rubbing the back of his neck. "when you were on the fire escape."

I gave him a wide-eyed look, then blinked. "You got those slags?"

He inclined his head.

"Yeah." I cleared my throat, "yes, I'll look."

Arius stood up doing something on his phone. "I'll have Felix go get the files."

"Are we still limiting who comes and goes from here?" Emil asked him

Arius set his phone down and picked up his cup. "Yes, personal guards, hand picked guards and minimal staff, all cleared by Troy and Crissy."

Emil looked relieved. "Good to hear. I'm not sure when Rena is coming over, but I'd like to believe its safe for her."

"We've done all we can do to ensure this, brother." Victor told him

I sat there quietly wondering what they were talking about. The size of the men in this room—if people weren't safe with them, where in the world would they be safe? They might all be royalty, but they were still twice the size of most males I'd ever seen.

A dark-haired man came through the door, he went to Arius and handed him a small tablet. Arius took it. "Thank you."

"Do you have the guards' lounge sorted out?" Paisley asked him

The man smiled, "Yes. Not that we expect to use it much."

Paisley grinned.

"Guards lounge?" Chase asked.

Alona smiled at him. "For when we women are here, so they're close at hand but not underfoot."

Chase raised one eyebrow. "I fear you ladies are ruining the best guards I've ever had."

Alona patted his hand. "But we *are* including them now and not just trying to be rid of them."

Chase sighed in a dramatic way. "There is that."

Arius came towards me holding up the tablet. "Just scroll through these and see if anyone looks familiar."

I took it and looked down. There was a man's face on the screen. It wasn't the one I told them about. I continued to look at it, I had no idea how to make the picture move or to scroll to another one.

Alona leaned over and slid her finger across the face and another face appeared.

Moving just my eyes, I looked at her hoping she understood my appreciation. She gave me a small smile.

Crissy jumped up. "Oh. I need a book." She grabbed her phone and sat back down.

No one else seemed to care that she'd just done that. I didn't know how she lived with her mind the way it was. I looked back to the face on the tablet. I didn't know him either. Placing my finger on his cheek I swiped it and his face slid off the screen. The next one I knew right away. I looked at Arius. "This is him."

Arius stepped closer and took the tablet.

Troy came over and looked at the screen. "I'll go see what I can find in his head."

"You can do that." I frowned. "How do you do that?"

Troy smirked. "I can read what's inside a person's mind."

I know my mouth dropped open, but I couldn't help it. "Pish. That's so much better than having their thoughts slam into my head."

Alona leaned forward. "You could go to the cells with them and help if you like."

The confusion must have been clear on my face.

She glanced at the red cuff around my wrist. "You could listen to what he's thinking and help Troy and Arius get locations," she shrugged, "answers."

I looked at the thing on my wrist preventing me from hearing others' inner dialogue.

"We can keep the exposure down." Arius said in a light tone, "so the only thoughts are his, no others."

I gnawed on my lip. I hadn't been able to hear anything when I'd been in the cube. I looked from Troy to Arius.

A man came into the room. Crissy jumped up and ran to him, taking the book he had. "Thank you." The large man left again. She stood there in the middle of the room and flipped through it. "It *is* Latin." She closed the book so quickly it made a loud *whup* noise. Spinning back around she looked at Rafael. "Arcus is Latin for—"

"I know, sis." He said quickly.

"Oh. You do." She sighed. "Okay. I didn't know you knew, and I wanted to explain why it was important."

Rafael motioned to her chair. "I know."

She nodded her head enthusiastically. "Okay. That's good, right. That you do." She went over and sat down.

I looked to see if Alona or Chase knew what that was about. Chase looked slowly from Crissy and Rafael to Troy. Troy had a slight smirk on his face. Alona sent her king a questioning look. He smirked and gave his head a slight shake.

"As intriguing as that is," Chase said as he stood up, "They're both thick-headed." He smiled at me while motioning to Troy and Arius. "You won't hear a thing from them." He motioned around the room. "Everyone else will stay here."

I took a deep breath and looked down at my wrist. Did I want to find out what that slag did with the missing women? Moving just my eyes I glanced around the room. I didn't need to hear the thoughts of all present, their anxious looks said it all. Blowing out a breath, I looked to Chase and gave a slight nod.

Chapter Six

I blinked. Just like that I was standing in front of the metal doors. The cubes were on the other side. I let go of Chase's arm.

"Did the cuff make porting easier on your system?" Chase gave me an inquisitive look.

I shook my head slowly. "My head didn't fill with white noise, but I still want to spew."

"Ah," he glanced at Troy, "we've been trying to come up with a way to help those new to porting not want to throw up."

Holding my hand over my churning stomach and shook my head briefly. "Considering what that really means, I don't think you're going to succeed."

"You may be right."

Arius opened the door and walked in without comment.

I blew out a breath, trying to keep my apprehension under control. I was going to do this. Intentionally try to hear what someone was thinking. I could count, on one hand, the number of times I'd done that. I was only listening to the doctors and attendants to try and figure out how to get out of there. I thought about that as I quietly followed the brothers through the aisles of cubes.

"How are we going to do this?" Troy looked over my head to Chase. "Allow her to hear, but not be seen?"

Chase gave me a brief look, "we could open the tray slot and have her stand near it."

Troy nodded. "It could work."

I was too busy trying to stay calm to add anything. I looked down each narrow hall as we passed them. "There are no windows," I said half to myself. "Do your prisoners get to see any daylight?"

Arius paused beside a corner to another row and pointed up. "We have ultraviolet light bulbs that are on a few hours each day." He did something on a pad beside the wall. "We can't have windows as too many people with abilities are here, outside the cells, and no windows mean no need to worry about someone breaking them out."

I couldn't find anything to argue with there. Having my own *ability*, I knew something like that could be possible.

"Go stand over there." Chase pointed a few feet down the hall. "You'll be able to see and hear, but he won't be able to see nor hear you unless or until you speak."

I nodded and moved to where he pointed. My stomach was in knots, pulse thrumming quickly. Pulling the scanner out of my pocket, I held it over the rubber bracelet on my wrist. I was really going to do this. I did as Paisley had shown me and the rubber fell off. Picking it up, I hugged it to my chest with the little scanner.

Chase stepped closer. "Whenever you're ready, we'll open the slot."

I took a deep breath and blew it out slowly. "I've never done this." I looked at him, then away quickly, "on purpose."

He touched my shoulder gently. "If you can help us end what they're doing, you may feel entirely different about it."

I nodded. "I don't know about that, but let's do it."

"He's an emotion feeder, it's probably how he knows what not to say to alarm women." Arius glanced to Troy.

Emotion feeder? Did I want to know? I was almost ninety percent sure I didn't. Was that a *skill*? The more this day went on, the more I felt like I'd had a complete and utter psychological meltdown.

…Kara…

I blinked and looked at Chase. "Sorry?"

"Are you ready?"

I looked back to the man on the other side of the see-through wall. He wasn't as large as the brothers, but he'd wasn't small either. If I'd been asked to describe him, I wouldn't have been able to pick anything unusual, he was plain looking. If you didn't count his eyes, which expressed nothing but loathsomeness. His thoughts had been vulgar earlier— "No, but I'm not going to back down now."

Chase walked past me and pointed to a button on a small panel. "If it becomes overwhelming, push this and the slot will close."

I looked at the button and then back to him. "Okay." The fact that he was giving me a quick out, was not lost on me. Why he was showing me kindness escaped me though.

…Cupid…

I gave him a startled look. "I keep getting lost inside my head."

"It's not a problem." He gave me a patient look.

I realized he was confirming I was ready, again. "Oh, yes. I'm ready." I turned and looked at the man and heard a noise that told me the small hole was now open.

At the same time Arius and Troy walked into the cell with the man. Arius' posture screamed 'don't mess with me.'

"Do you know who I am?" He asked the man.

Slowly he nodded and looked away quickly.

…the freak with the hypnotic eyes…

My eyes went wide. Hypnotic eyes? *That* I would have to ask about.

"Good. You'll answer any questions, or you'll deal with me."

…as if…

I looked at Chase, he raised an eyebrow, I nodded to let him know I could hear what the slag was thinking.

Arius crossed his arms over his chest and stared down at the man. As intimidating stances went, that was a good one, I thought.

"We know you've been collecting up women…"

…and now I won't get my pick because I'm here…

It dawned on me in that moment that this was real. What they'd been saying about abducted women was true. I'd thought it had been my paranoia.

Chase touched my shoulder, bringing me out of my head. Later, I'd ask how he recognized it was happening.

"…where do they go after you take them down to the tunnels?" Troy asked in a calm voice.

…like I care. I'm not one of the sewer crew—they're like a bunch of rats down there…

I cringed. I would definitely not be helping them look into *that*. I focused to listen and not think about rats in a tunnel.

"How many are still at the apartment?" Arius asked him.

"What apartment?" The prisoner said quietly.

…they followed me? How do they know this? Nelson will have my balls for this…

Troy glanced at Arius and shook his head.

Arius smirked. "Don't go anywhere. We'll be back."

They went out and closed the door.

The man blew out a breath and put his hand to his forehead.

…I hope they've moved the last ones to the track. This is Wednesday. Shit. They'll still be there…

He paced to the other side of his cube, then his thoughts blurred with the panic he was feeling.

I looked at Chase and gave him a quick look telling him I wasn't going to get any more from this panicking slag.

With a slight bow, he closed the small slot on the wall.

I turned to see Arius and Troy standing behind me. "I didn't hear much." I pointed to Arius, "he thinks you're the freak with the hypnotic eyes." I paused when he didn't look concerned or offended. "Okay, I don't want to know." I blew out a quiet breath. "He's upset he doesn't get his," I made quotes in the air, "pick of the women now that he's locked up here." I glanced from Troy to Chase. "This-this is really happening isn't it? It's not some episode my paranoia has created to protect me from reality—is it?"

Chase motioned to the pacing man behind glass. "This is the reality we're dealing with."

My heart skipped a few beats. I hugged the red cuff against my chest. "Yeah, I was afraid of that." I shook my head to get back on topic. "He-uh, doesn't know where the girls go that are taken to the tunnels. Calls the crew a bunch of sewer rats." I closed my eyes for a second, to remember what else. "Um, he's worried you followed him to the apartments and Nelson will have his-uh, balls for it."

All three men looked at each other.

"Of course it's Nelson." Troy said quietly.

"We could probably end this if we got our hands on him." Chase mused.

I didn't know who that was and decided it wasn't my business. I looked back at the man. "He's worried the women at the apartment won't be moved to the track before you guys get there."

"Track?" Chase looked at Troy.

Troy shook his head. "I couldn't see anything clearly." He gave me a patient look, "was there any more?"

"No. His thoughts were garbled after that." I shrugged. "That happens when strong emotions are riding someone." I moved my hand in a circle beside my head. "It becomes alphabet soup up there with emotion."

Arius pulled out his phone. "I'm calling Ellis and Abe, see if they know of any abandoned tracks or remote ones."

Troy nodded, "ask the girls as well." He looked to Chase. "We need to get to that apartment."

Chase nodded and motioned for me to go back in the direction we'd come. "We'll need Kara to show us where."

I started walking.

"We'll do that at the time. I don't want to tip them off we're coming." Troy said walking on the other side of me.

I looked from one to the other, then realized I hadn't put the cuff back on and still wasn't picking up anything.

"Hopefully their *recruiter* back there isn't on a regular schedule and being missed." Chase added quietly.

I paused. "So-you're going to that apartment building? How will you know which apartment?"

They turned and looked at me.

"We'll find a way." Troy stated.

"Even if it involves knocking down each door." Chase said with a grin.

"Oh." I frowned and started following them again. That was good. The kings were going to such lengths to find abducted women. I'd never really thought of what royalty did. For some reason I thought they were just fancy representatives of a nation. I rolled my eyes at my own corny thoughts. There was nothing regal now in the modern days. Too much reading of old books, that's what was my problem...

...cupid...

I jolted and looked at Chase.

He gave me an apologetic look. "I did try speaking to you first."

I shrugged. "I'm really not used to conversations *with* people." I looked at the floor. That made me sound like a complete loser.

Chase chuckled. "I was asking if you'd like to finish eating and hang out at the palace while we attend to some arrangements."

He had my complete attention at eating. "Eating any time is good." And that was the lame answer I gave him.

We went though the metal doors again. Chase stopped and motioned to the bracelet I still held. "You may want to put that back on. I don't know how many of us will still be in there."

Chapter Seven

I spent the next few hours wandering around a palace. I wasn't sure what it looked like outside, it could have been a medieval castle, but they called it a palace. Not that architecture mattered. I was still trying to grasp it was happening and had a few moments in my head of *'Holy fraggle! I'm in a palace.'*

The women had shown me around but many had to go rest. That left Alona moving from room to room instructing a few men where to place furniture. I guess when you have a palace you can redecorate it whenever you want. I'd never seen the amount of furniture they had here. When you've lived as I do, a bed is all you have if you're lucky

Chase had taken me to the city long enough for me to show him the building, then he'd brought me back to his beloved and vanished again. A very small part of me wanted to be there when they found the apartment, the rest of me didn't, so I hadn't even asked.

When Alona had to go see her father, she left me sitting on a balcony that overlooked the vast countryside. She'd told me I could wander around if I wanted. I'd sat there for a while on the balcony, wondering which direction the city was and how had I never spotted a freaking palace on a mountain before. That thought spurred more curiosity and not being cat I decided to walk to the end of the balcony and see if I could find the city.

There wasn't an 'end', and as far as I could tell the balcony went all the way around the palace. I paused again after the second corner and looked out over the landscape. There was a large colony in the distance. The buildings weren't tall enough to be the city, and as far as I could tell it was way too clean to be *the* city. A noise beside me, had me spinning around. A large man came out of the glass door and walked to the edge of the railing and looked over. He just stood there. A guard perhaps? I looked him up and down. He was wearing a sword at his waist. A sword! Shouldn't modern day guards of royalty be carrying a gun? He didn't move as I headed toward him. Did I want to speak to him? Probably not. As I approached, he looked at me and bowed his head slightly. I opened my mouth to tell him I wasn't part of the royal family, then thought a quick smile would keep me out of trouble. My track record with speaking usually got me into more issues than not.

I glanced over my shoulder as I reached another corner, he still stood there. Rounding the corner, I spotted another large man standing like a statue. He also wore a sword. Now I had definite questions. Whether I should ask or not left me undecided, so I prompted my mouth to stay closed and say nothing as I moved by him.

Out over the railing was more vast countryside, a few smaller built up areas were visible, but once again nothing like the over-populated city. I had no idea where I was. I paused when I saw movement at the base of the mountain. There were people on horses. Horses, not cars. Frowning, I glanced back to the guard, debating long and hard if I wanted to strike up a conversation. The tension in my stomach won and not was my decision.

Continuing on, I looked inside the glass doors running along the balcony. As far as I'd noticed, the rooms were all empty. What could they use those for? Parties? Did royalty throw parties? I gnawed on the inside of my lip. I needed to find some up-to-date articles on the royal family when I got back to the city. I looked out as I went around the fourth corner, still no city. Here the countryside was more built up then the others, but there were no skyscrapers or bridges. Where the fuzz was this palace located?

I was back to where I started, I sat down facing the landscape. I looked over fields, trees and lakes and it was probably the most peaceful thing I'd ever seen. I glanced at the door, debating if I should wander through the palace. Sighing, I sat back. I didn't want to take a chance on doing something wrong and wind up back in the cube.

I still couldn't believe that I had intentionally listened to another's thoughts, and I felt good about it. I don't know if I'd ever want to do it again, but this time had helped other people.

Bethany came out through the glass doors, looking like she wasn't quite awake. "How are you doing?" She asked as she sat down on the large cushioned chair across from me.

"I'm sitting on the balcony of a palace."

She nodded. "It's like something from a movie, I know. I'd tell you that you'll get used to it, but you won't really. I still stop and think 'wow this is really happening'."

For all of them being princes and princesses, they were more down to earth than half the snobby dirt bags that thought they were truly special on this planet. I realized she was sitting there looking at me patiently. What had I missed this time? "So, after they go to this apartment, do I get my gear back?"

"Honestly, I don't know the plan. I'm only up now because I have trouble sleeping when Leone is gone."

"Gone?"

"He went with the Kings, Emil and Arius to the apartment." She yawned, "I'm going to get some juice and try to wake up. Did you want to come?" She stood up.

I got up. "I didn't want to wander around on my own and possibly get lost or do something I shouldn't." I followed her through the large empty room.

She pulled her phone out of her pocket. "Hi. Yeah, I'm here with Kara, we're..." She stopped walking. "Where? Okay. I'll meet you at the top of the stairs." She tucked the phone back in her pocket and jogged toward the stairs.

I quickly followed.

When we reached them Daxx appeared in front of us. "Come on, we're meeting Crissy in the tower."

Bethany looked at me. "What about Kara?"

"She's safer with us." Daxx put her hand on my arm. "Eyes closed, deep breath." She said quickly.

Bethany made a face but did it.

I closed my eyes, then my stomach bottomed out. I opened them to see we were in a tower, just like those described in books, complete with stone merlons and the spaces to look out, crenels, I think they were called.

"So much for this anti-nausea gadget working." Bethany held her hand over her stomach. "I don't think I'll ever be port friendly."

Crissy appeared beside her. She was holding my bag. "Rafael dropped it by the table and ported to the armoury." She said. "It's very heavy." Dropping it, she turned to look out from the stone ledge.

"What's going on?" Beth moved over beside her.

"A small group is moving to the lower tunnel." Daxx said as she pulled her phone out of her pocket.

The other two women did the same. Beth took an earpiece out of her pocket and put it in.

"We're in the tower." Daxx said.

I realized they were all communicating through the phone. Like Rafael had been when I'd shot him...

"She's here with us." Daxx looked out between the merlons. "Yeah that's what I figured."

"I thought those entrances were sealed." Bethany said quietly.

I went over to see what they were looking at. We were a lot higher up than I'd thought.

"Where are you guys?" Daxx asked sounding impatient. "Really?" She shook her head. "We port inside, why doesn't..."

"Shouldn't they have thought of that before placing the barrier there?" Beth looked at Daxx who was still shaking her head in disbelief.

"I can go down..." Crissy's shoulders slumped slightly. "Okay. I'll stay here."

Daxx turned back to Bethany. "Can you do anything from this distance?"

Biting her lip, Bethany stood on her tiptoes and looked over the edge again. "If they placed a ward so magic can't work, then definitely no."

I moved closer and leaned between the merlons, looking down I noticed there were large wooden doors in the side of the mountain, just below us.

"We can see them now." Daxx informed whoever was on the other end.

I looked to see six men walking along the side of an old cracked road, trying hard to blend into the grass beside it.

"How far are you?" Beth gave Daxx a worried look.

Crissy pulled a small pair of binoculars from her pack. "I'm looking." She said softly.

The two other women paused.

"One is carrying a large duffle bag. No." Crissy made a strange sound. "Purple eyes." She hissed.

Daxx and Beth both looked over the edge again.

"We have Kara's bag." Crissy said. "I picked it up."

Nodding, Daxx went over and picked up my gear.

"She hit you from five stories up." Crissy said.

I cringed, I was pretty sure Rafael didn't need reminding.

"She has a point." Daxx set my bag in front of me. Touching her ear, she gave me a serious look. "This is your shot at redemption." She pointed toward the wall. "The guys are on the way with Paisley and Autumn, we have to stall them until they get here."

I gave her a wide-eyed look then glanced to Bethany. "How?"

Squatting down, Daxx opened my bag. "With this."

I took a deep breath and turned to look out at the men sneaking up the mountain, then back to her again. "I can distract them, but I'm not hitting them."

She nodded quickly. "That will work." Motioning to my bag, she touched her ear again. "Kara is going to keep them busy." She grinned. "Take that up with Romulus, we didn't place that barrier."

I knelt down and pulled out my bow, assembling it as fast as I could. Pulling out the quiver, I stood up. I couldn't put it on my back and have my arms clear the stones on either side. I looked at Bethany and held it out. "Hand these to me."

She came over and took it.

I pulled out an arrow and moved over, checking that I had enough room to maneuver without hitting the merlons. Unfortunately, the base of the crenel was made for much taller people.

"Oh. Here." Crissy ran over and pulled what looked like an old wooden box seat over.

Hoping it held my weight, I got up on it. It was perfect, making me the height I needed.

"Quinton asks that you don't hit them when they get here." Daxx grinned.

I knew they were kidding, but that would be my luck. Shoot another royal brother.

Nocking the first arrow, I checked the grass in front of where they were walking. It wasn't moving, so there wasn't much breeze on that level. Aiming a few feet in front of the first man, I released it. He jumped back into the man behind him. I didn't pause to watch as Beth placed another arrow into my open hand. I landed that one beside the second man. I continued, changing sides and directions and ten arrows later they just stood there, not moving in any direction.

"They're afraid to breathe." Daxx laughed.

"There they are." Beth said. "Distract them, Kara, aim in front of them again."

Beth handed me another arrow. I aimed and put it an inch from the one man's foot.

Right after that, Autumn and Michael were there. My jaw dropped as I watched Autumn take the man down in a blur of movement, then Michael leaned over him and he completely vanished. Just gone.

I couldn't look away when I noticed Rafael was using a sword. An actual longsword, not a cute little sabre, and he was using it against a man that was wielding a weapon that looked like an axe and hammer.

My FOS started climbing. This wasn't the middle ages. Why were these people using weapons like that? Not that I supported weapons at all... I glanced down to the bow in my hand. I wasn't one to judge. I used a bow or throwing knives in a time when most of the population had a gun hidden somewhere on their person and a switchblade in their pocket.

I turned back to see Rafael and Victor were taking on the last two as Quinton, Michael and Autumn were moving around the man waving his hands around.

"Can you freeze him, Paize?" Daxx sounded worried. She scowled. "Romulus better hide so I can't get a hold of him."

I glanced at the quiver Beth held and pulled out one of my precious bodkins. Nocking it, I zeroed in on the man waving his hands around.

"Kara's going..."

"Less talk." I said quietly. I didn't want to be distracted right now. I had to make sure this shot went between Quinton and Michael without hitting them. I watched the one waving his hands, there was no way I could predict where they were going to go next. His mouth was moving rapidly, his expression was malicious. I moved slightly to the right and released. A second later he howled and put his hand against his cheek that the bodkin tip had nicked. I lowered my bow slowly.

Quinton spun around and looked right up at me. Autumn was grinning as she landed a spinning kick on the other side of his face and he slumped to the ground.

"That was beautiful." Daxx sounded very excited.

Rafael moved over to stand beside Michael, in his hand was the arrow that had stopped the man from hurting the others. He turned and looked up at me. My heart flipped inside me, he didn't look angry, but he also didn't look happy I had helped. Autumn turned around and waved her hand, then gave me a thumbs up.

Stepping off the box, I took my bow apart and placed it back in the bag. As exhilarating as helping these people was, and surreal as being among royalty seemed to be, I just wanted to be on my way.

"Come on, we'll walk down to the courtyard." Daxx said.

"Yes. No porting." Bethany said as she handed me back my quiver.

I paused and saw how empty it looked, deciding if I was allowed to go, I could accept the loss of my arrows.

Chapter Eight

The sun was starting to set as I sat watching the others arrive. A few just appeared, but most came through a door or gate. Was it weird that someone appearing out of nowhere wasn't startling me now?

"You get Romulus on the phone *now*. I want to speak to him as soon as possible." Quinton was telling a man I didn't know.

"I thought those of royal blood were able to bypass the wards?" Paisley asked to Victor. "We can port inside the palace and use our abilities, why couldn't we port outside the gates?"

Victor rubbed the back of his neck and shook his head. "I'm not certain, but we're going to find out." He looked in my direction. "If Kara hadn't been up there, they may have had the opportunity to use what was in that duffle bag."

"What was in it?" She asked.

"The science team is examining it now, but at first glance it seems to be some sort of explosive."

Explosives? They were going to blow up the palace? Or blow up things to get to the palace? My heart regained a steady pace of too fast again. What was going on here? I looked at the swords across Victor's back, then glanced over at Quinton to see he wore the same. Again, *what* was happening? I looked back to Victor and Paisley.

Her eyes went wide. "They were going to blow up the gate?"

"At the least." He said abruptly, then turned to meet Troy and Chase as they came outside.

They were all dressed alike, dark avenging angels. I saw that the Kings actually fought in person. Weren't they supposed to just tell someone else to do that sort of thing?

Chase listened to Victor, then turned and looked at me. He was smiling as he walked toward me. "I hear you had some fun and excitement."

I felt the need to stand up in his presence. "I don't know if I'd go so far to call it that."

He inclined his head. "Thank you for lending aid." He motioned to the glass doors. "We're just going to grab a coffee or three. Come have some chocolate milk."

In the corner, I kept quiet drinking my chocolate milk. Why did it taste better than any I'd ever tasted before? I took another sip. And how did Mitz know and bring it to me again? I licked my lips and watched everyone else in the room. They were talking in small groups, too many conversations to follow any one.

Autumn and Michael came in the door, walking close together and looking happy. In her hands were my arrows. She came over and set them on the table.

"That was an epic shot." She grinned. "Quinton said he heard it go by his ear."

I almost spit out the milk I'd been savouring. "I held my breath, hoping neither moved."

Michael smirked. "There wasn't much chance of that happening. We were being held in place by the mage."

Autumn snarled, "until you freed us. I should have kicked him again just for using that hoodoo crap on me."

"Oh-that's," I frowned, "what that weird hand waving does?"

"Or worse. Usually worse." Michael said in a serious tone.

"Did Chase tell you?" Autumn smiled. "Four women were rescued from the apartment. Thanks to you."

That made me feel good. "Were they okay?" I stood up. "I know I said most of those taken were mindless twits—but I didn't mean I *wanted* anything to happen to them." I felt I should clarify that.

Michael nodded. "As far as we can tell, they are fine."

Autumn looked as relieved as I felt. "They'll be okay now at one of our safe houses."

I took a deep breath and exhaled. They'd gotten the man stalking women and taking them. Rescued some of the women. And, I'd helped them. In my mind, my debt for shooting a prince should be paid.

"If you can show us which tunnel entrance you saw them use, we'll follow that lead up as well." Michael motioned to Arius across the room.

I nodded. "So, I have an odd question, well maybe odd to you, but for me it's normal to want to know." I paused when Arius and Leone came over. "How do I know if I run into any more of those people taking women?" I held up my arm with the red cuff on it. "I mean if I can't hear what they're thinking?"

"Their wrist," Michael stated, "they'll have a device a bit bigger than yours." He pointed to the little Fitbit on my other arm. "Stay away from those."

I looked at Leone, then Arius' wrist, then turned back to his wrist. They were all wearing devices a bit bigger than the one I had on.

He grinned. "We've run into a few issues lately, so now we all wear them in case we can't port or wind up in trouble and need a fast out."

My mouth dropped open, I held up the hand with the Fitbit on it. "So, mine works like that? I thought this was to monitor me."

"No. That one is so you can safely stay here."

"Here?" I looked around the plant-bare solarium.

Michael nodded. "Yes, here in Alterealm. Your scan said you were human and we wanted to be sure you would survive when you left the cells."

Everything went loud, then muted silence immediately after. My heart felt like it stopped. "This is Alterealm?" I felt breathless. I *had* lost it completely. "*Of course* I did. How could any of this be real?"

"Are you all right?" Leone stepped closer.

I put my hand up to stop him. "No. No I'm not all right. Stupid, stupid brain. I thought I was done having strange delusions. How many years does it take for their fracking drugs to wear off?" I looked down at the small band they'd given me in the clear cube. "Should have known the second I *came to* in that room that this was all inside my head." With a vibrating hand, I pulled off what I'd thought was some sort of monitor, or lie detector, I had thought that briefly too. "Of course it's not." I dropped it on the floor. Then put my hand over my forehead. "You're just having a complete psychotic episode, you silly ignoramus, Kara." I laughed. "Porting and mages waving their hands and chanting spells." I snorted. "Most entertaining delusion yet." I walked past the giant men my mind had created. Well, at least I made them interesting, if not a little larger than life.

My illusionary Chase stepped in front of me, a concerned look on his face. I laughed. "Twin kings—*woo*, my mind worked overtime this round." I shook my head and patted him on the chest. "It all seemed so unreal but still very real." I gave him a sad look. "Only the craziest ever think of a place called Alterealm. I guess I've finally caved in." I shook my head. "So many wanting to get back to Alterealm." I wanted to cry suddenly. "Guess I made it before they did."

"What's happened?"

I spun around and looked at Rafael standing in the door looking very stern again. "Son of a bucket!" I rushed toward him. "That's why your walking around like nothing happened. When you should be lying in bed cursing the wound on your backside." I stopped at the step and looked up at him. From two steps below he looked twelve feet tall. Apparently, my mind felt the need to create giants. I grinned up at him. "Because you're not real and I didn't shoot your tush!" I put my hand over my mouth for a second. "I've been doubting my own accuracy since I saw you walking around like I hadn't shot you." I blew out a breath "I do feel better knowing that, really." I looked around. "A palace." My next thought had me slumping my shoulders forward. "Please don't let me come to in some dumpster. I really, really don't want reality to come crashing down like that." I said quietly.

Turning, I ignored all the figments of my very creative, broken imagination and walked out the glass doors that weren't really there into the pretty courtyard. Soft lights spread a gentle glow all around. At least my mind thought of practical things like being able to see in the dark. I could still smell the lavender. I hoped that scent was real, because as soon as I woke up to my bleak reality, I wanted to get something that was lavender scented. I went over to the nonexistent stone bench and sat down. If I just sat here for a short while, and didn't feed this fantastic delusion, reality should come back quickly.

I heard movement behind me but wasn't going to turn around and encourage the fantasy to continue. Out of sight, out of mind. I didn't know if that saying was true, but now seemed a good time to test it out.

Rafael stepped in front of me, he was holding the Fitbit I'd taken off. I wasn't putting it back on. He squatted down so our faces were level. "Kara."

I looked into his blue eyes, they weren't shooting fire at me or glaring at me, they were just soft, almost pretty, blue eyes. I exhaled loudly.

"Your mind hasn't fractured. This is not an illusion at all." He held my gaze, not looking away.

"It has to be." I told him softly. "How could I hear people—crazy people by the way, think of nothing but getting back to Alterealm." I sat straighter. "I looked it up when I got out. It doesn't exist."

Alona walked over and sat on the bench with me. "There's a reason you couldn't find it."

I nodded slowly and looked back to Rafael. "Because it's not real."

He gave me an understanding look. "It's very real and has existed through the ages."

"You couldn't find it because it's an alternate realm." Alona said slowly. "Another world that exists in addition to ours."

I dragged my gaze from Rafael back to her. "That's not possible."

She gave a slight shrug. "Neither is hearing what people think or feeling their emotions."

I opened my mouth and then closed it. "How could another realm exist, and no one knows?"

"No one from your realm knows," Rafael said quietly. "Those from mine know all about yours. My family protects yours from things like mages waving their hands creating magic and many other things that shouldn't happen on your side."

I bit my lip and studied him for a moment. "If that's true, why were people locked up where I was, thinking of Alterealm?" I leaned closer. "They *were* crazy." I tapped the side of my head. "The things I'd hear them think," I shook my head, "there's no way it was real."

He smirked. "I'm sure some of them were crazy. Or they ended up that way when they got stuck on that side and were locked up." He tilted his head. "You can hear what's in people's heads and you were thought to be crazy."

I opened my mouth and then closed it and frowned at him. What he was saying made sense. "Do you lose a lot of people that get stuck and can't get back?"

"More than we care to admit."

I turned to see Chase standing behind Alona with his hands resting on her shoulders.

Crissy came over and stood beside Rafael for a moment, then she dropped to her knees and sat there. "I was locked up and drugged and tested," she nodded, "so many tests." A tear rolled down her cheek. "They thought I was crazy because of all I see." She shook her head, "no one understood." She smiled up at Victor as he came over. "Here. It's okay, who I am." She smiled. "I'm allowed to be me."

I'd heard what went on in her head firsthand. "I don't know how you do it, but I'm glad you got away too."

She nodded.

Bethany came over with Leone. She held up her hands and bright lights the color of flames came off her palms. She smiled. "I'm allowed to be who I really am here too." She looked up at Leone, "and I've never been happier."

I took a deep breath and looked around at them as I exhaled slowly. "*This* is crazy." I said quietly then looked at Rafael.

He tilted his head to the side. "And for the record. You *did* shoot me."

I groaned. "Out of all the things I thought my mind had concocted, I was hoping that was one of them and it didn't really happen."

He shook his head.

"Sorry?" I offered.

"I think we should find Kara a room, so she can rest." Everyone turned to see Mitz standing in the doorway.

Troy looked down at me. "That's a good idea."

"Take the night, have a long soak in the tub, get some rest." Chase said. "Then in the morning we'll explain more."

I gave him a look. "There's more?" I stood up slowly. "What else could there be? Mages that can freeze people, men wanting to blow things up?" I looked around at them. "You guys vanishing or porting…"

Paisley came over, she was carrying my bag. "There is *so* much more." She held my bag out to me, "But after your meltdown, I think you should get some rest before we explain."

I took my bag and put it over my shoulder. "I wouldn't mind that bath."

"What room are we using?" Autumn asked. "I don't think she'd be comfortable in the one with *the* closet," she glanced to Michael, "it has no windows."

He nodded. "I'm sure here would be better than the lower chambers."

"I've already brought some clothes and put them in one of the rooms on the second floor." Mitz informed them.

"I'll go get her a phone with our numbers in case she needs to reach anyone." Quinton offered.

Chase glanced to him and gave him a brief nod.

I looked at the thing I'd dropped on the ground. "Do I need to put that back on?" I pointed to it.

Rafael lifted his hand and looked at it.

"I don't believe that will be necessary." Victor said giving Chase an odd look.

"She doesn't need it." Crissy said, then turned. "I need to go to my tower. I can't find all the pieces."

"Of?" Daxx asked.

"I'm not sure." Crissy picked up her pack from beside the glass doors. "Dark eyes, blue hair...but almost white," She sighed, "and something lost that wasn't really lost and doesn't want to be found." She nodded. "Oh and a big cat." She pulled out her phone. "I think I need a book about big cats." Typing on it she walked into the solarium.

I turned and looked at Chase, then to Daxx.

She shook her head. "Not even I can translate that."

"Big cat?" Quinton rubbed the back of his neck. "I swear if Hubert starts using animals, I'm going to gut him like a chicken." He spun on his heel and walked toward the gate. "I'm going up to talk to the guards in the tower. *Someone* find Romulus so today doesn't happen again."

Everyone was silent as they watched him walk across the yard.

"Well." Alona motioned to the door. "Let's go get you settled." She yawned. "Before I fall asleep."

"See you at breakfast." Chase inclined his head to Troy, then followed his beloved.

Chapter Nine

Opening my eyes, I lay there staring at the ceiling. I didn't know how long I'd slept, but I had. This wasn't all in my head. I'd decided. There was no way I could dream up how good soaking in the tub had felt. I'd never actually seen one of those deep tubs with the fancy feet either, so I couldn't have imagined it. Or this bed. I most definitely could not dream how comfortable this bed was. Realizing that helped me to understand that there was no way I could come up with the people I'd met in the past day. Even the deepest recesses of my mind didn't have images of giant men.

The ceiling was covered in an ornate pattern. There wasn't a single stain or crack. Why would someone make a ceiling that fancy? I turned just my head and looked around the room, then back to the ceiling. I supposed it was so one could lay here and look at it.

Lifting my arm, I studied the red rubber band around my wrist. An inhibitor to block skills. *Skills*. I still wasn't willing to label my curse as a skill. These people had given me the option to hear people's thoughts or not. I couldn't even picture what my life would have been like if I'd had this all my life. The last three, since I'd been out of the asylum, the minds of crazy people hadn't been as hard, but being able to walk into a crowd while having this would have made things easier. I lowered my arm. Then again if I hadn't had this *skill* I wouldn't be as good with the bow or knives and I valued the ability to defend myself—or others as it turns out.

Something vibrating on the bedside table had me jumping out of the bed. I scrambled up and stared at it. The phone. They'd given me a phone. Leaning over it I looked down at the screen. It was lit up and said Daxx. I had no idea how to answer it. Picking it up, I then noticed it gave me two options a green circle and red one. Shrugging, I put my finger on the green one and swiped it like Alona had done with the faces yesterday.

"Hello?"

"Hey. Good. You're up."

It was Daxx. I nodded, then remembered she couldn't see me. "Yes."

"Did you get any sleep?"

I looked at the bed. The blankets were still mostly tucked in, as if I hadn't moved the entire time. "I think so."

"Great. Grab some clothes from the closet and get dressed, I'll be there shortly."

The phone went silent in my ear. I lowered it and looked down. I'd just talked on a phone. Rolling my eyes, I set it back on the table. So maybe in today's world that wasn't a big deal, but it was a first for me.

I looked down at what I was wearing. It was similar to the two-piece outfits I'd worn in the asylum, except it was new, soft and not grey. I lifted my arm and sniffed the sleeve. Okay, it smelled nothing like what I used to wear.

I went over to the closet and stood there looking at the clothes. Mitz had said they were mine. There was no way I could fit this in my bag when I left. I bit my lip. I was going to fit as much as possible though.

Kneeling, I opened my bag and took out my bow and quiver and looked in the bag. Maybe I could get another bag from Mitz? Looking back at the clothes, I sighed. How was I going to pick? They were all brand new—I'd checked after my bath. None of them smelled of anything but that new material smell. Yes, it was weird that I knew something like that, but in my entire life the closest I'd ever been to new clothes was smelling them in the stores as I walked through, wishing I could buy some.

Okay, figure out what you're wearing now and then the rest later. I nodded. As far as avoiding thinking about the day before, I was doing a good job of it so far. At some point it would sink in and then things would get unpredictable. More than once I was consumed with anxiety as I replayed my breakdown last night. It was surprising they hadn't tossed me to the curb after that. If there was even a curb that was. I still had no idea where we were. Alterealm told me nothing other than it was a place that no one knew about—yet here I was.

I stood in my door holding my bag, now much heavier than it had been, when Daxx came down the hallway.

She waved a hand. "Wasn't sure if porting in front of you would bring on another incident like last night."

I cringed. "I can't say for sure what will, or won't, cause that."

She stopped in front of me. "I understand. When I first arrived here, I thought I was in limbo between life and death." Daxx smirked when I gave her a startled look. "Long story." She looked at my bag. "You won't need that. We're going to the women's cave, where we all hang out male free." She nodded.

"Cave?"

"No. It's a room. The guys named it women's cave." She rolled her eyes. "It's more like our combined office."

"Oh." I set my bag down and looked at it. "Just leave it here?"

"Yeah, we'll be back later." She motioned inside the room. "Just thought we could fill in a few blanks for you."

I pushed the bag away from the door with my foot, then stepped out and closed it. "Am I going to be able to deal with the information?" I gave her a nervous look. "My freak out scale is on a hairpin trigger now."

She chuckled. "I understand that." She held out her hand. "I have to port us there, it's a long ride from here to the there."

"It's not in the palace?"

Daxx shook her head. "No. Actually some of us have just started moving back in here, so all the offices and important spaces like the practice room are still down below."

I nodded. "Okay." I blew out a breath. "I'm not fond of this porting."

"No one ever is at the start." She took my hand, then stood there. "Full disclosure. The lower chambers are underground, but you've been there."

I pulled my hand back. "I have?"

"The cells, Victor's office…"

"Those are underground?" I clasped my hands together.

"Yeah. Have been for," she waved her hand, "hundreds of years. If you are uncomfortable, I'll get you outside, deal?"

I inhaled slowly. I'd already been in the cells and hallway. It hadn't seemed like it was underground, except for no windows, which now made perfect sense. "Deal."

Just like that I was standing in a hallway. I took a deep breath and blew it out slowly. "This porting thing is just…"

"I agree."

I turned to see Bethany standing in the room beside us.

She smiled. "If being in a room without windows gets to you, tell us, before you…"

"Go into meltdown." Autumn finished for her.

I stepped into the room. It was huge, not office like at all. Not that I'd been in a lot of offices, but they usually didn't house what this room did. There was a sitting area—that was bigger than my apartment, if I still had one. A group of desks and chairs were near the center. Two fridges, one filled with wine I could see through the glass. There was a stereo and large television. I didn't know what the one corner was, covered in what looked like the same stuff the cubes were, but the far end of the room had a large target, complete with knives sticking out of it. *Strangest office ever.*

"Welcome to our girl space." Paisley said looking up from her phone.

Alona gave me a wave from the one of the loveseats. "This is where you will find us," she frowned and looked at Daxx, "we should get her a porter that takes her from the palace to here at least."

Daxx nodded. "I already asked Troy."

"Makes sense, now that we are splitting our time between the two areas." Autumn waved a bottle of water around, "this room isn't bad, but I prefer the guards' training yard." She shrugged, "more air and sunlight there."

"You just like it because you get to help train them now." Bethany said going to a small fridge.

"That too." Autumn waved to the fridge. "Help yourself. We bypassed the long drawn out breakfast to come and talk to you."

Before I could move, Mitz rushed past me carrying a large tray. "Here you are, loves." She went and put it on the table surrounded by the loveseats. Straightening, she gave me a smile. "There's chocolate milk in the fridge."

"You could join us, Mitz." Autumn perched on the arm of one of the loveseats. "Take a break?" She cocked her head to the side. "Do you ever take breaks?"

Mitz gave her an affectionate look. "I had far too many years of doldrums, don't you worry, I'm absolutely animated now that my boys have found all of you."

I stood there and watched as she gave each woman a loving appraisal, then she turned to me. "If you require anything, let me know." She smiled at me and the tender look in her eyes made a lump appear in my throat.

I cleared my throat. "Th-thank you." I offered her what I hoped was a genuine smile.

"Absolutely animated." She turned and was gone from the room faster than anyone could speak.

"She makes me tired." Daxx said, going over to a coffee machine.

"Mmhmm." Alona replied.

Crissy jumped up from an empty corner and came over and looked at the tray. "I think Mitz is wonderful."

"She is." Paisley came over and sat down, then patted the cushion beside her.

I glanced at the fridge and my feet were moving toward it before I decided I wanted that chocolate milk. "How does she know what I like?" I mused as I opened the door and saw three cartons of milk.

"We have no idea." Alona answered. "She knew my favorite type of wine."

"What I eat or don't." Autumn chimed in.

"It's the same for all of us." Crissy said. "No one else understood three pieces of toast like she does."

I went over and picked up an empty glass, planning to just take that much, but ended up filling it and taking the whole carton with me. Setting it on the table, I sat on the edge of a loveseat. After a small taste, I looked around at the women. "I'm so far out of my comfort zone right now."

"We've all been where you are." Bethany told me with an understanding look.

I took a moment to study each of them. I couldn't see how they could understand how I was feeling. How could they know all the emotions and turmoil inside me that went with sitting down in a normal atmosphere with people like this—for the first time in my life? I opened my mouth to tell them when Bethany held up her hand.

"Would you like to hear our stories of arriving at Alterealm or get to the need to know facts first?"

I took another sip of my milk. I really loved this milk.

"She needs to know we understand." Autumn nodded. "After hearing how we ended up here," she grinned, "you'll feel like your story is boring." Smirking she glanced at Paisley, "well except for the arrow in Raf's ass part."

I was willing to listen to anything they had to say, as long as it didn't dwell on the fact that I'd shot a prince in the tush.

Daxx sat there looking into her cup. "I was chasing a bail jumper and the next thing I know I'm sitting on dusty orange ground." She raised her eyebrows, "nothing as far as I can see but orange dusty, nothingness." She took a small sip. "I thought I was in limbo waiting to die. Then Quinton, who didn't look like he does now, came along." She shook her head, "he's talking about mages and night walkers and I'm thinking please let me wake up now." Daxx sat back, "It gets more complicated from there, but when they told me another realm, it strangely felt right." She chuckled, "after waking up with a tattoo in the middle of my back one day, anything was possible."

Crissy nodded. "I saw the tattoo before I met her."

"It does fit pieces together, doesn't it?" Alona said quietly. "You need to understand a few small details before I tell you my story."

I looked slowly from the excited Crissy to Alona. "Details?"

She gave me a soft look. "Yes. To start with people from here live longer than normal."

I poured a little more to the milk into my glass, buying my brain a few seconds to process. I didn't want to have another episode in front of these people. Too many and they'd write me off and put me in another facility, or worse. I took a deep breath and let it out slowly, trying not to think of what worse could be. "Oh?" I finally said when I noticed they were watching me with wary looks. "How much longer?" I held the glass tightly between my hands, trying not to give into the nervous urge to trace the guard on my hand.

Alona looked at Crissy. "Victor is five hundred?"

Crissy nodded, again excitedly. "Soon he will be five hundred and one."

"They better not have a ball for birthdays." Daxx mumbled.

I looked down slowly and watched the milk in my glass. Five hundred. That was—I didn't know how I felt about that.

"Kara?"

I looked over at Paisley.

"Are you all right?"

"I don't think I've ever been all right." I rolled my eyes at her. "I have trouble distinguishing between what's happening and what is from my head." I looked at Alona, "When you said longer, I was thinking one hundred...five hundred, that's—" I turned to Crissy. "How old are you?" She looked around eighteen.

She looked from me to Alona, then to Daxx. "I'm twenty-five." She frowned. "I don't know how long I'll live now though." She smiled and lifted her left arm, "with this."

I looked at her tattooed arm, not even sure if I wanted to know what that meant. One bizarre thing at a time. Minimal words I told my mouth. Curbing my habit of blurting out my sardonic opinion was in my best interest. Saying what I thought wasn't going to buy me any favors here. I needed to focus on something else for a moment. Get some questions that wouldn't leave me alone. "Having heard your thoughts, I have to ask, how do you cope with that?" I bit my lip, hoping that didn't come off as rude as it sounded out loud.

She sighed. "I don't know, I just do." Giving Daxx a nervous look, she slid from the arm of the loveseat to sit on it. Mostly. She still looked like she was going to spring off it. "I see things." Crissy tapped the side of her head. "In my head." Pointing to the corner with the plastic walls, "I write most of it down." Shaking her head, she moved off the seat and squatted beside the loveseat. "It's never ending pieces popping into my head." She nodded and looked at me.

"She has hundreds of visions a day." Daxx explained. "and more than once she's saved our butts by giving us forewarning going into something."

"Yeah if I can figure them out." Leaning forward, she took a piece of fruit off the tray and put it in her mouth.

"You figure out enough." Paisley said with a gentle look.

"Not to mention you have a photographic memory on top of that. We never have look up anything on the internet anymore." Bethany said giving her a big smile.

Eyebrows raised, I looked at Crissy. "That explains *so* much."

Alona chuckled. "Probably felt like you were hit by a truck when her thoughts were popped into your head."

I nodded.

"Her emotions are just as rapid." Alona said.

"I'm getting better, with the walls so I don't affect you, Alona." She frowned, then turned to me. "I don't know if I can pause the images when I'm near you though."

I lifted the hand with the red cuff on it. "With this you won't have to."

Tilting her head she studied me. "You really don't want to have an ability, do you?"

I shook my head. "Helping last night is the first time I've used it," I rolled my eyes, "except to get me out of that asylum."

"I'm glad you got out." She nodded, then took another piece of fruit. Getting up, she went over to the corner and started bouncing a rubber ball against the wall.

"It helps her process the visions." Alona said in a hushed voice.

"I wish her luck with that." Taking a sip, I flicked my gaze from woman to woman.

"I'll go next." Autumn said quickly. "I'm the most recent addition to Alterealm." She grinned. "Before this I lived in the back of a gym."

I'd heard of worse things. "It's out of the weather."

"Right." She sobered. "Joe's Bronze Ring, you may have heard of it."

"I know where it is. I don't go in places with mostly men though."

Alona gasped. "I just realized you'd hear their thoughts. You poor woman."

I made one of those noises that was like an exclamation mark, because that's all I had to say on the thoughts of men.

Autumn gave her head a shake. "I used to think my story was bad, but what your family did to you is worse."

"Your family was like mine?" Was it possible that there were other parents out there that just dropped off their children and never returned?

Autumn shrugged. "Wouldn't know. As far back as I can remember is when I was six. I was alone on the streets then." She gave her head a slight shake. "But I'm here now."

"How did you end up on the streets at six?" I leaned forward. How could another human to someone so young?"

"No idea." She smiled at Paisley, "but thanks to lab geeks, I have a blood sister."

I looked at Paisley, then back to her. I knew my mouth was wide open. "You're sisters?"

She nodded.

"And you found out here?" I paused before I said it out loud. Once the words came out, there was no going back. "In another realm?"

"Yes." Paisley laughed, "and we have more relatives here than we know what to do with."

I sat back. "How did you end up going from a gym to here?"

Autumn looked angry for a moment. I was afraid I'd overstepped somehow. It was one of my skills, saying the wrong thing.

"The bastards got me." She said quietly. "Drugged me during my morning run."

"Which, uh, slags are that? I don't know if you've noticed, but there are a lot of them out there."

"The ones taking women." Bethany said.

Autumn nodded. "Same ones you were following. They shackled me, brought me here to Alterealm," she snorted, "they learned the hard way to never try that again."

"She kicked their asses, even in chains." Daxx said with a big grin.

My jaw dropped again. "Why-why are they collecting up women? Human trafficking?"

Daxx shook her head. "Worse."

I frowned, "Worse?"

"They're breeding people to men with Alterealm blood." Daxx informed me.

"Holy mother of pearl!" I covered my mouth. "Who-why? Is there a female shortage over here?" My FOS stared to escalate rapidly.

"No." Paisley moved over closer and put her hand on my arm. "No, there isn't. It's nothing like that."

"It's that Hubert douche we mentioned yesterday. He's totally insane and wants to take over Alterealm and start his own following." Autumn said in a low tone.

"And many more horrific things." Alona added.

Holding my hand over my erratic heart, I blew out a breath and looked to Autumn. "I'm so glad you got away."

Autumn nodded and looked at Paisley. "We both did."

My head snapped to look at Paisley. "They had you too?"

She nodded slowly, the expression on her face changing to a more somber look. "I woke up on an island filled with the lunatics."

"An island?" My eyes felt like they couldn't be opened any further.

"Which we shut down." Daxx told me.

"Oh. Oh good." I swallowed the tightness in my throat and took another deep breath.

"Some don't get away." Bethany said quietly.

I looked around. "You got those girls from the apartment."

"We've gotten many from places they were stashed all over the city." Alona said. "But sadly, we're not in time for some."

"What-what..."

"Emil's daughter was also taken." Paisley interrupted. "She's pregnant."

I jumped up and paced to the other side of the room. Stopping I stared a wall with a map on it, not really seeing, just trying to process.

"Kara." Alona was beside me. "We're not telling this to upset you."

I glanced at her. "It's hard to unhear that." I took a deep breath and exhaled slowly. I'd been on the other end of being forced to do something. No choice in the direction of your life. Most of the time I avoided getting in the middle of things, or tried to. Sometimes I couldn't go the other way, no matter how much I told my legs to run. But this—this happening to women was... I looked at the floor, even with my vast knowledge of words, I didn't have one that adequately described how wrong and awful this was. "Can-can I help find the rest?" I looked back to her, then turned and watched the other women watching me. "I can-can do something. Listen to thoughts or even stick arrows in people, I don't like to harm others, but some..."

"Have it coming." Autumn finished.

I nodded.

Alona put her hand on my arm. "Let's finish talking and then we'll figure out how your useful skills can be put to use."

I nodded briskly. Never in my life did I think I'd want to use my curse. I started to walk back. "Is Emil's daughter all right? I mean..."

Autumn was kneeling on the couch watching me. "She's coming to terms with things. She's going to have the baby and come over here and live in the palace."

I went around the loveseat and sat back down. "A guarded palace will be good." Picking up my glass, I took a sip. My mind was churning with what they'd told me. I didn't know this woman, but she must be incredibly strong.

"You good?"

I looked at Autumn. "I don't think I will recover from knowing that."

She gave me a hard look. "Good. Retribution is a great motivator."

"I don't know about retribution, but I understand being made to do things you don't want or deserve, and these women are worse off than I was, so I have to do whatever I can."

Autumn nodded slowly, I could tell she was feeling what I was saying by the look on her face.

Taking a jagged breath, I looked at Paisley. "How did you get away? Did you have to fight them too?"

Crissy came back over, a puzzled look on her face and sat on the floor beside the loveseat.

Paisley grinned at me. "No. I jumped off a cliff into the water. Arius pulled me out."

"I saw her." Crissy said. "I was afraid she'd drown."

"You guys were there?"

Daxx shook her head. "Crissy had a vision of Paisley in the water and told us. They got there in time."

I held my breath for a moment as I processed that. Exhaling all at once, I stared at Paisley. She only nodded. Turning, I gave Crissy an appraising look. "You see things in advance?"

With her excited expression she nodded, then she frowned. "I just wished they came with instructions to put together."

"I don't envy you."

She shrugged. "It's just me. I don't know what to do without it."

Everyone turned to look at Bethany.

"Oh," she smiled, "my turn." She bit her lip and gave me a look I didn't understand. "My story is," She winced, "very different than the others."

Alona laughed. "Just a bit. I can still see you threatening Victor and calling Raf Tarzan."

Beth's face flushed. "Hind sight, huh?" She took a deep breath then looked to me. "I'm a witch," she held up her hand and red sparks came off it. "I use magic." She closed her hand and they were gone. "My best friend got mixed up with Hubert's mages and ended up being put in the cells here." She paused and watched me.

If she was waiting to see if she had my attention—what else would hold it after her saying that? I nodded, just in case she needed some visual cue.

"So," she said softly, "I was told by one of Hubert's idiot mages that the royals," she motioned to the other women, "would trade someone to get my friend back."

I nodded again, more than intrigued.

"I mesmerized Leone from a distance…"

I frowned.

"I got inside his mind," she said quickly, "and talked to him non-stop. Then I lead him to a house in this realm." She looked sad for a moment. "It was a trap. They warded, a spell of sorts, the house so he couldn't leave."

My eyebrows went up. There was such a thing?

"Then I realized after talking to him that I was so far on the wrong side of all of this—but it was too late. So, I wandered around Alterealm's," she sighed, "endless fields to get help."

"That's when she ended up in the cells." Autumn nodded.

"Yes," she rolled her eyes. "Trying to get through to you guys was not easy."

Daxx snorted. "Getting anything through the men's heads is a hard task."

I looked back at Beth. "Clearly you're forgiven."

She brushed the hair back from her face. "It was a bit bumpy for a while, but yes."

I put my hand against my cheek and looked at her for a moment. Dropping my hand, I picked up my glass. "I feel a bit better about shooting Rafael now."

"I'm just happy you're on our side." Daxx said as she got up and went toward the coffee brewer. "When I thought Willis Hubert's men were using bows and arrows, I was ready to go buy a gun."

Paisley nodded. "It was frightening until we realized you weren't."

"I wasn't very calm myself." I took the last sip of the milk, then debated if I wanted to fill the glass again. Deciding not, I picked up the carton and went over to the fridge and put it in. I wasn't ready to sit back down but went and stood near them. "How did you end up here, Crissy?"

I wasn't sure I could handle much more but asked despite my better judgement.

Crissy smiled and looked at Daxx.

"I brought her." Daxx said. "We've known each other for a while. We knew she'd be okay here, because she could see mages and through their magic."

I started tracing the leather on my hand without looking down at them. "See them?"

"Their eyes." Alona replied.

"Oh." I frowned. I'd seen their eyes too, I thought. "So-so something like that makes a difference?"

Alona nodded. "Yes. Most cannot. Although we are starting to piece together that all of us," she motioned to the others, "have at least one parent with Alterealm genes."

It took my brain as few moments to put that together. "You think," I looked at my hand for a second as I continued tracing the finger guard. "You think one of mine did too?"

She nodded. "There's a strong possibility."

"Oh." I sat on the arm of the loveseat. "Does that mean I'll live longer or," I looked around at the others briefly, "what does that mean?"

"Do your eyes change color?" Alona asked with a serious look on her face.

I shook my head. "Not that I know of."

"Then it more than likely is just in your DNA, nothing more." She smiled. "Which is a good prelude to my story. My father was from here, my mother from our side." She sat there looking at me for a few moments. "I am much older than I appear to be," she smirked, "at least I hope so."

I studied her for a moment, she didn't look older than thirty. Actually, if I didn't take into account her eyes, which showed a longer history then the rest of her, her appearance wasn't much older than mine. "You don't look much older than I am, or how old I think I am."

Alona smiled. "Bless you." Her expression sobered. "I'm ninety-eight."

The room was silent. All the women were looking at me as I digested that number. Victor was five hundred, Alona was ninety-eight. I cleared my throat. "You look great." Was the first thing my mouth thought to say.

"Thank you." She leaned forward and set her cup on the table. "This is the part where I put your internal freak out meter to the test."

Again, complete silence. I wasn't sure if warning me was good. Just the thought of my FOS climbing, accelerated my heart rate and had it climbing. I blew out a short breath and gave her a quick nod. Better to get it over fast, I thought. I held my hands clasped tightly together in my lap.

"You've seen the mages with their glowing purple eyes."

I nodded, feeling like I was vibrating with nervous energy.

"Well in this realm, there are other colors eyes can change to." She was speaking slowly in a soothing tone.

I didn't feel soothed in the slightest. I felt anxious.

"Talk fast or she's going to have a meltdown before you get to the rest." Autumn said quickly.

With a slight nod, Alona looked at me, her eyes locked on mine. "Other than the magic users, the color of the eyes denotes a variance of how one sustains life."

Her wording was not making my FOS go down.

Alona glanced to the floor briefly then looked back at me. "Mine are red."

Her eyes were red. Not blood shot red, not tinged red, but glowing, bright blood red. I straightened and then froze, just looking at her eyes. With jerky movements I looked to the other women, their eyes hadn't changed, then snapped my head back to Alona. Still red. "And-and," I swallowed the lump in my throat, "and you sustain life how?"

"Mmm," she held my look, "that's the part that will set off your built-in panic meter." She whispered.

I held my breath, not moving at all as she opened her mouth far enough, I could see tips of fangs. Fangs. *A fang is a long, pointed tooth. In mammals, a fang is a modified maxillary tooth, used for biting and tearing flesh...* Now was not the time to recite definitions from dictionaries I told my brain. Tearing flesh. My brain reiterated. "Uh..." I stood up and backed up a few feet.

"It's not as you think." Alona said.

I frowned, her eyes were no longer red. "I think," I swallowed, trying cue my mouth to secrete saliva. "I think fangs are a modified maxillary tooth, used for biting and tearing flesh." I nodded quickly.

"Yes." Crissy jumped up. "In mammals that is what they are for." She nodded. "Alona isn't an animal that needs to hunt prey to survive." Her expression was one of excitement again. "I looked it up." She grinned. "I like fangs. I wanted to know how they just appeared." Crissy's expression grew somber, "and the anatomy of Alona's and all the other essence feeders isn't anything like an animals' fang..."

I couldn't process what she was saying. "Essence feeder." I whispered. "The man that was taking women was an emotion feeder." My mind was scrolling through words quickly. "I only know two definitions of feeder." I looked at Alona, "and you are not a container filled with food."

"Tell that to her mate." Daxx snorted, then shook her head quickly. "Sorry." She lifted her hands. "It's the hardest thing to understand over here," she grimaced, "maybe not the hardest, but..."

"Definitely the most bizarre." Paisley finished for her. "When Arius showed me his fangs, I thought..."

"Vampire." Beth nodded.

I backed up another foot, trying not to give into the fear that was building up inside me. "Your," I looked from Paisley to Beth, "husbands have fangs?"

Beth nodded. Paisley as well.

"All of the guys do except Chase." Autumn said nonchalantly.

My head snapped back to Alona.

She shrugged. "It's true. Chase's eyes go yellow. He's an emotion feeder."

In a blur I turned and walked toward the corner with the target. Every word they'd said since I'd stepped into this room started flashing through my mind. It was so much, *too much* to deal with. Because finding out that Alterealm was a real place wasn't bad enough, now I had to cope with—my mind stopped. An image frozen in it like someone had taken a snapshot of it. I turned slowly and looked at the anxious women behind me. "Are there green eyes? Bright not-natural green?"

Daxx frowned. "Yes."

I put my hand on my forehead. "I thought it was the drugs. When I kept seeing them, I thought it was because of the wacked up meds they were pumping into me." I shrugged, "they didn't help with hearing thoughts, but sometimes they made me hallucinate..."

"Someone in the asylum had green eyes?" Autumn stood up.

I nodded. "Yes. What does that mean?"

"It means they were locked up with a smorgasbord." Daxx said sounding appalled.

"What?" I hugged my waist, feeling dizzy and nauseous suddenly.

"Green means they are life suckers." Autumn said. "If they touch someone..."

Eyes huge I covered my mouth with both hands. More than once people collapsed, that had seemed perfectly normal—well as normal as some in that intuition could be. I dropped down to squat and hugged my knees.

"Kara?"

I shook my head, not able to say anything just yet. This was all real. This had been real when I'd thought people locked up me with complete lunatics...and they'd only wanted to go home.

Bethany came over and sat beside me on the floor. She didn't try to touch me. I appreciated that she recognized that it would send me over the edge.

"It seems you've been exposed to Alterealm long before you came here." She said quietly.

"I thought-it was all so," I took a deep breath and exhaled slowly, "how could I know it was all real?"

"You couldn't." She leaned over her legs so she could look into my eyes. "There's no way you could have known."

I held her dark eyes. "I thought they were all insane."

A look of compassion appeared on her face. "Some may have been."

"I wanted out," I whispered, "and they just wanted to come home."

She nodded, "maybe the guys can look into that place and see if some are still there."

I let out a shaky breath. "I can't go back."

"You don't have to." Daxx came over and held her hand out to me.

I looked at it for a moment and then took it and let her help me to my feet.

She titled her head, an apprehensive look on her face. "This is not the way we pictured this talk going."

Releasing her hand, I nodded slowly. "I just feel like I've been whacked upside the head with all of this."

"You need to eat something to level out your blood sugar." Paisley suggested, "I think the speed your heart was going probably depleted any energy stores you had."

I gave her a skeptical look. "That's putting it mildly."

"Come sit." Alona patted the cushion beside her. With a sigh, she turned toward the door. "You may as well come in Chase, your hovering in the hall is starting to grate on my nerves."

Chase leaned around the doorframe and smiled at her. "I intended to, beloved," he waved his hand around, "but it seemed an inopportune moment to barge in." He inclined his head to me.

Taking a deep breath, I went over and sat down again. Paisley handed me a small plate with fruit on it.

"Is there a reason..." Daxx was interrupted when her phone rang. She answered it. "Still in the girls cave..." She frowned, "about?" She nodded. "I'll tell the others." She tucked the phone back in her pocket. "We are to go to the dining room. Its urgent."

Everyone turned and looked at Chase. He gave them a slight shrug. "Don't ask me, I was lurking here."

Autumn turned to me. "You okay being underground a bit longer?"

I paused holding a piece of fruit in front of my mouth. I'd been so agog with everything they were telling me I'd forgotten I was underground. I set the fruit back on the plate. "It doesn't feel like underground."

She gave me an abrupt nod, then motioned to the door. "You can come with us then."

Chapter Ten

The dining room was bigger than the soup kitchen on the southside. It should have been called a dining hall, not room. I sat in the chair and looked at the wall, at some point there had been portraits hanging there. Many, if the dark spots were any indication.

"Alona had them sent to the palace to be hung there again." Autumn leaned closer and told me. "It was only proper, or something."

It made sense to me, I supposed. I glanced to the men at the other end of the table. "Are meetings always held in the dining room?"

She made a noise, I couldn't define. "Yeah. They need a room just for meetings instead of bouncing from office to the practice room, or guard training yard."

I watched Troy and Chase as they spoke to two people in black robes. The man held himself stiffly, his face was cold and, well reminded me of Victor. The woman in the robe was almost as tall as the males with white spiked hair. "Are they priests?"

Daxx snorted, sitting down on the other corner of the table. "No. They're part of the elder's council."

I looked at her. "Elder? Usually implies someone of greater age." I watched Victor go over and bow his head in a respectful way. "They're older than Victor?"

"Yeah. A lot older we're told." Autumn answered softly.

How could someone be 'a lot' older than a person that was five hundred? I quickly forgot that thought when all five of them turned and looked at me. "Why are they looking at me?" I wasn't really asking anyone.

"I think I'll go find out." Daxx got up and walked toward them.

Bethany sat down in the seat she'd vacated. "Any ideas what this is about?" She looked at Autumn.

Autumn shook her head. "Michael's emotions have been iceman for the last few hours."

"Uh," Beth sighed, "that can't be good." She glanced at her phone. "Leone messaged on the way here and said he had to go take care of something and would be back later."

"Did he say what?" Autumn asked.

Beth shook her head. "No. Which is unusual."

"Something's up." Paisley said sitting down beside Autumn. "Arius is in beast mode and said he'd be unreachable for a while and I was to stay here or in the palace, nowhere else."

"I was told the same." Beth said.

"Ditto." Autumn mumbled.

Frowning, Daxx started walking back toward us. "Kara, while we wait for a few of the others to arrive, could the kings have a word with you?"

I glanced around to the others in the room. Quinton and Emil were looking at a tablet and talking to some man I didn't know. Rafael was standing near the door talking to three large men that looked like pirates. Alona was speaking with a woman I hadn't seen before. There was too much going on in this room. I touched the red cuff under the table and was very thankful I had it.

"I'll go with you." Autumn stood up.

Daxx nodded and stood beside Bethany.

I got up slowly, and moved down the table, not sure why they'd need to talk to me. There was a room full of people, a whole realm of people that served them, why me? I stopped a few feet away from them.

Chase winked at me, then motioned to the two in black robes. "This is Elder Segos and Elder Drusla."

I wasn't sure which was which because they both bowed their head as he said it.

"We've been discussing a few matters and think you may be able to help." Troy said with an unreadable expression on his face.

Moving just my eyes I looked at Chase for a second and then back to Troy. "With?" I couldn't think what *matters* I could be helpful with.

"I have to say," the female elder nodded to Autumn then smiled at me, "hearing of your shot at the palace yesterday is quite impressive." She glanced to the other elder. "Don't you agree Elder Segos?"

He inclined his head. "Indeed, a precision shot such as that requires great skill."

So Drusla was the women, I surmised from that exchange. "You want me to shoot someone?" I inhaled through my nose slowly, then exhaled. "The idea of hitting anyone— seriously harming another being bothers me, but," I looked at Autumn, "having a few blanks filled in, I could be persuaded to help in that way."

"Noted." Troy said abruptly. "However, that's not the help we were referring to."

I frowned. "Oh."

Elder Drusla looked at the red cuff on my arm. "The inhibitor is working? You can't hear what we're thinking?"

"I doubt she could, Elder Drusla, without it. Our minds are too disciplined…"

Chase waved his hand, "That's not the point, Elder Segos." Chase gave me a questioning look, "there are a few thoughts we really need to know." He looked at Troy for a moment, "to end this for good."

I bit my lip and looked down at the red band. I'd helped once by listening and I had told the women I would do it again, but I couldn't prevent the feelings of panic that went with it. "I can try," a thought hit me, I looked at Chase, "one at a time?"

He nodded. "For now, yes."

For now? My FOS jolted up a few points. I glanced briefly to Autumn. "I don't know if I can handle more than one or two at a time."

Autumn gave Elder Drusla a look. "Then we'll make sure it's only one or two."

The elder inclined her head.

"I think we should start with Eunice." Troy said in a low tone.

"Eunice?" I remembered Autumn mentioning that name—before my freak out at the office.

Autumn's expression hardened. "She's our ticket to Hubert. She's in the cells."

"Thanks to you, princess." Elder Segos bowed his head to her.

"Yeah, I still have a few things to settle with her." She looked back to me. "She says she doesn't know what's going on. Doesn't know how she ended up in the cells." Crossing her arms over her chest, she glanced briefly to the elder. "We need to know if she's full of it."

"She could lead us to her brother Nelson." Chase offered with a shrug.

"Is-is Hubert the same person as Nelson?" The kings had said they needed to get Nelson to end this.

"No." Victor crossed his arms over his chest. "I suspect if we find one, we'll find the other."

I nodded slowly, processing. "I can-can try to see if this Eunice has any useful thoughts."

"Excellent." Elder Drusla smiled at me, then bowed her head.

I needed to ask someone why people kept bowing to me. Was it some sort of custom here, or an acknowledgment? I needed to know.

"We'll set that up after we find out about the details of this message." Victor nodded abruptly and glanced at his phone. "My brothers are on their way back from the communication center now."

I frowned. Message? I turned to ask Autumn what that was about when Michael, Arius and Leone came into the room, a tall man in black robes with them. His long hair was black with pure white streaks going through it, his eyes almost as dark as his hair. He glanced to me as he approached us, my heart pounded hard in my chest from his dark appraisal.

The brothers stopped, the older man didn't. He went right up to the kings and bowed deeply for a few seconds. "Your majesties."

Victor inclined his head. "Elder Marinus."

Straightening, the man nodded. "I have just confirmed the message is authentic."

"What is it?" Troy's whole posture changed.

"The communication is from Solrelm, Night King." He bowed his head again.

Chase's easy posture stiffened. "Solrelm? That's," he shrugged, "I can't even remember the last time we heard from there."

"It's very rare, indeed, brother." Troy turned back to the older man. "What is it they want?"

"An audience with the royal family." Elder Marinus told him in a low tone, "it sounded urgent."

Troy rubbed the back of his neck and glanced to Victor. "Set it up as soon as we're able to arrange security."

"Very well. Shall I limit their attendance?" This time he looked to Rafael.

Rafael came over to stand in front of him. "I'd prefer no more than three."

"That's three more than I'd like." Quinton said quietly.

Ignoring him, Rafael continued, "Elders and personal guards present outside the doors."

The elder nodded. "Very well. I will ensure it is arranged."

"I'll call Ira and get him to have escorts ready." Rafael pulled out his phone and walked over by the door.

From silently observing, I noticed the men in the room seemed to know what was going on, and judging by the looks on the faces of the women, they did not. I bit my lip and debated, for about thirty seconds, about taking off the rubber inhibitor and listening to see how that was possible. How did none of the women know a thing about Solrelm, wherever that was. And more important why did I want to know?

All three elders bowed their heads and left through the other door. Victor went over and closed the door and then turned around and looked at the men that had been talking to Rafael. They inclined their heads and went out.

The woman Alona had been chatting to, bowed and quickly followed them.

Arius glanced to the man Quinton and Emil had been talking to.

"Ellis can stay." Chase said.

With a nod, Arius closed the other door.

"Okay now I'm a bit concerned." Alona said quietly and went to sit beside Daxx.

The door behind Victor opened and Crissy came though it. She stopped and looked at the other closed door and frowned. "What's wrong?"

"That's what I'd like to know." Daxx stood up, "what is the deal with this Solrelm place? I've never even heard it mentioned before." She waved a hand at the door. "and this is the first time those doors have ever been closed."

"I was wondering the same thing." Alona leaned forward on the table.

Troy rubbed the back of his neck. He straightened and looked at Daxx. "It's not going to help Kara's current state of mind to go into great detail about it right now."

I looked from him to Daxx, then back. "What do I have to do with it?"

"Because," Chase moved over to stand beside his twin, "you've just found out another realm other than the world you live in exists."

"And we may have left out a few details in the past when discussing various topics with our mates," Troy added.

"Oh?" Alona gave Chase a hard look.

"And here I thought the secrets and guessing games were all behind us now." Daxx crossed her arms over her chest. "What don't we know?"

Arius looked at Paisley, she raised one eyebrow at him.

"That there are more than the two realms." He said quietly.

"How many more?" Paisley asked him.

"There are six in total." Victor said without preamble. "Your world," he looked at me, "Alterealm," he glanced at the twins, "Solrelm is yet another..."

"This meeting is with people," Bethany waved her hand, "or whatever from another realm?"

Leone nodded and then glanced to Daxx. "I've only ever been at one other meeting with them, so it's not even something I think about day to day."

"There's information in the library. A whole section about the other realms." Crissy stood up.

"And you've never told us?" Daxx asked her.

"How do I know what you want to be told and not be told?" She shrugged, "if you make a list, I can tell you." Crissy frowned, "but I don't know how you'd know what you want to put on the list if you don't know."

Everyone paused and looked at her. I felt better knowing they didn't quite understand that either.

Daxx shook her head abruptly. "We'll—deal with that later." She turned and looked at Troy, an unhappy expression on her face. "So, other than you didn't tell any of us," she waved a hand to where the women were sitting, "that there are more realms." She paused for a moment and looked at the floor, as if she'd lost her train of thought completely.

"You watch over our realm," Paisley looked at Arius, "does this other one have a job?"

"What is this Solrelm? Its purpose?" Bethany asked.

Arius studied her for a moment. "They do."

"Creeps me out." Quinton stated bluntly.

Mitz came in the door the elders had gone out. "Sorry to interrupt, I'll need the ladies at the seamstress shortly to alter sashes before the meeting."

"Sashes?" Daxx crossed her arms and looked at Troy.

He cleared his throat. "We'll have to be more formal for this..."

"Formal how?" she growled.

Troy's lips twitched. "A robe to go over your clothes."

"No bodice and gown?" Daxx clarified.

Mitz chuckled. "Only if you wish." She turned and looked from Troy to Chase. "Robes, sashes and amulets only?"

Chase looked at Daxx for a moment. "I think that would be wise, lest Kitten stab her king."

Mitz smiled. "I'll tell them to leave the crowns in the vault." She looked at me. "You'll be wanting Kara to attend?"

Troy, Chase and Victor all turned to look at Rafael.

Rafael's brows drew together as he glared back at them.

"Oh," Alona said softly while smiling at Rafael.

"I knew it." Autumn nodded.

Knew what? I looked around at the others trying to decipher what they were talking about. Most in the room were looking at Rafael with smirks on their faces.

Heaving an audible sigh, Rafael stomped over to the door and opened it.

"Raf, where are you going? We have to get security sorted out." Leone gave him a hard look.

Rafael stopped and turned around. His expression wasn't a good one. "I know." He lifted his hand in the air, then dropped it. "I don't want any of this." He glanced at me, his blue eyes moving over me slowly. "*But* we can't leave her just sitting outside the damn doors. So I'm going to get an amulet for her to wear. *Temporarily.*" He heaved another big sigh, "so I don't have to listen to the questions why she's in the chamber without one," he turned on his heel, "and the blah blah blah."

It was quiet for several seconds as everyone watched him go out the door.

"Blah blah blah is new to his vocabulary." Chase said looking at Victor.

"I think there are many things in his world are about to be new." Victor said, looking amused.

"Okay, ladies, lets get to the seamstress's quarters." Mitz clapped her hands together.

Chapter Eleven

Before I could figure out what was going on, I found myself in a long grey robe with elaborate black suns and moons embroidered on it. The material was soft and reflective, almost shiny, but not quite. Everyone was standing in a room of chairs waiting for the elders to arrive. Adjusting the red sash, I looked again at the large emblem of a shield and sword on it and wondered what that was supposed to mean. None of the other women's sashes had that on it. Daxx had a large moon and small sun on hers. Alona's was the opposite to that. Crissy's had something that looked like the scales of justice on it, and Paisley's was similar only a sword was in the middle pointing down. I frowned when I noticed Victor's matched Crissy's. What did these symbols represent?

I looked at the door again, debating if leaving was a better option for me. Outside the door stood large armed personal guards for the women. Chances of them letting me just walk away? Less than zero, according to my calculations.

"You doing okay?"

I looked away from the door to Autumn. Her sash had a book of some sort with a sword through it. I studied the pendant she wore hanging out of her robe and noticed it was the same. "I'm not sure why I'm here." I rolled my eyes and motioned to what I was wearing, "in this meeting or whatever it is."

She snorted. "Join the crowd."

"Don't you want to see people older than ten centuries?" Alona asked as she adjusted her sash.

She had a point. It's not like I'd get that opportunity again in my life. Then again, I'd only just found out that there were people that lived that long. "They're all over one thousand?"

"Yep." Daxx pulled at the collar of her robe. "That's what we're told."

"I wonder how old they are." Bethany was playing with her pendant that hung over her sash. Matching symbols of two swords crossed with the sun and moon on either side for Bethany, I mused in my head. Still not knowing what all of it meant.

"Elder Varus is two thousand, six hundred years old." Crissy said as she fidgeted with her pendant. It looked like she was having a hard time standing still and doing nothing. Knowing the flow of her mind, I could understand why she would have a hard time being idle.

Paisley looked at her. "Did you read that?"

Crissy shook her head. "I asked Victor." She nodded. "Elder Varus is the oldest and that's why she's the head of the council." She glanced over to the where the men stood chatting. "Elder Landry is the youngest, he's only eleven hundred."

"*Only*." Daxx murmured and rolled her eyes.

I was going to meet people that were *that* old. I was struggling to make it to twenty-six and they had survived hundreds, and more than a thousand—or two.

"Each brother has a mentor on the council," Crissy was talking fast, but quietly, "I wonder if Emil has one now?"

All conversation stopped when Rafael came into the room. With long strides he came toward me. My heart started beating faster. The first time it had happened, he was glaring at me in the cube, then again when I watched him wield his sword in his warrior garb. Now, in a non-threatening robe like my own it was happening again. I turned to say something to Autumn, then noticed the women had moved a few feet away, leaving me standing there by myself. My level of panic elevated.

Rafael stopped in front of me and looked down at me. I couldn't figure out what he was thinking, his expression was completely closed off.

His sash had the same thing on it mine did. I stood there staring at it, puzzling out why they would do that. Clearly the matching symbols between the men and women meant they were a couple. Why would they want to portray Rafael and I were? And why was it necessary I was at this meeting? With people from another realm...

He held up his hand, a silver chain with pendant dangling from it.

I looked at the pendant. It had a shield with a single sword, pointing up on it. On either side of that there was a sun and moon. It was the same as the larger one around his neck.

"*This* is my mates' pendant." He said quietly. "You need to wear this to be in these chambers."

I stood there, then realized he was waiting for me to take it. "Why do I need to be here?"

Rafael's jaw clenched, his expression going blank. He held the pendant closer to me.

Glancing out of the corner of my eye to Autumn, she gave her head a quick shake. Hesitantly, I took it from his hand. "I'll return it when we're finished."

His blue eyes moved over my face, I thought for a split second they softened. Without further comment, he spun on his heal and walked over to Michael.

"Well, that was something." Alona gave me a gentle smile as she came over and took the necklace out of my hand. Stepping behind me, she put it around my neck.

"Guess that arrow broke Rafael's charm." Daxx said as she crossed her arms and stood to study Rafael.

"Definitely not what I expected." Bethany whispered.

"She did shoot him in the butt with an arrow." Paisley had moved closer as well.

"Yeah." Autumn smirked. "I think his *pride* is more damaged than his butt was."

"Damaged describes so much more than his pride." Chase said as he moved closer. He motioned around the room. "We've graduated to a new arrangement in these chambers."

I looked around at all the chairs behind tables. Along the back was a long table with at least a dozen chairs behind it. I watched Alona look down the long tables that were set up to curve from one end to the other. I didn't stop to count chairs but guessed there had to be close to twenty. Going off how fancy they were compared to the others, it must be where the royal family sat.

"Are our guests using those chairs?" Alona asked.

I followed the direction she pointed to see four chairs at the end of the room.

"Yes." Chase pointed to the opposite end where two more chairs had been placed behind a table. "The archivists will sit there." He looked bored. "Official meetings such as this are transcribed for the journals."

"You guys should join this century and tape them." Paisley said glancing up from her phone.

Chase grimaced. "That would be a sight, your papa-elder's face in the archives for all to see."

Crissy shook her head. "I like that they put them in journals to read."

"Of course you do." Daxx said, then sighed. "When is this rigmarole starting?"

Just then a door on the far end of the room opened.

"Now." Chase answered.

Twelve people came out of the door wearing the long black robes. They moved to stand behind the long table and stood beside their chairs. In unison they all bowed.

"Your majesties." The woman in the middle with long white braid said.

I looked down the length of the table, trying to see if any of them looked as old as a thousand. They didn't. Which was probably okay, if they aged normally it would likely not be pretty to see.

"Our guests will be arriving shortly." The woman said looking at Chase. "They are adjusting to our realm." She offered a polite smile. "I thought it prudent for us to precede their arrival and meet the new members of the royal family."

"A meet and greet of sorts, of course." Chase motioned to the curved table. "Perhaps you can give us a hint as to how we're supposed to be formally placed along our new table too."

Elder Varus nodded. "Elder Landry has overseen the new arrangement of the chambers, I will let him assist there."

A man with long brown hair and gentle eyes bowed his head. "It would be my pleasure." He glanced down the length of the table. "It would save time if we introduced ourselves as well."

"A wonderful idea, Elder Landry." The woman with red hair smiled. I didn't know how old she was, there were a few grey streaks in her hair, but nothing made her look older than a thousand years old. "I'm Elder Udela." She looked right at me as she said it, then bowed her head.

I didn't know if I should smile or…

"Elder Drusla." The woman I'd met earlier stated abruptly.

Next to her was a man with light brown hair, he didn't look fifty, never mind older than a thousand. "Elder John." He looked at Michael and bowed his head.

Next to him was Elder Landry, he motioned to the man that had reported to the kings in the dining room. "Elder Marinus." He said in a deep tone.

The man beside him was Elder Segos, who bowed his head abruptly before stating his name. "Segos."

Watching him for a second, Elder Varus turned to look on the other side of her.

A man with white hair, very little black still showing, nodded. "Elder Moire."

Next to him, the man with the long wavy grey hair made an elaborate motion with his hand before bowing his head. "Elder Nodin."

Elder Udela was beside him, she turned to look at the man beside her.

He squinted at all of us for a few moments, before smiling a stiff grin at Paisley and Autumn. "Elder Roan."

The woman with dark hair and haunting white eyes bowed her head gracefully. "Elder Faran."

Last at the table was a happy looking woman with curly white hair, it bounced as she nodded. "Elder Arian."

Elder Landry came around the table into the center where we stood. He walked to the far end of the curved table. Skipping two end chairs he motioned to the next one. "Prince Emil, if you would."

Emil raised an eyebrow. Without comment, he went around the table and stood beside the chair the elder had motioned to.

"Prince Quinton, The Huntress's Captain." Elder Landry motioned the chair beside Emil.

"Perhaps we can forego the long titles at this point." Troy suggested. "So we can all find our chairs before our guests arrive."

Elder Landry inclined his head. "As you wish." He stepped to the next chair. "Prince Arius."

With long strides Arius went to the chair, Paisley followed him and stood at the chair next to him.

The elder nodded and stepped to the next chair. "Princess Autumn."

With a quiet snort, Autumn went to the chair. Michael followed her and stood in front of the chair beside her.

"Very good." The elder said in a hushed tone. "Huntress." He looked at Daxx. She nodded and went to the chair. Troy, Chase and Alona followed and took the next three chairs.

The elder walked along and motioned to the chair beside Alona. "Justice."

With a stern look, Victor moved to take that spot. Crissy was right beside him.

"Enforcer." The elder looked at Leone.

Leone smiled and took Bethany's hand and went to the chair.

The elder stood there and looked at me.

"Kara." I said nervously, not sure if he knew my name.

"Princess Kara and our Captain of the guard."

Before I could correct him on the princess part, Rafael took my elbow and steered me around the table.

I stood beside Bethany, she gave me a reassuring smile.

"I have to say, princess, I'm quite excited you're here."

I looked to see Elder Udela looking at me. I needed to correct this princess thing…

"I too have telepathic abilities." She smiled at me.

I didn't know what to say to that. I'd never met anyone that had the same problem as I did. Why was she looking so pleased about it?

"Can you hear our thoughts?" Elder Varus asked.

I opened my mouth to say something, when Chase answered.

"Kara is wearing an inhibitor at the moment." Chase looked down the table at me. "She finds too many thoughts overwhelming," he motioned to Crissy with a smile on his face, "and our seer's thought capacity almost debilitated her."

"Oh. Yes." Elder Udela nodded. "I remember how hard the first few hundred years were for me." She heaved a loud sigh. "It was a very trying time." She held up her arm, her robe fell down her arm to reveal a thin band on it. "When Elder Arian designed this, I was elated." She taped her finger against it. "With a touch I can hear or not." She smiled again.

I looked at Chase, then back to her. "I…"

"We'll get some tests done in the lab and get the witches working with my team to design a personalized one that will work for you." The elder with the bouncy curls said.

"Thank you." Chase answered before I could process what they were saying. "She has agreed to assist us with Eunice."

Elder Udela's eyes widened. "I tried and wasn't able to weed my way through the mush in her head." She held up her wrist. "I fear the last two thousand years with this have let me be a little too selective and my skills are too unpracticed."

"Maybe you're just getting old." Elder Drusla leaned forward and smiled down the length of the table at her.

"That could be." Elder Udela laughed.

I didn't know if I was supposed to speak. I bit my bottom lip, trying not to. Blurting out the wrong thing in a room full of leaders and royalty probably wouldn't be the best thing. In truth I had no idea what the frack was happening...

"I am quite intrigued with the Princess Kara's skill with a bow." Elder Marinus said. He glanced to Rafael, "perhaps we can discuss reinstating such weaponry into the security protocol, Captain."

I looked up to see Rafael's jaw twitching, he didn't look happy at all to be talking about what I could do with an arrow. Maybe they didn't know I'd shot him in the tush.

"I think that's an excellent idea, Elder Marinus." The scary looking Elder Segos said nodding his head. "It hasn't been used in the realm in well over a thousand years and could be useful again."

"I have some ideas for arrow tips that stun and incapacitate." Elder Arian said loudly, looking completely animated.

"Intriguing." Elder Drusla said with a smirk. "Once we find out what Solrelm wants of us, I think we should begin tests to help Princess Kara with her telepathy and have her do some teaching in archery."

"I agree on both matters." Elder Varus said, then turned to look at Troy and Chase.

Troy nodded his head. "I'm inclined to agree." He turned to Chase.

Chase looked down the table at me, an understanding expression on his face. "I think if this is what Kara wants, we'll make it happen."

What Kara wants? I had no idea what I wanted. No idea what was happening. They were going to help me further so I could or couldn't hear people's thoughts. I frowned, I guess that meant I wasn't going to be keeping the red cuff. Teach archery? What did I know about teaching anything?

"I think we all need to get out of Kara's face." Rafael growled. "She didn't even know Alterealm existed a few days ago. She's been through hell. Tortured by the human doctors—everyone just needs to back off and let her adjust."

My mouth was hanging open as I stood there looking up at him, but I couldn't think beyond my shock to close it. Where had that come from? That was the most I'd heard Rafael say, and he was defending me. The man that had been shooting darts of hatred at me with his eyes yesterday now was defending me.

"As you wish, Captain." Elder Varus bowed her head. "We'll proceed when the princess has settled more."

A man came in the door to my left. "They are ready." He inclined his head to the royal family and then to the elders.

"Show them in, Ira." Troy said, then he sat down.

Everyone else sat down, Beth tugged on my hand so I would as well. I was about to meet more people from a third realm. I honestly didn't know how I felt about that. More had happened in my life since I climbed that fire escape than in the last ten years.

Two men in grey robes came through the door at the other end and sat in the two chairs there.

Beth nodded to something that Leone told her, then leaned closer to me. "We do not stand when the Solrelm representatives come in."

I looked at her and nodded. "I don't even know why I'm here." I whispered.

Rafael turned and gave me a hard look.

I closed my mouth and clasped my hands in my lap. My hand felt naked without the leather finger guard. Mitz had me put it in my pocket, she said nothing weapon related was worn into the council chambers. I didn't mention the four knives at my ankles, deciding my own comfort level was more important than walking into a situation I didn't know anything about, without a way to defend myself if needed. I took a deep breath and then looked at the door, waiting, all I had to do was sit here and not freak out. I could do that. I hoped I could do that.

Chapter Twelve

I was still sitting there mentally coaching my mouth to stay closed and soothing my FOS to stay low enough that I didn't do anything that would land me back in the cells. Although, I had a few moments to think that being in the cells was the safest place for me—

The door opened again, and the same man came in. He stepped to the side, then bowed his head. "Princes Bastian and Trendan and the Commander of the watch, Sigor."

Three men walked in. The first thing I noticed was they weren't as large as the man, Ira, but they weren't petite people either. I didn't know which ones the princes were and who wasn't until two sat down and the third waited. The last man to sit must be Sigor.

"Prince Bastian." Troy said in a respectful tone.

The man closest to us bowed his head. "King Troy, a pleasure." He had short black hair, that went in any direction it wanted. He didn't look anything like a prince, then again neither did any of the people sitting at the table to my left. He didn't look at Troy as he spoke, just glanced down the table at each person sitting there.

"Prince Trendan." Troy inclined his head.

The man with the perfect blond hair bowed his head. "King Troy, thank you for agreeing to this meeting."

I briefly glanced to the commander, his entire aura screamed death-to-you, like Victor's had on our first encounter. He wore a black robe with no embroidery. The two princes wore deep purple robes, only they were sleeveless. I wondered if they were called a gown instead of a robe.

All three had a tattoo on their left shoulder. What was it with other realms and tattoos? These didn't cover the whole length of their arm though, just the upper deltoid. Without making it too obvious, I tried to make out what it was of. It looked like someone had taken a brush and black paint and made a circle, not quite completing the top of it. In the middle it looked like an eight on its side, again the ends not quite meeting. I looked up to the man who's shoulder I was focusing on to see him looking at me. His eyes were the darkest blue I'd ever seen, then I noticed the ring around that dark blue wasn't black, like all eyes I'd ever seen, it was white but not as white as the rest of his eye.

"Bastian." Prince Trendan said quietly beside him.

Bastian cleared his throat and looked away from me. "Sorry. Soul distraction."

His brother looked at him, then briefly glanced to me. "Your majesties, elders," Trendan bowed his head to the elders, "Our commander has detected an anomaly we're quite frankly not clear how it's happening."

"That's concerning." Elder Arian said quietly.

"Quite." Prince Trendan nodded. "We've consulted all of our seniors and they are unable to give us the answers."

"Your seniors didn't have the answers?" Elder Varus leaned forward in her chair. "We're," she motioned down the table, "mere infants in comparison to your oldest residents."

Prince Trendan nodded, his perfectly placed blond locks didn't even move when he did that. "Yes and yet they can't figure it out."

"And you think we can?" Elder Nodin asked.

"That is our hope…"

"Drop the proper speak and political posturing and get to the point." Quinton blurted out.

I was glad he did, and from the looks of a few of the others so were they.

Chase smirked. "I agree with my brother. What is the issue?"

"Someone is screwing with our barrier." Bastian stated looking at Chase.

"Shit." One of the brothers beside me said bluntly.

Elder Arian looked like she wanted to jump out of her seat. She looked at the man, Sigor. "Did you bring any data?"

Sigor tuned to look at Prince Trendan, he gave a quick nod. Sigor stood up and pulled out something that looked like a phone and walked down to the end of the table where Elder Arian was.

She stood up and took the device and started looking at it. "Oh dear." She whispered.

Elder Varus stood up and looked at the two archivist's "I need you to leave. We will submit a summary for the archives later."

The two closed their books and stood up. Inclining their heads, they turned and went out the door without a word.

Troy leaned forward on the table. "Elder Marinus, I need you and Elder Roan to contact the other realms and see if they report the same thing."

Elder Marinus nodded and got up, walking quickly to the door. Elder Roan was right behind him.

Prince Bastian stood up. "It's happening here too, isn't it?"

Victor answered before Troy could. "Yes, and we know who is responsible."

My heart was skipping in my chest. I clasped my hands in my lap and squeezed them. What the pish were they talking about? Barriers? *A fence or other obstacle that prevents movement or access.* My mind quickly referenced. I had to be thinking the wrong thing. Maybe it meant something else here. I looked at Beth, her eyes were huge as she sat there. That did not comfort me at all. A hand touched mine. I looked down to see Rafael's big hand over mine in my lap. I looked up at him, he was watching the others, not even acknowledging he was doing it. It made me feel oddly better, but not at the same time.

Michael stood up and rubbed the back of his neck. "They have to be working with someone from your realm to even know where to begin to do that."

"You're saying someone from our realm is doing this?" Prince Trendan stood up as well now.

"They'd have to be to know the best locations to do it." Elder Arian said, then looked back at the device Sigor had given her.

"We've been so busy with other," Prince Trendan waved his hand, "issues lately, we missed this entirely."

"That's not at all surprising." Victor stated. "We've had our hands full here as well."

"You're going to want to look at inner staff, and any staff with families that have a less than favorable history." Leone looked to Michael who nodded.

Releasing my hands, Rafael leaned on the table. "When they said the barrier between, we thought it was just ours." He looked down the table at Troy.

"Is it possible the lawless faction is behind this?" Prince Bastian asked his brother.

"Nothing would surprise me. They've really ramped it up lately." Trendan pulled out his phone. "I need to inform mother and father immediately and have them transported to a secure location."

Bastian nodded. "Only Tor and Ulric are to know. Have them escort and stay until we get back."

Nodding, Prince Trendan walked over to the corner of the room.

Daxx pushed back from the table and got up. "We need to get the teams to up their game and get moving." She looked at Quinton.

He stood up. "I was just thinking the same thing. I'll go to the yard and get it started." He lifted his chin to Troy. "You need to revisit the heads of all we've brought in. There has to be something we're missing."

Arius got up. "We need to find Nelson." He kissed the top of Paisley's head, then turned to the door. "Raf, we're going to need Kara to visit Eunice as soon as this is wrapped up and find out what's inside her sick mind. If she can lead us to Nelson, we'll get Willis Hubert too."

I looked from him to Rafael. He was nodding but didn't look at me.

"Kara, *princess* Kara." Bastian said quietly and stepped over to stand in front of the table. His dark eyes searched my face. "You're a mind reader?"

I shook my head. "No. I hear what people think."

He grinned. "Can you hear what I'm thinking?"

I held up my arm, so the cuff would fall, and the red cuff was visible. "Not while I'm wearing this."

"It's probably a good thing." Trendan said coming back over. "My brother is fascinated because your soul isn't blended with your mate's. It's a puzzle and he *loves* a good puzzle." He rolled his eyes.

I looked at him then back to Bastian. "I-I don't understand. My soul?"

Bastian gave me a big grin. "Yes, your lovely soul."

Rafael stood up, making a low growling sound.

Eyes-wide I looked up at him. He'd just growled like an animal.

Leone moved over and put his hand on Rafael's shoulder. "Let's go give Quint a hand."

Rafael looked at him, then shrugged off his hand. "I'll be there after I take Kara to the cells to see Eunice." He held his hand out to me.

I looked to Beth, she gave a slight nod. Placing my hand in his, I stood up.

"I'll come with." Chase said and stood up.

"I'm in." Autumn said. "I want to know if she's faking this."

I didn't have time to think as Rafael pulled me by the hand and walked out of the room quickly. He kept going after we were through the doors.

Autumn and Chase caught up.

Rafael went around the next corner and stopped. I almost walked into him.

"We'll be there in a minute." He said and looked at Chase and Autumn.

"As you like." Chase inclined his head, then gave me a reassuring smile. "His bark is much worse than his bite," he shrugged, "or so I'm told."

I watched them walk away. As soon as they turned down a different hall, Rafael released my hand. I looked up at him. I didn't need to hear what he was thinking to know he was very conflicted right now.

"You can take off the robe now." He said as he undid his own and pulled the sash over his head.

I took off the sash, then undid the robe. "Oh, your necklace." I reached behind me and felt for the clasp. Fumbling with it, I managed to undo it and held it out to him.

His jaw was clenched as he took it. "Look I know you don't know what the hell is going on," he shook his head, "I don't think you should be dropped into all of," he waved his hand around, "this, but if you can give us something that will end it all, then I'd be stupid to stop that."

Stop that? How could he stop it? Something inside me snapped. "This?" I waved a hand around. "I don't even know what *this* is." I took a deep breath, trying to stay calm and failing for the most part. "I thought people were taking women," I scowled at him, "I don't know what this barrier stuff is." I pulled the robe off and shoved it against his chest, "and what is this soul blending horse pucky? What is that even?" I waved the sash around, then added it to the robe he now held. "Witches and magic bands and teaching archery," I wanted to stomp my foot, but was able to control myself enough to not do that in front of him and look like a child, "I don't know *what* is happening."

"Ah," Emil walked up to us, "I'm with her on most of that." He crossed his arms over his chest looking from Rafael to me, "my life was dull, even predictable until I met my brothers." He gave me a gentle look, "it's been organized chaos since then."

"I just," I looked up at one, then the other as they towered over me, I shook my head. "I just need a few moments." I turned and started walking down the hallway. I stopped when I reached the hall Chase and Autumn had turned down. I didn't know where I was going.

"Take that hall and keep going straight, it will take you to the cells." Emil called out.

Turning down the hall, I started walking fast. With my head down, I watched the patterns change on the carpet as I moved over it. I didn't know what I was supposed to be thinking. Who would with all of this dumped on their head? Barriers, that were important, and it was bad they were being messed with, why—I had no idea.

Soul blending... I stopped and glared at the carpet. How did that Bastian guy know anything about my soul? Taking a few steps, I shook my head and huffed out a breath. I believed people had souls, but not like they were something tangible that you could touch or see.

I started walking again, I'd figure that out later. Lifting my arm, I looked at the red band. Did I want them to make me something like that elder had? Something that enabled me to listen or not... that was something I never thought I'd have to consider, like *ever*. So did I? If I wasn't going to be allowed to keep the inhibitor cuff when I left, something like that would be good to have. I shrugged, okay I wanted my own off switch.

How long was this hallway? Taking a deep breath, I pushed the thought that I was walking in an underground hall out of my head. I'd seen these people fight, as scary and medieval as it was, not to mention amazing to see—so why did they want me to teach them how to use a bow? *It hasn't been used in the realm in well over a thousand years...* Elder what's-his-name had said. My brain stalled for a half second on the thousand years part. A hundred years times ten. Giving myself a mental poke, I moved past that. I suppose the fact that I was a quarter of one of those hundred years and knew something useful for them was a good thing. A compliment in some obscure way...

"You look like you're about to implode."

I jolted and looked up to see I'd reached the double metal doors and most of the royal family stood there. Chase smiled at me and then looked behind me. I turned to see Emil walking slowly down the hall.

He shrugged, "thought I'd give you space."

I huffed out a breath, wanting to thank him, but not saying anything.

"Where's Raf?" Chase asked.

"Poof." Emil said flicking his fingers into the air.

"He's probably at the yard with Quinton and Leone." Michael said.

"Or he's running with his tail between his legs," Emil said, motioning to me, "Kara went off on him like an explosive device."

"Ah, and I missed it." Chase gave me an amused look.

Emil looked to the others. "I didn't know everyone was going to be here."

"Not everyone will be, we're waiting on Michael." Victor stated. "Crissy will be in her tower when Kara takes off the inhibitor."

I mentally blew out a deep breath. Crissy being around when I took it off wouldn't have helped me focus.

Michael came out of the cells. "Good. Saves me chasing everyone down." He opened the case he carried and pulled out one of those things they wore on their wrists. He looked at it, then handed it to Emil. "They've all been programmed to land you at the palace or the landing room here." He took out a second and after checking it gave it to Daxx. "The women's take them to their cave instead of landing room. The guards are programmed as well." He gave the next one to Troy.

I was surprised when he gave me one. I looked at it.

Autumn stepped closer and popped it open to show me the buttons. Michael handed her one. She took off the old one and put the new one on.

Closing the one I held, I put it on my wrist that wasn't covered by the red band. I didn't know why they were giving me one, but it made me feel like I had some control over where I was.

"Did anyone else feel like our neighbors from Solrelm didn't share everything?" Emil asked looking around at the others.

"I'm inclined to agree." Victor said glancing up from his phone.

"We need to call an informal meeting with one of them." Chase leaned back against the wall and crossed his arms over his chest.

"For?" Michael gave him a strange look.

"If they're able to zero in on a specific soul…"

Victor put his phone in his pocket. "I've never really delved into how it works."

"Oh." Crissy looked excited, "it explains it in their book."

Chase looked amused. "They have a book?"

She nodded. "There's one for all the other realms," she shrugged, "more for this one." Eyes huge she looked at Victor. "Do you think they have a library with books about their history?"

Victor smirked. "You are not getting a library card to all the other realms, heart, I fear our chamber couldn't house the books you'd bring back."

"That would be silly," she grinned, "I still have a few rooms in Alterealm's library to go through." She pulled her notebook out of her backpack and started down the hall.

Michael gave her an amused look. "Back to this meeting."

"We want this off the record I assume?" Victor asked, watching Crissy walk away.

Chase nodded. "For now, yes."

"I'll get in touch with them. I'm thinking Prince Bastian would be the one we wish to speak with." Victor turned and opened the door to the cells.

Autumn moved closer to me and held out her hand, smirking.

I frowned, not sure why.

"I know you have knives on you. No weapons in the cells." She said.

I didn't know how she knew, but I couldn't argue with the reasoning behind it. Shrugging my shoulders, I bent down and pulled the knives from the straps on my ankles. Straightening, I held them out to her. She took them and handed them to Michael.

Giving her an amused look, he glanced to me. "You can pick them up on your way out."

I half expected some lecture or him confiscating them completely. I looked at Autumn, then Paisley. "Do you carry weapons?"

Daxx snorted. "They *are* the weapons."

Troy tilted his head and looked at Daxx.

She sighed and raised her hands. "I'll leave it in the office."

Chase moved over to the door and opened it. "Let's go see what Eunice has tucked inside her head."

Chapter Thirteen

I hugged the cuff to my chest after I took it off. Only Chase and Autumn were standing here with me. I wasn't sure where the others had gone. Here I was again, willingly using what had ruined my life. I blew out a breath slowly, trying not to have *that* moment where I wondered what having a childhood and family would be like. Giving myself a mental smack, I turned to look at Autumn. "Who is this Eunice?" I glanced to Chase. "Besides being the sister of the one of the creeps you guys are hunting."

He leaned against the wall. "She's the one that was holding the women on the island, and as far as we can tell was in charge of rounding them up."

I glanced to see Autumn's look harden. "She told them to shackle me." She continued to look at the wall that we couldn't see through yet. "She almost blinded me with poison she blew into my eyes." She snarled, "she had to cheat and doesn't fight with honor." She turned to look at me and for a moment I was glad we were on the same side. "She poisoned her blade and I could have bled out if the doctor hadn't had the cure."

Chase straightened and came over and put his hand on her shoulder. "You still kicked her ass injured and unable to see."

She gave him a hard look, then smiled, "I did." Turning back to the glass wall, she motioned to it with her chin. "She's saying she doesn't know what's going on now. How she ended up here." Crossing her arms over her chest. "I need to know if she's pretending to be an idiot, or if it's one more scheme or," she looked at me, "if she's telling the truth."

I nodded slowly. "Okay." I hugged my waist, then turned to Chase. "Maybe if they ask her what the last thing she remembers is, I will be able to hear if she is faking it or not."

Chase nodded. "I'll go tell Troy to try that." He walked out of the area.

"Thanks for doing this." Autumn said quietly. "I know you don't want to." She gave me a softer look. "I know you don't like being able to, but," she shrugged, "have you ever thought there was a reason why you can? That somewhere in all of fate's plans you were given that for one reason only?" She nodded. "I had times where I cussed at my life. Thinking it was so unfair." Autumn glanced to the floor for a moment. "They didn't last long. No time for pity parties on the streets." She nodded and crossed her arms over her chest. "Then I found out about," she waved her hand around, "this and it hit me. I was a warrior for a reason. Being here. Stopping this is the reason."

Biting my lip, I looked at her. She wasn't wrong. "I've never thought there was a reason for it." It felt like tumblers clicked inside my whole body. "I always thought there had to be a mistake, a fluke for life to do this to someone." The wall changed and we could see inside the cube. I looked at the redheaded woman sitting on her bed. She didn't look like a malicious insane person. She looked lost, in the way I'd seen so many at the asylum look. "I guess now is when I find out if that's true or not."

Autumn nodded and crossed her arms over her chest, she didn't look away from the woman inside the cell.

For her own safety, I thought, that woman better hope she never gets out of there. I glanced to Autumn quickly as Troy,

Victor and Arius stepped into her cell. Being on her bad side could be bad for anyone's health. I pushed the button to open the slot in the wall.

Eunice scrambled to her feet and then did a low curtsy to Troy. "Your majesty."

…Willis would have a coronary if he saw me do this…

…I can't disrespect royalty, despite my brother and his friend's delusions…

"Sit down, Eunice." Troy said in a flat tone.

She quickly sat down, then looked at Arius. "Did the blood tests show anything?"

…please let this nightmare end…

Arius shook his head. "Nothing to confirm drugging."

Eunice's expectant expression changed to defeat.

…no that can't be. Incompetent lab rats…

"There has to be something." She jumped up, then bowed her head when the men straightened. She held out her arm. "This. What is this?" Shaking her head, she glanced at Victor. "I *know* it's the Hubert family crest, but why do I have it tattooed on my wrist?" She rubbed her hand over it. "When did I get this?"

…this infernal thing won't stop itching…

…how is it possible I got a tattoo and don't remember…

…if this is Willis' idea of a joke, I'm going to…

Victor turned and looked at Arius for a moment, his expression not changing. "You don't remember getting it?"

Eunice shook her head quickly.

…would I be asking if I remembered?

"No. I didn't even notice it until the scrapes on my arms healed." She frowned, "which if anyone could shed light on how I got those, I'd be grateful."

…maybe I was injured and have a concussion. That would explain so…

"What is the last thing you remember clearly, Eunice?" Troy asked then crossed his arms over his chest, looking down at her with resilient focus.

She stepped back and sat down, looking at the floor.

...what is the last thing I recall with clarity?

...I'm going to claw this out of my skin...

She rubbed her hand over her wrist again. "I-uh," she squeezed her eyes tight, "we," she looked up at Victor, "Nelson and I, we were trying to reason with Willis." She looked annoyed. "Mostly *I* was, Nelson would never openly go against Willis..."

...talk about impossible feats. There is no reasoning with that old goat...

She shook her head. "After millenniums of trying to prove the gods chose the wrong family, we'd—I'd conceded that if," she looked up at Troy, "if there had been an error, we would have proved it in that time."

...I'm sorry, brother, but it's true...

...is a pounding headache a sign of a concussion?

...what if it's worse than that. All those years of battle could have damaged something...

...focus Eunice, get your ass out of this cell...

A look of pain filled her face, she put her hand to her temple. "You have the mates mark—all of you? I don't know when this happened."

...lucky bastards. What I wouldn't give for that connection...

...the fates are cruel, there will never be a woman mated to a woman...

She gave Arius a hopeful look, "the prophecy has come true and I don't know how or-or when."

...the doctor needs to remove this or numb it...

Looking at her arm, she brushed her hand over her wrist.

"When were you and Nelson trying to reason with Willis?" Victor asked.

Troy was oddly quiet, I wondered if that meant he was doing his seeing into her head. Blinking I focused on listening and not thinking about things that didn't matter.

...think, think, think, when?

...what was happening?

Eunice took a deep breath, a serious look of thought on her face. "Uh, the years seem to blur together so much after the first five or six hundred."

...the whole realm was in a dither over something...

She exhaled and looked at the floor, "there was a celebration," lifting her arms, she rubbed her temples, "anniversary of the coronation for our twin kings." Dropping her hands, she looked up at Victor.

...I still can't believe I followed Willis blindly and believed he thought the prophecies were rigged. One maybe, but hundreds...

"How many years?" Arius asked, his tone so quiet it was barely audible. "How many years were we celebrating?"

...these questions are getting annoying...

"Fifty." She gave him a hesitant look, "we didn't attend, of course, but..." She stopped when the three men straightened and looked at each other. "What?" She stood up.

...why are they looking at each other like that?

"What?" She gave Troy a panicked look, "how many years have you been king?"

...I swear if I've lost more than a few weeks, I'm going to crack Willis upside the head. His childish pranks are getting ridiculous...

Troy looked slowly from Victor to her. "We just celebrated one hundred and sixty years."

...they're not joking...

...one hundred sixty years...

Her mouth dropped open. Her eyes were huge. She put her hand over her mouth and stumbled back until she hit the bed. Landing on the edge of it she gave him a horrified look. "A hundred and ten years."

...oh my god...

...what is happening?

She looked at Victor. "How-how have I lost over a hundred years." With a shaking hand she brushed it over her hair pushing it back from her face.

...this can't be happening...

"I'm over nine hundred years old." Her voice cracked as she spoke.

...does Nels know? Of course he does. He knows everything Willis does...

...brother what have you done to me?

...oh no. No, no...

...They did it. They found Arwan...

"We'll be back momentarily." Victor said, opening the door.

...I feel sick...

"Could, can I have some water please?" She asked without looking up from the floor she was focused on.

...how could they do this to me?

...I thought it was a joke, Arwan couldn't possibly still be alive...

...when did he find him? Why didn't he tell me?

I heard the men walk back into the space but couldn't take my eyes off Eunice. I wanted to say I'd never heard such helplessness from another before, but that would be a lie. What I hadn't done before was watch it while I was hearing it.

Eunice slid off the edge of the bed to the floor and pulled her legs up to her chest.

...oh Willis. You stupid, stupid man...

...you've gone completely mad...

...how could you be so lost in your vengeance to do this to me? Nels, I'm your last relative...

She started crying. In her grief I couldn't make out any thought that made sense.

Taking a ragged breath, I pushed the button to close the small door. I just stood there looking at the woman on the other side of the wall. The reflection changed and then I could see her. Exhaling, I turned to see most of the royal family standing there looking at me.

"She's not faking." Autumn said.

I knew it wasn't a question but nodded slowly anyway. "She's not." I looked at Chase. "She was pretty snarky at the start." I watched Autumn rub her hand over her tattoo. "There's something about her tattoo, it's itches and drives her crazy."

Michael gave me a hard look, then turned to look at Autumn.

She looked at her wrist on the arm her tattoo covered. "I didn't have it long, and it wasn't the real deal…"

"I'm calling Romulus, he better have good answers." Michael pulled out his phone and walked out of the area we were in.

"Call the lab tech, witches, hell all of the science people and get that mark tested." Chase told him as he walked away.

Michael held up his phone and waved it but kept walking.

"What did you hear?" Daxx asked.

I clutched the band to my chest. "She thought maybe she had a concussion at first, then that Willis was playing some sick joke on her." I looked at Troy, "she broke when you told her it's been over a hundred years."

"So she doesn't remember all the horrible things they've done, that she's done?" Paisley asked moving closer to Arius.

I shook my head. "No. I don't think she does." I looked at the cuff I held. "She doesn't know what's going on, only knows her brother and Willis have done something awful."

"Do you think we'll be able to get some locations from her, or ideas they suggested before this happened to her?" Bethany asked.

"I don't know. I don't see why," I shrugged, "she wouldn't want to help. After she's calmed down,"

Autumn snorted. "You've never seen her the way I have."

I understood where her hostility was coming from. "I don't think she remembers when you fought, or anything for over a hundred years."

"How is that possible?" Daxx asked looking to Troy.

"We'll see if she does." Autumn spun on her heel and walked out of the area.

"Shit." Arius followed her quickly.

Chase moved over and did something on the panel, then we could see Autumn walking into Eunice's cube.

Eunice looked up, then stiffened and pulled herself to her feet. She frowned at Autumn then her gaze paused on the part of Autumn's tattoo showing below her hoodie sleeve that was pushed up. She bowed her head. "Princess." She stood taller, taking a ragged breath, her eyes darting between Arius and Autumn. "Is she your mate, prince Arius?" She gave him a weak smile. "Congratulations on the good fortune of such a lovely mate."

Autumn didn't look impressed. "Do you remember fighting me?"

Eunice jolted like she'd been hit. "I-I, we did? What," she glanced to Arius nervously, "what reason could I have to fight you?"

Autumn sneered at her. "Because you wanted me for yourself."

"I," Eunice paused and looked her up and down, then bowed her head to Arius quickly, "who wouldn't." She whispered, "I'm so sorry, warden, I-I…"

Autumn made a sound of annoyance and turned on her heel, brushed past Arius and left the cell.

"Eunice," Arius waited for her to look at him, "we're going to look into that tattoo of yours."

She inclined her head. "Thank you." She looked at her wrist, then rubbed her hand over it. "It's rather distracting."

"I'll be back later. I need you to think of where your brother might be hiding. Any locations you used to evade us in the past." Arius crossed his arms over his chest and looked at her until she glanced back up at him.

"I," she rubbed her hand over her forehead, "I can't believe this is happening." She nodded slightly, "yes. I'll try to recall locations." She had a distracted look on her face, her eyes were hollow. "I'll-bring a map." She frowned. "Warden," Eunice winced at her hard tone, "Prince Arius, Willis is-is, he needs help. Nels just follows him blindly…"

Arius looked at her for a moment more, then turned and walked out.

Chase pushed the button again. "Someone needs to find out how Willis was able to bewitch her for the last eleven decades."

I inhaled sharply. "She thought of someone named Arwan?" I bit my lip wondering it I said it right. "That she'd thought him being alive was a joke?"

Chase looked at Troy, then they both turned to look at Victor.

"Who is Arwan?" Emil asked.

Victor took a deep breath, his chest rising slowly. Exhaling, he gave Troy, then Chase a look of trepidation. "Arwan is the most powerful mage known throughout history." He glanced at Emil then, "he's older than time and for the most part I believed he was a fable created in a writer's mind."

"So this Arwan is real?" Daxx asked.

Bethany turned and looked at me, a scared look on her face. "There are stories in the witch's journals about him. From," she brushed her hair back from her face, "thousands of years ago. He's alive?"

"Eunice thinks her brother found him. Sounded like he'd been searching, or at least they'd discussed looking for him." I looked at Chase. "She thought, he did it. He found Arwan."

Chase closed his eyes for a second, then looked at his twin. "We need the council called back." He nodded. "Now."

Alona went over and wrapped her arms around Chase.

The waves of fear coming off these people had my FOS climbing to a dangerous level.

Troy turned to Victor. "Did you reach Prince Bastian?"

Victor nodded. "He said he couldn't get back over here today, but is willing to meet with us, in secrecy as soon as he can manage it."

Troy nodded. "Okay." He looked at Michael as he walked back into the area. "Get Romulus, Clairee, the head archivist and historian rounded up. Have them at the elder's chambers within the hour." He paused, a look of thought on his face. "And find the oldest living resident of Alterealm, we're going to want a private sit down with them."

Michael frowned. "What's happened?" He looked at the wall Eunice was behind. "What did you find out?"

Autumn finally looked away from the wall she couldn't see through. "She's not faking. Hubert did something and she's lost over a hundred years."

The shock was plain on Michael's face.

Autumn went over and touched his arm. He looked down at her with affection and concern evident in his eyes. "And apparently they have some mage that's only the most powerful mage *ever*."

Michael's brows drew together as he looked over at Victor.

"Willis Hubert found Arwan." Victor supplied.

"But he's dead..." Michael zeroed in on me. "He's not dead?"

I shook my head. "Eunice doesn't think so."

"Fuck me." Michael whispered and then hugged Autumn into his side. Kissing the top of her head, he looked back at Troy. "I'll get all of the heads of departments and factions to the chambers."

"I need a drink." Chase said and motioned to the way we'd come in.

"I'm with you there." Emil said.

"Call Rafael, Quint and Leone and get them to the solarium." Troy said as he took Daxx's hand and walked out into the hall. "This is a fucking game changer."

I fumbled to put the inhibitor back on. Keeping my head down, trying to process what was going on. I'd agreed to help. What had just happened was so far from helping, I didn't know what to do. Bethany came over and held the one side of the cuff for me. After it closed over my wrist, like a comforting blanket, I looked at her. "Listening in was supposed to help." I whispered.

She looked at Emil, who was clearly waiting for the two of us before leaving. "It did." Her brown eyes connected with mine again. "Everyone is just thrown by this." She offered a slight smile, but it didn't reach her eyes. "We've been trying to figure out how they were doing all of it…" she let out a shaky breath, "now we know."

"Is Rena safe where she is? Should we bring her over sooner?" Emil asked, not really looking at either of us.

Beth motioned to for us to leave. "I think she's okay where she is now." She gave him a gentle look. "No one can bypass Alona's security there."

He nodded slowly. "Yes. Okay." He rubbed the back of his neck and started walking. "For three hundred years I had questions, now I'm starting to wish I was still clueless."

"I think," Beth walked between us, "we were all meant to be here. Now. To stop this from happening and destroying this side and," she huffed out a breath, "destroying many realms and countless lives."

For the first time in my life, my anxiety settled. That paranoia that plagued me was absent. My FOS was humming but evened off. My heartbeat was steady, my nerves calm. If I'd been someone that believed in a faith or religion, I would have taken this as a sign that I was meant to be here. That I was destined to be as fate intended me to be. I didn't believe in any of that, and yet I knew with absolute resolve this is where I was supposed to be.

Chapter Fourteen

I stood in the room, breathing. Just breathing. I needed a few moments to settle inside myself. I'd told Daxx I needed to use the bathroom, then had run up to my room and now I just stood here. Pulling the hand guard out of my pocket, I put it on without looking at it. My gaze was stuck on the robe and sash laid out neatly on my bed. Had Rafael done that, or had he given it to Mitz? I didn't know why I needed to know a small detail like that.

Shaking my head, I went and sat on the end of the bed. Small details seemed to be tying in together and turning out to be huge things the past few days. I had so many questions right now. It would be selfish to blurt out 'excuse me, what about this?' when there were so many serious revelations to be dealt with. I was being petty sitting here thinking only of myself.

Standing up, I closed my eyes and took a deep breath, trying to assess how I felt. My FOS was still low. Opening my eyes, I looked around the room. How was that possible with everything I'd found out in the last twenty-four hours? Any sane person would be running and screaming 'get me out of here'. I smiled, then chuckled to my own thought. Since when did sane describe anything to do with my life.

Nodding, I walked to the door. Time to find out what all of this meant. People as old as the kings and Victor looking panicked about this Arwan guy didn't bode well for some twenty-five-year-old *completely human* girl with a sketchy past.

I opened the door and then froze. Across the large hallway Rafael was coming out of a room. Closing the door he stood there. He was dressed in his battle gear again. I'd never really thought leather was sexy, not that I'd ever owned any, but the black hide looked good on him. I tried not to ogle him in an obvious way but found it hard not to. The black vest he wore was form fitting and depicted quite clearly how much muscle was under it. Snapping out of it, I stood there like a startled animal, hoping he wouldn't notice. So, of course he did and stood there doing much the same thing I was. I looked at the door.

He pointed to it. "It's my room."

Mitz had placed me across the hall from the man I'd shot? I nodded, not knowing what to say.

He stepped into the middle of the hall. "I'm guessing you found out something from Eunice? We were just heading out when Quint got a call to get here now."

Feeling awkward after appraising his body, I turned and started walking toward the stairs. "I don't understand all of it."

Rafael walked beside me. "Eunice isn't faking?"

I shook my head. "She has no memory of the last hundred and ten years."

He stopped and looked down at me. "Seriously?"

I stood there, hands clasped together. "I heard her thoughts clearly."

He ran his hand over his short hair. "That's crazy. I'm only eight decades older than that."

Starting at his black leather boots, I looked up his form until I reached his eyes again. He did not look a hundred and ninety years old. "And you're the baby brother?"

He snorted. "Unfortunately." He motioned to keep walking, a look of urgency on his face now. "How is that possible? For her to lose that much time?"

"I don't know. It has something to do with her tattoo and someone called Arwan." I looked up to see him frowning at the floor as we walked. When his eyes went wide, I knew he understood.

"Arwan is a myth. Some wizard guy stories were written about."

We started down the stairs. "Apparently he was and is very much real. Victor looked concerned."

Rafael paused and looked down at me. "Victor?"

I nodded, but kept going.

"Shit, that's not good." He said under his breath.

At the bottom of the stairs I stopped and looked up at him. "Why are you being so nice to me?" It was a legitimate question. "I shot you."

His look darkened for a moment. "Yeah, you did. And I will hold it against you for the rest of my life because my brothers will *never* forget or stop harassing me about it. And when you live as long as we do, that could be a hella long time" He took a deep breath, then huffed it out all at once. "I can't—I don't know how to explain it." Rafael's blue eyes searched my face. "I don't want to freak you out." He shook his head. "My heart got stuck in my throat the two times I saw you lose it," the hazy confused look in his eyes cleared, turning them a lighter shade of blue, "I don't know what to do about it and you need time to digest all of this," he smirked, "I don't think there's a name to describe it from your perspective." He motioned to keep walking. "Later on, I'll try to explain it to you."

I didn't know if what he said was supposed to make me feel better or more confused, he really hadn't explained anything.

"Just-just let me know if you need anything, okay?" He placed his hand on my back as we walked, not rushing me, just keeping it there.

I nodded. "Okay." I wasn't going to ask, then my mouth had other ideas. "Can you at least tell me why I keep getting called Princess?"

He inhaled a sharp breath, dropping his hand away from me. "Just go with it for now." He gave me a smile that could have charmed the feathers off a bird, then walked ahead of me into the solarium.

Most in the room watched me when I walked down the steps, a few glances to Rafael followed. I stopped at the table and looked at the food sitting on it, trying to assess if I wanted to eat, and also keeping my back to everyone meant not seeing people stare at me. My stomach was tense, but walking away from free, non-spoiled food seemed like a dumb thing to do, so I picked up a sandwich and turned around. No one was looking at me now.

I went over and sat in the same chair I had before, finding a small piece of comfort in repetition. If twice could be call that. I took a bite of the sandwich, pleasantly surprised it was egg salad. Foods with mayonnaise, not spoiled, was a rare taste for me.

Autumn came over and sat in the chair beside me, leaning on her knees and looking at the floor. "Thanks again for doing that." She sat up and took a deep breath, then exhaled it slowly. "I wanted her to be faking it so bad," she grinned, then shook her head, "now I can't even muster up any anger for retribution."

I chewed slowly thinking of what to say. Swallowing, I looked at her. "That's good, right, not being burdened with those feelings?"

She nodded slowly, "Yeah, a clear mind is good, but I really did want to lay a beat down on her for what I went through."

I recalled what she'd said. "I'm glad you're okay."

She studied me for a moment, then she jerked her chin toward Rafael. "Everything good there?"

I looked at Rafael as he spoke to Troy, a serious expression on his face. "I don't know. He's not mad at me, completely, but he's very confusing."

She chuckled, "yeah, that seems to run in the family." She stood up and put her hand on my shoulder. "Track down one of us girls, if you want the answers to his confusing mumbo jumbo or the stupid things he does."

I watched her walk over to Michael, she said something to him and he smiled. Both glanced to me, then gave each other a look I could only describe as lost in love.

Alona and Chase came down the steps. "Sorry for the hold up. We popped over to check on Rena and the security system."

Emil stood up, a concerned look on his face.

"Everything is fine." Alona gave him an understanding smile, "Chase just wanted to assuage my worries."

Emil nodded. "Thank you for checking in on her." He motioned around the room. "I was going to after someone explains what this new discovery means."

"Explanations would be good." Daxx sat down and looked around at the men.

Troy motioned around the room. "Everyone, take a seat. We have a short time before we have to be at the council chambers."

"We're going back to see the elders?" Rafael went over and stood by the glass wall, crossing his arms over his chest.

"Yes." Chase placed a kiss on the top of Alona's head when she sat down. He didn't sit, just stood there with his hands on her shoulders. "Kara has found the answers to our questions."

I gave him a startled look. I had?

"Which questions?" Quinton asked.

Troy rubbed his hand across his forehead. "The main one that's been plaguing us," He glanced around slowly, "how Willis is managing to do half the things he has."

"And?" Leone put his arm around Bethany and pulled her closer to him.

"Eunice believes Nelson and Willis have found Arwan." Troy said quietly, looking around weighing the reactions to what he said.

"She hasn't been playacting about not knowing how she ended up in the cells." Victor said glancing to Crissy briefly, "she's lost over a hundred years, recalling nothing."

"How is that possible? No magic works that long." Quinton scowled and crossed his arms over his chest.

"That's what we're finding out." Michael told him. "Kara heard her thoughts clearly. We think it may have something to do with the Hubert crest tattooed on her wrist."

"So it's some kind of magic through the tattoo?" Leone asked glanced down at Bethany for a moment, then back to Victor. "It would have to be some powerful spell."

Troy sighed, "the kind of power Arwan has."

"You really think he's alive?" Quinton looked from Victor to Michael, "after this long?"

"I always thought the stories were just myths." Rafael stated.

"Myths derive from the truth." Victor told him. "I remember the elders and our grandfather searching for him. He'd just vanished without a trace."

"So how do we find him and stop him?" Daxx asked.

"That's why we're meeting with the elders and several of the leaders and heads of departments at the chambers." Troy told her, his eyes lingering on her for a few moments.

"They'll know?" Paisley got up from the chair and went over and wrapped her arms around Arius' waist.

"If they don't, then we are all in dire trouble." Troy said quietly.

"We need to check everyone brought in since this started and see if they have the tattoo." Rafael straightened away from the wall and went to the table of food.

"Are tattoos recorded on the intake file?" Quinton looked to Arius.

Arius shook his head, "no. Only the mates mark is." He pulled his phone out, "I'll get them started on it." He lifted his gaze from the phone and looked to Troy, "it's going to take some time to check them all."

Troy nodded, "have them flag any whose behavior has changed drastically as well."

Arius nodded and kept typing on his phone.

"Maybe this tattoo could help us find the traitors I couldn't see." Crissy gave Victor a hopeful look.

Victor's look was affectionate as he nodded to her. Then he turned and looked at Michael, "I don't know if they'd be so callus to send someone in with the Hubert crest in their skin, but we can look into that."

"Maybe Kara can help."

I looked at Bethany.

She was looking at Victor, "if they've somehow managed to hide their intentions from Crissy seeing, maybe their thoughts will give them away."

"I don't understand." I said, not even pausing to wonder if I should say anything. "I mean I get me listening to their thoughts, but I thought Crissy's visions were premonition like."

Crissy nodded. "Oh, they are." She looked over my head, "but I can see if people are bad too."

I waited for more explanation, then realized there wasn't going to be any.

Bethany grinned, "Crissy can see the aura that surrounds people."

I didn't know what to say to that. I had no real clue what they were talking about, then I remembered Crissy looking over my head when I was in my personal cube. "You can see mine?"

She nodded. "Yes." Crissy looked excited, "yours is filled with pure intentions, but," she looked at Victor then to Quinton, "you have a bit of that don't mess with me color like the men do."

"There's a color for that?" Autumn asked with a smirk on her face.

Nodding rapidly once more, Crissy turned and looked at her, "yes." She frowned, "I don't know if colors mean things or if it's just the feeling I get that go with the color..."

Autumn held up her hand. "That's okay, I will take your word for it."

I realized then that one of the main things that got me out of that cube was how much these people believed in what Crissy saw. I gave her a friendly smile. "Well, I'm glad you can see mine." I figured I needed to at least thank her. The way my mouth had been spitting out every thought in my head, I would have still been locked up if it hadn't been for her.

Arius put his phone in his pocket. "The guards are on it now." He shook his head, "never before have we had to keep going back over each person so much."

"I've been thinking about that." Troy crossed his arms over his chest and looked down at the floor for a second before continuing. "When we had the others come in and help dig through minds to track down those that hurt the women—" he paused to see if everyone was listening. "None of those that helped were vetted."

"You think we may have let one of Hubert's into the cells without knowing it?" Michael's expression hardened.

"It is a possibility." Troy said quietly.

"Should we check the guards that work the cells?" Paisley looked to Arius.

His jaw twitched for a moment. "Most have been with me down there since I took over," he gave Troy a serious look, "but I suppose we should be diligent and make sure."

Troy nodded. "After the meeting, we'll start checking all who have access to any part of the chambers, and palace."

"What about their families?" Bethany asked. "Could they be leaking information to a family member and not even know it?"

Rafael shook his head. "We can't have Kara listen in on every resident in the realm." He gave Troy a hard look. "We need to prioritize. Do those with access first."

Troy nodded. "I agree." He gave me an appraising look. "We'll do whatever you're comfortable with."

"I," I glanced to Rafael, a bit surprised he'd jumped to my defense so quickly. He didn't make eye contact with me. I looked back to Troy, "I'll do what I can." And I meant that. I'd agreed to after the girls had told me about the women, but now there seemed to be so many other facets that meant many could be hurt or worse. I may wish for some humans to be gone from this earth, but that didn't mean I was going to let it happen to innocent people too.

Troy turned to Michael. "Have them do their tests after the meeting so we can expedite Kara having her own personal inhibitor like Elder Udela."

Michael nodded. "If we can check the teams, that would be a load off my mind before we go exploring that tunnel Kara saw them using."

"Guards are first priority." Troy nodded, "they're closest to us then the others."

Chase moved away from Alona. "Grab a snack, even if you're not hungry, we have some long hours ahead of us and much to learn."

With somber expressions several bodies moved toward the food.

"Before I forget," Daxx stood in the middle of the room, then motioned to me when everyone looked to her, "Kara saw residents with glowing green eyes when she was in the psych hospital."

Troy looked to me, then back to her. He closed his eyes for a moment, then looked at his twin. "We're going to have to find that place."

The expression on Chase's face matched his brother. "Yes we do." He gave me a quick compassionate look, "without risking Kara being locked up again."

The bite I'd swallowed got stuck in my throat. I tried again and winced as it hurt.

"I'll check with our people on that side, see if there's a way we can get in without being committed to do it." Victor informed then, then turned back to speak to Crissy.

I didn't even know if I could find that place again. I hadn't really cared to know where I was running from, only that I got away. Taking a deep breath, I looked down at the sandwich in my lap. Did I regret climbing that fire escape? Should I? I lifted it and took a small bite. As bizarre as all of this was, some pieces seemed to fit. Someone held a glass of chocolate milk at my eye level. I looked up to see it was Rafael. I took the glass. "Thank you."

He nodded. "I know everyone wants to check on everyone, but I don't want you doing something you don't feel comfortable with," his blue eyes were locked on mine, "speak up if it's getting to you." He nodded.

"I just want to help so I can go back to peace and quiet." I gave him a hopeful look.

He grinned. "I think that train has left the station for good." With a shrug, he turned and walked back over to the table of food.

I sipped the milk. Still wondering why he'd brought it to me. I looked at him walking away, or more specifically where I'd shot him. I was kind of glad I hadn't done any permanent damage now. Looking away before anyone saw me, I took another bite of the sandwich. Maybe the elders would have all the answers and this could be over soon. I stared into the liquid in my glass, yeah because easy-peasy happened *all* the time in my world.

Chapter Fifteen

The two elders that had been sent to check on the other realms weren't back so we were waiting. My mind paused on the thought of realms. Other realms. I was still having trouble swallowing the fact that there were other realms. Five others existed outside of the world I lived in. Well, lived, until I climbed that fire escape.

Bethany leaned closer. "The woman Rafael is talking to is Clairee, the leader of the witch's temple."

I looked at Clairee for a moment. Aside from the cloak she wore, she didn't look like a witch. Then again, neither did Bethany.

"Victor and Michael are talking to Ira. He's in charge of the guards' house, or the guards in general, I guess. He's also Mitz's mate."

I studied the man for a moment. He looked a bit older than Victor in appearance and almost as cold. I didn't see him with Mitz, but I didn't see Victor with Crissy and he adored her.

"The odd-looking man is Romulus, he's the head mage or whatever they're called." She smiled. "I don't understand that mage stuff."

The man looked, greasy, was the only word that came to mind. He had eerie eyes and I was really glad I couldn't hear his thoughts.

"The small man is the doctor," she paused, "I'm not sure why he's here, but I'm sure there's a purpose."

The man didn't look like any doctor I'd ever dealt with; he looked compassionate and caring. The doctors I'd dealt with didn't at all.

Bethany pointed to the other end of the room where two men sat. "That's the top archivist and historian."

Leone came back to his chair and leaned down between Crissy and Bethany. "Crissy could the something that was lost be Arwan?"

Crissy looked over his shoulder at nothing for a moment. "I don't think so." She frowned, "it is a person but not a mage." She nodded. "I see those differently. Oh," her eyes went huge, "they wear a stone on a chain around their neck." She bit her lip, "it's brown, like amber only it's not. I'm going to ask Bronx to help me find books about stones after this." She got up and went to the man standing at the wall behind her chair.

It was the same man that had brought her the Latin book. He was big in a scary way and looked like a pirate. I glanced down to the other end of the table to see large intimidating men standing behind Paisley, Autumn and Daxx. There was one behind Alona as well. They all just stood there, not looking around or even appearing bored.

Turning in my chair, I saw there was one behind Bethany. He glanced at me briefly, then back to whatever he was focused on in the room.

"That's Mac." Bethany whispered, "my guard."

It made sense. Princesses and queens should have guards.

"I guess he's yours." She looked behind me.

I turned to see a large man a few feet behind my chair. He had short black hair, normal green eyes and a long thin goatee. His arms were the size of tree trunks.

"His name is Bartholomew."

I almost jumped out of the chair when Rafael spoke from beside me. I hadn't heard him come over.

"I need a guard?"

Rafael nodded. "You do now."

"You got her a guard named Bart?" Beth asked. "I wonder what his last name is."

Rafael gave her a blank look.

She shrugged. "I couldn't resist."

Before I could say anything else, the two elders came in the door at the end of the room. They quickly went to their chairs, bowed their heads to the kings and sat down.

Arius and Mitz came through the other door.

Mitz sat at the other end of the table beside Emil.

"I guess that makes sense," Bethany said quietly, "she's in charge of the kitchen and housekeeping."

Leone looked over our heads at Rafael and smirked. "And she's part of the royal family."

"She's our aunt." Rafael said.

Beth looked from Leone to Rafael. "Your aunt?"

Rafael nodded. "We didn't see her much before mom and dad died, but since then she's always there."

"I think her and mom may have had some kind of falling out because she wasn't around much for the first forty years of my life, but the last hundred and sixty, she's around every corner." Leone smiled and glanced down the table at her.

"It must have been hard losing her sister." Beth said quietly.

"Yeah." Leone looked at her, affection in his eyes, "she's a lot like mom. They were twins, not identical, but still there's got to be some kind of connection with twins."

Bethany nodded. "I had no idea she was your aunt."

"She doesn't want the recognition, or to be called royal." Leone said then turned to watch Victor and Michael come back to their chairs.

I looked to where Mitz sat. She was talking to Emil and looked as she always did, happy.

"I must admit," Elder Varus said loud enough that all the soft voices hushed, "I'm quite concerned by this sudden meeting." She looked at the two men sitting at the other side of the room. "This meeting is off the records until I say otherwise."

The man closest inclined his head to her.

Victor stood up. "Before we discuss any of our findings, I must ask that all present reveal their forearms and wrists to be examined."

Michael nodded and pulled a small box off his belt.

They went around the table and stood by Rafael.

"All of us?" Elder Drusla asked.

"Yes. We've discovered something and must perform our due diligence." Victor answered.

Elder Drusla accepted what he said and pulled up the sleeve of her robe and rested her arms on the table, palms up.

Victor and Michael went and stood in front of the doctor first.

I realized they were looking for tattoos like the one Eunice had. I pulled up my sleeve and was going to put my arm on the table when Rafael put his hand over mine and stopped me. He shook his head.

I looked at him for a moment then he let go of my hand and watched his brothers walk around the room. I noticed Elder Udela touch the bracelet she wore before putting her arms on the table. A look of focus appeared on her face.

I traced the leather on my hand in my lap and wondered if I'd ever have the control to take on a room full of minds without flinching.

She looked right at me and smirked.

I couldn't help smile back. She heard what I thought. Maybe there was hope for me after all.

When Michael and Victor sat back down, Elder Segos gave Victor a curious look.

"Is there an explanation to follow?" He almost looked amused, or perhaps that was just him when he wasn't being cold and scary.

"Yes." The elder with the judgemental look said. "An explanation would be welcomed," he waved his hand around, "to have so many in these chambers without…"

Chase stood up, "this isn't an elders council, Roan, this is just a room large enough to hold all of us."

Elder Roan frowned, "I see."

Chase took a deep breath and sat back down. "This is a collective brainstorming session, because we are in deep shit here, people."

Elder Varus raised her hand, a concerned gaze locked on Chase. "Perhaps we should save questions for after the brothers explain why we're here."

Chase inclined his head to her and then turned to look at Troy.

Troy sucked in a breath and then nodded slowly as he exhaled. "Elder Moire, have the other realms been contacted?"

"Yes, my king. They are all looking into it to see if their borders have been affected." Elder Moire looked concerned. "It's not something they've felt the need to monitor."

"Understandable." The Elder with the curly hair said. "It's never been an issue in all of time."

"Keep me up-to-date when they get back to you." Troy told Elder Moire. He turned and looked at Victor.

Victor stood up. "We have much to discuss in this meeting, so I'm going to get to the point quickly." He motioned down the table in my direction. "Kara was able to ascertain that Eunice indeed has no recollection of how she came to be in the cells."

"Amnesia?" Elder Varus asked.

Victor shook his head. "No, I'm afraid not."

Elder Udela looked at me. "You were able to sort through her thoughts?"

I nodded. "Once she was asked the right questions, yes."

"How clever." She said, sitting back.

Victor looked at the Elders for a moment. "The last thing she recalls clearly is a coronation anniversary celebration," he looked at Troy and Chase, "the fiftieth anniversary."

Elder Nodin sat forward. "That was one hundred and ten years ago."

Nodding slowly, Victor crossed his arms over his chest. "Yes. She has no memory of anything she's done in all that time."

"How is that possible?" Elder Segos didn't look amused now.

"Magic?" Elder Varus asked. "Who is strong enough to maintain a spell that long?" She looked at the leader of the witches and mages, neither looked or responded.

"She thought of only one name." Victor said quietly. "Arwan."

There were audible gasps in the room at the mention of that name.

Elder Varus looked at me. "Eunice knew it was Arwan?"

I nodded slowly, "that's what she thought. They did it. They found Arwan."

"That's," the mage Romulus stood up, then put both hands over his face. Shaking his head, he dropped his hands. "He hasn't been seen for thousands of years."

"Could he do that?" Elder Segos asked. "Disappear for that long?"

Romulus' complexion paled. "Yes. Yes, he could live this long without ever being seen or detected." He took a ragged breath, "over half our teachings are rooted in his brilliance."

The room was silent. I looked around at the others to see their reaction to this news, they varied from shock to teary eyes.

"How does this relate to you checking our arms?" Elder Roan inquired softly.

Arius stood up. "Kara was able to hear how much the tattoo Eunice has is bothering her. It's not recent, so healing wasn't the issue."

The youngest Elder leaned forward. "The tattoo of the Hubert family crest?"

Arius nodded. "We're checking all that have been brought to justice since this began." He lifted the tablet and looked at it. "None at the start had it," he looked to Victor, "or they were too low in the ranks to matter. A few of our celebrities have it and it was never noticed." He looked back at the screen. "We're still checking, but almost all of the recent intakes have it, some are almost invisible and hard to see, but they're there."

"You believe Arwan is connected to these through magic?" Elder Arian asked.

"We suspect there might be a connection." Arius looked at Autumn, "there is no other explanation as to how Eunice could do what she has and not remember it."

Elder Varus looked at the shocked looking mage. "How do we locate Arwan?"

Romulus shook his head. "You don't, not if he doesn't want to be found."

"There has to be something that can be done." Elder Nodin stated.

Arius looked at the screen in his hand once more. "Out of the number with the tattoo, only some have memory issues." He turned and looked at Troy, "I believe those that were opposed to Hubert's plans or parts of them were spelled to believe, as Eunice was." He looked down at Paisley for a moment. "Those that were in agreement didn't need to be magically persuaded."

"How many of our celebrities weren't magically persuaded?" Troy asked in a solemn voice.

Arius cleared his throat. "Not many. Marcus, Davis a few of the ex-guards we got in the tunnels beneath the palace."

Quinton stood up and glared at Romulus. "Mages."

Romulus' eyes were huge. "I-they…"

"You will have all of your faction listed in your registry report to be screened, as soon as you are able to arrange it." Victor ordered, coldly.

Romulus nodded. "Yes. I'll call them all to the arena."

Victor glanced at the leader of the witches. "The same for the members of your temple, Clairee."

She nodded. "Of course. I will have them all paged to the temple by the end of today."

"We'll need you both to test the tattoos and see if you can detect what was used." Troy said watching Romulus and Clairee.

They both nodded without comment.

Quinton sat down. "How do we stop Arwan?"

All eyes turned to look at Romulus again.

His face flushed. "I-I don't think you can." He wiped a hand across his brow. "There are so many casts he could be spinning to never be found, even if he were, I can't think of a way to…"

"Give it some thought." Elder Segos said in a cold tone.

Romulus nodded and dropped back down into his chair. "I don't think he's stoppable." He mumbled.

Elder Varus turned to the two men sitting alone. "If either of you have any insights into the matter of stopping the most powerful mage to ever live, feel free to share."

"I think there is only one way to stop him." Elder Drusla said in a calm tone.

Elder Sego glanced down the table to her and nodded.

"And that is?" Elder Varus asked.

"End his life." Elder Moire stated in a low tone.

The atmosphere in the room was heavy in the silence. No one spoke. Looks of trepidation were passed from person to person. I didn't understand exactly what a mage could do, or why this particular one was worse, but if the people in this room were afraid, I was pretty sure I shouldn't be involved in any of this. What could I offer in all of this?

Chase leaned closer to Alona and hugged her against his shoulder. I realized she'd be physically feeling the emotions in the room. Pushing back from the table, I went down to her and squatted down beside her chair. I held up my arm with the inhibitor on it. "Do you want this?"

She gave me a teary-eyed look. "No. You need it."

I looked at Chase, the expression on his face was a combination of pain and fury. He leaned his head close to her. "Beloved, you are not required to stay."

Alona took a ragged breath. "I'm not leaving. The fate of everyone I hold dear is at stake, and I won't be excluded." She sucked in another breath. "I want to help."

Chase exhaled loudly and looked at me, indecision in his eyes. "Take the inhibitor my beloved." He said in a faint whisper.

Alona looked at me, sniffled and then looked like she was going to cry more. "What about you?"

I shook my head. "I'll manage." I looked around the room, trying to figure out where the spot was that put me the furthest from thinking minds. "I'll just stand in a corner." I shrugged. "If it's too much I'll leave, I'm not exactly priority here."

Alona sobbed quietly and nodded.

I stood up and reached into my pocket for the scanner to take it off. I looked at it in my hand, then looked around the room. "Try not to think." I said half jokingly, then nodded to myself more than the others around me and held the scanner over the rubber keeping me sane. It fell off. Chase caught it. I held my breath and handed him the scanner, then walked quickly down the table and around it.

...a true warrior always places their well being last...

...try not to think...

...I just did...

...maybe the hair is grey and not blue...

...Raf will go ballistic if she has a melt down...

...breath deep Kara, you can do this...

...one sign of stress and I'm taking her out of here...

"Come to this side, princess." Elder Udela stood up. "The elders have years of practice keeping their thoughts from me."

I nodded, holding my hand over my forehead, fighting the tingles of the thoughts invading my mind. I walked quickly past the four sitting together.

...I wouldn't survive going up against Arwan...

...absolutely amazing. Another unmatched warrior...

...rhodiola might help her control it...

...the captain's control is about to be tested...

When I reached the other side, Elder Drusla stood up and offered me her chair. I shook my head. "I'll just stand back here." I went to the wall behind the elders' seats. "I may have to exit quickly." I closed my eyes and took a few deep breaths, the hum was still there, but nothing was getting through, opening my eyes, I nodded to no one in particular. My breath caught in my throat when all of the elders stood up and bowed their heads to me. Unsure of what to do I looked over to Rafael only to see him standing at the end of the table with his gaze locked on me. I looked back to the elders and motioned to them. "Please sit." They did.

"I'm so sorry for all the drama." Alona said quietly, wiping a hand over her damp cheeks.

"Your comfort takes precedence, my queen." Elder Varus stated. Looking down the table, she motioned to Clairee as she spoke, "Elder Arian, the priority is to work with the temple and find the combination to help princess Kara have some peace of mind."

Elder Arian nodded. "I'll begin immediately." She looked to Rafael and nodded again.

Taking a deep breath, Elder Varus glanced down to me before turning back to look at the royal family. "I assume you're planning to check all staff with access to the royal family and main factions in our realm?"

Victor nodded. "We are starting with all guard staff and then the mages and witches." He looked over to me, "if Kara is able to cope with it, we're going to utilize her talents."

"I will assist as much as I can." Elder Udela said. She looked at me. "In cases where they can see me, however I'm afraid my status and position inhibit free thought."

I nodded. "Thank you." I slowly looked around at the hopeful expressions. "I'll try to help as much as I can."

"Your selflessness is humbling, princess." Elder Drusla turned her chair so it was at the end of the table and wasn't blocking where I stood.

I was trying not to have a full-on panic attack with everyone watching me. Without knowing why, I looked over at Rafael. His blue gaze was steadily appraising me. I don't know why but knowing he was on my side now made me feel calmer. He raised one eyebrow in a question of it I was all right. I nodded enough to let him know I was surviving this so far.

A chair scraping the floor had me turn to see Autumn had stood up. "I don't know if you elder folks are all knowing or get reports or what," she looked down at Michael for a second, he was smirking, "but Kara has been through it." She nodded, "what her family did to her makes me living on the streets look like a cake walk." She waved a hand at them, "maybe tap into your ancient memories or whatever and see if we can find her family." Autumn looked at me as she spoke. "Her last name is Coffey if that helps." Shaking her head, she zeroed in on Elder Roan, he wasn't looking offended by her words. "What she went through being locked up with crazies at ten, is disgusting. I want to have a one on one with whoever put her there." She nodded.

Daxx stood up. "While she was locked up, she heard others wanting to come home to Alterealm." Elder Roan looked at me quickly then back to her. "She saw people with glowing green eyes there too."

"Your saying members of our realm were trapped there?" Elder Roan's voice cracked.

Daxx nodded. "Yeah, that's what I'm saying."

He turned quickly to me. "Could you describe them?"

I shook my head quickly. "I don't," I huffed out a breath, "I don't know who the thoughts came from, there was so many," my heartbeat accelerated.

"We're going to find the asylum she was locked up in." Rafael's lethal tone brought all eyes to look at him. "If any residents from here are still confined, we'll bring them back." His look hardened when he glanced at me, "and justice will be given to those responsible for her torment."

Troy cleared his throat and stood up. "We believe if we can find Nelson Bosworth, we will be able to end all of this."

Elder Udela straightened in her chair. "Is Eunice willing to help locate him?"

Troy nodded. "She's expressed a willingness to share locations with us."

"I believe," Alona stood up slowly, "if we can find his mate, we may be able to find more details we need."

"He has a mate?" Elder Faran frowned. "A bonded one?"

Alona shook her head. "No. I believe she is as I am, and half Alterealm." She gave Chase a quick look. "They've only been together seven or eight months at this point, not much longer."

"Does she have anything distinguishable to help us locate her?" Elder Marinus asked.

Alona smiled, "she had a bright blue brush cut. It's quite unusual for a woman."

Emil leaned on the table and looked down at her. "Petite build, friendly disposition?"

Alona gave him a confused look. "Yes."

"Prince Emil, you've seen her?" Elder Segos inquired.

Emil nodded. "Yeah, she's regularly at one of my favorite..." he gave Quinton a quick look, "places."

"Is she usually alone?" Michael asked him.

Emil shrugged. "I've never really noticed who is with her. I just remember her because of her hair."

Michael nodded. "We'll set up a guard rotation to keep watch for her."

Elder Marinus stood up. "If this is all, I think we should adjourn, we have much to do."

Elder Varus stood up and looked around at everyone slowly. "Not a word of anything spoken in this room today is to be shared." She looked at me, "until we have checked everyone with access to the royal chambers and palace." She bowed her head to the kings, "your majesties, prince and princesses." Turning, she walked quickly from the room.

The rest of the elders did the same thing and all but Elder Udela and Elder Marinus left the room.

I watched Ira go over to Mitz and the compatibility I'd questioned was answered when he put his arms around her and held her, without her saying a word. He'd just known comfort was needed.

Rafael walked quickly toward me, then stopped and looked at the two remaining elders coming in our direction.

Elder Udela bowed her head, "I will do whatever I can to lighten your load while you're trying to ferret out traitors."

The man beside her inclined his head. "I will also be beside you each step of the way, princess, any conspirator amidst us is ultimately my failing."

Rafael shook his head. "Its no one's fault. There is no way we could have foreseen all of this."

The elder straightened to his full height. "I still feel accountable for it, Captain." He glanced at Elder Udela, "We've spent a thousand years trying to eradicate the Hubert line, they've always, since before my time, been trying to overtake the throne."

"Since before mine as well." Elder Udela admitted. "From all accounts in the archives, this has been ongoing since the dawn of the royal throne." She shook her head. "Right along with the Hubert line has been the Bosworth family, I believe if we can seize the remaining members to both we may finally live in a time the royal family and residents of our realm aren't in danger."

I wasn't picking up a single thought, which I was thankful for because what they were saying was so surreal to me. I was with people that had lived thousands of years and despite the amount of time they had, there had still be struggles and trials for them to beat. "I appreciate any help." I said quietly, then smiled a nervous smile. "I'm still struggling with all of this," I motioned around the room, "being real and that I'm here."

"You are stronger than most seasoned warriors, princess." Elder Marinus bowed to me.

I didn't know about that. I was currently just trying not to blurt out '*holy fraggle, this is really happening!*'.

"I was thinking, perhaps if we can set up an area with each faction we're screening that has some sort of wall or barrier that prevents us," Elder Udela motioned to me then herself, "from being seen, I could in fact help share the load with princess Kara."

Each time they said princess, Rafael gave me a quick nervous look. I held his look for a moment before he nodded and looked at the elder. "We'll arrange that."

"With your permission," Elder Marinus looked at him, "I'd like to oversee the arrangements to begin this as quickly as possible."

Rafael nodded. "The first group we're doing is personal guards, including all of the elders' guards."

Elder Marinus nodded. "A wise idea. With age we become too used to habits and those we've seen regularly. Familiarity does not ensure trustworthiness." He inclined his head. "I will begin there and have all the guards paged to meet at the guards' yard." He glanced to me, "and have a small area set up so you won't been seen." He turned on his heel and walked toward the door.

Elder Udela looked to Rafael, "I'd like to take, princess…"

"Kara. Just Kara." I said quickly.

She smiled, "Ismenia. Izzy," she winked at me. "I'd like to take Kara to see Clairee and Elder Arian to get her device sorted as soon as possible."

Rafael nodded. "Take her guard with you. I will meet you at the yard after you're finished." He looked at me, then to her for a moment.

She pointed to the door. "I'll wait over there."

I watched her walk away then looked up at him.

His eyes searched my face. "Are you okay?"

Hugging my waist, I looked up at him. "Honestly?" He nodded. "Other realms, barriers, evil mages, all this magic *stuff...*" I heaved a loud sigh. "Can I go for a time out in one of the cubes?"

He smirked. "I might request my own soon if we don't figure this out."

"Is it always like this?"

Shaking his head, he closed his eyes for a second. "No. Things are just crazy right now because we've been chasing our own asses in circles for months trying to figure out how all of this is possible." He looked at me, an expression on his face I didn't understand. "Thanks to you, we have more answers than we have since this began."

I felt awkward, no one complimented me—on anything, ever. "I'm just trying to help." I glanced over to Autumn. "The girls told me about Emil's daughter."

Rafael made a sound of annoyance. "Yeah. We'd all like to see a little justice for her."

"Justice, honor—I don't think I've ever heard those two words spoken or thought as much as I have since coming here."

He smirked, "there could be worse things."

I sighed, "That's true." I'd lived worse things.

"I sent Autumn to get your inhibitor back from Alona. *Wear it* until they figure a personalized for you one."

I nodded, I didn't have to be persuaded to do that.

Grabbing my arm, Rafael held it up and opened the device Michael had given me earlier. He popped it open. "At any time you're feeling overwhelmed, *use* this." His eyes bore into mine. "The top button takes you to the girls cave. The bottom one takes you to the courtyard at the palace. In case you feel like the walls are closing in again."

I looked at the buttons. It was strange he understood that happened to me.

"Kara." Dropping my arm, he lightly grasped my chin so I had to look at him. "Do you understand?"

Nodding was awkward with him holding my face so I whispered instead. "Yes."

...leave before you fuck this up...

His blue eyes darkened as he looked down at me. I couldn't look away.

...walk away now...

He nodded his head abruptly and released my chin. "I'll see you at the yard shortly." Turning on his heel he walked quickly through the door a few feet away.

Autumn came over and looked at the door. She held out the red cuff and device and grinned at me. "I recognize that fast-run-the-other-way walk."

I took the cuff and accepted her help putting it back on. "That's what he was thinking too, more or less."

She laughed, "at least you can hear what he's thinking behind his stupid moves."

I touched it once it was done up, feeling like it was a security blanket. "Hearing men's thoughts has never worked out for me in the past."

She snorted. "I still say it's a heads up most of us could have used."

I motioned to where Elder Udela stood. "I'm going with Izzy to see the witches and Elder Arian about my own off switch."

Autumn shrugged, "I'll come with. Michael is in iceman mode and busy setting up the meeting with mages." She shrugged, "it's better I stay out of the way so I'm less likely to kick someone in the face."

I'd seen her do that, and believed she would if required. "I wouldn't mind someone with me that understands what's going on."

Laughing, she started walked toward the elder. "I don't understand *any* of this. I just fight when they say fight."

Chapter Sixteen

I nodded, even though I had no idea what she said.

"Perhaps, Cyril," Elder Udela said with a smirk, "you could speak in layman's terms, so we have some idea of what you're saying."

Elder Arian stopped and grinned. "I'm sorry. You're right, Izzy, I get carried away." She took a deep breath and clasped her hands in her lap before looking at me. "I use the inner wrist because the skin is thinnest there," she lifted her arm and showed me hers, "so it reaches your system quickly."

That I understood. "Is it a drug?" I looked from one to the other, "I'm not really big on drugs."

Cyril shook her head. "No. It's a combination of technology, anatomy, herbology and witches magic." She grinned. "It's quite brilliant, I don't mind saying." She laughed. "And Izzy is a much calmer person since we discovered what really worked."

Autumn pulled her phone out and looked at it. "Michael needs me to help in the yard." She gave me a cautious look, "are you good here?"

I looked from Izzy to the other elder and then nodded. "I'm good. I don't have a meltdown scheduled for today."

Autumn smirked and got up. "I'll see you at the yard."

We watched her leave. I turned and looked back to see Izzy shaking her head.

Izzy laughed. "More than once I was mistaken for a lunatic when I went off." She gave me a serious look, "those moments when your inner thoughts get trapped in the thoughts of others and you don't know which way is up."

Inhaling sharply, I nodded. "Yes. I have meltdowns often." I frowned, "twice so far since being here." I motioned to the air around us. "I thought this was all inside my head." I frowned. "I used to have them so often, I thought it was all the drugs they gave me, but now I don't know."

Cyril Arian nodded. "That is why we do a complete workup of your blood. Make sure there isn't something lingering in there." She picked up the notebook beside her. "How long ago since you got out of that dreadful place?"

"Three years." I looked down at my hands, "it might be closer to four." I looked back up at Elder Udela's soft brown eyes. "I have no reason to keep track, really."

She nodded, a look of understanding on her face. "That you got out is the most important thing."

Elder Arian, Cyril, nodded, her curly hair bouncing. "Did you have any surgeries that you know of?"

I looked to Izzy briefly before looking back. "Surgeries?"

"Yes." She nodded again. "More than a few times we've found that those places tried to insert implants."

My heart jumped up into my throat. "Implant what?"

Cyril rolled her eyes, "silly ineffective devices they think will, fix," she made quotes in the air, "what is wrong with someone, when there isn't anything wrong."

I looked down the front of myself. "I don't think so."

She wrote in her notebook. "We'll get a scan and be certain." Setting it down, she held out her hand, "may I check your wrists?" She gave me an awkward smile, "to measure and be certain of scar free surface."

I looked down at the finger guard on my hand, then undid it. Setting it in my lap, I took the scanner out of my pocket, then removed the inhibitor. Pausing I looked at the device

Michael had given me. Blowing out a breath, I undid it and set it with the other bits on my legs. I held my hands out. She ran her hand up my one forearm, turned it and checked the other side, then did the same to my other arm.

Izzy leaned over and looked at my elbow. "What happened there?" She pointed to the scar.

"Oh." I turned my arm and looked at it. "After I thought I'd hid long enough, and my hair had grown back," I paused to watch Elder Arian measure my forearm and wrist and scribble it in her book. "I decided I needed a job. I was starving, cold, no home." I shrugged, "I found a job at an animal shelter, cleaning the cages and looking after the animals." She took my other arm in her hand and picked up her measuring tape. "I don't hear animals' thoughts." I glanced at the scar again, "I got a little to close and made one of the dogs nervous." When she released my arm, I clasped my hands in my lap. "I didn't tell them it happened, I didn't want the dog to be put down, so I had to treat it myself." I held up my arm and twisted it to look at the scar. "It was a bad location to wrap by myself."

"I think you're brilliant." Elder Arian lifted her face from her notebook. "Troy told us how you got out of there." She nodded. "I'm so glad you did."

Izzy nodded, a big smile on her face. "I'm so happy you're here." She gave the other elder a wide-eyed look. "In such a short time, she's already found answers."

"Yes. Answers we desperately needed." She frowned when her phone buzzed across the table. Picking it up, she studied it. "Clairee is unable to come here, she's knee-deep in rounding up witches as ordered, so we're to meet her at the temple."

"We'd better get there then." Izzy stood up. "We have much to do today, checking guards, witches and mages." She nodded.

I put the inhibitor and little device back on and stood up as I stuffed my finger guard into my pocket.

"I'll be along shortly. I want to go discuss the blood tests and scans with the doctor." Elder Arian picked up her notebook.

Izzy nodded and motioned to the door. "I'm afraid we'll have to walk, Kara, I don't have a porter programed for the medical wing."

I huffed out a breath. "That's perfectly fine. I don't *port* very well."

She laughed. "No one does at first."

The witch's temple was nothing like I had pictured. It wasn't a temple at all, just a normal building. A large building from what I saw as we walked across a lush green lawn. It had been hard to see completely with my guard, Izzy's guard and three other guards that had joined us as soon as we stepped outside. That was a lot of large bodies to see around. Izzy told me it was all perfectly normal to have that many escorts. Maybe normal in her world, but just being near others wasn't a *normal* thing for me.

The lobby of the building wasn't fancy, but it felt homey, modestly decorated with comfortable looking benches and plants. I didn't know what the scent was, but it made me feel the same way that smelling the lavender for the first time did.

The woman from the meeting came out from a room and smiled as she came toward us. She bowed her head as she got closer. "I'm Clairee."

"Kara." I gave her my best awkward, but friendly smile.

"I'm sorry I couldn't get over to meet with you." She looked stressed. "Trying to get all the witches in the realm here on short notice is proving," she glanced to the elder, "to be a challenge."

"It's not a problem, Clairee." Izzy smiled at her. "Kara was wondering how this works exactly." She held up her wrist to show her special band. "I've long forgotten the specifics."

Clairee nodded, "it's not that complex," she smirked, "okay, it is a bit complex. Elder Arian's device works with the natural pressure points in your wrist. Combined with proper herbs and magic, if you will, it helps you to control your ability."

I frowned. "I thought it was an off switch."

She studied me for a moment. "It could be called that, once you learn how to use it." Someone yelling could be heard from behind one of the doors across the room. Clairee looked at the door for a moment, then turned back to me. "Finding the correct herbs for each person is the hardest part. We have to find the one, or ones, that enhance calming for you."

I didn't completely understand what she was saying. "I'm not sure what that has to do with..."

Izzy touched my shoulder, then dropped her hand when I looked at her. "Abilities, such as ours are hardest to control when emotions are high."

I nodded, she wasn't wrong.

"They certainly don't get out of hand when you're calm." She gave me an exaggerated look, "the more you try to stop them the higher your heart rate raises, then that makes them get worse until you have a meltdown, as you said."

Clairee nodded. "Staying calm goes a long way in controlling when you want to hear or not hear another's thoughts." She smiled. "It works for some seers, those with telekinetic abilities that they can't control and telepaths."

The door the loud noise came from opened and a small woman came rushing out, toward Clairee.

"Excuse me." Clairee went over and listening to what the woman said, with her hands motioning frantically. Nodding, Clairee gave us a quick smile, then went to the room she'd come from.

I looked back to Izzy. "So does this work for people like Crissy?"

She made an o with her mouth for a second. "Sadly no. Controlling, or suppressing visions is a trickier business. In Crissy's case, if they're suppressed it's like the pause button was hit, so once the suppression is lifted, they all hit her like a tidal wave."

I nodded. "I've heard the mayhem in her mind."

She nodded. "Yes. I don't think any force natural or otherwise could suppress that."

I felt sad for Crissy.

Clairee came back out, a serious look on her face. She came back to us quickly. "Sorry about that."

"I explained how it worked a bit further." Izzy said.

"Ah, good." Clairee took a deep breath. She motioned to another door, "I have a few samples prepared." She started walking toward it. Izzy followed her.

Before I could move, the door the woman had come out of opened and Rafael came out. The expression on his face was as hard as the look I'd gotten the day I shot him. When he spotted me, he slowed. Looking toward the floor briefly, he took a deep breath, then started walking in my direction. The look was gone, but his stance and posture were rigid and angry.

Unsure if I should follow the women, or continue to stand there, I looked back to see Clairee and Izzy waiting in the doorway. When I looked back, Rafael's large body was right in front of me.

"Are you doing all right?" He asked, his tone conveying no emotion.

I nodded, wondering if I should ask him the same thing. "Cyril," he frowned like he didn't know who that was, "Elder Arian thinks they should scan and make sure I have nothing implanted in my body."

He raised an eyebrow. "What kind of implant?"

I clasped my hands together. "She said sometimes doctors do that trying to control what's wrong with people."

He scowled. "Let them do their tests. Make sure everything is as it should be."

I nodded. "Yeah, I was thinking the same thing."

Rafael took a deep ragged breath, his blue eyes moving over my face.

"Is-is everything all right with you?"

He closed his eyes for a second and jerked his head like he was annoyed. "Yeah. Fine." Pulling his phone out of his pocket, he looked at it. "They have the guards ready at the yard." He looked over to Clairee. "Are you finished here?"

I shook my head. "Clairee has samples…"

He motioned one of his large hands toward where she stood. "I'll wait here."

Giving him a wide berth, I went over to where the women waited, glancing back to see Rafael standing there with his hands on his hips glaring at the floor.

Chapter Seventeen

I turned to look at Rafael and Michael standing at the end of the partition, I shook my head. Izzy nodded at me, agreeing with my assessment of the guard on the other side.

"That will be all." Victor said in a cold tone.

We heard the door open and close.

Rafael moved to the other side of the barrier, where I couldn't see him. "How many more?"

"We're down to twenty." Troy said.

Izzy took a deep breath and exhaled. "I'd forgotten how tiring this can be."

"Do either of you need anything?" Michael came over.

Izzy shook her head. "I'll grab a snack before we head to the arena of mages." She smirked.

"I'm fine, thank you." I told him.

"Next one on the way in." Ira said.

I don't know how long we'd been doing this, but I'd heard a lot of confused guard's thoughts. Ira began each 'interview' by showing them a photo of the tattoo on Eunice's arm, asking if they'd seen anyone with it. The idea being that any involved with that Hubert man would panic, or at least think about something related to him and what they were doing.

So far I'd only heard rock steady, but confused male and female—much to my surprise—thoughts. Izzy looked like she was bored and I had to agree. That was shocking to realize. Doing this was so far out of my comfort zone, but to be so relaxed to the point of thinking about other things instead of focusing... like why was Rafael standing there looking like he'd rather be beating on something then anything else. Michael kept giving him strange looks, but I couldn't pick up his thoughts to know why.

"Sir, do you think they're among us? Those we've been trying to find?" A man asked.

I completely forgotten he was on the other side of the partition.

...if we have a way to recognize any involved, this could soon be over...

I glanced at Izzy, she looked over at Michael and shook her head.

...my wife will be happy to see more of me...

I heard a door open, then close.

"Last one." Ira told us.

The door opened.

Victor straightened from where he'd been leaning. "Kinsley, you didn't have to report to do this."

"I know," a woman answered, "I was coming into the yard when the Captain was telling the rest of the men, so I thought it best I stay."

...being on light duty is driving me insane...

"How's the arm?" Troy asked her.

"It's healing. Not as fast as I'd like it to, but I can't complain."

I wondered what a female guard would look like? Debating taking a peek, I decided they hadn't wanted anyone to know we were here listening in, so I really shouldn't.

...ten times a day I regret declining the quick fix with royal blood...

...I can't have the rest of the guards think I get special treatment though, so suck it up...

Michael went around the partition. "I'm glad you're here. We're going to need a female guard at the palace soon and I think you'd be perfect for it."

"It was my understanding all the palace positions were filled."

...of course I want to work at the palace. It's a palace...

I smirked at her thought, happy to know I wasn't the only one gobsmacked by a real palace.

"This will be as a personal guard." Troy told her.

"I'd be honored, my king."

...personal guard? I wonder to who. I know the guys have the princesses...

"Our brother, Emil's daughter is going to be moving into the palace and after the island, we feel a female guard would be best." Troy informed her.

...she may not like the guard being me...

...I failed her...

I glanced to see Izzy to see her eyes closed, pain etched on her face. I didn't know the connection. How could this Kinsley person be responsible for what happened to Rena?

"How, uh, how is she doing?" There was no mistaking the awkwardness in her voice.

"She's doing as well as can be expected." Michael informed her. "Autumn spends a great deal of time with her, as do the other women."

...that's good company for her, after Princess Autumn taking down Eunice, she'd feel safer...

Kinsley cleared her throat. "Just let me know when you need me."

I heard the door open and close.

Izzy brushed the side of the band she wore. She gave me a small smile, "I need a short break. I'll meet you at the arena for the mages." She rolled her eyes. "Being in their heads never proves to be dull." She got up and walked out around the partition.

"That went well." Ira said.

"I can't tell you how much better I feel knowing our guards can be trusted." Michael added.

"What of the two guards we suspected with the false information trap?" Victor asked. "They weren't here today."

"Shit, I forgot about them." Michael didn't sound happy.

"Give me a moment to check on their whereabouts." Ira said quickly, "since that time, we've been sending them all over letting them chase their tails."

...there has to be something important here...

...I can't get it to stay out of my head. Clairee better come up with something stronger...

I looked at the floor to appear like I wasn't listening but recognized the thought echo as Rafael's.

...grey hair like old? Is there a different kind of grey hair?...

"Raf." Michael barked.

"What?" Rafael glared in the direction of his brother.

"I asked what your thoughts were on Kara checking those last two guards later." Michael sounded annoyed.

Rafael glanced at me briefly, then scowled around the partition to where I couldn't see. He motioned toward me. "Ask her. She's right there." He stomped out of my sight.

I stood up and went around the opposite end of the makeshift wall. Victor moved out of my way.

Michael had his hands on his hips looking at Rafael. Giving his head a quick shake, he turned to me. "Would you be willing to see if you can help us find out about those two for sure?"

"You think they're traitors?" I looked down at the cuff in my hand, then decided other than Rafael's cryptic thoughts, the men in the room were able to prevent sharing theirs with me.

"There's a possibility, yes. We tried other means to flush them out but were only left with doubts and nothing proving their disloyalty." Victor told me.

I glanced to Rafael, who from his expression was still stuck in his own thoughts. "I can try."

Troy inclined his head to me. "We'll get that set up as soon as possible." He motioned to the door. "We need to get to the arena now. Romulus is having trouble keeping his mages waiting."

I nodded. "Izzy," he quirked an eyebrow at me, "Elder Udela, said hearing the mages thoughts is never dull." I took a sharp breath. "They don't think in bizarre riddles, do they? Like the one I shot?"

Troy grinned. "I have no idea. Personally, I dislike peeking in their minds because it's so cluttered up there."

That really wasn't the answer I was looking for. I started for the door, following Victor. "Is this arena in walking distance, or do we have to," I looked over my shoulder to Troy, "port?" I was hoping for walking.

"It's not far," Michael held the door for me, "a short ride."

I went out the door and down the stairs. Across the yard were horses. Beautiful, large equines. Forgetting I was supposed to be following the men, I went over to the midnight black one and held up my hand. "You are magnificent." I said softly. The animal looked at me for a moment, then shook its head and nuzzled my hand with his nose. I didn't look, but just from the animals' posture, I knew it was a male. "And you know you are." I grinned up at him while rubbing my hand over his muzzle. He was huge, my head barely reached his shoulder.

"You like horses?" Michael came up beside me.

I watched my hand glide over the beast's glossy coat. "I've never seen one in person before," I glanced at Michael, "I love all animals. He's beautiful, is he yours?"

Michael shook his head. "No, Odin is Raf's."

I smirked. "Odin? Like the god?"

Michael grinned. "We all pick names from mythology."

Odin turned his large head, almost knocking me back as he did.

I stepped around him to see he was watching Rafael walk toward us. I didn't need to hear his thoughts to know he wasn't impressed his horse liked me. "He's magnificent." I told him when he was close enough to hear me.

Giving me a questioning look, Rafael came over and patted his one on the shoulder. "You ride?"

I looked at the horse, then back to him. "Not yet, but I'm hoping." I offered my best smile.

"She can..." Michael stopped and looked at Autumn coming in our direction holding the strap to another large horse in her hand. The dark chestnut followed her with ease.

"Guard tried to tell me this horse, Athena had been saddled for me," she snorted, "it's not happening, Iceman."

Michael grinned. "I thought you might want to try riding on your own. Athena is very obedient."

Autumn gave him a hard look. "I don't care if she can sing the alphabet, I don't do animal," she waved her free hand around, "signals well." She stopped walking and the horse nuzzled the back of her head.

"She likes you." Michael said with a smirk.

Autumn looked behind her at the animal. "She's pretty likeable herself, but I'm still not getting on her back." She held the strap out to Michael.

He took it and smiled down at her. "You're coming with Hachi and I?"

She nodded, "until I grow a pair big enough to do it on my own."

Michael laughed and leaned down to kiss her on the forehead. "I'd prefer you didn't."

I looked at the chestnut horse standing behind them. "I'll ride her." My mouth blurted out before I could think it through. I nodded, feeling excited.

"I thought you'd never ridden before." Michael gave Rafael as quick look.

"I haven't, but," I motioned to the horse, "I may never have a chance to again." I moved around his so the horse could see me approaching. I held out my hand. "I don't know about you, Athena, but I'd be offended being labeled obedient. That's almost as bad as being called complacent." She nudged my hand with her nose and didn't object when I rubbed my other hand along her jaw. I looked under her chin to Michael. "Can I?" He looked over at Rafael. I turned to him, "please?"

Rafael took a deep breath, then exhaled. He motioned to the corner of the yard. "Ride her over there for a few minutes and make sure you can sit the saddle without sliding off."

I nodded. I had no idea what that meant, but I was all for doing it.

Rafael reached over and took the reins from Michael and turned to lead the horse to the corner.

I walked quickly behind him, trying to remember what I'd read about horses. Left side? *Mount and dismount from the left side.* I almost walked into Rafael's back when he stopped. Going around him, I went to the left side of the horse, then stopped abruptly when I saw how high the stirrup was. There was no way I could get my foot up in that.

"Steady, Athena." Rafael said in a soft voice. He came up beside me and before I could ask his advice in getting up there, he grasped my waist in his big hands and lifted me up in the air.

Biting my lip, to keep from yelping in surprise, I put my leg over the horse and grabbed the horn on the saddle. When Rafael let go, I looked down at the ground and decided it was a good thing I didn't suffer from vertigo or fear heights. Athena was quite tall. Rafael startled me again when he moved my foot and adjusted the strap so my foot could rest comfortably in the stirrup. When he went around to the other side, I leaned down onto my stomach and rubbed my hands along Athena's neck. "Proceed with caution until I get the hang of this please, girl." Patting her neck softly, I sat back up. Rafael flipped the reins over the animal's head and handed them to me. I took them and held them tightly.

"She'll follow your cues. Knees to go, steer with the reins. Just the slightest movement and she'll respond." He patted the horse's neck. "I trained her, so I know her well."

I nodded and squeezed my knees gently. Athena started walking slowly. It was a weird feeling the large animal's movements beneath me. Rafael walked beside us. "Is that what you do? Train horses?"

His expression didn't change. "I enjoy it, but no. I'm Captain of the guards, so that's what I do."

I pulled the strap of the rein to the right and Athena turned. "Oh. You're in charge of the guards?" I pulled on them and the horse stopped. "All," I paused when she pranced on the spot, "all of them?"

"Yes. All of them and the security in the realm."

I looked at him, then noticed I barely had to look down. "You're very tall." I said, not realizing I'd said it out loud until he smirked.

"Don't fall off. We'll be leaving in a minute." He turned and walked back toward the others.

I watched him walk away for a second, then nudged Athena to walk again. She did without jostling me too much. "Silly, really." I said quietly. I hadn't thought Rafael had such an important position, which was me making assumptions that because he was the youngest, he'd not have to assume such responsibility. Clearly not having a family or siblings of my own left big gaping holes in my knowledge of such things with. I looked over to see my guard, Bart, standing out of the way. He was holding the reins of a horse. Awkwardly, I turned Athena to go to him. Stopping her, I felt a moment of pride that I was doing this. "You're coming too?"

"Where you go, I go. My Captain's orders." He stated in a low tone.

I looked over my shoulder to see Rafael riding toward me. Right behind him was Michael with Autumn sitting in front of him, her legs over his. I would fall off if I rode that way, I thought. I turned back to Bart. "How do I make her do more than walk slowly?"

He got up on his horse, then looked back at me. "More pressure with your knees. Nudge her with your heels or clicking." Turning his horse, he road over toward other guards on horses.

Clicking? I had no idea what that meant. I frowned and looked down at the back of Athena's head. Clicking, I thought again.

"Ready?" Michael asked.

I nodded. "I think so."

Autumn grinned. "You're braver than I am."

Athena turned into the horse they were on, my knees skimmed by Michael's foot. "Or, I'm crazier." I said softly.

Michael grinned, then raised his hand toward men standing by a big gate. They turned and opened it.

I rode behind Michael and Autumn, they followed Victor. Rafael was beside me and Bart on the other side. I didn't know how many rode behind us, I was afraid to try and turn in the saddle and look. The silence was uncomfortable, but I took the opportunity to try and watch what the others did to make their horses go faster. For the most part Athena was just following along with the rest of the animals, like she knew I had no idea, and she was just going with the flow.

Troy's horse ran up until he was beside Rafael, he turned and smirked at him after the animal slowed to the same pace. "Quint isn't happy."

Rafael grinned a real smile and looked at him. "I owe Victor for agreeing to stick him in an arena full of annoyed mages, but its worth it." He lifted his hand in an annoyed motion, he hasn't shut up since," he paused and glanced to me for a second, "Kara got here."

I realized he was referring to Quinton harassing him because I shot Rafael. Most likely more to do with where I shot him, than actually being shot.

Troy laughed. "Daxx reluctantly agreed to not tell him all the mages magic was blocked while there."

Smirking again, Rafael nodded. "We owe her too."

"You know he'll get even if he finds out." Troy was leaning on his knee, still looking amused.

Rafael nodded. "He can try."

I took a few minutes, just absorbing that. The way they harassed each other and plotted against one another. I'd never really thought of what having siblings would be like, but I surmised if one were to have them, this comradery would make it more pleasant.

"You're doing good for someone whose never rode before."

I looked to see Troy was talking to me. "I think Athena is behaving because she knows I'm a novice."

He nodded. "She's a good animal." He glanced at my hands. "You didn't put the inhibitor back on?"

I looked down, I'd completely forgotten. "I guess I didn't." I looked at him, then to Rafael, before checking Athena was staying on track with the other horses. "Most of you are good at keeping your thoughts in your head." I gave Rafael a quick glance out of the corner of my eye.

"That's good to know." Troy's horse moved ahead of Rafael's, "might want to put it on before you go in the arena. There are some very annoyed mages in there." He made a noise and his horse sped up, running toward Michael.

Clicking. That was clicking? It didn't sound at all like *clicking*. I looked at my wrist, then put the reins into one hand so I could get the rubber band out of my jacket pocket. Holding it, I wondered how I was going to manage this.

Rafael moved closer and put his hand out.

Reluctantly I handed him the device and held my arm out. He put it around my wrist, without touching me.

"You should keep it on until they make your personal one." He gave me an odd look. "So you don't get overwhelmed."

I clamped my mouth shut, trying not to smirk. I didn't need to hear what he was thinking to know he didn't want me knowing anything inside his head. I nodded, then glanced ahead to see Michael, Victor and Troy racing toward a large dome. Grasping the reins, I made that *clicking* noise and prodded Athena with my heels. She took off. I held my breath, trying not to shout out something juvenile and leaned down, focusing on the rhythm of her motion so I wouldn't bounce off. It was wonderful. One of the most freeing and exciting things I'd ever felt.

I heard the pounding of hooves before I saw Rafael and Bart racing to catch up to me. Putting my head down further, I nudged her again, hoping she'd run faster. She did.

I had a quick moment of panic when the dome was fast approaching and I didn't know how to slow her without tumbling off. Before I could figure it out, she started to on her own. Autumn was standing beside Michael, her eyes huge and grinning. When Athena stopped, she pranced a little bit and shook her head. I couldn't stop smiling.

Rafael appeared beside me, he rubbed his hand along Athena's flank, then reached up and plucked me out of the saddle. He looked angry and I couldn't figure out why. When my feet touched the ground, I was a bit unsteady for a second, but caught my balance holding onto the stirrup. His blue eyes glared down at me for a quick moment, then he turned on his heel and walked to where Victor and Daxx stood.

I let go of the stirrup when Bart came and took Athena's reins. Autumn came over.

"You are crazy." She said, still grinning.

I giggled. "That was awesome."

Michael shook his head, giving Rafael a quick glance, then motioned to where they were. "Let's get you inside and behind the barrier before Romulus gets the mages lined up."

I nodded and followed him quickly. "Is Izzy here?"

"Yes, she had someone port her here." He glanced back at me. "We don't like our elders riding out in the open. Especially right now."

That made sense. "I didn't think we could port here." Not that I regretted riding.

"We can't once we port inside. Romulus has it blocked." He looked over to where Quinton stood, then stopped and motioned for me to go behind a short cement block wall. "You'll be able to hear thoughts around this?"

I nodded and moved to go behind it. "Yes. The only wall I've ever had it not work on are your cells." I smiled to see Izzy sitting on stool waiting for me.

Michael stopped. "Just let us know if you need a break."

Sitting down, I nodded again.

Rafael and Victor stood on either end of the wall with cold expressions on their faces.

"This is going to be similar to listening to poetry in another language." Izzy told me with a smile. "The more experienced the mage, the more their thoughts are a mish mash of unclarity."

I grimaced. "I can hardly wait."

"Can you hear me back there?" It was Daxx.

Izzy and I nodded.

"They can." Victor informed her.

"Okay Romulus, bring them in one at a time." Michael said.

"Thank the stars for that." I recognized Romulus' voice. "If I hadn't warded this dome against magic, we'd have casts flying about all over the place out there."

"You what?" That was Quinton.

Rafael smiled and looked down at his feet.

"Bastards." Quinton growled. "You too, Daxx. Oh. I'll get you for this."

I turned to see even Victor had a smile on his face.

"I'll, uh, go let the first one in." Romulus said in a hesitant tone.

Roughly fifteen mages later, I decided Izzy hadn't been wrong. The mumbo jumbo inside the mages heads was making me dizzy. It reminded me of a children's story I'd once read about ham and, green eggs I think I remembered, only it was much more complex.

"Next one." Troy said.

I watched Izzy take a sip of water and wished I'd thought to ask for something to drink.

"Milo," Romulus said, "we're looking for some information you may be able to assist us with."

"Oh. What is that?" A wheezy voice replied.

I focused to hear his thoughts, there was something there, but it was like it was behind something that blocked it. I frowned and looked at Izzy, her gaze connected with mine, then a sharp pain stabbed through my head. Grabbing my head, I dropped it forward trying to figure out what it was.

"Michael." Victor said in a gruff way.

Someone was touching my hands. I opened my eyes to see Rafael kneeling in front of me, looking up.

"Pain." I hissed.

"Romulus, come here." Michael barked. "Elder Udela?"

Rafael's large hands covered mine. The pain was excruciating. I leaned down and rested my forehead against his trying to breath through it.

"Milo you worthless rodent, I told you nothing warded, spelled or enshrouded." Romulus said very loudly.

"What? Oh, this? It's to keep that Manton from learning a new cast I'm working on. The nosy busybody is constantly trying to steal my work."

"Put it in here. Now." Romulus barked.

The pain stopped. I didn't drop my hands or move. Just stayed where I was, panting for air.

"Elder Udela, are you all right?" Michael asked.

"Yes. Yes. That was unexpected." She said in a quiet voice.

"Kara?" Rafael whispered.

I opened my eyes to see his eyes a few inches from mine. Dropping my hands, I straightened so I wasn't resting my head on his. "I'm fine." I said, still trying to catch my breath. I rubbed my hand over my forehead. "What was that?"

Romulus came around the barrier and looked from me to the elder. "He will be punished for not following my explicit orders." He looked nervous.

"We're all right now." Izzy looked at me with an inquiring expression. I nodded. "Let's continue and get this finished, shall we?" She sounded as out of breath as I was.

Rafael continued to kneel in front of me. His brows were drawn together. He touched my hand. "Do you need to take a break?"

I inhaled slowly through my nose, then blew it out slowly. "No. I'm with Izzy, let's get this over with."

Giving my hand a gentle squeeze, he stood up then turned to Romulus. He pointed a large finger toward him. "I thought the place was warded?" He tone was low and lethal.

Romulus bobbed his head. "It is. I warned-warned the Justice that with my kind, there is always some loophole..." He stopped when Rafael stepped right in front of him.

"That better be the last loophole today, or you're going to be suffering through a ban, realm-wide for a month." Rafael snarled down at him.

Romulus's eyes went wider than I thought eyes could go. "A-a magic ban on mages? That would, that would..." he nodded quickly. "I will screen each one before they enter this space, Captain." He bowed his head and backed away a few feet, then turned and moved out of my vision.

"Milo." Romulus barked. "You get to be this months' screener in the cells with the Warden for that stunt."

"What? That's—but I can't cast down there." The wheezy voiced squeaked.

"Exactly. Next time I order nothing magic is to enter, you will remember to follow orders." Romulus' voice was pitched higher than normal. "Now. This. Do you recognize this? Have you seen anyone with it or any inkling of it's meaning?"

There was silence for a few minutes.

...might as well castrate me while he's at it. The warden and no magic, I will surely perish...

"No. it's a bunch of meaningless symbols. What amateur designed that?" Milo said, with disgust in his tone.

Checking the rest of the mages went off without incident, other than trying to pick through their strange thoughts. The witches at the temple hadn't yielded anything so far either. There were only two more to check.

Giving my head a quick shake, I turned my attention back to the curtain that we were sitting behind.

"Sephare, we're looking for information on this?" Clairee said in a quiet way.

...looks familiar, but I don't have any details for them...

I glanced to Izzy, her brows were drawn together, she looked over at Michael and shrugged.

"Clairee." He said in an even tone.

"Have you heard of Willis Hubert, Sephare, or Arwan?" Clairee asked.

...they're chasing fairy tales. They've wasted half my day for fairy tales...

Heaving a sigh, Izzy shook her head.

"That will be all, Sephare." Michael said.

"Estrid." Clairee said in a friendly tone. "We're looking for more information on this."

...I've seen that...

Izzy and I both sat straighter and looked at Michael.

"I think I've seen that." A quiet voice said.

...is that the same? Wait...

...is it?...

"Where did you see it?" Clairee asked.

"I'm not..."

...Elijah and his stupid video games...

...complete waste of time and space...

"I'm trying to remember if it's that, oh," she sounded distressed.

"Take you time." Troy said from the other side of the curtain.

...no, that stupid game logo has a round thing through it...

"I can't remember." She sobbed.

"It's okay, Estrid. Take a deep breath and think." Clairee suggested.

...I think it was at the day realms market...

...was it the day realms? Will I get in trouble if I'm wrong?...

"I think," she took a ragged breath, "I think I saw something like that at the market," there was a pause, "on the day side." She made a noise of distress. "But I can't remember for sure."

...*they don't look mad...*

...*I just want to go home now...*

"Were you there shopping? Do you remember what for?" Clairee asked.

"I, uh," there was another pause.

...*they're going to think I'm stupid...*

"No. Not really. There's a boy there, he helps at the crystal vendor's stand."

"Do you know his name?" Troy asked.

...*my face is on fire...*

"No. I've never spoken to him." She whispered.

"But it was around there that you saw it?" Troy asked in a gruff way.

"Yes."

"On a person or..."

"Oh. No. Not a tattoo." She interrupted Clairee. "I think it was on the side of a box near the crystal vendor."

"Is that all you remember?" Clairee asked.

...*I was so distracted by the boy...*

...*I need to find out his name...*

...*maybe Sibyl will go with me later...*

"Estrid? Is that all you remember?" Clairee asked again.

"Oh. Yes. I wish it was more." Estrid said quickly.

"You've done well. You can go now." Clairee said.

There was the sound of a door, then the curtain was pulled back. Clairee looked at Izzy then me.

"She's completely smitten with the *boy*." Izzy said.

I had nothing to add to her summary. I was tired, my head was starting to pound, and I wasn't sure if I was thirsty or wanted to throw up. I'd never listened to so many thoughts in one day, ever.

"She's still young." Clairee smiled, "very rare that her powers are this strong at her age."

"It's more than we've found all day." Michael stated.

Romulus had been leaning in the corner. "I am personally glad that those with the most power, and we depend on have been found trustworthy."

"I was hoping we'd find the snakes today." Autumn said as she got up off the chair. "A possible mark on a box isn't making me want to dance."

"It could be some sort of signal to Hubert's people." Michael suggested, crossing his arms over his chest and looking around at the others.

"It is possible." Victor said. "We're going to have to keep a watch and see to be certain."

Rafael nodded, his stance similar to Michael's. "Without tipping them off."

"This is very frustrating." Troy said, then sighed. "We know they're out there, but it's like they're ghosts."

"We still have the inner chamber staff to check, and those two guards." Michael reminded him.

"A ghost," Clairee whispered. She spun to look at Romulus. "A ghost!"

Romulus jolted like she'd hit him.

"Could he?" Clairee put her hand over her mouth.

"He could." Romulus nodded his head so fast it was blurry.

"Care to share?" Michael asked in a loud voice.

Clairee jumped an turned back to him. "Arwan." She nodded. "What if he's been coming and going undetected all this time."

All the men turned to look at Romulus.

He nodded, regret on his face. "If anyone can do it, it would be him."

"Are you talking about him cloaking others to walk among us?" Izzy stood up.

Romulus frowned. "It would have to be him. Only he is skilled enough and able to adjust for any situation."

"You're saying," Victor looked from one to the other, "the infamous Arwan has been walking among us all this time?"

Clairee bit her lip, a serious expression on her face before she nodded.

"It would explain how so many were recruited without our detection." Troy said.

"I must," Izzy turned to Troy and bowed her head, "with your permission, update the other elders."

Troy rubbed his hand across his jaw then nodded. "Yes. Tell them to think long and hard to see how feasible this is."

"I shall." She bowed her head to him and then looked back to me. "Kara?" She rushed toward me.

I don't know if it was the sudden motion or I was just beat, but I felt lightheaded.

"She's bleeding." Izzy leaned down in front of me and put her hand on my shoulder.

Bleeding? I looked down the front of me to see blood spots on my hand in my lap. Lifting my hand to my face, I touched the wet under my nose.

Rafael was right there on the other side of me. "Is this normal?"

I couldn't tell if he was asking me or not.

"I've never had it happen." Izzy said quietly.

Clairee was almost in my face. "Kara, is this normal?"

"Perhaps she's overdone it." Romulus leaned down between Clairee and Izzy to look at me.

I slide off the stool and stumbled back a few steps. Too many people in my face made me nervous. I wiped my hand across my face again, dizzy from moving so quickly. "I don't know," I looked at the blood on my hand, "why this is happening." I looked over at Izzy, and everything went fuzzy. My knees gave out.

"I've got you." Rafael said.

I found myself in his arms. "I don't know what's wrong." I slurred.

"Get the doctor to her room." Rafael said in a strained voice.

Then static filled my head, but I was spinning too much to care.

Chapter Eighteen

I opened my eyes to see Mitz sitting beside me. I was in a bed.

"There you are." She smiled at me. "You were just dehydrated, love, you'll be right as rain in no time." She patted my hand. "Just rest a while. I'll go get you something to eat."

I took a deep breath and then blew out a breath and closed my eyes again. I wasn't dying, that was good. When I opened them again, Mitz was gone. My head still felt strange, but I did feel better. Lifting my arm, I froze, it hurt. There was a needle in my arm. Scrambling up, I knelt on the bed. Staring at the bag, I tried to figure out if they were giving me drugs. Was that why my head felt strange? Peeling the tape up off my arm, I puffed out breaths like a breathing exercise, building up the courage to pull the needle out of my arm. Squeezing my eyes shut, I grasped the end of it.

"Hey," a hand closed over mine, "it's just fluids."

I opened my eyes and looked at Rafael. "I don't like needles."

He didn't move his hand from mine. "Then drink more than chocolate milk and we won't have to stick them in you." Gently, he moved my hand away from my arm.

I scowled at him, then frowned, trying to remember when I had a drink that wasn't chocolate. He was right. Other than that tea from Mitz, I hadn't.

Rafael sat on the bed and looked at me. "We'll take it out when the bag is empty."

Dropping down to sit on the bed, I looked up at the bag. There wasn't much left in it. I wonder how long I was asleep.

"Does that happen a lot?" His expression held concern, "you forget to drink and end up with nosebleeds?"

I shook my head. "It's never happened before." I didn't dare say the milk was better than any I'd tasted.

"Try to put water in a few times a day." He patted his chest. "You freaked me out standing there bleeding, going paler by the second."

"I'll try." I looked at my arm, then reached to pick at the tape. "What were they talking about before I started dripping blood all over the place?".

He blew out a breath. "Arwan. It's possible he's been cloaking himself. That he's been coming and going all this time."

"Cloaking?" I glanced to the bag, wishing it would hurry up and empty.

"Making himself invisible."

I touched the needle as I looked at him. "They can do that? Mages?" The idea of invisible people made the hair on the back of my neck stand up, not to mention my FOS notched up a few points.

"And witches." Rafael nodded.

I looked at the bag again. "That's kind of creepy."

Rafael snorted. "Everything with mages is creepy." He leaned closer and moved my hand.

I waited for him to chastise me again, but he didn't. Instead he put two fingers over the needle and pulled it out with his other hand. I jumped as he did. When he moved his fingers, I watched the blood spread under the bandage. Pulling off the tape, I moved to get up and get a cloth. Rafael grabbed my wrist and leaned over, licking my arm. My brain was didn't know whether that was gross and germy or too bizarre to describe. Pulling my arm from his grasp, and away from his tongue, I looked down to see it wasn't bleeding now—in fact there wasn't even a mark where the needle had gone through my flesh. I looked up to see him sitting there looking at me—with red eyes.

"Healing saliva." He said in a rough voice.

I frowned. "You know that's a huge paradox, right? Saliva is generally the most germ-infested secretion a body has."

"Not this body." His eyes went back to normal as he looked at me. "You're not freaked out with my eyes."

...stupidest move ever. Why did I do that?...

I pretended I didn't hear his thoughts. "Alona showed me that hers changed."

"What else did she explain?" He watched me carefully.

...don't drag this out. You have enough on your plate. This can't happen now...

"There was a mention of feeding, and," I looked at his mouth, "fangs." I shifted so I was further away from him. "I'm afraid my mind got suck on the purpose of fangs before much more could be said."

Rafael just sat there looking at me. His gaze moving over my face.

...shit. Damn grey hair again...

...I need to call Clairee...

I watched his expression change, like he wasn't even seeing me now, even though he was looking at me. "Are you all right?"

He jerked and sat up straight. "I'm fine."

I lifted my wrist to show I wasn't wearing the inhibitor. "Are you trying to figure out the pieces Crissy has seen?"

Rafael jumped up from the bed, then looked at my arms. His jaw clenched. He'd forgotten I wasn't wearing the inhibitor. He spun around and smashed his hand against the wall. I didn't know what the wall was made of, but it didn't crack despite how loud it sounded. "Don't be poking around in my head." He rumbled and then turned around to give me a hard look.

I shuffled to the edge of the bed and stood up. "I wasn't poking anywhere. I don't ask for this." I glared at him. I could see his chest rising and falling and feel the buzz in my mind of his thoughts. I wanted to hear but didn't want to at the same time. I pointed to the door. "Get out if you don't want me to know what you're thinking right now."

He glared at me, then spun on his heel and stomped from the room.

I jumped when his door across the hall slammed shut.

Chase leaned around the door frame and looked in. "Bad time?"

I blew out a breath. "No." I sat back down.

He stepped into the room with Alona. She gave me an understanding smile. Chase tucked his hands into his pockets. "I heard you had an interesting day."

I watched Alona go over and wrap the tube from the IV around the hook the bag was handing from. Picking the cap up off the table, she put it back on the needle.

"It was different." I told him quietly.

"I suppose it would be after the years you spent trying not to use your ability."

I shrugged, glancing out to Rafael's door.

Chase grinned. "At least you're not balking when it's called an ability now."

I gave him and earnest look. "I've never found it useful before."

Alona sat on the bed. "I hear it was very useful today."

"I'm still trying to figure out this cloaking thing." I looked from her to Chase. "Those mages, the stuff they think." I shook my head. "They're all a bunch of wackadoodles."

Chase laughed. "I think we should rename their faction to that. Instead of the mages' collective, we can have a collection of wackadoodles."

I smiled, pushing the hair back from my face. "The crazy people from the asylum were saner than some of the mages."

"I have no doubt." He nodded. "I'm sorry we missed it. We're taking turns sleeping around here with everything going on." He looked at my arms. "Clairee and Elder Arian working on your personal device?"

I nodded and rubbed my wrist, wondering if I should put the inhibitor back on. Looking up, I motioned to the bag on the table. "Clairee sent herbs I'm supposed to," I lifted my hand in the air, "see if any of them make me feel calm or peaceful." I looked at Alona, "I'm not sure what peaceful is supposed to feel like."

Rafael's door opened. He stopped and looked at me for a moment, clearly still not happy with me. Without a word, he turned and went down the hall out of sight.

"He's in a mood." Chase sounded amused.

I lifted my arm the needle had been in. "He licked my arm after he pulled out the needle." I stared at the unmarked spot. "That can't be sanitary."

Chase chuckled. "I agree, who knows where his mouth has been."

Alona gave him an odd look, then gave her head a slight shake. "Troy told us they think Arwan is cloaking himself and walking around."

I nodded. "That creeps me out. The idea of someone walking around you can't see." I frowned. "How are they going to find someone they can't see?"

"Very good question. I believe Victor is asking Romulus that right now."

Mitz came in carrying a tray. She gave me one of her caring looks. "You seem better." She set the tray on the bed. "I've brought you water and tea. I'll make sure you drink more than chocolate milk from now on."

She really was a sweet lady. "Thank you Mitz." I looked at the plate to see a sandwich, fruit and a few cookies. They always have food here, I thought, which was just silly, of course a royal family had food.

Going over, Mitz got the pole with the bag hanging on it and started wheeling it toward the door. "Let me know if you need anything."

"Thank you." I said quickly before she was out of sight.

"We're going down to the solarium for some coffee. Come down when you're ready." Alona said as she took Chase's hand and stood up.

"We've asked for reports from all the departments, so maybe we'll have some good news." He bowed his head to me as they walked out.

I looked at the food. Eating was not going to be a problem if the rumbling in my stomach was any indication. Getting up, I grabbed the bag of herbs. I'd sniff them while I ate and see if any of them made me feel 'good things', although eating did that, so how would I know?

Chapter Nineteen

The solarium now had plants in it. Maybe plants didn't fit, they were more like trees of all kinds and sizes spread out though the room. It was nice to see.

I didn't know what to do, so I sat in the chair and watched all the conversations taking place in the room. More than one guard had come and gone. Two of the elders were also here. It had taken me a moment to recognize them without their robes on. Elder's Marinus and Segos, I believe were their names.

The women would sit for a moment, then one or more would go to one of their men as they stood talking and drinking coffee. Autumn nodded to Michael and then came over to me. "You look better. Guess you needed some rest."

"And fluids that aren't chocolate it seems."

She grinned. "Yeah staying hydrated is important." She shrugged. "Your crash gave all of us an excuse to grab a nap though."

I lifted my eyebrows. "Glad I could help." I looked at one guard coming back in and giving Michael a tablet. "What's going on now?"

Sitting in the chair beside me, she leaned her elbows on her knees. "Gathering intel, I'm told."

"On?" I looked at my arm where Rafael had licked me. I didn't know why I kept doing that. Did I expect something to change?

"No idea. Hopefully it will lead to getting out of here though. I miss working out, so a little action would be good."

"I'm okay without action." I watched Clairee come in the room when Rafael turned and met her in the middle.

They spoke quietly for a moment, then both of them turned to look at me. Rafael still didn't look pleased.

"What's with *that* look?" Autumn turned to me.

I sighed. "We had a verbal altercation because I heard what he was thinking."

"A verbal altercation, huh?" She grinned and stood up. "Guess he should keep his thoughts under control." She jammed her hands into the pockets of her hoodie. "Raf's an all right guy." She watched Clairee and Rafael walk toward us. "He's pretty straight up, just ask him up front when you have a doubt."

I nodded, even though I didn't think that would happen. As they reached us, I touched my arm again where he'd licked me. His gaze followed the movement of my hand, then he looked right at the inhibitor on my other arm.

Clairee smiled at me. "Did you get a chance to try those herbs?"

I nodded. "Yes. I rubbed them on my wrist and inhaled their scent like you said."

"Did any of them do anything?" She clasped her hands in front of her.

I nodded. "Two of them did." I sighed, "I think. It could have been the cookies I was eating at the time."

Clairee grinned. "Yes cookies can invoke good feelings as well."

Rafael smirked and looked over at Crissy. "Some more than others."

I stood up, feeling tiny sitting near him. "I left the two that made a difference on the table in my room and put the rest back in the bag."

Clairee nodded. "With your permission I'll go collect those, so Cyril and I can get the first test device ready."

"Oh." I hadn't realized they'd do it that quickly. "Yes." I nodded.

"With any luck we can test it later on today." She bowed her head to me. "I will let you know." With a quick look to Rafael she walked quickly from the room.

"I realize seating is an issue here, but I'd like to cover a few things while we're all here." Troy said loud enough that all other conversations stopped.

"We need to have a room just for meetings." Daxx stated dryly. "And a schedule of where we're eating or whatever. I went to the dinning room before coming here."

Bethany nodded. "Leone and I almost did the same when we got the message."

Chase filled his mug and then turned to Alona. "Beloved, does a project such as that strike your fancy? Establishing where we're to do what, now that we have split our residences?"

Alona nodded, a gentle look on her face. "Yes. I would love to find a meeting room." She glanced to Troy, then back to Chase. "Here or the chambers?"

Chase waved his empty hand around. "Anywhere you decide works for me."

Alona looked happy. "I will get it done."

"I think we should figure out the meal thing too. Knowing where we're supposed to be would save a lot of time." Paisley said, looking around the room. "I think this would be perfect for lunches."

Bethany nodded. "I agree. And we could have breakfasts in the dining room like always."

Daxx nodded. "Yeah. That's a habit I enjoyed."

"May I suggest we use the dining hall here at the palace for dinners?"

Everyone turned and looked at Mitz, who had been standing quietly in the door.

"Dining hall?" Arius asked. "There's a dining hall here?"

Mitz nodded. "Yes. It would save me from bouncing around if lunch and dinner were in the same building."

Quinton lifted his cup to Mitz. "More food if Mitz is happy. I'm all for that."

Troy grinned at him. "Then that's settled. Breakfast at the chambers and other meals here at the palace."

Chase took a sip, then looked back to Alona. "And my lovely mate will find us a designated meeting space."

"But we're still having snacks at the meetings, right?" Leone asked.

Mitz laughed. "Whatever you need, love."

Leone nodded. "Okay I'm all for a room for meetings, because we've outgrown Victor's office."

"I for one, would enjoy having my office as my own again." Victor gave Alona an abrupt nod. "Let me know when you have found a location and I shall have maps and other required items sent there."

Alona gave him a huge grin. "I shall." She inclined his head to him.

"Might I request a few extra chairs in this meeting room?" Elder Segos looked at Alona and bowed his head, "my queen. I have enjoyed having more purpose recently."

Elder Marinus nodded his head. "As have I."

Alona looked at Chase, then back to them. "I will find a room large enough."

"With that settled, we need to share our findings." Victor put his cup down and crossed his arms over his chest. When no one objected, he continued. "We've had extensive tests run on Eunice Bosworth's tattoo." He glanced around the room, "it has been confirmed that there are still traces of magic within the marking."

"She's given us several locations they used to use. But as it was a century ago, we're not holding our breath Nelson will be at any of them. Also, the more she tries to remember, and fight the remaining magic, the more ill she feels." Arius rubbed the back of his neck for a moment. "Romulus and the science department have concluded that only a mage with extraordinary skills could do such a thing."

"Confirming that Arwan is still around." Michael stated in a low tone.

"Great." Quinton said and then sat down. "So how do we find him?"

Michael glanced to Elder Segos for a moment. "Elder Segos and Marinus had an idea and Romulus is currently testing to see if it is possible, but it's purpose is to detect magic that is otherwise undetectable."

"Huh?" Daxx frowned and looked at him. "How does that work?"

Michael shook his head. "I have no idea. All I care about is that it is doable, then we'll figure out what comes next."

Emil yawned, then got up and headed to the coffee pot. "I took the first watch watching for that Leila woman."

"Do you think she'll stick to her old habits?" Alona asked quietly.

Emil shrugged. "I've seen in there recently, so there's a good chance."

"I feel bad using her to find Nelson," Alona gave him a sad look, "but on the chance she's been spelled, we have to."

Emil nodded. "Any means to find that bastard, I'm all for."

"Do you think finding that, uh, slag is the answer?" I watch Emil smirk at me.

He pointed to Troy, then Chase. "They do, so I'm with them."

I took a deep breath. "Let's hope that if she's not openly a blatherskite, that her thoughts are easily heard then."

"Your vocabulary is quite eclectic for one with no formal education." Victor gave me a sincere look.

I shrugged. "When I kept getting sent to the solitary units, I finally realized it was because of the language I screamed at them," I rolled my eyes at him, "more than the fact I was screaming." I glanced down at the guard on my hand. "So," I looked back up, "I asked one of the nice attendants if I could read. Books weren't popular there, so she gave me a dictionary. I started reading dictionaries. I still do."

Victor smiled at me. "That explains some of the phrases you use." I smiled back at him. "I was around when they were frequently spoken."

"Most I was able to get my hands on were old." I pushed the glass away. "Today's are quite different."

Lifting his cup, he toasted me. "It adds a charming quirkiness to your personality." He glanced at Rafael.

Moving just my eyes to look at him, I wondered why Rafael was giving him such a hard look.

"So, we're looking into catching Arwan. What do we do until we can?" Autumn crossed her arms over her chest and held his look.

Michael gave a slight shrug. "Business as usual. We can't put everything on pause in the hopes we find a mage that doesn't want to be found."

Rafael nodded. "Doing that could be playing into his hand."

Leone kissed Bethany on the top of the head and went over to get more coffee. "I think we should find that tunnel Kara followed them to." He glanced at Daxx. "And we're still trying to find *the track* that they're taking women to."

Daxx nodded. "Tim is working with the teams to check out any possible locations we," she motioned to Crissy and Bethany, "can think of."

Leone nodded. "Good." He turned and looked at me. "Think you can show us where the tunnel is?"

I bit my lip. "On a map?" I gave Daxx a quick look. "I'm not really good with maps."

"If you can pick out a few landmarks that Crissy and I might know, we can get the guys to go look, bring back pictures." She suggested.

I liked that idea. "Yeah. There's a few stores and buildings nearby that are one of a kind."

Daxx nodded, then turned back to Leone. "Okay we'll go over it after this meeting and get back to you with a list."

Leone grinned. "Great." He glanced around the room. "I don't know about the rest of you, but I'm in the mood for a fight or two."

Autumn snorted. "I second *that*."

"I know we're all going a little stir-crazy right now," Troy rubbed a hand across his jaw, "but for security purposes we've had to be more careful."

"Yeah, yeah." Daxx mumbled, "we get it. Please don't go there again."

Troy smirked at her.

"If I may." Elder Marinus looked at Troy. Troy nodded. "I am quite interested in finding the facility that Princess Kara was held in." He looked at me. "If there is a chance some of our own are still being held there…"

Rafael looked down at me. "Do you remember what city it was in? The name of it?"

I bit my lip. "I have no idea the city it was in. I got on the first bus I could and didn't look back."

He nodded.

I closed my eyes, trying to the see it. "I don't remember a name anywhere I could see." I opened my eyes. "There was an emblem, or-or logo on the orderly's badges."

"Oh." Crissy jumped up from the table and came rushing toward me with her notebook. "Can you draw it?" She held them out to me.

I took them, glancing briefly at Rafael, he gave me a slight nod. "I can try." I moved over to the table and set the notebook down. Standing there I looked down at the blank page. Closing my eyes for a second, I pictured the badges I'd seen for so many years. Opening them, I held my breath and put the pencil on the paper. Moving without overthinking, I roughed out the letters and the two shapes that surrounded them. I exhaled and straightened it. "It was something like this." Before I could turn around Crissy was right there, almost on top of the table.

"I know this." She picked up the book and looked at Victor. "I've seen this." She frowned. "It's in my old notebook." She said quickly then vanished.

"Crissy has seen it?" I looked to where she'd been standing, then over at Victor.

"If she says she has, then yes." He nodded. "It is more than possible. She has seen something to do with each mate for my brothers."

I opened my mouth to ask what that had to do with me when she reappeared.

Dropping the notebook on the table, she leaned over it and started flipping pages. "It was way back," she mumbled, "after Daxx's tattoo, but before the twin sisters…"

I glanced to see that every person in the room stood patiently and watched her. I, on the other hand, wanted to shout and ask what she was talking about.

"Oh, here." She tapped a finger on the page.

I looked over her shoulder at it. Her drawing was much more detailed then my own. "That's it." It was like I was looking at a badge right in front of my face.

Grabbing the book, she spun around and waved it while looking at Victor. "I know where it is." She nodded. "The same city I was in before that lady with the flower." She looked excited.

Victor came over and put his arm around her and leaned down and kissed the top of her head.

She looked up at him. "Do you think I was supposed to go help Kara?" She bit her lip, a worried look on her face.

"I don't believe so, heart." He kissed her again. "I believe you were meant to see it, so we could find it now."

Crissy blew out a breath and looked relieved. "I can show you on a map where I was." She looked at me. "Where we were."

"It will take some planning and co-ordination." Michael said looking at Rafael.

Rafael nodded. "We're taking a full team." He turned and looked down at me, resolve etched on his face. "In case some of ours are there—and because we need their records."

I sucked in a breath, my nerves buzzing from the tone of his voice.

"Just make sure we're on *that* team." Daxx said, then held up her hand when Troy turned to her. She motioned to me. "Kara went through hell, but there might also be answers there the rest of us are looking for." Turning, she gave Autumn a quick nod.

"Yeah. If there's any record of anyone dropping their kid on the street…"

"Or doing experimental drug therapy on them." Bethany said looking at Crissy.

"Or vanishing grandfathers." Paisley gave Bethany a nod.

"We're going to search all their records." Alona looked at Chase. "Make certain our guards and your *team* are prepared for an extended visit."

Chase inclined his head to her, then turned to his twin. "That we will."

"Make certain there is room for a few elder warriors as well, Captain." Elder Segos turned to Rafael. "Answers we have long sought may, in fact, be in that very facility."

Rafael looked down at me, the nerve in his jaw pulsing. With an abrupt nod, he looked back at the elder. "I'll coordinate with your guards, so we're all on the same page."

"It seems this is a good juncture to break this meeting." Victor leaned down and looked into Crissy's eyes, then kissed her quickly on the mouth before straightening. "We have much to arrange." Without further explanation, he disappeared.

"I'll come to the yard with you and fill in Ira." Leone looked at Rafael.

Rafael nodded and then looked at me. "Get us those landmarks for the tunnel." He turned to Daxx. "I think we'll use it as a warmup." With a grin, he disappeared.

Daxx grinned. "Lots of ass kicking coming up." She pointed to me, "I need those buildings."

"She can tell you about them while we go exploring and find a meeting room." Alona said giving Chase an affectionate look. "I'll need input for this one."

Chapter Twenty

I just stood there gawking at the thrones. Real thrones. They weren't made of gold or anything flashy, but the carvings in them were intricate and even though they were well maintained, you could tell the age by slightly worn areas. They had to be older than the oldest elder, at least.

Alona went behind the thrones and pulled the material back. Behind them was a huge window. "This view is spectacular." She looked around. "We could place the thrones at the end," she turned and held her hands toward the far end of the room, "with a portrait of their parents there."

"I've never seen a portrait of them." Daxx said, "none from the dining room was of them."

Alona took a deep breath, the excited look on her face fading. "Chase says it was put away."

"Do you think we can find it?" Bethany asked looking around the room. "I'm thinking tables set in a big square, so we can see everyone."

"Like knights of the round table, only square?" Paisley asked with a smirk.

Mitz came into the room. She stopped and looked at the thrones, then looked away. Her smile wasn't as luminous as usual "I have a fresh batch of cookies cooling in the kitchen here." She looked right at Crissy when she said it.

"Oh." Crissy got up off the floor.

My mouth spoke before I could filter it. "I'm sorry about your sister, Mitz. It must have been hard for you."

Mitz looked at me, an expression I couldn't read on her face, then smiled. "My boys have been talking."

Bethany nodded. "Leone and Raf explained why you were at the last meeting."

Ah," she smiled, "the fact they've kept it to themselves this long is nothing short of a miracle."

"Kept what to themselves?" Daxx frowned.

"I believe I know as well." Alona said in a quiet way.

Mitz looked at her, "I wondered if they'd shared with you ladies." She gave Daxx a resolved look. "I'm their aunt."

Daxx's eyes went wide, then she shook her head. "It makes sense now. How you speak and they jump."

Autumn nodded, "I thought maybe she had a super-power."

Mitz grinned. "No super powers. It took a decade to get them to stop calling me Aunt Mitzine." She cringed. "Awful name." She laughed.

"I can't imagine losing my twin," Bethany shrugged, "if I had one."

Mitz nodded slowly, "it was the hardest time of my life." Clasping her hands in front of her, she looked at the thrones, "I had been at odds with Viola for a hundred and forty years before they were murdered." She sucked in a breath when the women looked shocked. "It was never confirmed that Willis Hubert was behind their deaths, but everything pointed to him." She looked sad. "You can't bring someone to justice if you can't find them." Her smile was faked, as she tried to put on a good front for us. "I regret those years without her. I missed so much of the boys growing up because of it." She shook her head, "I just couldn't forgive Theodore, even though she had." To the confused looks she sighed, "Theodore is the boys' father." She hugged her arms around her waist. "I couldn't forgive him for Emil," she sighed, "actually for Emil's mother."

No one spoke as she went over to the smaller throne and ran her hand over the arm.

"Having two true mates was so rare it was almost unheard of." She sat down on the platform in front of the thrones.

Two mates? Little cogs inside my head started clunking together. I blinked to bring my brain back to reality. Now was not the time to get lost in my head.

"Having a king with more than one queen was— scandalous." Mitz took a deep breath and then exhaled slowly, "I just couldn't get over Theo being unable to control his baser instincts at four hundred years old and resist marking Letti Brown."

Marking? What would that entail? Mates. Marking. Clunk, clunk, more cogs falling in place. I looked at the girls' arms, or more specifically, the tattoos on their arms. They tattooed their 'mates'. That was... I didn't have a holy fraggle kind of word for that.

Mitz shook her head, "as if I'm one to talk of such things." She laughed quietly, "I—the sister to the queen falling in love with her guard was *such* a taboo." Mitz smiled, tears shining in her eyes. "So, it wasn't frowned upon when Ira took a post as far from the palace as possible, then we were out of sight," she made quotes in the air.

I sat on the floor, feeling like my whole body was lost in some foggy place. I looked around to see that most of the other women had sat down too. I was willing to gamble it wasn't for the same reason I was sitting.

"They knew about Emil before they died?" Bethany asked.

Mitz nodded, "yes. Theo had to go over often, or Letti would have gone mad, and he may have as well, and we didn't need a mad king on our hands." She shook her head, "After Theo's death, Letti vanished." She looked distressed. "If ever there was someone skilled at staying hidden, it was her." Glancing at the throne beside her, she continued, "Ira and I tried for years to find her, find Emil—" She looked to Crissy, "but, we weren't able to track their name changes at that point."

"What was she like? Your sister." Bethany asked in a soft tone.

Mitz smiled, "beautiful, gentle, caring," she laughed quietly, "nagging, annoying, to a sister." A tear rolled down her face, "I was only able to see her for a few short minutes before she passed." She wiped her face and nodded. "I'm so glad I did." Inhaling a sharp breath, she stood up. "I should get back to the kitchen."

Everyone stood up slowly.

"Mitz," Paisley gave her an understanding smile, "we were thinking of turning this into *the* meeting room," she glanced to the others, "we don't exactly fit in the offices now."

Alona nodded, "and not rushing through a meal would be nice," she rolled her eyes, "keeping meetings out of the dining rooms."

Mitz nodded and looked around. "It would make good use of this room." She grinned, "Chase and Troy will never sit upon a throne."

"We were going to leave the thrones and wondered if there was a portrait of their parents we could place in the room." Alona gave her a hopeful look.

Mitz nodded slowly. "I think they'd like that, to have their parents watch over them during discussions about the realm." She nodded her head quickly. "I will have it brought out of storage." Pausing she looked around at each of us, then bobbed her head abruptly and walked out of the room.

"That was…"

"Yeah," Autumn interrupted Daxx.

Paisley looked at her. "I had no idea."

Bethany exhaled a deep breath. "Same."

"Chase left out so many details." Alona wiped her damp cheek.

"I didn't even know." Crissy said, the surprise clear in her voice.

"They are so lucky to have her." Autumn turned and looked at me. "What's wrong?"

I opened my mouth and then closed it. Where did one start? "I think…" I looked around at each of their faces, "I'm missing pieces to a very complex puzzle."

Autumn snorted.

"I think we'll need wine to explain those pieces." Alona said, "just as soon as I contact the movers about what to bring for this room." She started typing on her phone.

"*That* talk." Daxx nodded, then took a deep breath.

"I think we should make a slideshow for that talk." Paisley looked at Bethany and grinned, "it would be so much easier."

"Gloves." Crissy nodded. "We should get her gloves."

I was learning to ignore the random things Crissy said, but this time the others were nodding their agreement to her statement.

"Gloves?" I gave Alona a curious look.

She nodded. "Do you like wine?"

I frowned. "I've never had wine."

"That's a travesty we need to correct." She nodded. "Immediately." She looked around at the women. "The cave, balcony or hot tub?"

There were several hot tub replies.

Alona nodded. "Someone take her to *the* closet and find her a suit." She vanished.

Chapter Twenty-One

I'd never been in a bathing suit before, probably because I'd never been swimming. I looked around as the rest of the women stepped down into the hot tub, which was closer to the size of a pool than a tub.

They looked so good in their suits. I was thankful for one thing as I undid the soft robe. I'd shaved my legs that first day in the fancy tub. On odd thing, yes, but I would have looked like an ape standing next to them if I hadn't.

"You look great." Bethany said with an encouraging smile.

I looked down at the blue one-piece suit they'd chosen for me. "Thanks." I said, not really meaning it. "I've never been," I motioned to the hot tub, "in this much water before."

Autumn held her hand up to me. "We won't let you go under." She grinned at me.

I believed her and accepted help into the warm water. When I sat down, I couldn't help closing my eyes. It felt wonderful. If something could wash away stress, this was it. When I opened them Alona held a fancy glass in front of my face.

"It's very mellow." She told me with a smile.

I took the glass and a small sip. I wasn't sure how it was mellow, it was tangy and tart to me.

"It tastes better after the first glass." Crissy nodded.

I set it down and turned back to the women. "I'm," lifted a dripping hand, "struggling." I gave Daxx a hopeful look, "and I'm hoping I'm drawing all the wrong conclusions."

She snorted, "Doubtful, but let's find out."

Paisley nodded. "What conclusions?"

I looked at the tattoo on her arm. "The tattoos. The Mates? Tattoos."

Paisley lifted her arm and looked at it. "They are something, aren't they? Arius and mine are identical. I don't know how it does it."

Beth nodded. "And no two couples are ever the same."

I looked at the glass and wondered if another sip was warranted. I wasn't sure but found the glass in my hand anyway. "You get tattoos when you get married?" I cringed. How would that be a good way to start a marriage?

"Ah," Alona sighed, "so much to explain."

"Again." Daxx murmured.

Autumn gave me a serious look. "We don't *get* them, they appear on their own."

I watched her, then took a drink. "Appear."

She nodded. "I know it sounds whack—and it is, but yes. They're not there one minute, then they are."

"Just like that?" I took a few more sips and looked to see all the women nodding. "Okay." I couldn't doubt all of them. "How?"

"Only true mates' tattoos will appear." Crissy said with a smile, "and finding your true mate is rare." She nodded, looking serious.

"Mitz said the king had two." I had to know.

Daxx frowned. "It is. I'd rather shoot myself in the foot than have two."

Alona smirked. "Thankfully none of our prophecies have foretold of us having more than one."

"I don't even know how that would work. The connection with Leone is strong…" Bethany frowned, "the idea of two like that is exhausting."

Paisley nodded, "their father wouldn't have had an easy time."

Daxx snorted, "Fidelity is so ingrained after the tattoo, I'm sure he must have thought he'd lost it."

"Fidelity?" I took another sip, wondering how that had anything to do with a tattoo.

Alona smiled. "Yes. Once true mates are bound, there is no cheating or unfaithfulness."

I paused on that. There was nothing bad I could think of for that. "That's—" I didn't have a word for it. Something Crissy had said popped into my head. "Why do I need gloves?"

Crissy rolled her eyes at me. "So Rafael can't mark you until you are ready."

The sip of wine I'd taken went down the wrong way. I coughed and sputtered, almost spitting it out again. "What?" Was all I could squeak out as my throat burned.

"Rafael is your mate." Crissy smiled at me. "The prophecy says, the last brother of nine will stand stronger with his arcus mate at his side. Only she will be able to bring him the peace he's long sought." Crissy nodded. "I wasn't sure until I found out that arcus is Latin for archer," she frowned, "I wonder why Raf needs peace? Peace from what?"

Daxx pointed at her. "You knew all this time and didn't tell us?"

"I didn't put it together until the men asked if Kara was going to council meeting." Alona said quietly.

"Same." Bethany nodded.

"It was a done deal for me when I saw her sash." Autumn grinned.

I finished the glass in one gulp and then held up my hand. "What do you mean? I'm-I'm Rafael's mate? Do I get a say in this?" I paused when Alona got up and filled the glass I was waving around. "I don't-I can't—" I closed my eyes for a moment to regroup. I opened them and looked at Alona. "I can't even be near men, never mind this mated as one thing—"

Alona smirked. "I've never thought of it that way," she looked at Daxx, "I suppose with the bond we're quite similar to mated as one."

Daxx nodded. "Just don't tell the guys that."

I found myself taking another sip. "Bonds? There's a bond?"

Paisley nodded. "Mates bond. We can tap into what other is feeling, although the guys most of the time don't transmit *any* feeling."

I laughed, only it came out sounding more like a giggle. "There won't be any bond between Rafael and I. He threw a fit when I accidentally heard what he was thinking earlier."

"Oh? Was it bad?" Bethany asked.

I thought about it. "No. But he still hit the wall, literally with his hand, and told me to stay out of his head."

"Rafael did that?" Daxx asked.

I bobbed my head, feeling a little like jello for some reason.

"That doesn't sound like Rafael." Crissy frowned.

Alona raised her glass in a dramatic ay. "Being close to ones' mate tends to bring out the worst traits in a person."

Autumn laughed abruptly. "I'll drink to that." She raised her glass and then took a drink.

"It's true." Bethany said giving me a sympathetic look.

I took another drink, thinking briefly that Crissy had been right, this did taste better after the first glass. "I think he's hiding something." I hadn't meant to say that out loud, then froze when they all looked at me suddenly.

"Oh? Have you heard what?" Alona leaned closer.

I shook my head. "No. I try not to *hear*, but a few things aren't adding up." I stopped and laughed loudly. Louder than I'd intended. "Okay. *None*," I waved my hand around, "of this adds up, but he is hiding something."

Daxx toasted in the air. "They all hide something." She paused with the glass near her mouth. "I think fate brought you to us," She motioned with the glass around to the other women, "to even the odds because you can hear when the men are full of it." She nodded, "you can give us a heads up."

I shrugged. "If I could hear half of them, maybe, but I can't." I looked at the inhibitor on my wrist, hoping it was okay that it got wet. "I've heard Emil, Chase—when he wanted me to," Alona smiled at that. "Michael," I grinned at Autumn, "who was less than impressed he'd had a moment of weakness and let his guard down. And Rafael," I frowned, "a few partial thoughts in the meeting when I took," I held up my arm, "this off, but other than that, their minds have walls of steel."

"Damn." Daxx took a drink. "That's so annoying."

"I'm glad we don't know everything they think." Paisley said. "It would be boring then."

Bethany grinned at her. "Says the woman that calls her mate beast."

Paisley blushed.

I went to take another sip and realized the glass was empty. My head was fuzzy, I didn't remember drinking it. I set down the glass before Alona filled it again.

"Rafael doesn't want this," I motioned in the air, "mates' stuff. He told me." I shrugged. "He just doesn't know what to do about it yet."

"I don't think it's optional." Daxx glanced to Alona.

Alona rolled her eyes. "Michael didn't either and look how that ended."

Autumn grinned. "It was a few rough rounds."

"You almost dying a few times didn't make it easier on him." Bethany tilted her glass at Autumn.

"Dying?" I looked at Autumn.

She bobbed her head, "Blade through the gut, that poison…"

"Don't forget about the elixir when you broke your ribs." Paisley added.

Autumn snorted. "As if I could forget that." She looked at Bethany, "your near-death incident made your life less smooth too, I've heard."

I looked form Autumn to Bethany.

Bethany sighed. "I fell off a fire escape and broke," she motioned up and down her half-emerged body, "everything."

My mouth dropped open.

"Here's to the magic of the royal blood." Alona lifted her glass in the air. The other women motioned with their glasses too.

"Magic blood?" I was trying to use logic in computing that, which was a mistake, because nothing related to any of this was logical.

"Their blood heals," Crissy nodded, "fast."

"But," Bethany pointed at me, "be warned there's a bond between you if you ingest it."

Paisley snorted. "Yeah that one needs to be in bold print in the 'welcome to Alterealm' manual."

"Manual?" I gave her a hopeful look.

She sighed. "The book we keep talking about writing."

"Oh. I'd hoped for a moment there was some sort of instruction manual on all of this. Not that I think I need to worry about it, but," I glanced to Crissy, "what kind of gloves?" There was no way I was going sign on for the mate thing. I didn't know how it happened, but if gloves somehow prevented it, I was wearing gloves.

"Oh," Crissy jumped up, splashing water all over. "I have some." She got out of the tub and went over to her pack. "I always carry them, so the cable doesn't cut my hands."

I opened my mouth to ask what cable, then decided I didn't want to know.

Crissy held up a pair of black fingerless gloves. "I'll set them with your robe." She put them down beside the white fluffy material, then turned back to the tub. As she went to get in, her foot hit her phone and it dropped to the bottom of the tub. "Oh." She looked at Daxx. "I just got that one."

Daxx grinned. "I told Troy we need water, sword and axe proof boxes for our phones." As soon as she finished her phone rang. She looked at it. "Speak of my devil." She set her glass down and hit the button. "Hey mate." She must have turned it on speaker, because we could hear Troy talk.

"Are you in the chambers or palace? We were just coming to find you."

"Chambers." She looked around and grinned. "Hot tub."

"Oh?" There was someone talking we couldn't hear. "Is there wine involved?"

Daxx smiled. "Yes, but we're all mostly sober."

"Mmm, mostly."

There were more voices in the back ground.

"Why are you looking for us?" she asked.

"Prince Bastian is coming over for a private meeting and in lieu of everything, we thought you ladies would like to be included."

"Smart man." Daxx nodded. "When and where do you need us?"

"It takes an hour for him to acclimate to our realm, so we'll meet at the elder's chambers." He cleared his throat. "This isn't a meeting with the elders however."

Daxx nodded. "We'll be there soon." She hung up.

Alona finished what was in her glass and stood up. "Are they hoping he can just zero in on Willis Hubert's soul, so we can go retrieve him?"

Daxx sighed. "I don't know, but if he can, then I say let's take it." She got out of the tub.

"I don't like cheating," Autumn climbed out, "but if he can, I'm all for stopping this."

I got out, wobbling a little and picked up my robe. Putting it on, I tucked the gloves in my pocket. "As long as his focus isn't on my soul again, I don't care what he does with others." My head was pleasantly buzzing, not in a bad way, just a different way then I'd ever felt before.

"I'm going to use the port device to go back and change." Bethany grinned. "My head is a bit fuzzy and porting is bad enough, never mind if I end up in the wrong place."

I looked at the device on my wrist. "How do I get to the Elder Chambers after I get dressed?"

"We'll meet at the solarium and go together." Autumn said then vanished.

"Here goes." Bethany held her wrist up and then pushed the device and was gone.

Opening mine, I looked at it, hoping I picked the right button I hovered my finger over it and closed my eyes.

Chapter Twenty-Two

I was still light-headed after I dressed. I had to sit down to put the knives in the straps on my ankles. I wasn't sure wine was my kind of thing at all. Putting the gloves on, I smiled as I flexed my hand. I wouldn't have to wear a finger guard with these. And I couldn't become a mate. Win, win.

I went down the stairs slowly, wondering how long this strange feeling was going to last.

By the time I reached the solarium, all of the others were already there. Chase smiled as I came in, then turned to Alona. "Was there a reason a wine meeting was required, beloved? Finding a meeting room didn't go well?"

Alona laughed. "We found a room. The *meeting* was because Kara had questions."

"Ah," was all he said, then he turned and looked at Rafael.

Rafael was looking at me, or more accurately at the gloves I was wearing.

"Questions answered?" Troy asked with a smirk on his face.

I realized he was looking at me when he said it. I thought for a moment. "Mostly." I shrugged, "if those could be answered.

"Mm," he nodded slowly, then looked at Rafael again, raising one eyebrow at him.

Rafael still didn't say a word.

I looked around. He knew what the talk was about. They *all* knew what the talk was about and yet none of them were going to say anything. I stood there scowling, moving just my eyes from one man to the next and so on; they were all just looking at Rafael.

Making a noise of frustration, Rafael put his hands to the sides of his head. "All of you back off." He dropped his hands and looked at Troy, then Leone and finally Michael. "None of you are qualified to offer your thoughts, suggestions *or* advice on this." He huffed, "I watched you all fail miserably when it was your turn."

Daxx snorted and Autumn echoed the noise.

I didn't know if it was the wine or I'd missed something. From where I stood no one had said a word out loud. I blew out a breath, feeling the light-headedness end just like that. In its place was a resolve, almost anger, but not quite. Before I knew I'd done it, I was standing in front of Rafael. "You knew *all* of this but told me 'just go with it' when I asked you." I poked him in the chest making sure I had his attention. "I've spent my whole life having to do things the way others told me I had to," I poked him three more times, "well, I'm telling you right now," another poke, "you can keep your mate's pendant," poke, "your mate's mark or whatever it is," poke, poke, "and you can keep your blood and bond." This time I thumped him on the chest with the heel of my hand, feeling that needed a little something extra, "to yourself." One more thump, just because. "The last thing I need is someone else trying to control me and I'll be a son of a bucket if I let it happen." I put my hands on my hips and glared up at him.

He didn't even look upset or annoyed I'd just thumped on his chest. I frowned as his blue eyes studied mine. He reached and put both hands on my shoulders, then my head filled with white noise.

Pushing away from him, I put my hands up and squeezed my head. "Don't *do* that." I ground out, then I looked around. We were in a very dimly lit, large empty room. "Where are we?"

"Shit." He stomped over and flipped on a light switch. "You had me so distracted I just ported us to my old room." He came back over and stood there with his hands on his hips. "I didn't need my brother's interference," he waved his hand around beside his head, "here, we can communicate and get inside each other's heads," he shook his and took a deep breath, "I thought this conversation would go better with just the two of us."

Get inside each other's heads. I shook mine. I didn't feel good.

"Are you all right?" The concern in his voice was clear.

I waved him off. "I don't think I like wine."

He grinned. "Don't tell Alona that."

I nodded.

"Look," he closed his eyes for a moment, then opened them to give me a soft look, "I didn't ask for any of this, and you certainly didn't."

I frowned.

"Don't get me wrong, I feel *very* drawn to you and I will never let anything happen to you, but the truth is," he lifted a hand, then dropped it. "I've got a lot going on right now," he tapped the side of his head, "and the last thing I need—you need—is a mate with all of this," he waved his hand beside his head, "going on." Taking a deep breath, he exhaled slowly. "If I don't get it under control, I'm going to lose my position as Captain of the Guard and," he hissed a breath, "and that can't happen."

That told me nothing, other than I'd been right and he was hiding something, but I wasn't going to complain. I nodded abruptly. "Okay. Good." For reasons I couldn't explain, I felt odd after everything he'd just said. "That's— fine with me. I don't do well close to," I motioned up and down his body, "men." I hugged my arms around my waist. "Their thoughts never match their actions." I added quietly.

Rafael frowned down at me. "That's all wrong." He said softly. "How could a man think of anything but you?"

I felt my cheeks heat at his words and wondered if that was because of the wine, too. Surely it had to be what caused that kind of reaction. Why would he say something like that after just saying he didn't want anything to do with me?

Rafael moved closer to me and I felt like my feet were stuck in place, I couldn't step back. He put his finger under my chin and gently tilted it up so I was looking into his blue eyes. "How any man could look into your beautiful grey eyes and think of anything but you," he shook his head, "it's insane."

I was sure I'd stopped breathing all together as he leaned down and brushed his lips over mine softly. "Just do me a favor," he whispered against my mouth, "until we get this sorted out," he brushed his lips over mine again, "don't go testing that theory." He kissed me harder. "It could be bad for their health."

In that moment I would have agreed to fly to the moon if he'd asked me. None of this made sense. He didn't make sense. I was never drinking wine again.

Rafael straightened up but didn't release my chin. He's gaze searched my face, then his expression changed. "You look like that was your first kiss." He frowned. "Have you ever been kissed? Have you ever been with a man, Kara?"

His tone was gentle, but there was something in his eyes that was hesitant.

"Yes and no." I mumbled, still feeling strange.

"What?" He smirked. "There is no yes and no to that, Kara." Rafael stood there looking down at me, waiting. I don't even think he was breathing.

I sighed. "Yes, I have been, but not really by choice." I rolled my eyes, knowing how dumb it sounded, "I don't think." His eyes darkened. "I was wacked on drugs and one of the orderlies..." I shook my head trying to stick to the facts. "Being around men doesn't work out for me." I waved my hand letting him know that was all I was saying about it.

"Wait." He leaned down so our faces were level, an intense expression on his face. "Orderly?"

I nodded.

"A man?"

I gave him a surprised look. "Yeah."

"A *man* that was to care for your well-being?" His voice was so low I had to focus to hear him.

I nodded. Wondering if something I had said hadn't been clear enough.

He continued to look at me for several tense moments, then straightened up and turned his back to me. He just stood there with his hands on his hips looking at the carpet.

I stared at his back, not sure what to do. "Rafael?"

He inhaled deeply, then turned to me. His eyes were red. "I can't imagine what you've been through in your short life—"

I found it odd I could see compassion in his eyes, even when they were red.

"But," he said softly, "I'm not here to make it worse. Tell me what you need—at any time and I'll see that it happens."

I didn't know what to say. It wasn't the fact that he'd just said he didn't want to be mated to me any more than I did him, or that a prince was pledging to, what, look after me? It was all of it and none of it at the same time. I couldn't think. Why couldn't I think?

Before I could find something intelligent to say, he was in my face again, lifting my chin up, our face so close I could feel his breath against my mouth. I held my breath.

"We need to be around the others. Now." He grasped my hand in his and walked quickly to the door.

I almost had to run to keep up with him as we moved through the endless hallways.

"So what has Raf breathing fire?" Daxx asked, sitting on the table between Bethany and I.

I glanced over to Rafael standing with Michael and Leone. He was moving his hand in a jerky motion, all of them looked mad. "I'm not sure what happened." I said slowly. And I wasn't.

Daxx nodded her head and watched Troy walk over to his brothers. A moment later he turned and looked at me, his expression grim.

"Something has them all in protective mode." She said quietly.

"Whatever it is," Paisley said in a quiet voice, "Arius took off to get a map."

"A Map?" Daxx shook her head. "What does a map have to do with it?"

A map. Pieces snapped together in my mind. A map for the asylum. He'd gone all red eyed strange after I'd told him about the asylum. "To find the asylum." I whispered. "I told him something and," I looked over to see Rafael standing there looking at me with his arms crossed over his chest, "I think it upset him."

Alona chuckled. "Yes, that looks like the 'someone has wronged one of our own' stance."

Bethany smiled, "that posture is for a lot of other things too. Like absolutely not."

"Over my dead body will you do that." Autumn grinned.

"That too." Daxx said.

Arius came back in carrying a tablet. He went over to Victor.

Victor nodded and glanced at Crissy. He held out his hand and she got up and went over to him and looked at the tablet. She nodded. He kissed the top of her head and handed the tablet back to Arius, who then nodded to Rafael. They were definitely a working unit.

"Looks like they've found where you were locked up." Daxx murmured quietly.

"Is that good or bad?" I wondered out loud. I honestly didn't know how I felt about it.

"I'd say good for those that are stuck there and shouldn't be, and bad for those holding them." Paisley said quietly.

Ira came in the side door and nodded his head to Victor.

"Let's take our seats, everyone." Victor said loudly.

I was still sitting in mine, so I turned around and stared at the empty chairs the elders usually sat in. As I did, Elder Marinus and Segos came in and sat down. They weren't wearing their robes this time.

Rafael sat down beside me.

Prince Bastian came in the door and bowed his head. "Sorry for the delay in getting back here." He looked at Troy. "Securing my parents took an odd turn." He sat down in the chair he'd sat in the last time and looked around. "I take it this is an unofficial meeting?"

Troy nodded. "It is."

"I hope all is well with your parents." Victor said.

Bastian ran his hand through his already messy hair. "It is now." He crossed his arms over his chest. "So, what can I do for you?" His dark eyes moved down the table looking at everyone. When he reached me, he lingered for a moment.

Rafael took my hand under the table and squeezed it.

Bastian looked at him and raised an eyebrow.

"Are you able to zero in on a particular soul?" Quinton asked.

Bastian smirked. "Right to the point works for me." He leaned forward and put his arms on the table. "Yes, but finding it first is the chore. Dark one's pop right out or the hot ones," he lifted a hand to the inquiring looks, "those close to crossing. But finding an exact one is still time consuming. Race is also a factor."

"I see." Victor answered.

"Whose are you hoping I can find?" He gave Chase an amused look.

"Willis Hubert." Chase said in a low tone.

"The man responsible for the uproar in our realms." Bastian didn't say it like a question. "And I'm presuming you'd like me to keep this off the official record, so to speak."

"If possible." Troy leaned back in his chair and crossed his arms.

"*If* I do this," he looked at Troy and then Chase, "I'm not saying I can find him, but if I do, there may come a time when I ask for a favor in return."

The room was silent. Victor looked to Troy for a moment. Troy inclined his head ever slightly.

"We would endeavor to assist you if it's within our means." Victor said firmly.

"That sounds like a loophole, if there ever was one." Bastian grinned and then suddenly turned in chair and looked right at me. "Princess Kara, with the intriguing soul unbound to anyone in this room, what do you say? Can I trust them to help if I ask?"

I'm sure I looked like a startled animal at that point. I looked down the table at the others and then back to him. "They are very honor bound."

"Yes." Bastian grinned. "That they are." He sat back in his chair and placed his hands in front of him on the table. "I will see if I can hunt down this soul you're searching for." He shrugged. "I'm sure it's very stained by this point, so it shouldn't be impossible."

"What of an ancient mage's soul?" Victor asked. "Are you able to see theirs?"

Bastian smirked. "A young one perhaps, and old one would be a difficult task, but an ancient mage? I'm afraid they don't have enough soul left to trace." He shrugged, "the longer they practice their magic the more they give up."

"Are-are witches the same?" Bethany asked quickly.

He smiled at her. "You have nothing to fear with yours, little witch. Your magic is so pure your soul is like a blinding neon light."

Bethany looked relieved.

The prince tapped his hand on the table. "If that's everything, I'll go start searching." He stood up.

"Don't you need details about Hubert?" Daxx asked.

He shrugged. "Not really." Bastian inclined his head to Troy, then Chase. "You'll be hearing from me." Without another word, he spun on his heels and went to the door Ira stood beside.

The men got up after he left. Victor looked at his phone and glanced to Crissy. "Give me a few minutes."

Crissy nodded. "I'll go to the cave and wait."

Rafael released my hand and got up. He nodded to Leone. "Let's go check on the team watching the tunnel."

Leone nodded and kissed Bethany. "I'll be back by dinner."

One by one the men left.

I continued to sit there, trying to figure out this soul business.

"Come on." Autumn said to me and motioned to the door with her head.

I followed the women to their cave, still lost in my own head about what Prince Bastian had said about souls. I sat on the arm of the loveseat.

"I don't know anything about this Solrelm." Bethany said, sitting down.

"I didn't like Quint's reaction to hearing they were coming here. Or that Bastian guy's answers." Daxx pulled the knives from the target and backed up. She tossed one, then paused and glanced at us.

"Have you read about them in detail?" Paisley looked at Crissy.

She shook her head. "I can when we get home."

"Home from where?" Bethany asked.

Crissy put her notebook into her pack. "Handing out protein bars and care packages." She smiled. "That's what Victor calls them."

Daxx stopped and looked at her. "On our side?"

Crissy nodded. "Yes. Victor helps me," she paused and looked into the space above Daxx's head for a second, "well, he guards me with other guards," she shrugged, "all cloaked by the witches, while I hand them out."

Daxx raised her hand, "wait. He takes you to the other side to hand out protein bars?"

"Yes." Crissy smiled.

Daxx was frowning now. "I've had to turn down thirty different bounties because I'm not allowed to go over there..."

"I think there's a big difference between handing out care packages to the homeless and tracking down bail jumpers." Autumn said with a smirk.

Daxx raised her hand. "Not the point."

"Perhaps Troy is concerned that Willis Hubert knows you're a bounty hunter and could be setting a trap for you." Alona offered with a smirk on her face.

"Where's all this logic coming from?" Daxx threw her hands in the air. "I'm going to find Troy." She turned and started for the door, "If he can't find someone for us to beat down, he's taking me over to do my job." Shaking her head, she went out into the hall, muttering. "Should be doing it in at least *one* of the realms."

She was still muttering as she walked down the hall, but we couldn't hear what she was saying.

Paisley looked at Alona. "Do we warn Troy?"

Alona smirked. "No. No, I think we should keep it a surprise."

"I guess telling her that Arius takes me over to check on Mrs. Stein all the time would be bad." Paisley looked from the door to Alona again.

She smiled. "I'm thinking most definitely bad."

The phone in my pocket rang, I almost fell off the arm, still not used to the fact that I had a phone, never mind that it rang. I looked at it, then slid the green button over. "Hello?"

"Kara, it's Izzy. Chase gave me your number. I was calling to ask if you could come to the labs and talk with Cyril about arrows but have just been informed by Michael that they have found Leila." She paused and spoke to someone with her. "Can you find your way to the elder's chambers to speak with her?"

I frowned. "I don't know what I could ask her."

She laughed. "Others will be doing the speaking, we're just there to listen."

"Oh." I nodded and looked at Autumn. "I can have one of the others take me there."

"Excellent. I'll see you shortly."

I hung up and stared at the screen.

"What's up?" Autumn asked coming over.

"That was Izzy. They've found Leila."

"Oh," Alona stood up, "this is a talk I'd like to be in on."

I nodded. "They want me to listen to her thoughts." I gave Alona an anxious look.

"She did seem sweet and sincere when I met her." She motioned to my arm. "Can I borrow that when you take it off? I'd like to be part of this discussion and not feel it."

I looked at the inhibitor and nodded. "I have to go back to the elder chambers."

"They don't have her in the cells?" Paisley gave Alona a puzzled look.

"I know nothing of the what's, I merely suggested they find her." She motioned to the door. "Let's go see what she can offer."

Chapter Twenty-Three

"She has no tattoo." Michael told Alona. "So we know she's not spelled by the same magic Eunice was."

"She knows what going on?" Autumn asked him.

"That's what Kara and Elder Udela can tell us." He answered.

Izzy nodded and looked at me. "Hopefully we can."

"I'm going in too." Alona announced. Chase tilted his head and gave her a look. Alona motioned to me. "Kara is going to give me the inhibitor when she takes it off." She gave him a stern look. "I can ask the questions." She tapped her chest. "I know what questions to ask."

Autumn glanced at Chase. "I'll be there, don't worry I've got her covered."

Michael frowned.

Autumn shrugged, "You big guys go in there and she's going to clam up. If we," she motioned to Izzy, Alona and I, "go in there, we might get somewhere."

Michael looked at her for a moment, then nodded. "Let us know if you need anything to validate what you're saying to her."

Autumn touched his arm and smiled. "Thanks, Iceman."

"We'll have the guards step out once you go in." Troy told me.

"Anything you can find out will help." Daxx said quickly.

I nodded. I took the scanner out of my pocket and held it over the cuff. It came off. I handed them to Alona and glanced at Izzy. She pushed the button on her bracelet, then nodded to me.

Chase helped Alona put the cuff on and then pulled open the door.

I followed Alona to see a woman sitting at the table Prince Bastian has sat at earlier. The woman had bright blue, spiked hair and I didn't need to hear her thoughts to know she was afraid.

"Leila," Alona pulled out a chair and sat down, "do you remember me?"

Leila looked at her for a moment, then nodded. "Yes. At the island."

...I wonder why we don't go there anymore...

Alona nodded. "Yes."

Izzy looked at me, then picked up her phone and typed something on it.

Leila ran her hand over the device on her wrist. "What is this for?"

Alona glanced at her phone. I realized that Izzy must have told her what we heard.

"It's a stabilizer." Izzy told her. "So you can be in this realm without repercussions to your health."

Leila's eyes went wide. "I'm here? I'm in Alterealm?"

Alona nodded. "Yes."

"Nelson said he'd bring me here when it was safe to do so." She looked around. "Is he meeting us here?"

...I can't believe I'm here...

...why am I here without him though?...

"Not just yet." Izzy said. "How did you and Nelson meet?"

Leila smiled, "It was the most terrifying, but wonderful thing." She looked at Alona. "You understand how hard it is to live longer then anyone around you?" Alona nodded. "And how trying it is to find somewhere safe to feed," she waved a hand, "without anyone catching on." Alona nodded again.

I had no idea what she was talking about. Safe to feed? I blinked so I'd stay in the present.

"A group of us had been rounded up," she put her hand against her chest, "I was so scared. Then Nelson tells them there's been a mistake and I'm not to be included among them." She smiled. "He was quite intimidating at first, but he's really quite sweet."

Izzy coughed. "Excuse me." She said quickly.

"What about Nelson's sister, Eunice, you get along with her?" Autumn leaned closer.

Leila nodded. "She's a little brusque at times, but we get along well enough. She's away on business right now..."

"What sort of business?" Alona asked.

...I don't understand all of these questions ...

"I can't remember if Nelson shared any of the particulars."

... he's going to be cross with me. He doesn't like me talking about things...

Izzy typed on her phone.

Alona looked at the phone in her hand. "Do you and Nelson stay with the others or do you have your own place?" Alona gave her a small smile. "I was concerned about that during our meeting, living with strangers."

"Oh," Leila smiled, "no everyone doesn't live together, that would be awkward. A few do, but Nelson and I have our place."

...don't share locations...

"Is it in a nice neighborhood?" Alona smiled again. "I live across the bridge; the view is spectacular."

Leila nodded. "I imagine it would be. Nelson isn't fond of heights, so I'm afraid we're on the ground floor. Its a lovely neighborhood though, we're two doors down from the most delightful bakery." She smiled. "Waking up to that fresh smell of bread in the morning."

"I'd be fat living that close." Alona smiled.

...I do like her...

... I wondered why I hadn't seen her again...

"Your business trip, it was successful?" Leila asked

"Quite." Alona replied. Then turned to Autumn

Autumn nodded and leaned on the table. "I have some hard questions for you, Leila." Autumn nodded, "you seem like good people and nothing pisses me off more than someone being taken advantage of."

Leila nodded.

...she's very straightforward...

... Nelson would like her...

"I'll help if I can."

Autumn nodded again and typed quickly on her phone. Setting it down, she looked at her. "Do you know what was happening on the island?"

Leila looked at Alona for a moment, before turning back. "We housed many women there, to keep them safe."

Slowly nodding, Autumn held her look. "From who?"

Leila frowned.

...I didn't ask details...

"I'm not sure, Nelson told me they needed to be kept safe," she shrugged, "I assumed from husbands, gangs..."

"They weren't safe there." Autumn gave her a steady look. "They were being held there against their will."

"That's-that can't be right." Leila shook her head.

...horrid, why would they say that?...

"Did you ever go up to the top and see for yourself?" Alona asked her.

"No." Leila looked distressed, "there was never time. Nelson is very busy with his work. He's an advisor to a very important man."

It was sad that she held such esteem for a man like that.

"Willis Hubert?" Izzy asked.

Leila nodded. "Yes. Yes, that's right."

"We rescued women from that island." Alona said in a hushed way. "They were forced to," Alona looked at her hands holding her phone, "have relations with men."

Leila blanched. "That can't be—Nelson..."

"She's not lying." Autumn told her.

...that's not right...

...Nelson said they needed protection, so they were hid...

The door opened and Michael stepped in.

Getting up, Autumn went over to him and took a tablet from him. He spoke to her quietly. She nodded and came back over and sat down. She handed Alona the tablet. "On this are some pictures of girls that were forced to leave the island with men."

Alona did something on the screen, then held it for Leila to see.

...Kara...

...shit, I don't know if I'm doing this right...

I turned to look at Autumn, she stared at me.

...they found receipts in her purse from the bakery. She has no phone. We need an address...

Her eyes sparkled.

...we're so close to getting Eunice's brother I can taste it...

"Why would you show me these?"

I turned back to Leila. She was distraught.

"Because you need to know the truth. Nelson's lying to you. They're all lying to you." Autumn's voice was steady.

Leila shook her head.

...I need to talk to Nelson...

"Eunice isn't on a business trip." Autumn said as she pointed to the tablet. "She's in one of the cells here in Alterealm. She remembers nothing. Nelson had his own sister spelled so she'd go along with Willis Hubert's sick plan."

Alona turned the tablet again. "There's Eunice, pacing in her cell. Right now."

Leila leaned forward and looked at it. Her emotions were plain to see on her face. She frowned, then shook her head. "This can't be right."

...how could all of this happen...

...I thought he cared about me...

...it's a lie...

I looked at Alona and nodded.

She reached over and turned the tablet off. "We need to find Nelson, Leila. We have to put a stop to women being hurt."

Placing her hand against her chest, Leila nodded as a tear rolled down her cheek. "I can't—" She turned to Autumn, "I just-thought..."

...how could I be so stupid?...

Closing her eyes, she put her hand against her forehead for a moment. When she opened her eyes, she looked at Autumn. "What do you need me to do?"

Autumn nodded her head slowly. "Do you know where Nelson is right now?"

Leila looked at the tablet. "What time is it?"

Alona glanced at her phone. "Four p.m."

Leila clasped he hands together on the table. "He's always home by six for dinner with me. Some nights he's not there long..."

...what's going to happen to me now?...

I didn't know if I was supposed to talk, but I blurted it out anyway. "We'll keep you safe."

Alona glanced at me.

Autumn shrugged. "You may be under house arrest for a while, but we won't let Nelson and his flunkies come after you."

Leila gave her a shaky nod. "We're two doors down from the Dutch bakery on Clive avenue, number three fourteen."

Autumn typed on her phone.

Alona put her hand on hers. "Thank you."

"Is your home warded?" Izzy asked.

Leila shook her head. "No. I didn't want any of that magic stuff in my home."

"Do you have any sort of signal to let Nelson know all is well, or isn't?" Izzy sat forward in her chair.

Leila shook her head. "No. No one knows where we are. Nelson wanted our place to be excluded from the list of safehouses they used." She put her shaking hand over her mouth. "It was our home."

Izzy gave her an understanding look. "Thank you for your help. I can't begin to explain how dire the situation could have become if it continued."

Leila gave her a bleak look and brief nod.

She was so stunned, I wasn't picking up any thoughts at all.

Alona picked up the tablet and stood up. Autumn did as well and lead us from the room.

The entire royal family was outside the door.

"We got his address." Autumn said with a big grin.

Alona nodded and hugged Chase. "He'll be home within the next two hours."

Chase hugged her. "Let's not keep him waiting."

"Did she know?" Paisley asked. "What's really going on?" She looked at me.

I shook my head. "No. He managed to keep her in the dark and away from just about everything."

Izzy nodded. "He thoroughly conned her."

"When do we go?" Autumn asked.

Michael gave her a cautious look. "You're not going. The last time you saw Nelson we pulled a blade out of your guts."

"Yeah," she gave him a look, "I'd say we're overdue for a face to face."

"I believe what your mate is failing to say is we need Nelson alive and functional." Troy said.

"He'll be alive." Autumn scowled at Troy, "and mostly functional."

Izzy looked at her phone. "I'm afraid I have to borrow Kara." She gave me a big smile. "Cyril has your device ready to try and still needs to discuss arrows with you," she frowned, "or was it bows?"

I glanced over to Rafael. He gave me a slight nod. "Okay." I bit my lip. The idea of having a device that would allow me to control if I heard or not, with just the push of a button was pretty exciting.

Izzy smiled at Troy. "Come find us when you have Nelson. If we're lucky we'll be able to get all the answers we need from inside his head," she shrugged and glanced to Arius, "one way or another."

Troy nodded, a not so pleasant smile on his face. "You will be called first."

Chapter Twenty-Four

I rolled over on my stomach and played with one of the lavender blooms a few inches from my face. After several failed attempts at using my new bracelet, we'd decided to call it a day. I'd come back to the palace, to sit and clean any debris from my arrows. Instead I found myself laying here thinking of, well, the overwhelming number of things I'd learned and experienced in the last few days.

Picking up another arrow, I checked the nock for any damage. One chip out of it would change the course it flew.

"You look deep in thought."

I looked to see Alona walking toward me. "So many thoughts, but none at the same time."

"Ah," she sat down a few feet away from me, "I understand those moments." She looked at the arrows laying around me. "How did your training session go?"

I sat up and looked at the bracelet on my wrist. "Not great. The dose was wrong, I almost knocked myself unconscious the first time."

She gave me an understanding smile. "I guess it's one of those things that will take time to find the right dose?"

I nodded. "It's very weak now." I picked up the arrows and started putting them back in the case. "Elder Udela said she did knock herself out at first." Kneeling, I picked up my bow. "I'm to try and keep it off as much as possible, except at times like Crissy standing beside me, so my body can adjust." I gave her a worried look. "I'm afraid to do that around too many people."

Alona nodded. "I can relate to that." She held up her arm, where she still had the inhibitor on. "I'm cheating right now. With Chase off with the men to get Nelson, I didn't want to distract him if I had a moment."

I frowned. "I don't understand how that works."

She got up and brushed off her skirt. "It's hard to explain." She motioned to my bow. "Bring that, Chase told me to show you something when you were done."

Picking up my gear, I followed her through a large wooden gate.

"This is the outer courtyard - or something like that. Maybe lower court." Alona grinned. "I'm not sure, I haven't mastered palace lingo yet." She stopped and looked at me, "at one point in my life I was hiding in back alleys, how could I ever know I'd be part of a royal family?" She chuckled softly, then continued.

I realized then that it was true, what the women had told me. They were just as much an outcast in our society as I was. The path we walked was well formed, but unmanicured. It hadn't been used in a long time. I should really ask more about the history here, why a palace sat here empty. The only problem was when I asked questions it led to more things that I wasn't sure I wanted to know about.

Alona stopped and motioned with her hands in front of her.

I looked to see targets set up on the other side of a the high walled in area. There were three targets, set up at different distances. I smiled. "Chase did this?"

Alona smirked and shook her head. "Rafael did this."

I looked at the targets again. "Why would he do that? He keeps saying one thing, then doing something completely different."

Alona started walking toward the targets. "That seems to be a male thing, I believe." She motioned to the targets. "Is this close enough?"

I nodded. "Yes. Its perfect." I was bubbling over with joy inside and had to keep my head down so I didn't do something lame like literally jump for joy-. I set the case down and opened it. Pulling out an arrow, a field tipped one, I took my bow off my shoulder. I flipped the sight and nocked the arrow. "Elder Arian is making me stun arrows." I pointed the arrow at the ground in front of us. "So I don't have to injure, just incapacitate. She said something about grab tips too." I grinned, feeling like an excited child. "I've always wanted to try those, but they were out of my price range." Exhaling I tried to regain some calm. "We went over how to weight the shafts—" I glanced at the ground for a second, "I felt smart talking to her."

Alona raised her eyebrows. "They're very good at customizing weaponry and listening to input."

I nodded and raised the bow. "I'm all for not shooting anyone." I drew back on the string and lined it up, raising it slightly, I released it.

Alona clapped softly when it hit the center of the furthest target. "I could never do that."

Lowering the bow, I looked at her. "Would you like to try?"

Her eyes went wide. "Yes, I would."

"Left or right-handed?" She'd need to use one of my gloves.

She shrugged. "I'm adept with both."

I took off my right glove. "My bow is set up for the right." She put the glove on.

Getting another arrow, I handed her my bow. "Practice pulling it back a few times."

"Hey."

We turned to see Autumn coming toward us.

She motioned to the targets. "Nice set up."

I nodded. "I'm happy to see it. Gives me something to do instead of thinking."

Autumn grinned. "Yeah, I get that. I use the same method, only I kick a pole instead."

I winced. "Up close fighting I can't do."

Alona huffed out a breath. "This is quite a bit harder than I'd imagined."

I turned back to her. "You'd need a slightly longer bow, because of your height." I shrugged. "I have the tension set high on mine too.

She nodded. "Kudos to you, for making it look so easy."

I grinned. Holding out the arrow, she took it. I moved over and stood beside her, pointing to where she needed to put the arrow.

"Rafael gave the nod for you to train some of the guards that aren't skilled at hand to hand combat." Autumn said with a grin.

I gave her a surprised look. "I didn't know it was up to him."

Autumn laughed, "he is Captain of the guard."

Nodding to Alona when she lifted the bow, I kept my attention on what she was doing. What Rafael had said about losing his position popped into my head. "So the jobs, they're real, not honorary?"

"Very real." Autumn said. "They earned them; they weren't given them."

"Oh." I moved closer to correct Alona's stance. "Turn more." I told her. "So, if they earned them, I guess they work hard to keep them?" Alona looked like she was focusing intensely. "Now draw it back tight. Look right there." I pointed to the site, "then move it up a slight bit and release. Exhale as you do. Keep your eye where you want to hit, not on your hand." I said quietly.

Alona released the string. "Oh." She exclaimed when the arrow hit the top of the base holding the closest target. "Well it wasn't where I was looking, but I still came close." She grinned, then raised the empty bow again.

I moved to adjust the way her hips were facing. "You want to line up your hip and shoulder."

"So not my thing." Autumn said. "Yeah, the guys stay on top of their game all the time to keep those positions." She shrugged and crossed her arms. "They don't want to rule from a golden throne."

...I don't know what's the matter with me...

I glanced to the grass, trying not to see whose thoughts I picked up. They speech echo sounded like Alona.

"I don't think this is my thing." Alona said in an abrupt way.

...I haven't felt the urge to bite someone in thirty years...

Alona held the bow out to me. "I must go. I will see you both shortly when the men return." She handed me my glove, gave us a plastic smile and quickly walked back toward the path.

Autumn watched her walk away, then motioned to the bow. "Can you hit the furthest one from here?"

I smiled and leaned down to get an arrow. I'd have to find out more with the fangs and feeding. Under any other circumstances I'd freak out if someone was thinking about biting me, but Alona seemed more distressed about it then I was. Rolling my shoulders, I shrugged off the thought and nocked the arrow. "Pick a ring."

Autumn turned toward the target. "Second from the center."

I exhaled and turned to it. Bringing it into the sight, inhaling I drew back, then exhaled and released.

"Yes. Nice." She said as the arrow hit the ring she'd selected.

I smiled. I'd never had someone admire my skill with a bow.

Frowning, Autumn pulled her phone out of her pocket. "Guys are back." A hard look appeared on her face. "They got Nelson."

Autumn didn't give me time to pause after porting us outside the cells, she whipped the door open and was almost at a run by the time we reached the area everyone else was waiting. Michael grabbed her by the shoulders before she got three steps into the space.

I paused and glanced at the bracelet on my wrist. Was I ready to try and cope with this many people? I shrugged. Most of them hid all their thoughts, so this would be a good time to practice 'tolerance' as Izzy called it.

Michael gave Autumn a steady look. "I know you want to have a moment with him, but we need him breathing and coherent." He continued to hold her shoulders and look down at her.

...I can't even trust myself to be near him after what he did to her...

With an abrupt nod, she leaned her forehead against his chest. "I'm good."

Giving her a look, he nodded, then dropped a kiss on the top of her head.

Autumn spun to Troy. "Did you look?"

Troy shook his head. "Not yet. We're waiting on some screening first to see if he's magically spelled."

Autumn crossed her arms over her chest and turned to glare at the man standing in the middle of the cell.

"Where's Alona?" Daxx asked.

Chase heaved a deep sigh. "She's feeling off," he waved his hand around, "possibly from wearing the inhibitor. The doctor is running some tests."

"Oh. I hope she's okay." Bethany said.

Was that why she'd wanted to bite me? Backlash from suppressing her empathy? I hoped that's what it was, because I wasn't volunteering to sate her craving if it wasn't. I turned to study Nelson. He was as large as the men hovering behind me. His shoulder length black hair was slicked back to lay flat on his head. If Victor's cold appearance could be called scary, then this man was terrifying. He stood there, looking bored. As I watched him, his eyes slowly went white.

"Did you know?" Troy said in a quiet voice behind me.

I turned to see Victor looking at Nelson and shaking his head. "No. There was no record of his feeding class."

Not understanding I glanced to see the men giving each other looks.

"Arius," Chase said in a low tone.

Arius nodded. "On it. I'll go get the cuff."

I turned to Daxx, she looked slowly from her mate to me. I raised my eyebrows in silent question.

"He feeds from a distance, doesn't have to be touching anyone." She told me with a serious look on her face.

...because he wasn't a scary enough bastard already...

My eyes went wide. "Is that worse than green eyed feeders?" I needed to talk to Crissy about the differences, if anyone could break it down methodically it would be her. Well, between the distractions she injected into every sentence at least.

"It's not worse, but it's not good either." Quinton explained. "They get amped up when they feed."

...too bad we can't knock him out and let Troy look...

My lips formed an o, but I didn't voice the holy frack my mind was shouting. "So-so a cuff will stop him from feeding or?" I felt the like only one here that didn't understand anything.

"I don't understand it either." Bethany said.

Paisley turned to watch Arius walk back in carrying a black cuff like the red inhibitor I'd wore. "Black?"

He nodded. "He won't be able to feed while we're in there."

She bit her lip. "I didn't know there was something to stop that."

Arius gave her a gentle look. "They can't wear it long, but it will help us not hype him up while we're in there."

Hugging her waist, she nodded. "Do you need my help getting it on him?"

Arius glanced at Nelson for a moment. "We may." He turned to Leone. "Get the science team here to test for magic, call Clairee too."

Leone nodded and pulled out his phone as he walked away.

"We're going to have to do this all at once." Victor said walking closer to the wall and giving Nelson a slow appraisal. "He's strong and disciplined." He turned to Troy, "it would be like capturing me I believe."

Troy raised and eyebrow, "I pity any that ever tries." Turning he looked around. "Where is Crissy?"

Victor looked back to the man behind glass. "She is observing from the office." I looked up to see his expression darken. "After the incident at the palace, I don't want her near Nelson. He wanted her taken out, so we know they have insight into her tipping us off in past situations."

"They'll have to go through me to get to her." Autumn said with a cold resolve.

"Elder Arian and Clairee are on the way." Leone came back. He waved his phone around. "And a few more elders are on route."

"They've been trying to get Nelson for a few millennia," Rafael said quietly, "this is a big win for us."

Michael nodded. "Now we just have to get the details out of him." He looked around Quinton to Troy. "Any ideas how we're doing that yet?"

Troy rubbed his hand against his jaw. "I'm trying to puzzle out the best way." He glanced to Bethany, "we could have him mesmerized."

Leone looked at his mate then back to Troy. "I don't know if Beth messing in his head is a good idea. He's got to be well versed in magic."

...I don't want her anywhere near him. In any way...

Troy nodded. "He's very disciplined, so I have doubts that even Arius' skill would work."

Arius nodded. "I'd have to have a specific objective as well, suggesting he tell us all he knows would be hours of endless rambling." He turned to look back at the man in question. "Similar to how Eunice was able to fill her mind with garbage when Troy was trying to look."

"We distract him then." Autumn said. "It worked on his sister."

I still didn't know if it was my place to speak up, but as keeping quiet had always been an issue for me, I motioned to the man behind the glass. "Maybe his sister and Leila could be the distraction." I shrugged when everyone turned to look at me. "Someone talk to him about them and Izzy and I can listen while," I motioned my hand up and down Troy, "you do whatever it is you do."

"It could work." Chase turned to Victor. "Who do we get to distract him?"

Victor was quiet for a moment. "It can't be one of us brothers, he'll be defensive as soon as he sees us."

"I'll do it." Autumn nodded. She shook her head to Michaels sceptical look. "I took down his sister, I talked to his mate."

...back me up, Kara...

I glanced at her quickly. "Autumn did very well with Leila." I said nodding. "I think she can be removed enough to not let anything he," I motioned to Nelson, "might try distract her."

Autumn gave me a quick nod, then turned to Michael. "Have the video of Eunice and one of Leila ready in case talking doesn't work."

Michael held her look for a second, then inclined his head. "I'll go get a tablet." He turned to Rafael, "can we move Leila somewhere with a camera?"

Rafael straightened away from the wall. "I'll call Ira." He looked at me for a moment, then walked out of the group, down the hall.

Walking past him, coming toward us were four Elders. Cyril, Izzy and Elders Marinus and Segos. A shiver went down my spine as I noted how menacing the two men were.

Izzy gave me a quick smile. "I've been looking forward to this for a few hundred years." She turned to look at Nelson. "We had to keep Enota under wraps so she couldn't come here and settle a score with Mister Bosworth."

I gave Chase a quick look.

...Elder Drusla...

...she went toe to toe with Nelson and had to retire from battle afterward due to injuries...

"One can't blame her," Elder Segos stated, "retribution festers into revenge after this long."

Izzy nodded. "I agree, Wulf, but we need him alive, so she'll just have to fester a bit longer."

Elder Segos nodded, but didn't say anything else.

"Do you have a plan, my kings?" Elder Marinus turned to Troy, then Chase and inclined his head.

"Of sorts." Chase said with a smirk. "We're waiting on the tests for magic, then we're going to inhibit his feeding." Elder Marinus nodded, clearly not surprised by how Nelson fed. "Then Dynamo," he motioned to Autumn, "is going to chat with him to distract him while Troy takes a look."

"We could listen as well." Izzy looked to me.

I nodded. "That's the plan." I glanced down the hall, wondering if I could find my way out of the cells. Being surrounded by this many people was starting to make the walls close in. "I'll be back when I'm needed." I started walking in the direction we'd come in. Glancing over my shoulder, I was surprised no one was following me. Turning back to figure out how to get out of here, I walked right into Rafael.

He grasped my shoulders to steady me. "What's wrong?"

I stepped back. "I just need a few minutes not surrounded by people." I glanced up to see his blue eyes filled with concern. "I'm not used to being around," I lifted my hand, then dropped it, "anyone."

He nodded and motioned down the hallway. "You can go out into the hall."

I nodded and went in that direction.

Rafael walked at my pace along side me. "Is your bracelet working?"

I lifted my arm and looked at it. "It's off right now." I glanced to see his expression become more guarded. "The dose or whatever was too strong at first, so I'm supposed to work on building resistance and only use it when it's overwhelming." We walked through the double metal doors into the hall. "Thank you for the target area." I blurted out.

He nodded. "I thought you might need somewhere to practice," he shrugged, "Autumn and Elder Segos convinced me our security could use the addition of archery." Rubbing a hand over his short hair, he looked down at me. "A lot of weaknesses have been brought to light lately."

I didn't need to hear what he was thinking to know he thought the blame fell to him. "From what I've heard, everything has been tested lately." I looked at the floor, then back up to him. "I'm still creeped out by the idea of someone we can't see walking around."

Rafael's expression of self doubt changed. "Yeah. The entire mage collective and witch's temple are working out how to find him."

I fidgeted with the seam in the glove on my left hand. "I'm sure they'll figure it out." I cringed, "I didn't understand half of what they thought." I shrugged, "so we'll work on something for other areas while they do that."

He kept looking at my hand. I wasn't sure if it was the glove he looked at or the bracelet I wore.

My mouth hadn't gotten the memo to check with my brain before speaking, again. "I don't understand why you're worried about losing your position of Captain of the guard." I regretted it as soon as I spoke the last work.

His expression hardened.

"Do you think everything happening is some failing on your part? That's a pile of crumbs." I didn't give him a chance to reply. "From what I've observed, your brothers all have some responsibility in protecting this realm too. No one could have foreseen all of this happening." The last part was pure conjecture on my part. I was just filling in blanks and pieces from all I'd heard and learned since finding out there was more than one realm. I clamped my lips together, waiting for the fallout my mouth often caused.

Many emotions flashed through his eyes. He glanced at my hands again.

"I haven't heard a thing you're thinking, if that's what you're worried about."

He looked visibly relieved. "I can't explain why—" He frowned, "I don't know if I want to explain it to anyone, but," he rubbed his hand back over his hair again. "I'm the youngest of too many powerful, talented and braggart brothers." He shook his head. "I know you can't relate," he blew out a breath. "I had to train harder, work endlessly and earn this position. To be seen as more than," he made quote marks in the air, "the youngest brother." Rafael's gaze connected with mine. I could see painful memories. "I've invested a lot of blood, sweat and even tears to get this rank and hold it."

...why do I want to explain everything to her all the time...

...that's just what I need, a weakness...

Years of practising a blank face came in handy. I didn't look away from him or do anything to let on I'd heard him. "Let me know if I can do anything to help," I motioned in the air, "you work out whatever is wrong so you don't have to worry about your position." I shrugged, "or show any sort of weakness to your over-bearing brothers." I wasn't sure if what I'd said would mean anything or not. What did I know about family? Zilch. Natta. Not a thing.

Rafael smiled down at me, a real smile that made me understand that if he chose to use that sexy smile to his advantage, his target wouldn't stand a chance. "You do get it."

I smiled back, so my mouth wouldn't confess I had no idea.

With an annoyed look, he glanced at his phone. "They need you back in there."

It felt like I could feel my nerves tightening. I took a deep breath, then nodded. "Okay."

"Hey," he cupped the side of my face in his large hand, making sure he had my attention – as if it could be anywhere else. "Don't do anything you're not comfortable with."

Standing there looking up at him giving me such a gentle look made me want things I knew I'd never be allowed to have—like someone to be close to. The fantasy lasted about three seconds. "Then I'd live in a box hidden away from the rest of the world." I whispered, "because my life is one uncomfortable moment after another."

His jaw clenched together briefly, his gaze moving from my eyes to my mouth. "Then we'll have to work on that." He leaned down and gently kissed my lips.

Before that could register, he straightened up and stepped back. "Let's go see if we can find out where Willis Hubert and Arwan are hiding."

I followed him blindly though the mazes as I processed everything. When he stopped, I looked up to see everyone standing there, anxious expressions on their faces.

"Everyone clear out. Kara doesn't need to be picking up any thoughts other than Nelson's." Rafael said in a stern voice.

Chapter Twenty-Five

As everyone came back into the space, Rafael was watching me carefully. "I'm good." I told him, then pushed the button on my bracelet. "I just need a minute in off position." I said glancing at Izzy.

She nodded and did the same, then turned to Elder Segos. "That worked very well."

He bowed his head to Autumn. "Princess Autumn pushed all the right buttons."

Autumn grinned. "He wasn't happy his sister knows what he did."

"No. I think he's more afraid of repercussions from her than anything the royal family could do to him." Izzy said with a grin.

"He truly loves Leila." I told them.

Autumn snorted. "Yeah, he almost went berserk when I told him we had her."

I frowned, still not sure I understood. "He's never fed from her." I looked at Chase, seeing if that fact was significant.

Chase looked surprised for a moment. "We can safely say he's fallen hook, line and sinker."

I didn't understand the reference, but everyone else seemed to.

"I guess it's true." Victor said in a light tone. "Even the most disciplined body has a weakness."

As everyone turned to look at Nelson in his cell, I looked over at Rafael. He wasn't looking at the prisoner, he was watching me with a look of concentration on his face. Dragging my gaze away, I looked at Autumn again. "When you mentioned the track, he thought of the train line at the end of a tunnel."

Michael and Rafael looked at each other.

"It's not a race track. It's a location at a track." Michael said.

Rafael nodded. "Has to be one no longer in use." He turned to Leone. "Do we have the plans for that tunnel that Kara followed them to yet? We need to see if there's a track near it."

Leone was typing on his phone. "Finding out right now."

Alona came in and leaned against the opening, hugging her arms around her waist. Chase straightened away from the wall and gave her a look, she nodded back, and he returned to what he was doing.

Daxx turned around and looked at Troy, who was standing silently looking at the floor with a blank expression on his face. "What is it?" Daxx went over to him. "What did you see?"

Troy took a deep breath. Exhaling slowly, he glanced at Victor before looking down at his mate. "If I'm not mistaken, Nathas Roan."

Chase pushed past Victor. "Excuse me? As in the only child of Elder-squinty-eyed-Roan?"

Troy nodded slowly. "The very same."

Paisley looked from Troy to Arius. "What does he have to do with any of this?"

Arius moved close and put his arm around her. "I think what Troy is hinting at is he didn't *disappear* on the other side."

Paisley looked up at him for a moment, then turned her head quickly and looked at Autumn. "You mean he meant to never return?"

Autumn's expression darkened.

"How do we tell Elder Roan this?" Alona asked, her eyes filled with concern.

"With a musical greeting card." Chase suggested.

She scowled at him. "I was being serious."

He shrugged, "so was I."

Bethany held up her hand. "If," she motioned to Paisley and then Autumn, "what they suspect is true and he is their father," she held up a hand and red sparks flew off it, "imagine his shock when he finds out that his daughters are going to bring him to justice."

Autumn snorted. "Oh, I'll bring him all right," she turned on her heel and started walking, "in a body cast."

Michael took a short breath, giving Troy a quick look, he shook his head. "Meeting in the practice room in a half hour." Turning, he ran after Autumn.

I didn't hear what Bethany said as we came into the practice room. I don't know what I expected for a *practice* room, but this was much more. I went to the wall on the far side, filled with weapons. Wooden, practice ones, but still weapons that probably hadn't been the *in* thing in hundreds of years.

Someone came up beside me, I dragged my focus from the wall to look up at Victor. "You guys really have been around forever." I motioned to the wall and smirked. "The Sumerian's called, they want their weapons back."

His lips quirked like he wanted to smile but couldn't. "Says the woman who shoots arrows when the rest of the world is shooting guns."

Quinton came over. "Sarcasm?" He raised his eyebrows at his brother. "From you?"

Victor grinned. "Perhaps I'm cracking under the pressure."

Quinton rolled his eyes, "yeah, right."

I turned to see Autumn and Michael in the far corner. She had her hands taped and was soaked in sweat. Michael was just clad in his jeans and was covered in a sheen of sweat.

"I'm glad it's his job to calm her down." Quinton said softly.

"Yes." Victor nodded, "I would have to agree with you there."

"What's up with Alona?" Quinton asked him. "She still feeling ill?"

"I'm not certain." Victor turned and looked over to Chase and Alona, who were huddled together.

Chase looked concerned and Alona looked determined. I made a note to stay away from their thoughts for a while. Couples thoughts during conflict were scrambled and usually made me dizzy.

Victor looked up, then grinned.

I followed his eyes to see Crissy sitting on a beam by the ceiling. There were three ropes hanging down from it. She'd climbed up there?

Crissy's head came up and she looked down to Victor, pointed to her waist and nodded.

"She's secured?" Quinton asked.

"Yes." Victor pulled his phone out and looked at it, then headed for Leone and Bethany.

Quinton gave me a nod and walked toward Troy and Daxx as they came in the door.

I looked around some more. On the other side of the mats was a board marked with targets. I went in that direction.

Arius and Paisley came in through a different door near the targets. His hair was wet, she was holding his hand and smiling up at him. I was glad the bracelet was still on so I couldn't hear the thoughts that were sure to broadcast from the way they looked at each other.

Reaching the target, I pulled out the five throwing knives and stepped back about fifteen feet. I held one across my fingers in my right hand, weighted differently than mine, I adjusted and took a breath. Tossing the first one at the target, I barely hit it. Scowling, I tossed another, and then the third. They didn't come any closer to the target.

"It takes practice with the knives." Emil said coming over to me.

I nodded. "They're weighted differently then mine." I squatted down and set the remaining two knives on the floor. Pulling up the cuff of one pant leg, I took the two blades out of the case on my ankle. Getting up, I tossed the first knife without hesitation. It hit on the right side of the bullseye. I threw the second one and heard the scrape of metal against metal as it sunk into the target right beside the first one.

"Ah, no practice needed." Emil grinned at me.

Chase come over clapping softly. "I may have to start calling you bullseye."

I cringed. "Please don't."

Emil picked up the two knives I'd set on the floor and went over to retrieve my knives. He turned around. "Why knives?" His eyebrow raised, waiting for my answer. "I understand arrows."

I took my knives from him. "For those close-up moments when I don't have time to assemble my bow."

He nodded. "Good reason."

"All right, everyone."

We turned to look at Troy.

"Considering what we learned from Nelson today, it's been decided we're going into the tunnel tomorrow."

"After examining the layout of that tunnel system, we've ascertained it would be more prudent to take two separate teams." Victor crossed his arms over his chest. "The tracks at the exit of the tunnel will have one team." He glanced to Michael. "Welsley will be leader for that group."

Michael nodded and pulled his shirt over his head.

"At the center is the old work caverns used as the main tunnel when the trains first went in." Leone told him.

"So, it's a maze of entrances and exits?" Michael put his arm around Autumn as they walked over.

Rafael nodded. "Its going to be chaos. Both teams will have to take a witch and a mage," he shrugged, "we have no idea what we could come up against."

Daxx looked at me. "Think you can handle being down in tunnels?" She glanced at Rafael briefly, then continued. "If the maps we have are right, there's a great location to watch from up high." She nodded and tuned to Autumn, "Kara stopping any strays with her bow would save a lot of chasing."

Everyone turned to look at me. I bit my lip. "I-honestly-I don't know. I don't do well underground."

Chase raised an eyebrow at me. "You've been in the underground chambers most of today."

Autumn waved a hand around. "This is not dark and musty like the real *underground*."

I took a deep breath and exhaled. "Will this," I lifted my arm with the porting device on it, "work down there?"

Michael looked to Victor. He nodded slowly. "If she's at the location Daxx mentioned it should."

Daxx looked back at me.

"I'll try." I nodded, mentally taking stock of how I felt about that.

"Keep the women in mind." Bethany gave me a serious look. "I think about the women they've taken, it helps."

I nodded, still not convinced.

"And if we don't stop them from bringing down the barriers, thousands of people will die when they do." Quinton shrugged, "I won't mention the mayhem that will occur when the realms mix."

All eyes were on him.

"Thanks for putting that into perspective, brother." Leone said, a grim expression on his face.

My FOS was topping out at a nine now. "The women." I said quietly. "I'll focus on the women."

"I suggest we all take a few hours, rest, eat a meal, then head over to the *new* meeting room." Victor said. "Where we will then have a hard conversation with Elder Roan."

Chase grinned. "I will be there, with bells on."

Alona closed her eyes briefly. "Come, king, lets go have a quiet dinner together."

"Ah," he bowed his head to her, "it would be my pleasure, Duchess."

Rolling her eyes, she took his hand and started pulling him toward the double doors.

Quinton turned to Emil. "I'm going to the palace kitchen to beg for food." He looked at me, then Rafael, "Anyone care to join?"

I sat on a stool sipping chocolate milk. The kitchen was, like every other room in this place, huge. Other than the size, it didn't look any different then any other kitchen, there was just more of everything. More stoves, more shelves and more sinks.

Emil and Quinton sat with me. They were discussing some sparring match in the guards' yard. Rafael was talking to Mitz as she worked at the far side of the room. He kept smiling down at her and seemed to be enjoying whatever they were talking about.

On the other side of the room, there were three women taking dishes from crates and putting them on shelves. Every few moments one of them would look over at Rafael and Mitz.

Checking I wasn't being watched, I pushed the small button on my bracelet. I stopped and stared at the glass in front of me, shocked that I had just done that. A week ago, I would have been exiting the room as fast as I could so I wouldn't hear anyone's thoughts, and now I was acting like it was my right to hear others innermost whispers. Scowling at the glass, I picked it up and took another sip.

...I didn't think I'd like having this much family, but I'm glad I was found...

I kept my eyes focused on the countertop. I knew that had come from Emil. As far as I knew, I'd never heard anything Quinton thought.

...I can't believe he's off the market...

...not that I want to settle down, but Prince Rafael was so fun...

I took another small sip and took my time savoring the flavour, so I wouldn't react and look at the women.

Rafael laughed at something Mitz said.

...I'm going to miss him...

That wasn't the same person as the earlier thoughts, I concluded. Completely different feel to it.

Quinton turned and looked over at Mitz, then sighed and turned back to Emil.

Rafael went over to the fridge and took out a bottle of water. Turning around he came toward me.

...I wished he'd look at me that way...

Again, a different person.

...the princess is lovely though...

Stopping on the other side of the counter, he leaned over to set the a bottle of water beside my glass of milk. I looked at it and then back to him. He tilted his head, an amused expression on his face. I watched him look at the blocker on my wrist and tilt his head.

...hydrate...

Releasing the bottle, I opened it and took a drink as I looked at him.

He grinned.

...thank you...

Setting it back down, I shook my head at him, trying not to smile back to his beaming grin.

"Here you go, loves." Mitz set a large tray of sandwiches on the counter. "I'll have this kitchen up and running by dinnertime tomorrow."

Quinton heaped a plate with food and stood up. Leaning down he kissed the top of her head. "Thanks." With a nod, he waited for Emil to get some, then they walked out.

"Eat in the courtyard?" Rafael asked me.

I nodded. "Yes." While realizing I never thought I'd be doing such a thing, not in my life.

"Don't forget your water." Mitz said with a grin.

Chapter Twenty-Six

"Your mother was beautiful." Alona said softly.

Chase hugged her against his side. "Yes, she was."

I stood off to the side, out of the way and looked up at the portrait now hanging behind the thrones. The couple in the portrait were regal and elegant. The king sat on the throne, his black hair dark against the silver crown. I couldn't decide which brother most looked like him, they all had some feature in common. The woman standing beside him was a young version of Mitz, her long, wavy red hair hung gracefully down her back.

"I don't want our official portrait to be formal like that." Alona told Chase. "I want it by the lavender gardens, perhaps sitting on a bench." She smiled at him. "Dressed to the nines with crowns gleaming in the sunlight."

"You will look ravishing, beloved." Lifting her hand, Chase kissed it tenderly.

"What official portraits?" Daxx asked loudly.

Chase gave his twin a quick look. "All royal members have them painted once mated."

Daxx turned to Troy, her hands on her hips. "I am *not* wearing a gown or a crown."

Troy opened his mouth, then closed it.

She turned to Troy. "As the *long-awaited huntress queen*, I'll be in my leathers for ours."

Smirking Chase looked at his brother. "I think that's fitting, don't you brother king? The night king and his queen in their battle attire."

Troy nodded slowly. "I'm actually liking the idea."

Daxx gave a quick nod, then turned to look at the room.

Chairs lined the back wall, with a table making a large square in the middle. Off to the one side was a large map and several smaller ones.

"I approve of using this room," Victor motioned to the thrones and portrait at the far end, "with our parents overlooking the proceedings."

"Yes. Well done, Alona." Troy nodded.

Alona smiled. "It was the perfect space for meeting."

Someone cleared their throat.

Elder Roan stood in the open doorway. He bowed at the waist, "your majesties."

"Its no longer the throne room. Its now just our council room." Victor said.

"Or, war room currently." Leone grinned at him.

"I was told I was required to be here at this time." Elder Roan inclined his head, "how can I be of service?"

Chase took a step forward, but Alona put her hand out and stopped him before he could go any further.

"Please take a seat." Troy motioned to the table. "Any one is fine, there are no formal seating arrangements here."

The next few minutes were filled with the sound of chairs scraping the floor. Even with all seated, half of the large table and chairs were empty.

"Your majesties."

I turned to see the rest of the elders standing in the doorway.

"Come in and sit down." Chase told them, then gave his mate a curious look.

Alona smiled at Elder Roan. "I thought perhaps we'd include all in this, to save repeating our findings."

Elder Roan nodded, "as you wish my queen."

"This is a perfect room for large meetings." Elder Landry said looking around.

"Yes," Elder Varus nodded, "and very fitting." She lifted her chin, motioning to the portrait.

I glanced to Izzy, she gave me a small smile. She had been there with Nelson and knew what was coming. As did the elder's Marinus and Segos, who, I noted, didn't look as enthused as the others.

"Findings?" Elder Drusla asked in a stern voice. "What you discovered from Nelson Bosworth?"

"Yes." Victor nodded, then looked at Troy.

Troy sat forward in his chair. "Before we get to that, the teams will be hitting the tunnel from the city as well as the exit tomorrow."

"My king," Elder Segos stood up. "I would like to be part of that."

"Wulf," Elder Varus said, "as an elder, you do not participate in warfare any longer."

The hardened warrior shook his head. "I took a seat on this council to do my part in protecting this realm and others." He looked around at his peers. "I have been *sitting* in that seat for three hundred years, Dyota, I think we can all agree that every blade in required in this battle. Winning is imperative to all who survive. My blades will be included in ensuring this victory." He shrugged. "Should I fall, there are more than enough others with the proper credentials to fill my seat." He bowed his head to Troy and sat down.

Elder Varus looked at Troy and then Chase. "While I agree with the importance of ending this, I can not agree with members of the elder's council fighting in it." She took a deep breath. "Your inclusion is entirely up to our kings."

Elder Marinus stood up. "I offer my blade for the good of the realm." He inclined his head and sat down.

Elder Drusla stood up, looking excited. "Don't think you two get to have all the fun." She bowed her head abruptly to

Daxx. "My service will always be available for any battle our Royals take part in." She sat back down.

Daxx turned to Troy, who looked down the table at Victor. Victor gave a slight nod.

"It would be our honor to fight alongside all three of you." Troy turned and looked at Rafael.

Rafael nodded. "We could use more seasoned fighters at the exit end of the tunnel with Captain Welsley."

Elder Drusla gave an abrupt nod.

"We would be honored." Elders Segos looked very pleased.

Elder Faran looked at Crissy, "has our seer any insights into this battle tomorrow?"

Crissy looked at her for a moment. "Nothing complete."

"Ah," the elder looked pleased, "inconclusive visions are the best ones, as the fates haven't decided, so the outcomes can still change."

I had no idea what that meant. I looked over at Paisley, who gave me a shrug. She didn't either.

"What else did you find from Nelson?" Elder Moire asked. "Anything of Arwan or Willis Hubert?"

"I'm afraid not, Ryce, there was no hint of that in his thoughts." Izzy told him.

"Were you able to see anything, my King?" Elder Moire asked Troy.

"I did." Troy said in a quiet tone. "It answered many questions on several levels."

"Oh?" Elder Roan leaned forward, "and how is that?"

Troy cleared his throat. "For as long as we've been aware of the situation with Willis Hubert, we have been trying to figure out how they were able to infiltrate our inner chambers and information system." He paused and looked at Michael for a moment. "The revelation pertaining to Arwan, and the possibility that he has been walking among us cloaked all this time," he looked at his own hands clasped in front of him on the table, "has filled in many gaps and theories."

I watched most of the elder's nod and agree with their king, excepting those present in the cells during the questioning. They were all looking at Elder Roan, knowing what was coming.

Troy continued. "I was able to see someone in Nelson's memories that, to be honest, shocked me more than anything I've ever seen."

"I've been seeing something lost, that isn't." Crissy interrupted, "then I saw more pieces and it's not a what," She nodded and leaned over to pick up her pack, "it's a who." She opened the bag and started rummaging, "there are more pieces, but they don't fit yet," she pulled out a textbook, "I'm still working on those." She nodded and took out a worn notebook.

I looked to see all the elders hung on her every word. They didn't seem confused or annoyed but were giving her their absolute attention. I realized then what Crissy had said was true. Here, in this other realm, she was not only allowed to be herself, but accepted and respected.

Flipping through the book, she nodded when she stopped on a page. "I didn't know the face," she shrugged, "how could I, there are too many faces in my head." She turned more pages in her notebook, "some appear, and I never see them again." She stopped and looked up. "I had to get a book about stones, and thought it was a tiger's eye I kept seeing." She shook her head, "but it wasn't." She held up the text book. "It was a star sunstone." Crissy set the book down and held up her notebook so everyone could see the sketch. "It's very pretty and he still wears it."

Elder Roan leaned forward onto the table, his already pale skin blanching even further. "Princess," he swallowed visibly, then looked at Troy, "my king, who did you see?" His voice sounded breathless.

"Nathas." Troy said clearly. "I saw your son, Nathas Roan."

Elder Roan covered his mouth for a second. "Is-is he…"

Troy shook his head. "He was very much alive."

The shock on the Elders face was clear. "What-what," he looked from Troy to Crissy, "what is the connection?"

"My friend," Elder Marinus looked across the table to Elder Roan, "Turbert, we do not have any details at this time."

Elder roan nodded.

"He could be spelled, as Eunice was." Izzy offered.

"Yes." Elder roan whispered, then looked back to Crissy, "May I see your sketch? What you saw?"

Crissy nodded and knelt on the chair, she stretched to hand the book to Bethany, two chairs away from the shell-shocked elder, who reached for the sketch.

His hands shook as he studied the drawing. He nodded and gave the book back to Bethany. "It is the pendant his mother gave him when he was a child." Taking a deep breath, he looked at Troy. "I'd like to go tell his mother, her child, missing for eighty years, is not dead."

Troy studied him for a moment, then turned to Victor.

Victor sat forward in his seat, "while I can not begin to grasp what you are feeling," he quickly looked to Elder Varus, "we must ask that you keep this information between your mate and yourself."

Elder Roan just sat there.

"Turbert," Elder Varus gave him and empathetic look, "until we understand the scope of Nathas' involvement, no one else can know."

Elder Roan nodded slowly. "Yes. Yes, of course. I-I understand." He stood up slowly.

Elder Nodin got up. "Allow me to accompany you, old friend."

Elder Roan nodded, pained emotions easy to read on his face. He turned to the door, then paused and turned back. He bowed his head. "Your majesties."

The room was silent as all watched him leave.

"I feel like I've been hit with a laser blast." Elder Arian said quietly.

"We're all stunned, Cyril," Elder Drusla said, nodding her head slowly.

Taking a moment, Elder Varus smoothed her hands over her hair as if she felt unkempt, yet there wasn't a hair out of place. "Was there anything else?" She finally asked while looking at Troy.

Troy shook his head. "Nothing of importance."

Rafael stood up. "As you know we're planning a take a team to the facility where Kara was held." He looked down at me for a several seconds before continuing. "Aside from warriors, we're going to need others to go with us."

Michael stood up. "We're not certain in what state any from Alterealm will be in, if they're still there, but we'll need to be prepared for all possibilities."

"How are we going to decide who is from here?" Bethany asked.

Elder Drusla grinned. "I'm sure that seeing the entire royal family descend upon the facility will be all that is required."

Elder Arian nodded. "I agree, but I could whip up a portable scanner that would work like the one in the intake cells." She looked at Rafael, "in case fellow Alterealm residents are incapacitated."

Rafael abruptly nodded in acknowledgment. "If you could adjust one of the port boxes to send directly to the medical wing, that would make things easier."

"You can change mine." Leone said as he nodded at his brother.

The elder smiled. "I'll get to work on that immediately."

Elder John looked to Michael. "I will assist the medical staff to prepare for possible incoming patients and to prepare a contingency plan."

Rafael sat down.

The room was silent.

"If that's everything," Troy glanced around, "I suggest we adjourn until we meet at the guard's yard." He looked over at Elder Segos. "The team going to the exit point will be going over first."

Elder Segos nodded. "We will be there." He looked at Elders' Marinus and Drusla. They nodded in unison.

Chapter Twenty-Seven

It was almost too dark to see the targets, even with the torch I'd borrowed from the courtyard set beside them.

I couldn't sleep. I couldn't sit still. I needed to get a new dictionary to read. I released the arrow and gave myself a nod of congratulations when it hit where I'd aimed. I nocked the next one, then paused when I heard someone walking through the grass.

"I kept thinking I was lucky you'd missed and hit me where you did." Rafael's voice got louder as he moved closer.

I drew back on the string and aimed.

"But you didn't miss where you were aiming, did you?"

I released it and watched it hit the bullseye. "I don't miss my targets." I turned and looked at him, "not in a long time."

He just stood there and watched me.

"Although I kept doubting myself thinking I'd missed because you were walking around so soon after." I frowned. "How were you walking that soon?"

He tucked his hands into the pocket of his jeans. "You definitely did not miss. It was bleeding all over the place." He shook his head, "the pain when they pulled it out, I can't even describe it."

I stood there for a second, then decided he'd brought it up. "How?"

Rafael grinned. "Our blood. We heal quickly."

I nodded slowly. "Right."

Crossing his arms over his large chest, he gave me a serious look. "The worst part," he paused for a second, "the worst part was getting one of my brothers to replenish the blood I'd lost." My thoughts must have reflected on my face. "Only royal blood can replenish royal blood."

I nodded slowly, thinking there was a story there, how did his ancestors figure out royal blood was needed to replenish royal blood? I waited for him to continue.

"My brothers were too busy laughing to assist me." He frowned. "Chase was the only one not crying from laughing too hard—Chase doesn't normally donate blood to us fangers, so that was almost as big a shock as being hit by an arrow.

"Chase is," I tried to find the right word, "unique."

Rafael chuckled. "That's one way to describe him." He shook his head and motioned to the targets. "Why are you out here in the middle of the night?"

I took a deep breath, then went to get my arrows back. "I couldn't sleep." I pulled them out and turned to find him standing right next to me. I gave him an exasperated look, that he smirked at. "I'm scared and nervous about tomorrow."

He held out his hand for my bow as we walked back. "If you're uncomfortable in the tunnels, use your porter and get out."

I took a deep breath and nodded.

He stopped and turned back to the targets. "Now show me how to do this." Serious blue eyes connected with mine. "As Captain of the guard, I like to know every weapon my guards use."

I motioned to my bow. "My bow isn't the right size for you."

He shrugged. "Not that I'll know the difference."

I handed him an arrow. "Why are you wandering around in the middle of the night?" I pointed to where he should nock the arrow. "You should have a finger guard on."

"One won't hurt." He said as he raised the bow.

"Line it up there, then adjust your aim down for closer, or moving targets and up for distance."

He nodded. "I looked out my window and saw a torch down here."

I turned and looked up at the palace, where only one window was lit. I heard him release the arrow and checked the target. He'd hit it. "Is that where you were aiming?"

Rafael held the bow out to me. "Not even the same target."

I took the bow and tried not to smile. "Oh."

"I think I'll need a few daylight practice sessions before we start training the guards for archery." He looked at the target and shook his head.

We both started walking toward it.

"Are many being trained?"

"That's up to you." He pulled the arrow out and looked at it. "If they have no skill for it after the first few lessons, don't waste more time on them."

I disassembled my bow as we walked. "Okay."

"We have twenty that we've selected to start, I'm hoping there will be at least ten that become proficient." He motioned to the palace. "We'll place the trained guards here on watch and at a few of the towers by the chambers. At least until we've caught all of Hubert's associates."

I knelt and put my bow back into the bag. "It's worse than I've been told, isn't it?" When I put everything in it and zipped it up, he bent down and picked up the bag. He made it look lighter than it was.

"It is. Hubert's plan had been in place for decades before we knew anything. Could have been active longer, we have no way to know for sure."

We started walking. I stopped and look back at the targets. "What about the torch?"

271

"Leave it." Rafael looked around, "the area should have more lighting." He motioned to walk. "Its supposed to be warded, but after the last disaster, we should tighten security measures as well."

For a few minutes we didn't speak, just walked toward the gate.

"How are you doing," He looked down at me. "With all of this? You were dropped into it out of nowhere..."

I shook my head. "I think I was in it a long time ago." I looked up at the palace. "From birth, if the theory that one of my parents were from here is true. Then hearing the thoughts of those trapped in the same place I was."

"That's our failing, my family. How so many were born to the other side, or never returned, is a huge oversight on our part." We entered the courtyard. Rafael set my bag down and motioned to one of the stone benches. "After we realized how bad this situation is, Leone, Michael and I personally reviewed all the port records." He sat down and leaned over to rub his hands over his face in frustration. "There are hundreds of discrepancies." He shook his head, "from late returns, illegal crossings, missing people," he blew out a breath, "it's a colossal disaster."

I could see self-doubt and guilt in his eyes. "I'm sure when the guidelines, or whatever it's called, were established you weren't up against so many technological cheats."

He frowned at me.

I held up my wrist with the port device on it. "Obviously you are centuries ahead of my side in the technology field, but I'm sure it was easier to keep track of those," I wasn't sure of the word, "who went over to my side, it must have been much easier before everything became instant with gadgets and devices."

Rafael studied me for a moment. "I've never thought of it that way." He looked visibly more relieved.

"You can't regret it." I said quickly, "what's happening."

He raised an eyebrow at me.

I nodded. "If it hadn't, Daxx wouldn't be here, or Alona and the others."

Rafael smiled. "They have made our lives *much* more interesting, that's for sure." He looked at me for a long moment, making it feel awkward. "I wasn't very happy when I realized a woman had shot me."

I grinned. "Yes, your expression shouted that quite clearly."

He grinned. "I'm sure it was screaming when I figured out you were the one in my prophecy."

I played with the glove on my hand. "Crissy told me what it said."

"Having an *arcus* mate was so much cooler before her arrow was sticking out of me."

I couldn't help grin at his tone. "I'm sure it was."

Rafael's eyes glinted with amusement. "Fifty years of fantasies gone, just like that."

I laughed quietly. "I'm sorry I ruined your fantasies."

He still had a smile on his face. "I wish—" the jovial expression left his eyes, "I wish it could be different between us, Kara, but right now," he shook his head, "it can't."

Why did it bother me when he said it that way? I didn't want any sort of relationship either. "Well," I was hoping to make him feel better, "after the thoughts I've overheard from a few women in your kingdom, they will be *very* pleased to know that."

Rafael scowled, then rubbed his hand over his hair in an agitated way. "I can't," he looked at his large hand, "I'm almost two hundred," he shook his head, "I..."

I grinned. "I was afraid for a second you were going to claim to be a virgin. I didn't hear details about *that*."

His gaze searched my face for a moment. "Yeah. Okay," he nodded, "It's not for the reason you think." He sighed, then shook his head, "okay, it was, but," he motioned to his head, "I need times of—distraction." He shook his head, the expression on his face said he didn't like his own explanation.

"It was easier for me if my brothers thought I was sleeping with half of the female population."

We both turned when Autumn came walking through the gate mumbling as she looked at her phone.

"Out for a midnight stroll?" Rafael asked.

"Hey." She glanced up, a preoccupied look on her face. "Michael is busy with last minute stuff, so I thought I'd check the palace," she frowned, "grounds for security flaws."

"More lighting in the lower courtyard." He told her.

She nodded. "Got that one." Moving slowly, still looking at her phone she came toward us. "Michael told me to make a list for you and him. Paisley downloaded some note app on my phone." Her shoulders dropped, she held out the phone. "How do I save this? Because the last time I closed it, it was gone."

Rafael took the phone and looked at it. He stood up and held it where she could see the screen. "Right here." He pointed to it.

She looked relieved and took the phone. "I don't know why I couldn't just tell someone." She didn't look pleased. "My sensei used to say if you don't use it you lose it." She nodded, "that works for brains too I think." With an abrupt nod, she turned. "Don't stay up too late. Need you at the top of you game tomorrow."

Rafael sat down. "Hey, don't forget to fill out the appropriate forms and leave them on my desk for your security requests."

Autumn stopped and turned around. "Don't make me take you down in front of your mate, big guy."

He laughed.

Shaking her head, she turned and went into the solarium.

"I like her." I told him. "She says what she's thinking, or the little I've heard she does."

Rafael nodded. "Yeah, her integrity is rock solid." He glanced at my wrist.

I gave him a quick shake of my head. "It's off. It's just nice to know that there are some people that don't have ulterior motives, phony thoughts and are honest."

His expression softened. "I guess having an ability like yours only shows you the sides of human nature that need to stay hidden."

There was nothing I could say to that, so I nodded briefly. He'd summed up my life in one sentence.

"That makes my heart ache." He confessed. "To know that you've missed out on all the good things life has to offer."

"I have chocolate milk." I told him with a smirk, to try to lighten his mood.

Rafael smiled one of his charming smiles. "Yeah, that's right up there with chocolate ice cream."

I nodded, even though I'd never had chocolate ice cream.

His eyes studied my face. "You've never had chocolate ice cream? Wow, we'll have to fix that."

I laughed. "I hate to break it to you, but my life has been filled with a lot of tripe and there's too many things I've never had."

Nodding slowly, his look changed to contemplation. "We'll have to work on fixing that." He glanced at my wrist. "Turn off your blocker." He said softly.

I looked at it, then back to him, the expression in his eyes had changed again. He had that look he'd gotten when he'd kissed me before. "W-why?"

"Because," he said in a gentle tone as he picked up my arm. "I want to show you what it's like for someone to think," he pushed the button on my bracelet, "of you, just you. No ulterior motives or thoughts that don't match the actions." Lifting my hand, he placed a kiss in the palm of it.

I was afraid to breathe, to move for fear that this was only happening in my head.

He touched my chin and tilted my head up, then he moved much closer to me. "You're so beautiful," he whispered, his gaze moving over my face. His breath brushed over my mouth.

...eyes as dangerous as a siren's song...

His mouth brushed over mine. Moving slowly, he cupped the side of my face and kissed me again, lingering longer.

...a hundred times a day I want to kiss this mouth...

His mouth covered mine with small coaxing kisses, encouraging me to open my mouth.

...let me in. Let me taste you...

Between his thoughts and actions, my head felt light, in a good way that I'd never felt before. I opened my mouth and he deepened the kiss. His tongue dipped in to touch against mine. The kiss was slow and gentle. I stopped caring if I needed to breathe.

...so fucking sweet...

His thoughts made me dizzy. I wrapped my arms around his neck, not wanting him to stop. Putting his arm under my knees, he lifted me into his lap, without breaking the kiss.

...never felt like this before...

His hand grasped the back of my hair lightly and he held my head, his mouth was rougher.

...I want to taste every inch of her...

His thoughts had changed from thinking of me, to thinking about me. His actions, the tone of his thought echo, I felt like I was drowning. And I didn't care.

...her essence probably tastes like honey... smells too good...

Rafael growled in the back of this throat, then tore his mouth from mine. Holding my head, he cradled it gently in his large hand and rested his forehead against mine. Both of us were panting for air.

"So much," he kissed my forehead, "for an innocent kiss," he gasped out a breath.

I smiled, even though he couldn't see my face, "I don't feel innocent right now."

He snorted softly and hugged me closer.

I could count on one hand the amount of times in my life that I'd been held. It was a weakness I'd regret later, but now

I leaned into his arms, my head against his shoulder. "What is my essence?" I asked quietly. "I know it has something to do with the need for fangs, but," I lifted my head and looked up to see his eyes were red. I glanced to his mouth, knowing there were fangs in there.

"Essence is what keeps me alive." He answered honestly.

...I feel like a teenager unable to control his own body's reactions...

"You can think it if you don't know how to explain it. Often thoughts are easier then speaking."

His gaze flicked to my mouth, then his lips quirked. "I forgot you were listening." He grinned.

Before I knew I'd done it, my hand touched his bottom lip so I could look at his fangs. "Does it hurt? When you take someone's essence?"

...no, we can control how much they feel...

"I know you wouldn't hurt me." I moved my hand. "What happens if you bite someone and you don't like the taste..."

Rafael smiled wide. "We can smell it."

The shock had to be clear on my face because he gave me a cautious look.

Gently, he brushed the hair back from my neck and leaned down slowly. He kissed the side of my neck, near my shoulder. "right here." He whispered against my skin.

"And-and," I couldn't believe I was going to say it, "how do I smell?"

He kissed the same spot. "Like heaven."

"Did you already eat?" My brain immediately red flagged my mouth for saying that.

"Yeah, but I crave yours even when I'm nowhere near you."

"Oh?" I didn't know what to add to that.

"Mate perk," He whispered and lifted his head to look down at me. His eyes were blue again. "Fate's way of making sure we're compatible for a long life."

"Has fate ever been wrong? What if someone doesn't like how their intended mate," I frowned at my own thoughts, "tastes?"

He laughed quietly. "I don't know if that's ever happened."

"What if I don't taste like honey?" I shrugged, "what if I take like your least favorite food."

Rafael smirked, his eyes sparkling with amusement, "I'm sure you don't taste like liver."

With my eyes wide, I looked at him. "I could." Wait. What? Did I want him to bite me and taste my essence, whatever that was? This was definitely one of those things my mind could not have fabricated. Seriously, fangs. Essence. Liver-flavored essence.

Rafael looked at me, then to my neck briefly. "Even if you did, I guess I'd learn to like liver."

I knew he was joking, but he didn't smile. Neither of us did. Our eyes were locked together, breath shallow. "You-you should find out." I nodded hesitantly, "because now it will drive us both crazy, the wondering."

He nodded. "Yeah it could." His eyes started to change. "Right now?"

I nodded even thought my brain was saying, *wait, think this through.* I leaned my head to the side to rest in his hand. "Just-just go heavy on the no pain part."

He didn't reply as he leaned down to my neck again. His breath was hot, his lips soft as he kissed my skin again in that same spot.

I felt his fangs bite into me, but there was no pain at all. A shiver of awareness went through me and it wasn't what the logical part of my brain should have realized, that I was letting a man bite me with fangs. I enjoyed it. I held his head not wanting him to move away.

...*like no other*...

I only caught part of what he was thinking.

Pulling his mouth away, he licked over his bite, then grasped the back of my head and crushed my mouth beneath his. I felt a pinch of pain as his fang nicked my lip, but didn't care. Not knowing if I'd ever kiss another mouth with fangs again, I ran my tongue over the sharp teeth.

Rafael growled against my mouth and assaulted my lips again.

I was dizzy, never having felt this way in my life.

...fuck not now...

He tore his mouth from mine and pulled me against his chest.

...grey hair is almost blue...

...how is that possible...

Pieces all fell into place suddenly. I leaned back and looked at him. "You have visions."

He looked down at me and hissed out a breath. "You're bleeding."

I licked over my lip and tasted blood.

"I'm like a gangly teenager around you. I can't even kiss you right." He leaned down and licked over my mouth. When he straightened up again, his eyes were red.

I touched my lip with my tongue, there was no more blood. "I think you kissed me right."

Rafael made a strange sound that I wasn't sure what it meant, then pulled me against him again. "Yes. I have visions." He said quietly. "Not like Crissy does, thank the gods for that." Kissing the top of my head, he shifted so I was sitting on the bench again. "So much for thinking of only you." In a sudden move, he stood up. "This one won't quit. I keep seeing this woman with dark eyes and grey hair," he spun to look at me, "but not *old* grey hair, it's more blue," he rubbed his hands over his face, "but it's not grey all the time, its like the color fades into this blue-grey..." He stopped and looked at me. "It's driving me mad."

"Have you talked to Crissy? She's been having something similar, maybe the two of you could fit the pieces together—together." That had sounded better in my head.

"No." He blew out a breath. "I haven't."

"Well, have you talked it over with one of your brothers?"

He shook his head, looking annoyed and distracted.

I tilted my head and studied him for a moment. "Do your brothers know you have visions?"

"Yes," he rolled his eyes, "well, not to the extent that I do." He clasped his hands behind his neck and looked up at the dark sky. "If I tell them, they'll think I'm a liability."

I stood up. "I don't think they would."

"I can't take that chance." He went over and picked up my bag, "we should get some rest."

I didn't move to follow him. "Is that why you go to the temple? Are they helping you control them?"

He turned around and looked at me. "They're trying," he sounded so annoyed. "I can't have visions popping into my head in the middle of a battle. Lives depend on me. I have to stay focused."

I nodded. "I understand having things in your head you don't want. You should talk to your brothers." I suggested softly, not wanting to agitate him further. It bothered me to see him like this. "Has it ever happened when you're fighting?"

"No." He shrugged, "maybe during a practice skirmish." He gave his head a shake. "I can't take the chance." Rafael started walking toward the solarium.

I moved quickly to keep up with him. "Maybe it won't."

He glanced down at me but kept walking.

I continued. "Maybe your body knows when you need to focus and that overrides everything else."

We reached the stairs and started climbing to the second floor.

"There has to be something they can do." I held out my wrist with the blocker on it. "Like this. If they can make one for me, then surely…"

He shook his head. "It's not the same for visions. They can't supress them." Briefly he looked at me, "believe me, we've tried."

We were at my door already. I was a bit winded from trying to keep up with the speed he could move. "You should talk to your family, or the elders." I touched his arm, "they'd want to know and help you. That's a big burden to carry, Rafael." I smirked, "especially with how long you live. You shouldn't have to keep it hidden and all to yourself. You need to share it with someone."

Reaching past me, he opened my door and set my bag inside it. Straightening he touched the side of my face and gave me a look full of emotion. "I just did." Kissing my mouth softly, he stepped back into the hall. "Get some rest, Kara."

I stood there and watched until he went in his room and closed the door. Closing mine, I leaned back against it. I was going to have to rethink, well *everything*. Starting with this mate stuff. Being near him was like a drug, or, or something wonderful but possibly really bad for you. I frowned at the floor, that made no sense.

Puling my phone out of my pocket, I looked at it. Then my eyes went wide when I saw the time. Sleep. Definitely needed sleep. I'd been awake for almost an entire day, yet I'd never felt more energized.

Leaving a trail of clothes, I climbed under the covers. I was going to fight with a royal family in a few hours. Could life get any stranger?

I really hoped not.

Chapter Twenty-Eight

I stood out of the way as the room filled with many large people. We were in the armory, assembling to take our places at the tunnel. I felt sick. My stomach was filled with knots. I looked down at the jacket I wore, still amazed I was given something this nice. It was brand new made just for me. I liked that it was black, keeping clothes clean isn't one of my talents. The sleeves were loose but fitted enough to not interfere with the use of my bow. It had several pockets, inside and out, and a small pouch set in the back to not get in the way of the quiver case. I was given gloves too, the right was made with a thicker leather strip with two fingers padded to resemble a finger guard. The left glove had of rubber material on the palm, so my grip on the bow wouldn't slip. I'd never seen, or had, items like this before.

Elder Arian had brought me a quiver with my new stun arrows in it. They were very interesting, and truth be told, I couldn't wait to shoot someone and see how they worked.

"Fits good."

Rafael was standing in front of me, clad head to toe black leather, with half the armory strapped to his body. He looked dangerous and really, really good at the same time. I bit my lip so I wouldn't blurt that bit of information out.

He glanced at my wrist.

"It's off." I told him and watched a look of relief come over his face.

He nodded as his expression changed. "I, ah, had Mitz put extra, uh," he held his hands open in front of my chest, then jerked them away, "padding in the front so-so if you have to lean...." He shrugged, "so-so it's more comfortable for you."

I gave him a half smile. "Thank you."

He nodded a few times.

Chase stopped beside us. "Aren't you supposed to be the smooth one?"

Rafael gave him a blank look.

Chase held up his hands in supplication. "Leaving."

Clearing his throat, Rafael looked back down at me. "Oh," he suddenly dropped to one knee in front of me, "I had them add a few lined knife pockets."

I froze as he lifted the cuff of my pant leg and took one knife out of the strap on my ankle, then he did the same with the other.

Standing up slowly, he gave me a steady look, I noticed his eyes were a darker blue. "Right here." He murmured quietly as he slipped the knife into a pocket I didn't know was there. It was on a seam, or so I'd thought it was a seam beside the zipper. "You should be able to access them quickly."

I looked down at it, then touched it. "Wow, that's easier then bending down to get them."

He nodded again, his gaze flicking to my mouth a few times. "Did Beth give you your earbud?"

I nodded and touched my ear. "Yes."

"We'll all be connected once we're over there."

"That makes me feel better." I confessed.

"I need you to wear this." He held up the necklace with his pendant. "Any from here will know you, and respect who you are while you're wearing it." There was a vulnerable look on his face.

I nodded, then turned and lifted my braid out of the way.

Rafael reached around and slipped it around my neck, I could feel his hands brush against my skin.

"Just bite her and get it over with." Quinton said with a smirk as he stopped beside us.

I scowled at him. "A man with secrets should be nicer."

Quinton blanched. He glanced to Rafael, then walked the other way.

"I thought your blocker was off?" Rafael looked confused.

I shrugged. "It is. Everyone has at least one secret, right?"

With a big grin on his face, he looked over at Quinton. "I like your style, Kara."

Everything and everyone in the room stopped when Victor walked in.

"Ready?" Rafael asked me quietly.

"Not at all." I confessed.

Crissy came over and handed me two bars. "Protein bars." She nodded, then looked at my feet. "Are you wearing socks?"

I looked at my boots. "Yes."

She smiled. "Good. Socks are good." She turned and went over to Victor.

I looked up at Rafael.

He shrugged, "No idea."

"She's interesting." I reached behind me and put the bars into the small pouch.

"That she is." Rafael reached over and picked up my bow where I had it leaning against the wall. He held it out to me. "Let's go."

I followed Rafael up the second flight of stairs.

"Who knew something like this was under the city." Paisley said in a hushed voice over the group call.

"This used to be the hub of the city." Victor told her.

Rafael stopped and turned to look at me. He motioned to the railing. I went over and looked down. It was a good vantage point.

He touched the ear bud he wore. Then reaching into his pocket, he pulled out a large carabiner on a strap. "I don't trust the railing." He clipped the one end to my belt, then grabbed one of the bars the railing was anchored to and yanked on it. When it didn't budge, he clipped the anchor end to it.

"We're in place at the main tunnel." Michael reported.

Rafael touched the ear bud again. "Give me a minute to get there." He touched my cheek. "Kara's in place." His eyes asked if I was okay.

I nodded.

Dropping his hand away he looked to Bart.

The large man nodded.

"No one will get near her." He said in a gruff way.

"On my way to you." I watched Rafael run down the set of stairs leading toward the tunnel.

"No one without the silver crest leaves the tunnel, Kara." Autumn's tone was even.

"Got it." I answered, watching Rafael disappear into the dark tunnel. I looked at the silver patch on my shoulder. It was a moon and sun and I was glad they'd come up with a way for me to know who was with us and who wasn't. Shooting another royal family member and rendering them unconscious probably wouldn't end well. .

"Elder Segos, we are entering at this end, now." Victor said quietly.

"As are we this one." The elder replied.

I glanced back to Bart he was checking both sides of the stairs. Giving me a nod, he moved over and looked down below us.

"What the..."

I frowned trying to figure out who had spoke.

"Are those mages?" That was Leone.

"Romulus, we have a situation." A voice I didn't know said.

"Situation?" That was Romulus.

"It is like a mage's convention down here."

I figured that must be the mage that was with our team.

"He's not kidding." Daxx said.

"What is wrong with their eyes? Shouldn't they be purple?" I recognized Quinton's voice.

"Hold. What color are they?" Romulus asked.

"Still purple, but with a white glow." Rafael informed him.

"Oh, damn."

"Oh damn?" Quinton asked

"Like I stepped in something, or oh gods that's really bad?" Chase asked

"The latter. They're probably low-level fledgling mages." Romulus said

"So good for us?" Daxx asked

"And they're channelling a more powerful mage, I was trying to add." Romulus sounded winded. "Each one you take out makes the remaining stronger."

"How is that fair?" Bethany asked.

"Change of plans cupid. We're going to need you and your stun arrows down here." Chase said. "You can take out more with your shots then we can with a sword."

I didn't pause to think or ask questions. "On my way." I unclipped the rigging and started for the stairs Rafael had taken. Bart ran alongside me.

"You are her second skin, Bart." Rafael said in a low tone, "or the only thing you'll ever guard again is the toilet at the guard house."

I looked up to see his brows furrow.

"Captain." Was all the large man beside me replied.

"Yeah, no pressure, Bart." Alona said.

Someone snorted into the mic.

"What are they doing? The mages?" Romulus asked.

"Fifteen in a circle facing outwards." The man answered. "One in the middle. Guards all around them."

"We'll deal with the guards." Michael said.

"Shit. Okay." Romulus sounded like he was struggling. "The middle one is the strongest, he'll be controlling the rest. You need to take him out."

"They are holding people here, but we can't get to them." I recognized Elder Drusla's voice. "They've warded it."

"Cowards." Someone hissed.

"This ward is replenishing with each layer I unravel." Romulus said. "You need to distract the puppet master."

"The what?" Quinton growled.

"The mage in the middle." Romulus answered with a strained voice.

"Right." Paisley said.

"Babe?"

"Arius if you tell me to go hide somewhere in a safe corner, I'm going to get cranky. Bethany and I are our best chance right now." Paisley said quickly.

I kept running through the dark tunnel I'd watched Rafael go into.

"I was going to say, see if you and Beth can distract the mages once we engage the guards." Arius said with amusement in his voice.

"Oh. Okay." Paisley answered.

Bart put his hand on my shoulder to slow me down. I saw the others crouched along a wall and moved slowly toward them. Rafael motioned for me to move beside him. I did quickly. When I reached him, I looked to where he pointed. Down a ramp there was a large opening and a circle of men with their hands held out like they were meditating, only they were standing with their glowing eyes wide open. A shiver ran down my spine.

"Why aren't there guards up here?" I asked and looked up at Rafael.

"That's a good question." Michael said.

"The mage is really struggling here, *family*." Emil's voice was in my ear. "Perhaps you could work on that distraction?"

Troy nodded. "As soon as Kara is ready, we'll rush when her arrows start flying."

Rafael moved over, so I was closest to the wall. "Can you kneel and still aim?" He asked. "You'll be less visible."

I nodded and got down on one knee. Setting my bow down, I took the case off my back and rested it against my knee. Picking up the bow, I pulled out an arrow and nocked it.

"Sixteen mages, twenty arrows." Daxx said. "You've got this, right?"

I nodded. "Say when." I raised the bow.

"Let us try to slip down the other side of the ramp. As soon as they see us, let them fly." Rafael said moving away from me.

I nodded again. There was no time to think or be nervous.

"Bart you stay with her." Chase said.

I heard blades clearing cases but didn't look away from the target I'd selected. Drawing the string back, I took aim and held. I was going to have to clear some of the mages in the outer ring to get to the one in the middle.

One of the guards below jumped, and looked up the ramp. I released the arrow. Grabbing another, I nocked it and had just enough time while I drew back to see the first man I'd hit was laying on the ground. I aimed at the next and released. He went down.

I could hear the clash of metal but didn't dare stop to see if everyone was all right.

I repeated the process three more times before the mages were on to me. The next arrow hit some sort of invisible barrier.

"They're on to me," I said to no one in particular.

"Find a new location." Daxx grunted.

I picked up the case and got up, moving to the other side of the tunnel. It was darker over here. Dropping down, I grabbed an arrow while trying to keep track of how many I had left. I took aim at one of the mages on the far side with their back to me, then released it. I hesitated long enough to see that it took him down.

"Romulus, our mage is laying unconscious on the floor." Quinton said.

I hit another and he dropped to the floor.

"Almost," Romulus paused, "it's down. How many are left?"

"Too many." Michael grunted into the mic.

My next shot hit another barrier. "I have to move again." I got up and ran halfway down the ramp, spotting a break in the wall. "Bart, stay low." I ducked into the crevice and looked out. Hooking the quiver on the clip at my waist, I grabbed an arrow, took aim and released. I ducked back into the hole in the wall hoping they wouldn't see me.

"He's down." Bart reported.

"I zapped one to the cells." Daxx reported. "Puppet master's strings will be broken there."

I hit another one.

"Alona!" Daxx said loud in my ear.

"Got him" Alona hissed out a breath.

"Criss, you and Bronx follow Michael to check out that tunnel." Daxx instructed.

"Okay." Crissy answered hurriedly.

My next two shots hit their barriers again. "Move back up." I told Bart. We ran quickly. If I could keep them guessing where I was, I might have enough arrows to finish the last six.

"Six left." Bethany said.

I managed to take out two more before one of my arrows completely vanished while in flight. "Five arrows left." I told them as Bart and I ran back to the hold in the wall. "Last one vanished." I added, so they would know what I was up against.

"We need backup." Michael said. "Eight guards in the tunnel heading to you."

I took a deep breath and exhaled slowly as I nocked the next arrow. Leaning out, I found a target and released it.

"He's down." Bart told me.

"Leone, behind you." Rafael barked.

I took the next shot and watched as we moved to see the mage go down.

"Beth, see if you can hit him." Paisley said.

"Trying. He's deflecting it." Bethany said breathlessly.

"Thanks, babe," Arius said.

"Back to work beast and watch your back this time." Paisley answered.

"Arius, there's a giant down here." Quinton sounded like he was running.

"On my way." Arius answered.

I tried to stay close to the wall and take out another, but the next two arrows vanished again. "Last arrow." I informed the others. Gritting my teeth, I let the last one fly and watching, hoping it hit. It did and he went down.

"We have women on their way out." Elder Drusla reported.

"One mage left." Paisley said in a strained voice.

"He'll be strong." Romulus told us.

"No shit." Daxx growled.

Now that I had no arrows, I slipped the quiver onto my back and slung my bow over my shoulder. The sound of metal on metal and grunting and scuffling registered in the earbud. I hadn't heard it when I was focused on shooting. I wasn't sure what to do, I had no skills in hand-to-hand fighting. I watched Autumn spin and kick a man in the head, he fell back. She hit him again, then punched him in the face.

Daxx's guard went flying to the ground. I saw her step in front of him and glare at the remaining mage. He'd done that without touching him. With a growl Daxx charged for the mage. Three men blocked her.

"They know magic doesn't work on me, they're blocking me. I can't get near him." She pulled out a second blade. Her guard was back on his feet right beside her.

I started running down the ramp, Bart right beside me, his sword held out in front of us.

The mage raised his hands again. I looked down at my wrist as I ran, wondering if it would help if I could hear him. Probably not, I decided. Bethany's red flashes arced off his darker ones. The whole area glowed orange. Freeing up my hands as I went, I adjusted the bow so it was well out of my way. If I timed it right, I could get there, and have one of my knives in my hand before he spotted me.

"He's doing something to deflect my freezing him." Paisley said with a growl. "I'm afraid if it bounces off whatever he's doing I'll hit one of you."

"Keep trying, babe. If you're not looking at us, it shouldn't take." Arius was out of breath.

"Ok, I hope you're right."

I ducked around a short wall, later I'd stop and freak out knowing I was underground, running into a fight.

"I can't keep him occupied much longer." Beth said sounded frantic.

"They're purposely keeping those of us with the port boxes away from him." Leone growled.

"I'm out of arrows, but if I get close enough, I can disable one of his hands." I ducked as I sped past Troy and a very large man trying to chop each other to bits.

"I'm not," Chase grunted, "opposed to you chopping off the hand, cupid."

I didn't want to chop off anything. I also didn't want to let him continue what he's doing. I slid on the damp surface, pulling the two knives out of the hidden pockets. The mage was still waving his hands around. I glanced quickly to Beth, she looked like she was in pain. I moved quickly along the wall, he turned and saw me just as I was about to throw the knife. The knife left my hand. I kept moving, hoping whatever he was doing, he couldn't do if I was running. A bright light flashed in front of my face. Something moved over me, and I fell forward.

My hands were freezing. Huffing out a breath, I blinked to clear my vision. My hands were in snow. I looked slowly around me. I was in snow. There was no snow in the tunnel. Getting to my feet, I turned every direction. As far as I could see there was nothing but snow. "Where the *fak* am I?"

Chapter Twenty-Nine

Opening my coat, I pulled out my phone and checked. I still had signal. I dialed back into the group as fast as my cold fingers could manage.

"What do you mean gone?" Rafael yelled into my earpiece.

"She just vanished." Bethany said, out of breath.

"I'm here." I said.

"Are you okay?" Paisley asked.

"I think…" I looked around me again. "I think so."

"Where is here?" Chase sounded like he was running.

"Uh, I'm not sure but I think I've been banished to," I looked in the other direction, "Canada?" I was trying to decide if I should start walking or stay where I was. I could see my breath in front of my face.

"What?" Rafael said.

I nodded, to myself.

"Why do you say Canada?" Daxx blew out a breath. "Is there a sign?"

I shook my head. "I'm standing in snow." I watched large flakes fall in front of my face. "It's snowing."

"Snow?" Michael asked in a quiet way.

"I've never seen snow outside my head." Crissy said quickly.

"It's white." I tucked the other blade back into the pocket. "How do I get back?"

"Use your porter. Open it and push the button." Victor said something else, but I didn't catch it.

I looked at my wrist. "Okay, hang on." I tucked my phone back into my pocket and lifted my cuff up. Opening the thing on my wrist I pushed the button. Nothing happened. I was still standing here getting snowed on. I pushed the other button. Same thing. "Nothing happened."

"That's not very encouraging." Alona sounded worried.

"I'll head to Michael's office." Rafael sounded like he was running.

"We'll clean up here." Quinton said.

"What good is going to Michael's office going to do?" Autumn asked.

"The tracking software is only installed on his system." Rafael answered.

"Tracking software?" Daxx said in an unamused way. "You put a tracker on her? I thought we'd…"

"A tracker has been placed in all of our porter bands." Victor said with no emotion at all. "including my own."

"Since when?" Leone asked.

"The new bands we gave out a few days ago." Chase said in a tone that sounded very much like a king's order.

"After what happened to Paisley," Arius said quickly, "we didn't want to take chances."

"I'm all for it." Leone agreed. "So, I don't have to look for shimmering magic dust again."

I frowned. "So, you can find me?" I was starting to shiver. The shock of being here was wearing off.

"Will you be alright until they do?" Alona asked.

"Do you see anything but snow?" Autumn wondered.

I turned and looked around, seeing past the snow falling in front of my face. "Some trees, but no buildings or anything else."

"Do you still have your knives?" I heard a door close as Chase spoke.

"I've got three." I did up my jacket as far as I could and put my hands in the pockets. "Did you get that mage?"

Someone chuckled. "Your knife in his hand stopped all incantations." Quinton told me. "Just not before the flash that hit you."

"Should we, I hate to say it," it was Emil, "be asking why there? Did he mean to send her there or was that portal his own escape and why?"

"Damn. He's right." Troy said.

"Troy and I will go to the cells and see why he sent her there." Arius said.

"The rest meet in Michael's office." Troy added.

"Would she be safer in the trees?" Paisley asked.

"Kara, turn off the inhibitor so you can hear any thoughts of anyone nearby." Alona suggested

"As a warning?" I started walking toward the trees, I was cold and hoped the movement would help.

"Yes. Find some sort of shelter and listen." Daxx said quickly, like she was in a hurry.

I shoved the cuff of my jacket up and pulled the glove down so I could hit the button. "I'm hoping I'm alone. I have no arrows and just three knives left." Looking all around to see if I was still alone, I moved in the direction of the trees again. "It's off. How long will it take to find me?" I rubbed my hands together. My gloves were designed for archery, not cold.

"That will depend on if any of the guys have been there, or close by, before." Daxx explained.

"Oh? They have to know somewhere to go there?" I checked behind me. So far, I wasn't hearing any thoughts.

"Yes." Autumn answered with no further explanation.

I stepped forward and sunk up to my knees in snow. The next three steps were the same. I looked back to where it had deepened as I moved away, now realizing I was walking down a slight slope. My jacket, as much as I loved it, wasn't very warm. "Good call on the extra padding, Rafael." I said as I tried to pull the sleeves down further, but Mitz had made it so sleeves didn't interfere with using my bow. I stopped, listening.

"It wasn't for the temperature." His voice was strained.

"I hear something." I stopped and looked all around me.

"Inside your head?" Chase asked quickly.

"No." I took a few more steps. "It sounds like a whine or a soft moan."

"I don't like the sound of that." Beth told me.

I kept walking, trying to ignore the bite of the snow on my legs. "I think it's an animal." Pausing, I listened with my mind to be sure. There were no thoughts to hear.

"Animal?" Alona asked. "Be careful."

Nodding to no one, I pulled one of the blades out of its hidden pocket. Cold steel on my skin was not going to help me warm up.

"It's going to take some time to get to you." Michael said, distractedly.

I stopped again. "You know where I am?"

"Yes." Rafael answered, "and you weren't far off on your guess."

"Really?" I tried to figure out which way the sound was coming from. Did I want to go toward or away from it? "How long is *some time*?" I started in the direction I thought the cry was coming from.

"We're trying to ascertain who has been closest to your location." Victor's clipped answer was the only response.

"That doesn't sound encouraging." I cocked my head to listen again. "Can we get the mage guy to send someone here?"

"We're still waiting on Troy and Arius to get information from him." Paisley said quietly.

"I'm sure the knife through his hand is somewhat distracting at the moment." Quinton sounded amused.

I winced. "Right." I stopped abruptly and stared at the ground in front of me. "There's blood on the snow."

"Blood?" Daxx asked. "How much blood?"

I followed it slowly, a knife ready in my hand. "Not a lot, but enough to leave a trail."

"Kara be careful. If it's an injured animal…"

"What kind of animal?" Crissy sounded breathless. "A cat. A big brown cat?"

"How big are we talking?" Emil pondered.

It was good that they were in my ear and I wasn't alone, but right now I needed to focus. "Less talk until I find out."

"Yes, she needs to be able to hear." Autumn said abruptly.

The line went silent. "It is smudges, not drops." I told them. I stopped when I saw brown fur in the snow a few feet ahead. I held my breath as I moved closer, hoping it wasn't too gory.

I crouched down and moved around, hoping not to surprise it. It cried again, then froze when it spotted me. It wasn't a large animal at all. "It's a cat." Its dark eyes were huge as it watched me. I crouched lower and held out my hand without the knife in it. "Hey, little guy." I crooned, "are you hurt?" It didn't move, so I crept closer. "It's okay." I stopped when it was still a foot out of my reach. "I'm not going to hurt you." I dropped to my knees, ignoring the cold and pulled my glove off. I stayed still with my hand out. It raised its face and sniffed. "It's okay." I said again softly. Low to the ground, dragging its belly in the snow, it moved a few inches closer. I couldn't see any blood coming from the red spots on its paws. "That's it. I have lots of time I'm told, we can take our time." It moved closer and smelled my hand. "See I'm perfectly harmless."

Someone snorted on the other end of my earpiece.

It was shaking as it moved closer. "It's okay." I smiled. "You're just a baby." I didn't know what sort of baby, but if I could get it to trust me, it would fit in my lap. It touched its nose against my hand. "There you go." I crooned. It inched closer. The blood was wiping off its paws. "I don't think the blood is from it." I said in the same soft tone over the mic. "I think maybe the mom was hurt, or worse."

"Just keep an eye out for a parent." Victor told me.

Moving my head slowly, I looked around. "I don't see or hear anything." I moved closer. I didn't move my hand. It needed to make the first move to trust me. I understood that. Slowly I reached my other hand behind me and tucked the knife in my back pocket.

It was close enough now that I could get a good look at most of its body. "I don't' see any injuries." I put my hand down on my knee and waited. Staying low, it came over and nudged my hand with its nose. I slowly touched its head. The dark blue eyes watched me carefully, but it didn't tense or move away. I ran my hand down over its head to rest on its shoulders. It didn't cringe.

I didn't rush it to move closer. It wasn't shying away from my hand, so I continued, while looking for any sort of injury. "Oh, I was wrong," I whispered, "you're not a little guy, you're a girl."

It took a step closer, rubbing against my hand as I pet her. "We're kind of out in the open right now." I scooped her up, pulling her into my lap. "Let's go over there and use those trees for shelter." I stood up slowly, hugging her against me firmly without making her feel trapped. She leaned into me and put her chin on my shoulder. "You're a solid little thing." I said softly. "We can use each other to stay warm."

"Okay, Kara, the guys have found a starting point to get to you." Daxx reported.

"Starting point?" The cat was generating enough heat to warm my hands.

"None of us have been *exactly* where you are, but Victor has been about five miles away. Unfortunately, it's far so a few ports are required." Daxx explained.

"I'm going to get Elder Arian to program a tracking program for a phone." Leone said.

"I'm getting blankets and a few supplies." Alona said.

I finally reached the trees. "Blankets are good." I told her. Most of the trees had no leaves, so they weren't going to offer much shelter. I saw a tall, I couldn't remember what it was called… "I'm going to go sit under a big tree, like a Christmas one to get out of the snowfall."

"How are you doing?" Rafael asked.

"Cold." I pushed my face closer to the cat. "The cat is warm though."

"Okay. Keep watch for other animals." He told me.

I ducked under the low branches, shivering as snow fell down the back of my neck. My bow got caught, so I had to back out and take it off. I did and tossed it under the tree, the quiver case too. "I will." I told him. The bottom branches were closer to the ground then I'd thought. "The branches on this tree have sheltered the ground, there's hardly any snow under it."

"We'll be there soon, cupid." Chase told me.

"You can't go, brother." Victor's voice cut in abruptly. "As Troy can not. We are going into a completely unknown situation. We can not put either of you at risk."

"He's right." Rafael said. "Nothing would weaken the realm more than to lose one of their kings before twins are born."

"Fine." Chase said. "I will help plan the trip to the asylum, that I'm allowed to go on."

"Thank you, brother." Victor said.

"Troy, anything from that mage?" Daxx asked.

"I'm afraid not. He was just a puppet, and has no memory of snow either." Troy said in an even tone.

"Lucky him," I rubbed the top of the cat's head, trying to keep her calm. To keep me calm.

"There was a small inn here." Victor said quietly.

"Can we rent a snowmobile of some sort of vehicle there?" Rafael asked.

"I believe so." Victor stated. "Heart, can you go get me some cash?"

"Here are some warmer jackets." Bethany said.

"Be there in five with the programmed phone." Leone reported.

"You can't wear them over the jacket, Raf." Michael sighed. "You shouldn't take them."

"Get me a bag." Rafael said. "We have no idea if this is a trap. I am not going in there unarmed."

"I'm inclined to agree." Victor responded.

"I brought the money." Crissy said.

"Thank you, heart."

I was shivering less, or it felt like it. "I keep hearing beeps." I looked around us.

"Check your phone battery." Paisley told me.

Shifting the cat, I undid my jacket and pulled out the phone. "Where do I look for battery?"

"Beside the signal lines. It will look like a cylinder." Paisley sounded distracted.

"It has a line on the bottom." I stared at the phone wondering if that was good or bad.

"You remember that little cube I gave you?" Bethany asked.

"Yes." I moved the phone to the hand I was cradling the cat with and reached into the pocket again and got out the cube. The cat was passed out

"There's a small tab on it, that's a short charger jack. Plug it into the bottom of the phone."

I nodded and followed Beth's instructions. "A lightening bolt just appeared on the battery symbol."

"Put them both back in your pocket. Cell phones do not the like the cold." Bethany said softly.

I put them in the pocket and zipped up my coat again. Shifting the cat, I cuddled it close.

"That gives her an hour." Bethany's voice waivered.

"We should be there by then." Victor snapped.

"Kara, we'll be off the phone while we're porting, but know that Victor and I are on our way." Rafael's voice showed his stress.

"Okay." I nodded to no one.

"Do you need anything else?" Paisley asked.

"I wouldn't say no to hot chocolate." I said half jokingly. "For the record, it's never boring with you guys."

Someone snorted. "We aim to entertain." Chase said solemnly.

"Here's the phone." Leone was out of breath.

"We're leaving now." Rafael told me. "See you soon."

"My face feels like it's burning." I hadn't meant to say it out loud.

"Movement helps warm you up." Paisley told me. "But she's sheltered from the snow where she is."

I pushed my face into the cat to borrow some warmth. Its fur was wet, but still generated heat. She smelled like the wild. I couldn't have described it if someone asked me to, I just knew that's what it smelled like.

"Eating creates body heat." Crissy said.

"That's great, Criss, but she can't run to the corner store and grab some snacks." Daxx told her.

I lifted my head. "That's why you gave me the protein bars." I said, "you knew this was going to happen." I leaned forward and felt for the zipper on the pouch. It was hard with gloves on and cold fingers, but I wasn't taking them off. I finally found it.

"Did you know, Crissy?" Bethany asked her.

"I didn't *know*, know. The pieces were all over the place." Crissy sounded distracted. "I knew it had something to do with Kara, I saw arrows." She mumbled for a moment. "And cold. I didn't see the snow."

I opened the bar and took a bite. It was dry and tasted strange, but I chewed it anyways. The cat lifted her head and looked at me. "You want a bite?" I held it out to her. She sniffed it, then leaned back with her nose scrunched up in an expression that looked like *eew*. "Not your kind of snack, huh?" I took another bit and chewed it slowly. "Should have sent a drink too, Crissy…"

"We have a situation." Victor's voice cut off what I was going to say.

"What's wrong?" Troy asked.

I realized then that all of there were there all the time, just not talking. They were doing this for me, so I wasn't alone. Maybe it was the protein bar, but my throat was suddenly too dry to swallow. Probably the bar.

"The inn is closed and boarded up." Victor said, again with no emotion in his voice at all.

"Shit." Leone said quietly.

"We are checking the out-buildings to see if some form of transportation has been left behind." Victor said, sounding preoccupied.

The bland substance in my mouth became drier. I forced myself to swallow it, then sat waiting. What if they couldn't get to me? How long would it take if they walked? Would be dark by then? I didn't know if I could sit in the dark. My body was already going numb from the cold. I hugged the cat closer to me. The day I'd met this royal family, I'd been thinking of leaving the city to live in the middle of nowhere in the wild. Fate had just shown me that was a bad idea.

"Is Raf on the call again?" Michael asked.

Victor cleared his throat. "No, I thought it best he focuses," there was a banging sound in the background, "his energy on gaining access to these buildings."

"We're looking at the map to see if there is anywhere else nearby, brother." Leone told him.

"Very good. I am going to mute my mic and assist Rafael with his task."

"We'll let you know." Leone said quickly.

"Kara, check your phone's battery level." Bethany said quietly.

I nodded and wrapped up the rest of the bar. Moving the cat away, it dawned on me how warm she was actually keeping me. Opening my coat, I took out the phone and little cube and looked at it. "The cylinder still has a lightening bolt on it."

"Okay. Unplug the cube and tell me what it looks like." Bethany's tone was calm and patient. I thought maybe it was too calm, like she was forcing herself to sound calm.

I did as instructed. "It's still just a line on the bottom of the cylinder symbol."

"Mm, okay, plug it back in."

I did an put it back in my pocket, along with the rest of the dry bar.

"The temperature must be affecting the charge." Paisley mused.

"Victor, how are you progressing?" Chase sounded like he was worried.

I hugged the cat and buried my face in her fur again. I'd never prayed before and wondered if I should try it now.

"We've located two snowmobiles," Victor said, "however, one starts but is low on fuel. The other has fuel but will not start." I could hear Rafael in the background but didn't know what he was saying. "Rafael is attempting to syphon the fuel from one to the other."

"Kara's phone isn't going to have power much longer." Paisley told him.

"Understood." Victor replied. "We do have an extra battery, but that won't be useful if we haven't located her." He was so calm. "Kara, describe to me where you are with details as precise as possible. Give us markers to look for."

I lifted my head. "I had to walk down to get to the trees, not a big hill, but enough that I sunk in the snow as the level of the ground changed." I closed my eyes. "There are lots of tall tress with no leaves and Christmas trees scattered throughout." I heard someone choking and coughing in the background. "Is Rafael all right?"

Victor cleared his throat, "Yes. Although he's not fond of the taste of gasoline. Pray that it has no water in it." He added.

The phone beeped in my ear. "I'm underneath a really big Christmas tree." I finished quickly in case the phone went dead.

"Very good. If you phone cuts out, listen for the sound of a snowmobile."

The phone beeped again. I nodded my head quickly, then straightened. "Wait, what does a snowmobile sound like?"

"A motorcycle crossed with a lawn mower." Emil supplied.

"Okay. Got it." A loud sound came through the ear bud, I winced.

"Like that." Victor said loudly. "We are on our way."

There was another beep in my ear. "Okay, I'll—" the background noise stopped. "Hello?" Nothing. "Hello?" My phone was dead.

It was eerily quiet now. Falling snow didn't make any sound. That was a fact that Crissy would probably know, I thought.

The cat stirred in my arms and looked up at me. "Help is on the way." I said softly. She butted my chin with the top of her head. It dawned on me that I couldn't leave her if they did find me. When. *When* they did find me. If her mother had survived, she would have come looking by now. I straightened my cramped legs and put her on them to look at her. Her eyes were huge. I ran my hands over her fur. "You're almost a golden brown or will be when we wash off the blood." She lay down and let me rub my hands over her some more. "You need a name." She suddenly tensed and dug her claws into my cold legs, which made me tense.

"It's okay." I picked her up and hugged her again. She was shaking. "What is it?" Her ear twitched. "What do you hear?" I listened. Shifting her more, I made sure I had access to the knives in my jacket, just in case. That's when I heard a motor echoing in the distance.

I struggled to get out from under the tree, which was harder then going in now with cold, stiff muscles. Bent over while holding a scared cat, I tossed my bow and quiver out from under the tree turned out to be a feat that tested all my skills.

Finally, I got out and stood up. I didn't hear the motor any more. Squeezing my eyes shut, I exhaled slowly. I wasn't going to panic.

It felt like I was dragging both legs as I walked out of the trees. When we cleared them, I looked up the incline to see two larger than life men, all in black looking down at me.

I grinned.

Rafael started running to me. He had no issues clearing the deeper snow with his height. Victor wasn't running, but he wasn't taking his time either. He carried a large bag with him.

The cat tensed in my arms as Rafael got closer. "It's okay. He's here to rescue us."

Reaching me, he wrapped a blanket around me and grasped my shoulders, looking me over. "Are you okay?"

I nodded, "Cold but okay. Now." He hugged me into his chest. I was surprised the cat didn't even object. I blew out a breath of relief, then inhaled. Stepping back, I gave him a look. "You smell like gas."

His expression changed. "Yeah. Syphoning fuel is harder than I thought."

Victor reached us. He touched the ear bud. "We have her and she appears to be unscathed." He nodded. "Yes, one moment." Setting down the bag, he reached into his pocket and held something out to Rafael.

Rafael took it and sighed. "Let me see your phone. If the girls don't get to hear your voice, they're going to melt down."

Shifting the cat, I opened my jacket and took out the phone and held it out to him.

Victor's lips twitched. Pulling another bag off his shoulder he reached in and pulled out a bottle of water.

I hadn't realized I was thirsty until I saw it. I held out my hand. He uncapped it and handed it to me. I looked from him to Rafael. "You guys look huge in those big jackets."

Rafael glanced at me as he put my phone back together. "We didn't have time to go shopping."

I grinned. "Does this sort of thing happen often? Because I think I need to upgrade my boots to something warmer. I can't feel my feet."

He tapped the screen, then tucked it into his pocket. Touching the ear piece, he watched me. "She's on now."

"Kara?" It was Paisley.

I felt relief again for the second time. "I'm here."

"Thank the gods." Chase said.

"We're just hydrating her, then we'll head back." Victor said. "We should be able to do it in one port if Rafael and I both think the same destination."

"You should catch your breath, Vic, that's further than it was getting to her." Crissy told him.

I took another drink while giving Rafael a look to ask what she was talking about.

He shook his head.

"Your concern is heartwarming, Cristy, I will be fine."

The whole time they were talking, Victor was looking all around.

Rafael took a drink, then frowned and reached over to tilt my chin to the side. "You have blood on your face."

"I do? Oh. It's not mine," I moved the blanket so the cats tawny face was visible. Tawny. I smiled.

"Whose blood is it?" Daxx asked.

Victor stopped moving and stood there. "I believe it is the mountain lion cub's blood."

I shook my head. "No, Tawny isn't hurt. It wasn't her blood."

"Tawny?" Leone asked in a strained voice.

"Oh gods, she named it." Troy whispered.

"Can animals port?" I looked from Rafael to Victor.

Victor glanced at his brother. "Smaller ones, yes. However larger animals do not react well."

"You're bringing it back?" Quinton asked.

I nodded. "If it had a living parent, I would have met it by now." I looked up at Rafael, he had hand hands on his hips and was looking at the cat.

"It's a wild animal, it will..."

I cut Michael off. "Yes it's a wild animal with *no* parents that now has the scent of human all over her. If she doesn't starve or freeze, she will be killed because *I held her.*"

"Michael, she has to bring it back." Autumn said. "Leaving it behind is the same as me on the streets at six."

"Shit." Michael hissed out a breath.

"She's right." Crissy said, "Kara, well, Autumn too."

Rafael and Victor exchanged a look.

I wrapped the blanket around both of us and looked up at Rafael.

His gaze held my stare for a few seconds. Taking a deep breath, he exhaled and moved closer, giving Tawny's head a little scratch. "Tawny, huh?"

I nodded.

Turning he looked at Victor again.

Victor smirked. "Michael, locate the veterinarian we use and someone that knows about large-breed cats. Bring them to the lower courtyard."

"On it." Michael said.

"I'll go find the vet." Leone offered.

"Find out what they eat when young." Rafael added.

I squatted down and set her on the ground, then poured a bit of water in the palm of my hand, offering it to her. Tawny sniffed it, then lapped it out of my hand.

"Yay!" Bethany squealed. "We get to have a cat at the palace. I've never had a pet."

Victor shook his head. "The *cat* will likely be a hundred pounds once grown."

"So, she'll be like a dog, but not." Autumn said.

"I've always wanted a pet." Crissy sounded breathless.

Victor closed his eyes, and took a deep breath. "We'll be there shortly."

"I can't wait to meet Tawny." Alona said. "Pets were never doable having to stay hidden and on the move."

"We'll see you at the lower courtyard." Chase added abruptly.

Victor picked up the large bag.

Rafael squatted down. "I'll hold her in case she freaks out when we port. This coat offers more protection from claws." He ran his hand over her lightly. She turned and looked up at him. "Come on, Tawny, lets get you back and checked over." His tone was gentle and persuasive. She went right over to him. He picked her up and held her securely in one arm. Tawny stretched up and rubbed her head under his chin.

I couldn't help but smile when I stood up.

Victor picked up my bow and quiver.

"Let me guess," Quinton said, "Raf just charmed a mountain lion?"

Rafael grinned as he wrapped his arm around me.

"It would seem so." Victor stated, then put his hand on Rafael's shoulder. "Lower courtyard, in front of Kara's furthest target." He looked at Rafael.

Rafael nodded.

"In three," Victor said, "two, one…"

My head filled with white noise, but I ignored it. When Tawny hissed and leapt from Rafael's hold, I dropped onto the ground beside her. She was hunched, breathing fast. I put my hand out. "That is the worst part." I told her. She made a soft chirping sound and came over to me. I scooped her up and set her on my lap.

Rafael picked up the blanket and wrapped it around my shoulders. He squatted down beside me. "You should go have a bath and warm up, then eat."

I nodded. "I will when they get here to look at her."

Resting an arm on his knee, he looked up to Victor.

Victor smirked. "I'm going to put our gear in the armory and check in at the cells."

Rafael nodded. Then looked back at me. "Turn on your blocker."

I looked at him to see him motion with his chin. I turned to see Crissy running toward us, with the others following her.

I pushed the button on my bracelet and looked back to him. "You should go wash off the gas."

"I'll wait." He stood up as the others reached us.

"Oh my gosh, she's adorable." Bethany fell to her knees and put her hand out to Tawny.

Crissy sat down beside me, smiling. "Her ears are so cute."

"Look at those eyes, she's gorgeous." Autumn sat down as well.

Leone and Rafael exchanged a look. "The vet will be here shortly." He watched Bethany pet the cat. "Some wild animal expert too." He added.

Rafael took off the heavy jacket and tossed it to Leone. With a sigh, he squatted down and scooped Tawny up, then held his hand out to me. "Come on, we'll go up to the courtyard and get you some hot chocolate."

I looked at him and smiled. This big tough man standing there holding a cat cradled in one arm while offering me hot chocolate. I nodded. "Okay."

Michael stood there with his arms crossed over his chest grinning at Rafael.

"Shut up." Rafael said with a smirk as we walked by him.

I was cold and still in the wet clothes and blanket as I sat there watching the two men examine Tawny.

"What's the verdict, doc?" Autumn looked impatient as she stood close by watching them with the cat.

I honestly believe she would have kicked them in the head if Tawny had displayed and signs of being distressed. The vet came over and handed Tawny to me.

"She's in good health for such a young cub in winter. She's little dehydrated and underfed, so I'm gong to send over some drops to add to her water to give her a bit of a nutritional boost."

Tawny started purring, which made me look at her. I had no idea wild cats did that. I'd have to look up more information about her. I looked back up at the man.

"She's between two and three months, I'm thinking closer to three though. Her eyes are still blue and won't change until around five months…"

"Her eyes change?" Bethany asked.

He nodded. "They'll turn an amber shade."

"But she's the right size for that age?" Daxx asked.

"That's hard to say without knowing the size of the litter. Obviously the more kits, the more the mother has to feed, so they're smaller until they hunt on their own." He jerked his chin toward Tawny, "she probably doesn't hunt yet, and would have been taken to kills to feed if the mother didn't drag it back."

Daxx nodded. "So, we have to feed her now? What do we feed her?"

"Raw meat mostly. If you're going to try some manufactured kibble, it will need to be introduced gradually."

"But meat is what she's used to eating?" I asked.

He nodded.

"Then we'll feed her meat." Autumn said.

"Does she still need milk?" Bethany sat beside me and looked at the cat.

He shook his head. "It's doubtful at this age. She would have been weaned around six weeks." He turned and looked at Troy who had stood back observing this whole time. "We have pens and are better equipped for large…"

I jumped up. "You want to lock her up?" I glared at him, then looked to Rafael and shook my head.

"She'll need room to run." Again, the man turned to look at Troy.

"Then we'll give her room to run." Autumn told him, then crossed her arms over her chest and glared at him.

Michael turned his head slowly from Autumn to look at the man. "I don't believe the animal will be going with you."

I looked at Rafael.

He sighed. "She'll be living at the palace. There's plenty of room to run out here." He motioned over his shoulder.

The man bowed his head slightly. "Call me if you have any questions."

Leone nodded and motioned to the door of the solarium. The vet and the man that wanted to cage Tawny walked away with him.

Mitz came out carrying a small metal bowl. "I'll go get her a water dish in a moment. I brought her some of the meat I'm cooking for dinner, the pre-cooked version of course." She set the dish on the ground.

I knelt and put Tawny on the ground. It didn't take her long to find the meat and grab a piece. She shook her head with it clamped between her teeth, then crouched down to eat it.

"I wasn't sure how small to cut it." Mitz said.

We all stood there watching her eat.

"I'd say that's about the right size." Troy nodded, then looked at his brothers. "We could use a hand in the cells."

Rafael smirked. "Let me go scrub off some of this gas and I'll be there."

I looked up, having completely forgotten how the day had begun. "Do you need my help?" I looked at Troy. "Do any of those mages know anything?"

Troy shook his head. "Not so far, I'll let you know if we need you to listen."

"First she needs a hot bath and something to eat." Mitz interjected in a way that didn't allow for objections or complaint.

"Go." Autumn said, "we'll keep an eye on her until you come back."

Chapter Thirty

I read the message from Autumn and smiled. Tawny was passed out on the blanket I'd used. That made me feel better. I'd worried while soaking in the warm water that she wouldn't be happy here.

I looked down at the brand-new pair of boots sitting at the end of my bed. They were almost identical to my worn, wet ones, only better. I put my foot in one. Perfect fit, maybe even better then the others. How did Mitz know my size every time? I couldn't even tell anyone my sizes, even if they asked me.

I was doing up the second boot when someone knocked on the door. "Come in." I called out, then stared at the floor. Having the freedom to welcome someone in was an odd feeling for me.

"Kara?"

I blinked and looked up at Rafael. "Sorry, lost in thought."

"As long as it's just thoughts and not a place." He gave me a brief smile, then held up his hand. "Brought you a new port device." He frowned. "We want to run some tests on the other one and see why it didn't work. It could be that the energy from the flash messed it up, but that doesn't explain why it didn't affect your phone."

I got up and took it. "Does this one have a tracker in it?"

He looked at me, then nodded.

"Good. In case I end up being sent to the great white wilderness again." I put it on. "You know, before today I always thought the best place for me was in the middle of nowhere, with no people." I put my hands on my hips and shook my head. "I'm not so sure about that now."

He nodded slowly. "I can understand your need for isolation." Looking at the dresser, he went over and picked up my bracelet. "I hope with this you will reconsider that."

I looked up at him as he took my arm and put the bracelet on. He didn't release it afterward, just stood there holding my hand, a serious look on his face. "It doesn't bother me that you might hear what I'm thinking now." He gave me small smile. "You know my failings," he shrugged, "the rest doesn't seem to matter."

"Your failings?" I quirked and eyebrow at him, "Is hearing thoughts *my* failing?"

Rafael frowned down at me. "No."

"Then how are your visions yours?"

"Mine aren't useful…"

"How do you know? Have you ever tried to put them to use?"

Releasing my hand, he shook his head and paced over to the dresser. "I did years ago, but I was never right."

He stood there, his back to me. I could feel the tingle of his thoughts but wanted to figure out what he meant without hearing what was in his head. Pushing the button, I blocked my telepathy. "I think if you tried to learn how to work with them, you wouldn't spend so much energy trying to control them—or so I'm told."

He glanced over his shoulder at me.

I smirked.

"Is that what they've told you to do?"

"More or less. Its great advice I'm sure, but unless they've lived it," I shrugged, "I follow Izzy's suggestions." I bit my lip, hoping for an idea that would help him. "Is there an elder that might know more about visions?"

Turning, he leaned against the dressed. "Elder Faran." He grinned, "but understanding what she says is a challenge."

I thought back to her cryptic addition to the last meeting. "Yeah I noticed. Although knowing now that she has visions explains a lot. I don't understand Crissy half the time."

He snorted. "She's not too bad once you figure out her tone, when she's mumbling or really abrupt, its usually something inside her head and doesn't realize she's saying it out loud."

"Oh." I nodded, "that does make it easier." I cleared my throat. "Thank you for finding me today."

He stood there, his gaze locked on me. "I've never been that scared before in my life. When you vanished, those few minutes before you called, felt like a hundred years." His expression lightened. "I will always find you." Turning his head, he picked up his necklace and pendant. Turing it over, he held it up. "I had this bow and arrow added to the back of my amulet roughly eighty years ago."

Eighty years ago. I looked at it, I hadn't really noticed it before.

He tapped the larger one on his chest. "It's on this one too." Straightening, he stepped toward me slowly. "Knowing you were out there, somewhere, got me through some bad times. I didn't work hard just to prove to myself to my brothers." He opened the clasp on the chain. "I wanted to be worthy of my mate when she got here." Reaching around me, he placed it around my neck.

"I thought," I inhaled, noting how good he smelled, "I thought you didn't want this mate stuff."

Clasping it, he straightened up and looked down at me. "I don't think it's a good idea for me right now, but sometimes we don't get a choice in life." He shrugged, "and what do I know, I'm just a man." He winked at me.

Smiling, I touched the cool pendant lying against my skin.

"Just wear it." He said softly. "It will stop questions and," he looked at it, "it keeps the part of me that I'm struggling to control happy, well mostly."

I frowned, "the part of you?"

He nodded briefly, then touched the back of his hand against my cheek. "Yes. Being near my mate without claiming her is a challenge." He smiled, but his eyes were still serious. "I'm starting to understand some of the strange behavior from my brothers as of late," he didn't grin this time, "don't tell them that though."

"I don't understand." My voice was barely more than a whisper. "I mean, I get this funny feeling when I'm near you, kind of a breathless and dizzy—"

He tilted his head and gave me an amused look. "Breathless, dizzy feeling?" The expression on his face changed, to something more heated and intimate. "You need to keep things like that to yourself, princess. I have a hard enough time keeping my hands off you without knowing how I affect you."

My breath froze in my chest from his words.

His whole demeanor changed again. "We should go get some lunch before it's gone." Leaning down, he kissed me on the mouth softly, then straightened up and motioned to the door.

I hadn't realized how hungry I was until I sat down to eat. I looked at the half empty plate in front of me. That had never happened since I left the asylum-I was always aware of my own hunger.

Alona leaned closer. "it's a nice feeling isn't it? Not worrying about your next meal." She understood.

"Yes." I said softly.

Autumn jumped up and went to the door. She opened it and looked down at Tawny. "Need some help little one?" She reached down and picked up the bulk of the blanket Tawny was trying to drag along with her.

Without pausing, the animal ran toward me, dragging the blanket still in her mouth. When she reached me, I squatted down to her level. She dropped the blanket and came over, rubbing against my hand. "You're adapting quickly." I looked up to see all conversations in the room had stopped and they were watching me.

Getting up, I picked up the blanket and put it under the large plant, almost a tree that was behind the table. Tawny followed me and jumped on the blanket. I bunched it up and she laid down and curled up in a ball.

"I've just had the perfect idea." Alona said with a smile. "You should take the suite on the main floor, just on the other side of the lobby. It has a small anteroom that leads out into an enclosed yard."

I got back up, noticing Tawny watched me, but didn't move. I sat back in the chair.

"There's a bathroom as well." Alona continued, "the smaller room could be Tawny's domain with easy access to outside."

I looked from her to Chase, "would that be okay?"

She waved her hand. "Of course, it is." She nodded. "I'll have the men move your things down." She grinned. "The family in charge of storage and moving have been bored for years, they're quite happy to rearrange furniture all day long."

"Instead of moving the furniture in the room down, let Kara select her own." Rafael said.

I looked across the table at him.

"Even better." Alona looked excited. "Another room for me to help decorate.

Chase laughed. "When you run out, we'll build some more." Turning he looked at Troy. "Speaking of bored staff, I've had a request to move the date of our annual meeting with the family accountant." He smirked, "or actually his grandson, who is taking over the position. Which I'm very thankful for, as his grandfather still refers to it as the royal coffers." He grinned.

Troy set his fork down and pushed his plate back. "I saw the request in the thirty seconds I've gotten to spend in my office." He frowned, "Is there a problem?"

Chase grinned, "It seems there's many," he waved his fork around, "obsolete positions we've been paying a monthly retainer for since—well, since we were born."

"What positions? Victor asked.

Chase nodded, "things such as drapery flockers." He smiled. "I had to look that one up. They flock our draperies to make them look fuller and plush." He set his fork down and pushed his plate to the side. "My question is, since there isn't a need for draperies in the underground chambers, what have they been flocking for the last two hundred and sixty years?" He smirked.

Troy shook his head, smiling, "that's a flocking good question." He sighed, then rubbed a hand over his forehead. "I guess we better set up a meeting." He looked at Chase again, "why would the accountant not bring this up in the last two hundred and sixty years?"

"We should have Mitz attend." Victor stated, "perhaps all of us." He glanced from one king to the other, "while I don't wish to remove anyone's income, we could perhaps come up with more pertinent positions for some of the obsolete jobs."

Troy nodded. "That's a good idea."

Daxx gave Victor a serious look. "We need to find assistants or secretaries or something. Troy's desk is filled with garbage most of the time." She looked at Alona, "someone could be going through that and creating a summary of pertinent information."

Alona nodded. "I agree." She smirked at Chase, "I don't know how they've managed all these years without one."

Chase gave her a daring grin. "We had nothing *but* free time prior to the arrival of all you lovely ladies—and all hell breaking loose with Willis and his maniacal schemes."

"Perhaps," Emil looked around, "Rena could be of assistance when she comes over." He shrugged, "she's been coordinating our moves, relocations and all the details for years. Its not an easy task keeping the four of us invisible."

Autumn looked at Michael, "it would give her something to do, and we can trust her."

Michael nodded and looked at Troy. "I feel like a lot of issues we're facing with Willis wouldn't have gone unnoticed this long if we had one person managing information instead of each of us knowing only pieces."

Troy sighed and looked at Chase. "He has a point. Father's systems are so outdated..."

Chase nodded. "Yes. We could find her a team of her own to help sort out the realm."

"It is amazing you men have managed this long." Paisley smirked, then motioned to Bethany and Daxx, "all of us need some sort of position or task." She looked at Arius, "once we've caught Hubert and shut him down." She smiled at Leone, "Alterealm's DJ isn't exactly a position that merits a lot of attention, or time."

Arius looked at Victor. "I know I could use help in the cells, aside from the guards, the data collected is growing and becoming overbearing to process.

Victor studied him for a moment, then gave a slight nod and turned to Troy.

Troy nodded. "The meeting could be a long one. Set it up for next week and let everyone know when." He rubbed two fingers over the bridge of his nose. "This week is already booked."

Chase shrugged, "but we're closing in on them."

"I hope that is a fact, brother." Troy said quietly.

Michael looked at me. "Before I forget, again, there is no record of the family name Coffey in Alterealm. So that's a dead end there."

I'd forgotten they were looking for my family. "That's okay." I offered him an easy smile.

"We'll find your file when we go to the facility." Rafael told me.

"How is the planning for that going?" Arius asked.

Michael motioned to Emil. "Our brother has been working with some of our contacts over there to set it up."

Everyone turned and looked at Emil. He set his glass down. "We're setting it up so it will be peaceful." His gaze stopped on me, "we can't storm in there and take over," he shrugged and turned to Rafael, "some residents actually *need* to be there."

"So how are we going in?" Quinton asked.

"We'll be going in under the guise of transferring some patients out. Our contact has relatives that marry-mated into Alterealm blood, in fact he is often over here to see his sisters, so he's helping to arrange things. He'll be able to go over each resident and their file with us there."

"That's not as much fun as kicking ass, but if we can get Kara some answers and some of our people out," Daxx shrugged, "I can play nice." She frowned at Troy, who was giving her an odd look and smiling, "what?"

"That's the first time you've said our people in reference to those from *this* realm."

She gave him a blank look, then shrugged it off, "And?" She huffed out a breath. "Don't get all mushy about it." Turning back to Emil, "when are we going?"

Emil stopped smiling, "I'll know more by this evening."

Leone leaned forward and picked up Beth's hand and kissed it. "I, for one, look forward to stopping Willis and Arwan *and* letting the girls get us organized."

Rafael nodded. "Yeah, the last fifty years have been hard."

"Hard how?" Daxx asked.

Rafael looked at him. "Other than running the whole guard, being the youngest of—them isn't easy."

"Oh-you've had it hard?" Quinton snorted.

"Living you with you guys is hard." Rafael said and looked to Leone for backup.

"How?" Arius crossed his arms over his chest.

"The pranks and jabs go beyond…"

"Like what? We've never been unfair." Quinton said.

"No? You putting the hair remover in my conditioner?" Rafael glared at him.

Quinton grinned. "Wasn't me."

"Dammit." Rafael shook his head and continued to look at him.

"Keep trying, another twenty years or so and you might figure it out." Chase said with a grin.

Leone rubbed his brush cut. "There's a reason I keep my hair this short."

Rafael looked at me. "I could ask Kara to help."

"Me? I didn't do it." I was trying not to smile.

"No. You could listen in and see which one did though."

I tilted my head and looked at him. "Wouldn't that be cheating? Breaking some brotherly code?"

"Only code we have is no one messes with our siblings—there's nothing about messing with each other."

Alona waved her hand around, glaring. "I'm saying this once—anyone messes with my toiletry items or Chase's hair and they will suffer my wrath."

Beth nodded. "What she said."

"I will freeze you for all eternity if one of you so much as cause a split end on Arius' gorgeous hair." Paisley scowled at the men closest to her.

Clearing his throat, Troy stood up. "I need to get back to the cells and poke around in a few heads."

"I'm heading there too." Arius stood up.

All of the brothers except Quinton, Emil and Victor mumbled some excuse and rushed from the room.

"No guilt here." Quinton said, then raised he glass and toasted to Victor. "I'd say the ones that bailed worked together to rid you of your pretty mane of hair."

Rafael studied him for a minute. "I will find out."

Alona laughed softly and waved her hand at him. "Go find some sort of royal task to do, we ladies need to help Kara furniture shop."

"I'm out." Quinton stood up.

Chapter Thirty-One

Bethany and I sat on the little stone patio outside my new room.

"This will be a great spot to relax after you have your furniture." She grinned at me.

We were sitting on the stones. I nodded, then looked back inside the door. "I can't believe the size of the room." I gave her a wide-eyed look. "My room, when I had one, was not even as big as the bathroom."

She chuckled. "Erin and I used to rent a one-and-a-half-bedroom apartment, Tawny's room is the size the whole apartment was."

"Half bedroom?"

"Don't ask." She shook her head, then turned back to watch Tawny chasing a grasshopper.

"I feel like I went overboard with the furniture I picked." Tawny pounced again, missing the insect once more.

"Don't. I've been to the storage warehouse and there are miles of furniture." She grinned, "like enough that we could change the furniture every week for a year and never see the same pieces twice."

"Why do they have so much?" My phone buzzed in my pocket. I took it out and looked at it.

Bethany pulled out hers. "I have no idea. I don't understand palaces and royalty. I lived in an abandoned building and foster care most of my life." She smiled. "Looks like we're going to where you used to live tomorrow."

I studied the message. *Trip to the asylum in the morning. More details at dinner.* I was conflicted about going back there. I didn't want to, but if those I'd heard for years were trapped, I wanted to help free them.

"You can probably pass on going over, no one will blame you."

I looked at her, then turned to see where Tawny had pounced off to. "I feel like I need to be there." I couldn't see her. Standing up, I brushed off my pants. "Face my demons from the past sort of thing."

She got up as well. "I get that." She looked around. "Maybe she's in those shrubs?" She pointed to the far side of the yard.

"She's been chasing that grasshopper since we came out." I started walking toward them.

"Guess she needs to practice her hunting skills."

I looked at her. "Do we want her to hunt?"

Beth shrugged, "I don't know, but it's a preprogramed instinct I would imagine."

I moved to the opposite end of the foliage, trying to look into it. "Tawny, where did you go?" I paused, then pushed my way in. On the other side of it was a hole in the stone wall, just big enough she'd be able to fit through. "Oh no." I wedged myself between the sharp branches and dropped down on my knees to look out it. I caught a glimpse of brown running through the grass.

I looked up at Beth. "What's on the other side of this wall?"

Beth shook her head. "I have no idea." She pulled out her phone and helped hold the branches for me.

I started for the large gate at the other end of the yard.

Bethany ran along beside me. "Leone, Tawny got out through a hole in the wall."

We reached the gate and it took both of us to pull the large bolts back to open it.

"Okay. No. We'll grab her before she gets too far and come right back." Bethany put the phone in her pocket. "Leone's sending Mac and Bart. We're not supposed to go outside without them."

I heaved on the gate, it was heavy and opened slowly. "I'm not used to that." We went out and started along the wall. "She will be lost before they get here."

Beth nodded as she jogged alongside me. "Look." She pointed.

Tawny bounced in the air, heading toward the trees.

"Maybe we should get her a collar with her own tracker."

I started running. "We may need to."

"We're outside the warded area." Beth said catching up to me. "I just felt it as we passed through."

Later, I'd have to find out more about these barriers and wards. Right now, I was too frantic to retrieve the animal I'd already rescued once today.

We ran into the tree, then stopped. Two men were there. One of them had Tawny and she was struggling against his hold.

"Oh, good." Beth huffed out a breath.

I looked at one man, then the other, neither had the silver crests anywhere I could see, so they were not guards. I put my hand out to stop Beth from going any closer.

"Two princesses, this must be our lucky day." The man not holding Tawny said.

Beth stiffened beside me and held her hands out from her body.

The man with Tawny grunted, then grabbed her by the scruff of the neck and held her out from him. I knew parents carried their cubs that way, but Tawny was still struggling and wasn't happy.

"I apologize for not knowing your names, your highnesses," he bowed his head, "but I can see from your amulets you're mated to our Enforcer and The Captain of the Guards." He grinned. "How fortunate for us."

"What do you want?" Bethany raised one of her hands and held it there.

I realized she was waiting for an opportunity to use her magic. She was glaring at the man holding Tawny.

"A simple exchange." The man pulled out a small gun and pointed it at us. "We'd hoped for a prince, but two princesses mated to royal brothers will allow us much more bargaining power."

My FOS was off the charts. I was cursing myself for not putting my new jacket back on. My knives were around my ankles and not easy to reach.

The man suddenly dropped Tawny. She took off into the trees.

"Why did you do that?" The man with the gun sounded annoyed.

"I don't—I don't know." The other one looked confused.

"Ah," he waved the gun at us, "one of you is the witch." He grinned. "You won't be able to bewitch me so easily."

Beth raised her hand, bright sparks arced off it. "Okay." She gave him a steady look.

I stood there feeling helpless. A feeling I didn't do well with.

The other man snapped out of it and pulled a blade from behind his back. It made mine look like baby knives in comparison. Everything happened so fast it was a blur.

Bethany flung a ball of light at the one holding the gun. He stumbled back.

I dropped down to get my knives and heard the gun firing and felt my side sting. Grabbing two knives, I threw one at the man with the blade as he lunged at Beth. It hit him in the thigh. Dropping to one knee, he howled in pain.

Bethany flung both hands above her head, then dropped them toward the man with the gun. It hit him, sending him flying backwards. The gun fired again. I didn't have time to pause, I pulled out   the other knife as I threw the one in my hand. Hitting the man holding the blade in the shoulder. He dropped his weapon and cried out again.

Out of nowhere Rafael and Leone appeared. Quinton and our two guards also stood in front of us. Mac and Bart lunged at the man with two of my knives sticking out of him as Quinton went after the other who tried to run. He didn't get five feet when Quinton tackled him to the ground.

I looked over to see Beth holding her shoulder as Rafael dropped down beside me.

Leone ran to Bethany.

"I've been shot." She said breathlessly, holding her hand over her shoulder.

"Let me see." Leone moved her hand.

Rafael was on his knees beside me, he looked down, then his eyes went wide with fear.

That's when the pain in my side registered. I looked down to see blood staining my shirt.

"How bad?" Rafael bent over and pulled up my shirt. He hissed out a breath and pressed his hand against my side.

Michael and Autumn appeared out of nowhere.

"Autumn, Tawny took off into the trees." I pointed.

She paused to assess the situation and then nodded and ran in the direction I said Tawny had gone.

Michael held a box up to the man with our guards. He vanished.

Quinton dragged the other man over, then Michael made him disappear too.

I was feeling lightheaded as Rafael pulled me into his arms

"Michael, call the doc, get him to my room. Kara's been shot and I don't see an exit wound." Rafael shifted me so he could carry me and hold his hand against my side.

Leone stood up with Bethany in his arms. "Beth too, but it just grazed her."

"Shot?" Quinton looked at me. "With a gun?"

I nodded, then rested my head on Rafael's shoulder.

"Cowards." He turned around looking at the ground looking for the gun.

Michael pulled out his phone and started after Autumn. The guards followed him.

"Hold on." Rafael said as he stood up.

My head filled with white noise, then I found myself on a bed with Rafael still holding me.

Daxx came bursting through the door. "Quinton called me." She rushed into the bathroom. "How bad is it?"

Rafael lay me down, then knelt over me. He grabbed my shirt and ripped it open.

Daxx came back out of the bathroom with towels and crawled across the bed. She handed Rafael a towel, then started wiping my waist off.

"No exit. Shit." He looked at the door. "Where the hell's the doctor?" He pushed the towel against my side hard.

I groaned.

"Sorry, honey." He leaned down and kissed my forehead. "Have to slow the bleeding until the doctor gets here."

"I know giving her blood is bad because we don't want to heal it with the bullet still in there," Daxx looked at Rafael, "but you could slow it with your saliva."

"Don't." A man came running through the door.

"Hurry up, Doc." Daxx said moving out of the way.

Mitz and Alona came running in with another woman I didn't know.

"Start an IV?" The woman asked.

The doctor nodded as he looked at my side. He pushed against my side and I yelped.

Rafael growled.

"Brother, contain yourself and let him do what needs to be done." Chase stood in the door.

Rafael gave him a hard look.

I turned to see the women with an IV needle in her hand. I tensed.

"Hey," Rafael gently turned my face so I was looking at him, "It's okay. Look at me." He said softly.

"Little poke." The woman said.

I clenched my teeth as she pierced my skin.

"That's it." Rafael whispered and kissed my forehead.

"I'm going to have to take the bullet out." The doctor said. "I don't think it's deep, we could transport…"

"Do it here." Rafael said in a deep tone. "Then I'll heal her."

"Very well. If someone could port Miss Rule back to get what I'll need." The doctor held a towel over my side.

"I'll take her." Daxx got off the bed.

I closed my eyes, feeling tired.

"The fluids will help with the blood loss." The doctor sat on the bed, still holding the towel on my side. "I'd like to administer a sedative until I'm finished, so she's not fully awake."

My eyes popped open.

Rafael put his forehead against mine. "I'll be here the whole time." He whispered.

"Tawny is in her room." Autumn same running in, Michael right behind her. "Bart and Mac are repairing the wall."

I felt better knowing Tawny was okay. I looked at Rafael and nodded. "Do it."

He kissed my forehead, then turned and nodded to the doctor.

"I'll be right here." He whispered and kissed me again.

Chapter Thirty-Two

"Kara?"

I heard Rafael and struggled to get my heavy eyelids to open.

"Come on, honey, open your eyes." He coaxed.

I managed it and looked into his worried blue eyes.

"Hey, there you are. How do you feel?"

I closed my eyes again. "Foggy." I whispered, then tried to lick my dry lips with a pasty tongue.

"Get her a drink." He said to someone.

I looked at him again. "My side is throbbing."

He nodded. "With good reason. Here," he lifted my head and held a straw by my mouth, "have a drink."

I took a few sips, then leaned back down.

"I'm sorry, Kara."

I turned my head to see Beth beside the bed. "I think you got shot when I was trying to knock the gun out of his hand."

"It's okay. We did what we had to." I told her.

She nodded and leaned into Leone's arms, still looking upset.

I remembered she got shot. "Are you okay?"

She nodded. "It was just a scratch."

"Kara."

I looked back at Rafael.

He searched my face. "I want to heal the incision." His eyes connected with mine. "With my blood."

"A transfusion?"

Rafael shook his head, "no, honey, you have to ingest it."

"That's yucky." I said trying to stay focused.

He smirked. "If I do, it will be like you were never hurt at all."

My eyebrows went up. "You're that good, huh?"

Chuckling softly, he kissed my forehead. "Yeah.

I considered how I felt about drinking blood. I honestly didn't know, having nothing to base my decision on. "I just drink a cup of your blood and presto I'm like new again?"

"We'll get to the logistics shortly." His tone was serious now. "Before I do this, I want you to understand that we'll have an emotional bond after I do. It will wear off in a few days, but I'll still be connected to you for a short time."

"Emotional bond?" I tried to focus on the expression in his eyes. I couldn't tell if he was afraid or worried, maybe both.

"Yes. I'll be able to sense how you're feeling."

"Will I feel what you do?" The pain in my side was increasing.

He shook his head. "That's doubtful."

"How is that fair?" I asked him.

"Its not." He told me. "I don't want to do something you'll be uncomfortable with."

I nodded, then offered a slight smile. "That's okay, I can hear what you're thinking, so that will even it out."

He smirked.

"I can't believe you're actually explaining it *all* to her before helping her. She's got to be hurting right now." Paisley said.

Turning, Rafael looked at her where she stood with Arius. "I have watched *all* my mated brothers make *all* the mistakes, Paize, I'm learning from their disasters."

Arius frowned at him. Paisley smiled.

"Smart man." Daxx said.

"Suck up." Quinton said in a gruff voice.

Rafael looked back at me. I reached up and touched his cheek. "On one condition."

He raised and eyebrow at me. "Name it."

"We take this needle *out* of my arm."

He nodded. "We can do that."

"Allow me." Alona came around the bed and touched my arm. She did it so quickly I barely felt it.

"Thank you."

She nodded, then moved back from the bed.

"Okay, everyone, get out." Autumn clapped her hands together. "I'll go check on Tawny." She told me with a nod, then waved her hand at the door. "Out. Let's go."

I lay there watching Rafael as he watched the others leave.

"Sorry for all the trouble." I said softly. "First you have to drink gasoline to come find me and now..."

He stood up and shook his head. "None of it is your fault." Standing there with his hands on his hips he looked down at me. "We've got patrols out looking for anyone watching the palace." He pointed a finger at me. "As soon as you're up to it, we need to get started on training the archers." He nodded, "if anything, this incident has shown us we need more watchers around the palace."

I nodded. "Guess you better give me that miracle blood then."

Rafael grinned and pulled his shirt over his head.

After the initial shock., I felt my cheeks heat up. I hadn't lived under a rock and I'd seen naked male chests before. Just not this close, or ones that looked *that* good. It was like he'd been sculpted, and each muscle was defined.

"Kara up here."

I looked away from his body to see him pointing to his face. I nodded.

"You don't drink it from a cup." He said quietly as he walked to the other side of the bed. "You have to drink it fresh, from the source," he winked, "the closer to my heart, the better."

My eyes flicked to his chest again. Was he saying I'd have to put my mouth on *that* chest? I felt my cheeks go red again.

Rafael lay down beside me, propped up on his elbow. "You're killing me." Reaching over he brushed the hair back from my face. "Why do you have to be so friggin' perfect?" He whispered.

I looked back to his face. "I'm not."

He gave me a hard look. "You are for me." He touched my hip. "Roll this way, carefully."

I bit my lip and moved slowly. The slightest adjustment made the throbbing pain worse. I hissed out a breath and closed my eyes.

"You're beautiful, sarcastic—a bit lippy at times..."

I looked at him again.

"Intelligent, strong, talented," he paused and studied my face for a second, "brave—perfect for me." Taking a deep breath, he exhaled slowly and reached behind his back to pull out a knife.

My eyes went huge.

"I'm going to nick my chest, you need to drink quickly because it will close fast." He held my gaze until I nodded. "We'll do it twice and then take a look at your side, okay?"

I nodded again, unable to think of a single thing to say that wouldn't come across like, yes *please* let me drink your blood.

"Ready?"

I looked at the blade he held to his chest. "Yes." I glanced away when he cut, then blood was running down his chest. Leaning closer, I licked. Closing my mouth around the cut I sucked gently.

Rafael hissed out a breath and held the back of my head.

I'd licked my finger once when I'd sliced it, but my blood didn't taste like this. *I liked this.*

When it sealed, I lifted my mouth away and looked up to see that his eyes were red. Without a word, he sliced into his own flesh again.

By the time it healed closed, I was held tight up against his body, and honestly didn't know who had moved.

Rafael took a ragged breath and tapped my hip. "Let's," he blew out a breath, "let's take a look." He sat up and pulled the robe, *I hadn't even realized I was wearing,* open and pulled the large bandage off my side. "How does it feel?"

I tried to think beyond the heated thoughts I was having. "It's not hurting anymore."

Leaning down, he touched his mouth over it, then licked along it.

I sucked in a breath and watched him. He looked up at me, his red eyes locked on mine. Lifting his mouth away, he looked at me and then down my half-exposed body.

"I have to go before I take this too far." He leaned down and kissed the same spot again. Getting up, he picked up his shirt. "Stay and rest for as long as you need." He studied me for a second. "I'll see you at dinner."

I lay there staring at the door after he'd closed it. Never had I felt the urge to be with a man. Never. Usually their thoughts repulsed me.

I looked down to see the robe gaping open. Lifting my head, I looked at my side. It was red, but other than that, there was no way to tell I'd been shot or operated on.

Putting my head back on the pillow, I took a deep breath. Reality returned in a second. Tomorrow I was going to walk back into the place I'd spent twelve years trying to get out of. I needed to find something to do or I'd be a complete headcase and totally useless tomorrow. I stopped and looked out the window. It was almost dark. How long had I been out for? I looked around, then realized I was going to have to walk through the palace, down the stairs to get to my room with my clothes in it. My room. In a palace. I shook my head. That was surreal, even if I was living it.

Chapter Thirty-Three

Standing inside the entrance, my heart was racing, I couldn't get my feet to move. We'd met the contact outside the building, then everyone went in together, all fourteen of us. The others were speaking with the administrator and as hard as I tried, I couldn't get my body to move beyond this point. I shouldn't have come. I shouldn't be here. My mouth was dry, I was sweating, all sounds around me were muted. I saw Rafael's head snap around and look at me. He knew what I was feeling. He turned around and looked at me. It was like he was moving in slow motion toward me.

I saw him in front of my face, his mouth moving but I couldn't hear anything he was saying. His touch against my face registered slowly, a feeling of warmth filled me. I didn't know how he was doing it.

"Hey," I heard his voice finally, soft, whispering and steady, "you're not the same girl that escaped," he said quietly.

I tried to lick my lips and speak, but I couldn't find the words.

"Slow your breathing," his thumb stroked the along my jaw in a hypnotic motion. Back and forth, back and forth. "That's it."

I tried to snap out of it, afraid they would see me behaving like this and recognize me.

"Relax, Beth is blurring us so they can't see."

I jerked my chin up and looked at him. How did he know? I looked back down, trying to sort out my head. Trying to wash away the memories flooding my mind.

"You're not alone here, we're all with you." His voice was almost mesmerizing. "Look at me."

I blinked and looked back up at him.

"You have the control. Push the button on your porter and you are out of here." His eyes searched mine, "you're in control, not them."

His words pushed through the fear, the panic. I took a deep breath, trying to force my body to function.

"Kara," his concerned eyes locked on mine, "I've got you." He nodded. "You're not alone here, you'll never be alone again."

Licking over my dry lips, I nodded in a twitching fashion. "Okay." I swallowed, then took another deep breath and blew it away.

Rafael was nodding slowly, watching me. "You're going to the file room with the girls." He said in a hushed voice, "looking for potential patients for our new program."

I listened as he reminded me of the cover story. I nodded again, feeling less unsteady.

"Put your earpiece in and dial into the group call, we're all right here with you." Leaning down, he held my gaze waiting for me to acknowledge what he'd said.

"Yes." I whispered. "I can do this." I said more to myself then him.

"I know you can." Leaning down, he kissed my mouth softly.

I fumbled in my pocket for the earpiece and put it in my ear. I nodded to him as he straightened. Pulling out the phone with shaking hands, I tapped the group button and then put it back in my pocket.

"Turn the earpiece on when we all go in." He told me, then turned around and put his hand behind my back to help me move forward.

"We're having to be stealthy and mind the scanner." Chase's voice said softly through the earpiece. "Victor is going to distract the administrator as we continue on without them."

Paisley looked up from the computer screen. "This is going to take a lot longer then we planned."

Bethany and I opened the top drawer of the filing cabinets that filled the room.

"Most of the files older than five years are still in paper form." Paisley turned around and looked at us.

Beth started at one end and pulled a file. "What are we looking for? There has to be a way to skim through these faster."

I glanced to see she was looking at me when she asked. "Ah, look for notations of delusions, hearing voices…"

"Believing in alternate realities?" Daxx suggested and turned to look through the window at us.

I nodded. "That would work too."

"Just rhyme off room numbers or names and we'll steer our guides in those directions." Michael said.

"I'm getting bad vibes from the staff, many more than from the residents." Leone abruptly commented.

I paused, staring at the folder in my hand, trying not to remember. A feeling of warmth filled me, like a big hug only no one was near me.

"Kara, what's beyond the big green doors?" Troy asked in a quiet way.

I blinked. "Isolation units." I frowned and looked at the folder in my hand.

"Paize, check on computer and see who is in there." Arius said. "My gut says some of our people might be held there."

"On it." Paisley said turning back to the computer.

Beth nodded and stood there waiting for Paisley to list off names.

"Quinton, you still keeping the staff occupied in that meeting?" Leone sounded amused.

"Yes." Quinton hissed, "thank the gods Emil's contact is doing the talking—no idea what the hell he's saying though." He whispered. "Five minutes and I'm out of here though."

I put the folder back and pulled out the next one. Opening it, I skimmed down the patient information sheet. 'missing' was written across the bottom of it, with a date. I flipped the page down to look at the first page for the name. *Karalene Coffey* I stood there staring at the name, then flipped the page up again and read the intake assessment information. "Karalene." I whispered. "I think my name is Karalene."

Beth turned around and so did Paisley. Beth came over and looked at the folder open in my hand. She gave me a pleasant look. "It's a pretty name." Slowly, she took the file and closed it. "We'll take this with us."

I nodded.

"Kara?" Rafael's voice broke through the static in my head.

I gave my head a quick shake. "I'm good." I cleared my throat and looked at Bethany. "What color is at the top of the file? Beside my name?"

"Orange." Beth said then gave me a strange look.

I nodded, then looked around at the bulletin board beside the filing cabinets. "If I'm orange, then," I ran my finger down a faded color chart, "from orange up on this are the files we should be pulling."

Paisley stood up, "scan all those in isolation. We have files to pull."

"Will do." Arius said.

"What colors?" Paisley looked at me.

"Orange, red and yellow." I said.

Bethany nodded and started pulling folders out. "You go through them, Kara, you'll spot it before we do."

Never in my life would I have imagined that my time in this place would be useful for something. I went over to where they were piling files and opened the first one.

"Entering the isolation unit now." Michael reported in a hushed tone.

"All clear in the back." Autumn said in a normal voice. "Porting out from here would be easiest."

I shook my head and closed the folder. This patient was here from an accident. Opening the next one, I turned to see Bethany and Paisley on the bottom drawer of the cabinets. I glanced at the pile, there had to be fifty folders to go through.

"Black beside it means?" Bethany asked.

Paisley leaned over her shoulder and flipped it open. "Deceased."

"Oh." Beth put the folder back.

"Two from isolation so far." Chase said in a normal tone.

"What is their state of health?" Alona asked.

"Poor." He replied.

"We're ready here." She replied.

Alona and Crissy had remained behind in Alterealm to help with those coming in. There had been some discussion of me staying behind, but I insisted I had to be here. The notion of facing my demons hadn't been far off.

I set the folder aside with the last two. "Let me know when you're ready for room numbers." Beth grabbed the pile of those we weren't going to scan and started stuffing them back in the drawer.

"Give us a few more minutes here. We're being slowed down by a staff member that doesn't think we should walk them out." Rafael said.

"Carry them out if you have to." Quinton suggested in a not pleasant tone.

"Coming to you, Autumn." Leone said. "Two to port."

"Let me know when." Alona told him.

"Will do." He answered abruptly.

"I don't even need to scan these." Chase cut in. "They recognize Troy and I immediately, I can see it in their eyes."

"I'm bailing on this," Quinton said. "Stay there Leone, I'll bring them to you to port to med."

"Understood." Leone said.

"Quint?" Michael said in a strange way.

"Yeah?"

"We found Detrick." Michael voice was hollow.

"What? He's here? Is he coherent?" Quinton sounded like he was running.

"I wouldn't say that, but he's alive." Emil said quietly.

I gave Beth a questioning glance. She shrugged; she had no idea either.

"He's been here for the last fifteen years?" Leone asked.

"So it would seem." Victor stated.

"You can return with him if you like, brother." Troy told him.

"No. He'll be in good hands with Alona until I return." Quinton said. "I'll stay until we're finished. I don't know how this happened, but however it did, we need to be sure it never does again."

Paisley gave Bethany a teary-eyed look.

"How many more?" Alona's voice was just as emotional.

"Four, so far." Michael said.

"I've got him." Quinton said. "Yeah, Deet, it's me." Quinton's voice was strained. "You're going home."

"First two, Alona." Leone said in a hoarse voice.

I snapped out of it and looked at the folder in my hand. *Wants to go home to some place called Alterealm.* I set it in the to scan pile. Bethany and Paisley were looking through the pile now too.

"We have at least fifteen here so far." Paisley said.

"Give us the list of numbers in a minute, we'll split up and pre-evaluate before we get the scanner to them." Michael told me.

"Should have brought more scanners." Leone said.

"We didn't understand the scope of the task." Victor growled quietly.

I set the file on the scan pile and it slid off the desk, scattering papers on the floor. Kneeling, I reached to pickup the pages when dark red print circled many times popped out on me. I picked it up and read it. My eyes went wide, I grabbed the rest of the pages and stood up. "The one with green eyes, I know who it is." I read the note in my hand again. "People have died near him more than once."

"He could have been starving and it was an accident." Leone offered.

"Or he's lost it and it a genuine lunatic." Rafael replied.

"He'll have to go to the cells for assessment." Arius' tone was cold.

"Change of plans." Chase said. "Sparky, write a list of rooms and give them to Kitten to run to us. We need to expedite our visit, the staff is starting to ask questions."

"Arius, suggest to any getting a little too curious to go wait in the staff lounge." Troy said.

"I've got it." Arius said.

"Sarg, you've got watch outside the office. Pack up those files ladies, then meet us outside the main activity area." Chase said.

I gave Bethany a quick look, not understanding who he was talking about. She smirked and started writing down the numbers from the files. Understanding that she was Sparky, I opened the folders and pointed to the number, then grabbed the next one as she wrote it down.

"Alona, the man coming over is my best friend, see if you can help him." Quinton said.

"I will stay with him until you can come back." Alona said softly.

I took a shaky breath and tried not to get emotional. Opening the pack, I held it as Bethany stuffed folders into it.

"The guy your man paid to drive the bus is asking questions, Emil." Autumn said.

"I'll come chat with him when I'm done here." Arius answered.

"Oh. Okay, good." She said.

The contact that had set this up for us, had arrived in an old bus with a driver, to enforce the illusion we were transporting patients away on a bus. It was a good plan, but my stomach was going to be in knots until we were all safely back home in Alterealm.

I froze standing in the doorway. *Home* in Alterealm. I'd never had a home before, not really. I looked at the pack as Bethany put it over her shoulder. In that file with my name on it, would be people listed who's blood I'd come from, but didn't know. I turned to see Paisley waiting outside the office, then back to Beth as she gave me a quick smile and walked to the door. These people could be my family if I wanted, I realized, brothers and sisters. What about Rafael though, I definitely didn't want him as a brother.

My phone buzzing in my pocket startled me. I pulled it out and looked at it, it was a message from Rafael. We were on a call together, but he's messaging me? *Meet me at the bottom of the stairs by the office.* Stepping through the door behind Bethany, I paused and then held the phone for them to see. Paisley motioned to the stairs with her chin and nodded.

They went in the other direction. I realized then that they all must have studied the layout of this place, because they seemed to know it better then I did. I rolled my eyes at the ridiculous thought. Of course, they knew it better than I did. Twelve years of my life had been spent confined in one wing of the entire building. I quickly went to the stairs and opened the door. Rafael was running down the steps toward me. He jumped down the last few and landed in front of me. Reaching, he pulled the earbud from my ear and pushed the button on it. Touching his own, he took a deep breath and looked down at me.

"Are you okay?" His concern was genuine, reflecting in his eyes as he watched me.

I opened my mouth to say I was, then gave him a quick shake of my head. "I- this is a lot."

Putting his hand against the back of my neck, he gently pulled me closer, then wrapped his other arm around me.

I wrapped my arms around his waist and rested my cheek against his chest. As I did a feeling of warmth and caring, although I didn't know how I knew what the feeling was, filled me and wrapped around me at the same time. I closed my eyes and just stood there listening to his heartbeat against my ear.

"We're almost done. They're taking several to be ported out now." He gave me a squeeze, then leaned back.

I looked up at him. "If you hadn't figured out the color system, we'd still be scanning everyone we walk past." His eyes searched my face, "you don't have to stay if you don't want to."

I shook my head. "I'll stay until everyone else gets out."

His expression was guarded as he looked down at me for several seconds. Taking a deep breath his touched his ear. "On my way. Arius get your ass there in case we can't knock him out." He said gruffly. He smirked, "that's your deal not mine." Then dropped his hand. "I have to go." Grasping my chin, he leaned down and placed a firm kiss on my mouth. "Go wait with the girls." Holding out my earbud, he pushed the button.

I took it and whispered, "Be careful."

His eyes lit up and he smirked, then ran up the stairs.

I put the earbud back in.

"...working our asses off up here and you're having a quick rendezvous?" That was Michael.

Someone chuckled. "Jealous much, brother?" Chase said.

I put my hand over my mouth as I walked down the hall to the main visitors' area. The mic had been on when I'd whispered to him.

"Arius, are you crawling here or what?" Rafael asked.

"On the stairs." Arius huffed out a breath. "Couldn't be on the main floor," he said breathlessly.

Someone snorted. "Try a few hundred steps in full gear." Michael said.

"Quinton, your friend is malnourished and dehydrated from the medication, but otherwise physically without injury." Alona said softly, "mentally will take some time however." She paused. "I thought you'd want to know."

"Thanks, Alona." Quinton's said in a monotone voice.

I went around the corner, then hit something I couldn't see. Something grabbed my arms, then Bastian appeared in front of me. I covered my mouth so I wouldn't scream.

"So sorry." He smiled. "Princess Kara, fancy meeting you here."

"Is that Bastian?" Troy asked.

"Yes." I whispered and continued to stand there like a statue looking at him.

He dropped his hands and tucked them in his pockets. "Entirely my fault," he waved a hand around, "my kind are very distracted in places like this."

"Why is he here?" Rafael barked into the mic.

I winced. "Why are you here?"

He raised an eyebrow, then smirked and leaned over, motioning to my ear, "may I?" He didn't wait for an answer, just pulled the earbud out of my ear and put it in his. "Well hello, Alterealm people." He grinned and looked behind him. "No, no I'm afraid duty called, so here I am." He nodded, "Yes. Even the clinically insane have need of my favors."

I glanced behind me, to make sure we were still alone.

"So glad I ran into you, or the princess. I'll pop by later for a visit, I have some news." He grinned a daring grin down at me. "Ah, of course, Captain." Bastian nodded, "here she is." He held the earbud out to me. "Later, princess." He disappeared right in front of me.

I put the earbud in and put my hand out in front of me and waved it around. I didn't touch anything.

"Kara?" Rafael didn't sound happy.

"I'm here." I started walking again, faster this time. "He just appeared out of nowhere." I whispered.

"Hate when they do that, bunch of show offs." Quinton said.

"Get to the visitor's area, we'll be there shortly." Rafael said.

I nodded but didn't reply.

"Alona, the rest are coming over one after the other. Shout if you need me to pause." Leone said.

"We've instructed them to step forward after they land, but some aren't very alert." Autumn added.

"How many?" Alona asked.

"Sixteen. In a row." Leone said, "we have to do it before anyone comes out.

"Okay, we're ready." Alona said.

"Arius, wait. He looks familiar." Quinton said.

"Victor is that…"

"I believe so." Victor answered Michael before he could finish.

"Holy shit." Quinton hissed.

"What are we missing?" Chase asked.

"The green eyed one is—was one of the palace guards that disappeared, uh," Michael stopped for a second, "before you were born."

"He's aged." Victor said abruptly.

"Probably came close to starving a few times." Quinton said.

"Okay, so you go in first, if he's still right in the head, he'll know you. Victor." Rafael said in a quiet way.

I reached the visitor's area and rushed over to Bethany, Paisley and Daxx. Beth put out her hand and I took it. All of their faces reflected my feelings, we couldn't get out of here soon enough. I turned to see most of the orderlies were in the staff area on the other side of the plexiglass. Emil and the man that had arranged for us to be here were still talking to them.

"Keep the needle behind your back, Michael." Victor said.

I spotted someone I wished I didn't remember. Blowing out a breath, I looked at the floor. I'd made it this far without losing it, I wasn't going to let it happen now.

Beth squeezed my hand. Emil stepped closer to the window and looked out at us. Everyone was paused, waiting.

"Do you know who I am?" Victor said in an icy voice.

I couldn't hear if the person replied.

"We're here to take you home." Quinton said gruffly. "You will land in the cells for the time being, but we'll be there shortly."

"Yes. The twin kings are outside the door." Michael said, his tone lighter than the other two. "You've missed much but get to go home now."

"See I told you standing where he could see us was a good idea," Chase said.

"Yes, and I'm sure he'd fall at your feet and revel in your glory— if he wasn't chained to the other side of the wall, brother." Troy said sounding amused.

"Porting him from here." Michael said.

"I'm ready at the cells. I'll hit the scan button." Crissy said.

I hadn't realized Crissy was at the cells. I looked at Beth, she shrugged.

"Let's get downstairs," Arius said, "this place gives me the creeps."

Someone snorted, "now you know how your prisoners feel when you stand there glaring at them." Quinton said sounding like his normal self.

Bethany let go of my hand, her shoulders dropped in relief.

Paisley turned and watched the doors the guys should be coming through.

"Ladies," Emil said. The three of us turned around and looked at him, he jerked his chin toward an attendant coming toward us from the room he was in. "She says she needs to see you and she's…interesting." He said.

She came over, glanced at the pendant each of us wore, then inclined her head slightly, when she raised it and looked at us, her eyes were red. With a smile, they went back to a normal color. She grabbed my hand and shook it and then walked away. I held up my hand and looked down to see a note in it.

"Her eyes went red." Beth murmured.

"Whose eyes?" Michael asked.

"One of the attendants, and she recognized our pendants." Paisley said.

"She gave me a note." I voiced as I turned my back to the room and opened it.

"Which says?" Chase asked.

"Call me. It's important. Your loyal servant. And there's a phone number." I told them.

"As I said, interesting. I referred her to you ladies as there are too many watching in here. We have about five minutes to clear out. Our friend is running out of things to say." Emil informed us.

"Do we have someone undercover over here?" Leone asked.

"Not that I'm aware of." Michael answered.

Troy and Chase came out the door from the stairwell and started toward us.

"Is there a name?" Victor asked.

I looked at it again. "No."

"Keep them in the room for a minute, Emil." Rafael said.

I looked to see him coming through the door and even beside his brothers, he looked larger than life to me as he came toward me.

He looked in the room where Emil was. "Which one, Kara?" Rafael's voice grated through the earpiece. "Is he still here?"

I looked at him as he crossed the room. "Rafael, we got the records we need to…"

"Which one?" It wasn't a question this time, not really.

Closing my eyes, I took a deep breath and then opened them and looked at the staff members they had horded into one room. "The one with the awful moustache."

Victor stepped in front of Rafael as he moved to go to the room.

Rafael smacked him in the chest. "This is *not* for you to do, brother." His tone sent shivers down my spine.

Victor inclined his head and stepped aside.

"Shit." Michael had been heading to the back where Autumn was, he spun on his heal and hurried back down the hall. "Turn him over to the authorities here, Raf, we can't interfere in *that* way. Not here, not like this." He caught him and grabbed his arm. "We can't send him to the cells."

Rafael shrugged off his arm.

I stood there, heart racing as brothers stood face to face, glaring at each other.

"This is *my* job," Michael said, "don't do it brother." His voice had softened.

"I'll handle it." Arius brushed past me. "He'll turn himself in, with a full confession."

Rafael looked at Arius as he went past him.

"Get your mate out of her nightmare," Arius said quietly as he opened the door for the staff members coming out.

Without a word, Rafael turned and came to me, taking my hand, he started walking quickly down the hall. I almost had to run to keep up. We went around a corner, he stopped and pulled me tight against him. "Hang on." He said quietly.

Squeezing my eyes shut, I clung to his shirt. My head filled with white noise.

"Sorry," he whispered, then kissed the top of his head.

I opened my eyes to see we were in the courtyard.

Stepping back, Rafael ran his hand over his hair. "I'm sorry I couldn't find justice for what happened to you."

I frowned, "can Arius do that? Make him turn himself in?"

Rafael paced a few feet then stood there with his hands on his hips starting at the ground. "Oh yes." He made a sarcastic noise, "and much more. Probably told him to hate himself for the rest of his life or," he flung his hand in the air, "something. Arius is *very* creative when he's programming people."

"Programming people?" I inhaled slowly, taking the scent of the lavender in. It made me feel calm.

"He can get inside a person's head and tell them to do things, and you don't remember him doing it." Closing his eyes, he exhaled.

"That's…" I couldn't put into words how I felt about that. "Later I'd like more details." I went to the bench and sat down. "I'm a bit shaky right now."

He jolted like someone hit him and turned back to me. "you shouldn't have been there." His expression turned to anger. "I don't know what the hell I was thinking to let you—"

I cocked my head to the side. "Let me?" I shook my head. "No one has that power over me, not any more. I *wanted* to go. *I wanted to help free people that shouldn't be there*, Rafael." I stood up, thankful that my knees didn't shake, and went over to him. "And thank you." I put my hand on his chest and looked up at him. "For helping while we were there, I don't know how you knew and were able to calm me down and reassure me when you couldn't see me, but," I nodded, "thank you."

His jaw clenched a few times as he looked down at me. "Through the blood bond. I felt your fear, panic…" He hissed out a sound of annoyance and pulled his phone out. "The others are waiting for us in the meeting room." He motioned to the door.

Chapter Thirty-Four

We walked into the room together. All of the others were already there. Rafael didn't say a word, just went over to pull out the stack of files from the pack Bethany had carried, then set them on the table. He pushed through them one by one. I knew the file he was looking for. Finding it, he picked it up and opened it.

I watched his jaw clench as he flipped through the pages.

"We need to get those files to medical, so they're aware of what was used on those people." Alona said softly. "Some of them are in bad shape."

"What does the doctor say about their recovery?" Troy asked.

Alona sighed, "it is too soon to tell."

"We need to speak to Detrick and Gudrun as soon as they're able." Michael said glancing to Victor, then Quinton. "I still can't believe Gudrun is alive."

Troy straightened up from where he was perched on the table. "I'd like to read through these files before we turn them over to the doctor."

Chase nodded. "I agree."

Quinton rubbed his hand over his brow, "I never knew what happened to Deet, he just vanished."

Victor crossed his arms over his chest. "We need to find out how that happened, as well as how this many people were being held in the same facility—I do not believe it is a coincidence."

"Especially with that woman with the red eyes being on the staff there." Arius added. "We need to find out what she knows."

Michael pinched the bridge of his nose for a second. "I'm concerned with trusting her, to start with, but we still need to call her."

Troy nodded. "We'll look into that tomorrow."

"If we have to start checking all facilities like that for missing people, it's going to be a massive task." Leone glanced at Rafael, who was still looking at the pages in the folder.

Rafael walked over to the wall with the maps on it. He stood there with his back to everyone looking at the file. "Daxx," he said abruptly, "do you know where this is?"

Daxx gave Troy a hesitant look, then went over and looked where he was pointing in the folder. "No, never heard of it."

Rafael nodded his head once. "We'll have to look it up."

"What are we looking up?" Troy asked in that tone that told everyone he was in charge.

Rafael turned around. "Where Kara's *family* is." He snarled.

Victor cleared his throat, "while I understand your need," he glanced at Michael, "to find answers for Kara, we have other tasks that must take precedence, brother."

Rafael closed the folder in his hand and glared at Victor then he pointed to Crissy, "if it was your mate, you would burn every building in your path to find justice for her." His tone was low and lethal.

Victor stood there without movement and looked at him. "You are right." He nodded. "I would do, and have offered to do so many times." Giving Crissy a gentle look, he turned back to Rafael, "she doesn't want to relive her past, only move forward with her future."

I held my breath and watched, not even sure of what I was feeling.

Rafael shook his head, "she deserves to know why she was dumped there." He said through clenched teeth.

"I'm with him." Autumn pushed away from the table she'd been perched on. "Kara deserves answers." She looked at me. "If she wants it, I'll help."

I bit my lip and turned my head slowly to see everyone in the room was looking at me. Every expression said it was my call, entirely my decision. I'd never had options in my life. I'd never had people that were *for* me and not against. I didn't know what I wanted. For the first eight years I'd wanted to see my family, wanted to know why. Why had I been put there. Why no one came to see me on visitor's day, ever. The next four years I didn't care, my only objective then was to figure out what I had to do to get out.

"Kara..."

"Give her space." Rafael told Bethany.

I looked at her, then to him. Today I'd gone back there, something I never would have dreamt I could have done. I wasn't courageous, not in the slightest. I looked at Rafael's steady gaze as he watched me, assessing my state of well-being. Turning I glanced to Chase, then Paisley, they were watching too. I couldn't even describe what the looks on their faces meant. They were concerned and worried but stood there waiting. Everyone cared what I thought, what I felt. I mattered. My opinions mattered.

My throat seized closed, my heart was pounding in my chest. I wasn't freaking out, not the way I normally did. This wasn't panic, this was pure emotion, one that I didn't think I'd ever feel. I tried to clear the invisible obstruction out of my throat.

Logic, I needed to work this out logically. I was standing in a room, in a palace. A palace in another realm. I looked at the floor, then around at the others. In this other realm there was a family—*family* that had taken me in. Taken me in even though I'd shot one of their brothers. I tried to swallow the lump in my throat again. And, *and* despite all *that* they cared about me.

I felt a tear roll down my cheek but didn't move to wipe it away.

"Chase," Alona whispered.

Chase moved across the room to her and put his arm around her. Alona's face reflected the emotional turmoil I was feeling inside.

"Sorry," I said softly. I didn't want to upset her.

She shook her head.

Bethany came over, "Kara, it's okay."

I nodded, tears now running down my face.

Daxx lifted her arms in a jerky motion and looked at Troy, then back to me. "Do you want us to hunt them down?" She nodded, a scowl on her face. "*I'll* hunt them down; you don't need to cry." She looked at her mate again. "Troy, she's *crying.*"

I shook my head. "No, no. It's not that." My whole body was shaking and I couldn't get the tears to stop. "I'm I-I know you would and-and it," I wiped at my face, "thank you." I nodded, not sure what else I could say. I looked at Chase, then to Paisley, "thank you."

Rafael came over quickly and gently took my shoulders. "Honey, it's okay," he said softly.

"It is." I grasped his shirt in both hands. "I matter." I looked up at him, the tears blurred his face. My voice was barely audible and I couldn't seem to speak. "I can't-I didn't," I shook my head, then gasped trying to breath, "I matter but it doesn't, not before—" I rested my forehead on his chest, "they're not my family." I sucked in a breath. "Not really."

"Raf." Chase said in a quiet warning.

"Come on," Rafael put his arm around me and coaxed me toward the door.

I walked, blindly following where he guided me. The tears were slowing, but the thoughts in my head weren't. I couldn't focus as all the thoughts hit me at once. I heard him opening a door, then closing it. Wiping my eyes, I looked around. It took a minute to register that this was my room. The rest of the furniture was here and it was beyond anything I could have every dreamed of. *My room.* I had a room here. The room was three times the size of anywhere I'd ever lived. I'd selected the furniture, not from a second-hand store or someone's discarded belongings on the curb, but beautiful, well-cared for furniture and it was mine.

The damn broke again and I started crying uncontrollably. I felt him guide me across the room, until something hit the back of my legs. I sat down.

Rafael dropped to his knees in front of me, grasping my face between his hands gently. "Honey, talk to me. What's wrong?" He kissed my forehead softly, "how can I fix it?"

That made me cry more. "You can't." I said, "there isn't." I shook my head.

He wiped the tears from my eyes, so I could see his watching me. The pain in them stunned me. "I don't understand."

I took a deep breath and blew it out, trying to catch my breath so I could speak clearly. "There's nothing wrong." I whispered, my voice cracking as I did. "It's all right. Just-just so very right."

The confusion was clear in his expression.

"I've never had anyone," I put my hand over my mouth when my emotions threatened to spill over again, "anyone that cared about what happened to me." I shook my head, "never mind so many."

Relief showed in his eyes. "*Of course*, we care about you. All of us."

"I don't know anything about all of," I waved my hand around, "this. Royal stuff. A palace and-and, what if I do something I shouldn't? I don't know how to have friends. What are the dynamics of family? How-how do I do what I should do if I don't know what that is? You-you all give me choices. I don't know what to chose. You ask my opinion like-like it matters. I don't want to let anyone down."

He gave me a soft look. "Even at my age, I'm still learning. No one expects you to know everything," he smirked, "we leave that up to Crissy." He kissed a tear rolling down my cheek with such tenderness I hiccupped and tried to breathe. "If you make mistakes, so what. You think we haven't?" His eyes reflected the most powerful thing I'd ever seen. Love. Understanding. "If you knew how epically we've screwed up in the last hundred or so years, you'd run the other way." Another feather light kiss to my face. "We don't expect perfection." This kiss was placed on one damp eyelid, "I don't care what you do, I will always see you the same," the other eyelid with a loving a touch, "even when I was pissed that you sunk an arrow in my ass, I still thought you were the bravest, most beautiful woman I'd ever seen." He smirked, "I wasn't happy about it in that moment either, but the more you revealed who you are, the more my anger was filled with something else." His lips gently brushed over mine, "pride."

Taking a deep breath, he backed up and looked at me with such compassion I had to take a breath so I wouldn't start bawling again. "I have a lot to learn in this life and I would like to do it with someone." Blowing out a quick breath, he gave me a nervous look. "I have never *not* known what to say to a woman, but with you I can't seem to speak, or I babble like a moron." He blew out a slower breath, then looked at my eyes and didn't blink. "Karalene Coffey I'd like you to be my mate, in all ways—officially bonded, tattoos and all." He visibly swallowed then inhaled deeply, "I know we don't know each other, but I feel like we've known each other forever. I think you're the answer to my prayers, If I prayed— the solution to my problems and the only thing I need to succeed in life and everything it throws at me." He gave me a nervous smile. "I'm sure I will piss you off and make you want to shoot me again, many, many times in the next few centuries, but I promise I will always listen to you, I will always support what you need and always, always be there so you're not alone." He squeezed my hands gently, a vulnerable look in his eyes, "you don't have to answer me now, but please think about it."

I felt like someone poured cold water over my head. I opened my mouth to tell him I would think about it and I thought he was crazy. Me? Why would he want someone like me? I had issues. A lot of issues. Probably more issues than even I knew I had. "Yes." My mouth said with great conviction. No explanation, no thought, just that one word.

He gave me a hesitant look. "Yes, you'll think about it?"

I shook my head. "No, I won't think about it." I wasn't lying. If I thought about it, I'd run away. All I needed to think about was how he made me feel. Even the small things like holding my hand when I was nervous or scared mattered more than anything I'd ever known in my life.

His brows drew together.

"Yes. I will be your mate." Was I insane? Maybe. Did I care if I was? No. Nothing had ever just *fit* like this did. He wasn't perfect and it did seem like he had as much baggage as I did, but I felt safe with him. Always.

Rafael leaned back, still holding my hands and studied my face, I think he thought I was joking. "You will be my life, not just my mate." His smile went beyond one of the charming ones I'd witnessed before. I felt like my bones might be melting. He grasped my face and kissed me. Not brief, not teasing, but so passionate I was sure my soul was being fused to his at the very moment our tongues touched.

Lifting his head, he looked at me with red eyes. "Now?" he nodded quickly. "Please say now."

I blinked, "I-I don't know how…"

He gave me a grin, a complete player's grin, "your body will know what you want. Do what feels good for you."

I felt my cheeks heat.

Standing, he gently pulled me to my feet. I got lost in his smile he. He helped me take off my jacket, and dropped it on the floor. My nerves caught up to my spring-loaded mouth.

"I don't know how this bond happens." I blushed, "I mean other than *that* what I'm assuming happens, happens."

Rafael kissed my mouth briefly. "Yes, *that* happens. Fate does the rest." He took off one of my gloves, then the other one. With his eyes locked on mine, he shrugged out of his coat and dropped it on the floor.

I stood there as if my feet were cemented in place, staring as he took off his shirt and tossed it aside.

Reaching over, he took the earbud out of my ear and tucked it in his pocket before undoing his jeans.

I swallowed while trying to remember how to breathe.

Without a word, he lifted my arm and took off my bracelet. Kissing my hand, he placed my palm against his chest.

I glanced at the warm flesh under my hand, then looked back to see he held a knife.

"We need to do a blood exchange." His voice was deeper, barely more than a whisper.

I nodded unable to speak through the sexual tension taking a hold of my body and the lust seeping into my brain.

...honey, you keep looking at me like that and this is going to go way too fast...

My face felt hot. I looked back into his eyes, they weren't blue but weren't red yet. "I'm nervous."

Leaning down, he kissed my mouth softly.

...me too. I don't want to screw this up with you...

I gave him a surprised look. "I'm pretty sure you know what you're doing."

"My past. Anyone in my past doesn't matter. There's only you from now on." He looked at my neck, then to my mouth. Taking my hand, he turned to sit on the bed. With a gentle tug I was sitting across his lap.

...only you...

My heart had never beat this fast before. I dragged air into my body and tried to blow it out slowly but couldn't manage that.

...don't overthink it, just feel...

I nodded, afraid to speak and say the wrong thing.

...after the blood exchange, you'll be able to feel what I feel...

Eyes wide, I looked into his eyes, to see he was telling the truth. "Do-do you have to cut me too?"

He shook his head, then his eyes went completely red. He smiled, making his fangs visible, then winked at me. "No cutting required."

I'd forgot he had fangs. How someone could forget something like that I wasn't sure.

Watching me, he cut into his chest above his heart. I heard the knife clunk on the floor, then he cupped the back of my head and gently guided me toward him.

Licking the trail of blood, I wasted no time closing my mouth over the cut. Rafael sucked in a sharp breath, his hands clenching in my hair. The gash in his skin closed quickly. I lifted my head to see his red eyes focused on me.

Still holding my hair, he pulled my head gently to the side and lowered his. I felt his breath brush over the skin in my throat. Without warning, he bit me then lifted his head, his hot breath feathering over where he'd bitten. When his mouth closed around the bite and he sucked, my whole body flushed, completely aware of him.

As he lifted his head, I turned mine and kissed him for the first time without him initiating. Feeling what I could only describe as lust ran through me. Breaking the kiss, I stood up, then gave him a gentle push so he lay back on the bed. I had no idea what I was doing, only knew what I wanted. Him. Kneeling over him, I leaned down and licked over his chest. He made a guttural sound that echoed through his chest as my mouth moved up.

...too much of that and I'll embarrass myself...

He grasped the back of my head and gently pulled so I would move up to his mouth. I may have been on top of him, but he was in control of everything from that point on. He kissed me in a way that made my head light, my body hot and my mind go blank. I reached down and undid his jeans, then let out a frustrated sound when I realized there was no way I could get them off of him.

Rafael sat up, me sitting on top of him. He broke the kiss and pushed my shirt up to expose my waist.

I pulled it over my head and tossed it aside. He undid my bra and pulled it off my shoulders just as fast. I gasped and hugged his head when his mouth moved over me.

...so beautiful...

When he lifted his head, I leaned down and kissed his neck as he had done mine, he lifted his chin giving me access. I attacked his neck with my mouth and teeth, unable to stop the feelings rushing through me.

Grasping my waist, he stood up. As soon as my feet touched the floor, he bent down and started undoing my boots.

I wasn't even sure where they landed when I kicked them off. Lifting the cuffs, he pulled the knives out and tossed them out of the way. I took over when he was trying to undo my belt and jeans, and pulled them off quickly. As soon as they hit the floor, he grasped my hips and bent, kissing the sensitive flesh of my stomach. I sucked in a breath and held onto his shoulders as my knees threatened to give out.

Feelings of lust, need, and about ten others I didn't recognize flooded me. Panting, trying to breathe, I looked at his expression as he stood in front of me.

...so consumed with you I can't think, only feel...

Even his thought echo was raspy with need. I reached for the waist of his jeans and shoved at them. He pushed them past his hips and down, then sat to untie his boots, and push them off each foot.

I leaned over and pulled the jeans from his legs. As I straightened, he grasped my hips again and leaned back, pulling both of us onto the bed.

Crawling up his body, until my mouth was level with his, I hesitated, not sure what to do next.

"You set the pace, honey."

...it's all you. Only you...

I nodded and wanted to ask what I should do when his feelings washed over me again. Urgency, and need so deep it hurt. Gasping, I raised up on my knees and was glad he helped me. As I lowered myself onto him, I forgot how to breathe. There was moaning and I didn't know if it was from my throat, his, or simply a thought. Everything else faded and no longer mattered.

I looked down to see the intensity, his red eyes heavy with lust, his chest rising and falling in an uneven rhythm. I looked at my hand, wondering if it mattered which one...

...*left*...

I held out my left hand, he closed his left hand around mine, locking our fingers together.

...*honey you need to move now*...

The urgency of his thoughts were accented with a blast of passion through our bond. I used our clasped hands as leverage to keep my balance so I could move, after a moment I didn't need to think, my body took over.

The noises, I realized were coming from my throat, echoed by his own. Tugging on my hand, he put his above his head, forcing me to stretch out over him. The friction from our flesh contacting only enhanced the feelings that consumed me. My body was reaching, but I didn't know what for.

...*let go and stop fighting it*...

Grasping the back of my head, he pulled it to the side and lifted his. He bit into my neck without preamble and the pain mixed with the pleasure had me crying out his name as my body flew over the edge. I think I screamed, but couldn't focus enough to know. My whole body spasmed and shattered into the most blissful feeling I'd even known.

Releasing my neck, Rafael, shifted and flipped me over onto my back without leaving my body or releasing my hand. He moved with sure thrusts and took my body back up for a second time. I squealed as he tensed.

I swore I was floating, actually floating. Sounds started to return and all I could hear was our breathing.

Rafael kissed my neck and rested his face on the bed beside mine.

...you're amazing...

He kissed my neck again.

...as soon as I can breathe, we'll do that again... slowly...

I smiled and turned my head to rest my cheek against his.

Lifting his weight onto his elbow, he pulled our still clasped hands up, so they were held in the air. I looked to see a tattoo that started at his shoulder, wound around his entire arm, through our entwined hands and all the way up to my shoulder.

"It's beautiful." I whispered.

"You're beautiful." He leaned down and kissed me, slow, lingering.

I felt him stir inside me and despite what we'd just done I blushed.

I had no idea what time it was or how long we'd been here. I didn't care either. I lay there with my head resting on him as we lay on the bed, shaped like a T. "Do you think my name is pronounced Kara-lean or something else?" I turned my head and looked at him.

"What do I know? My name is Rafael," he smirked at me, "could be worse though, could have a name like Eugene or Herman."

"Gah, I said that, didn't I?"

He chuckled. "You did, right after saying something about my buns of steel."

I grinned, then lifted and eyebrow, "they are very nice buns."

Music started playing.

"Ignore it." He said quickly, then rolled and pulled me up to lay face to face with him. Brushing the hair back from my face, he kissed my nose. "I think Karalene is a beautiful name."

"You say it like Caroline, only different." I played with the dimple in his cheek as he smiled at me. "I like it."

He kissed me softly.

"Can we go horseback riding again soon?"

Moving back, so he could see me clearly, he searched my face. "Yes. I'll have to arrange guards and lookouts, but you can do whatever you want." He gave me a serious look, "you know, that right? You're now very officially," He held up my tattooed arm, "a member of the royal family."

I looked at my arm, then back to him. "Really? I wasn't sure if I could do whatever I wanted."

"Only thing you are not allowed to do is ignore me if your safety is in question." His expression was serious.

I nodded. "Got it. You're the security expert."

He grinned. Turning, he looked at the little fridge in the corner. "What's in the fridge? Tell me there's water."

I leaned up on my elbow. "Yes. Chocolate milk too and snacks for Tawny."

Rolling he got up and went over to the fridge. I couldn't help but admire the view of muscle as he moved with grace to the other side of the room. "Your tush doesn't even have a mark on it." I blushed when he gave me a look over his shoulder. "Which I'm thankful for."

Coming back over, he handed me a bottle of water, then lay back down and took a drink from his own.

The music started playing again. With a loud sigh, he reached over the side of the bed, and rummaged around in his clothes and picked up his phone and looked at it. Heaving a sigh, he flopped onto his back and set the phone on his chest and tapped the screen. "Yeah?" Putting his arm under my shoulders, he pulled me closer.

"Ah, good, you answered *finally*."

It was Chase.

"First, Kara is well?"

Rafael raised an eyebrow at me in question.

I blushed. "I am fine Chase."

There was a pause. "I'm sure you are now."

I could feel him smiling through the phone.

"Is there another reason you're calling me?" Rafael asked.

"No, I just missed your sexy voice." Chase chuckled. "Yes, and I'm now getting that 'this is serious' look, so dinner has been pushed back for a short bit because Prince Bastian is on his way over."

Rafael picked up the phone and looked at it. "Where are we meeting?"

"Meeting room." Chase said.

He tapped my arm so I would move, and we could sit up. "We're bringing him to the palace?"

I sat up and looked around to see where my clothes might be.

"Yes. Fewer eyes on him here." Chase said something else, but it was muffled.

Rafael nodded and swung his legs off the bed. "Yeah, staff is limited here, no chance of others finding out." He stood up.

I sat there, clutching the sheet to my chest staring at him.

...don't start thinking like that or we'll never get out of this room...

My eyes snapped up to his face, my cheeks heated as he grinned at me. Smiling, I stood up, dropping the sheet. His gaze moved over me slowly.

"Brother?"

Rafael grimaced. "What?"

"I asked if you were on your way." Chase sounded amused.

Rafael nodded. "Yes." He tapped the phone and tossed it on the bed, then gave me a leering smile. "If it weren't important, I'd have food sent here and skip dinner."

"I'm starving now." I told him, "and I have to feed Tawny..."

He picked up his pants. "Fine, but unless the realm is on fire, we're coming right back here after dinner."

My face felt hot again. "Okay."

Chapter Thirty-Five

We paused outside the doors to the meeting room, Rafael pulled me closer and leaned down and kissed me, making my head spin all over again.

The door opened and Quinton stood there. "Never mind, he's right here." He looked at me, then to Rafael, "and from the moony eyes Kara's giving him, he's bewitched her."

Rafael chuckled and pulled me into his side and brushed past Quinton.

"I'd say it's a bit more than a bewitching by the mates marks covering their arms." Chase said with a big grin on his face.

I looked over to see Bethany and Paisley with huge grins on their faces.

Crissy streaked across the room and threw herself at me. "Welcome to the family." She squealed.

I hugged her back, very thankful I'd remembered to turn on my bracelet.

"This is wonderful." Alona said, then raised her eyebrows at me, "you will have to share details, as we like to discuss which brother outdoes the other, and who we place on the Neanderthal list."

Rafael kissed the top of my head, then headed straight for the coffee pot.

I went over to the table and looked at Autumn, "he proposed." I said feeling my face get hot when I thought of after the proposal.

"Excuse me what?" Daxx shoved by Troy and gave me a wide-eyed look.

"Oh my." Alona said with a big smile.

Leone rubbed his hand over his face and looked at Rafael. "You really did?"

Rafael went over to the fridge at the end of the room and opened it. He gave Leone a huge smile. "I *really* did. I made sure she *knew* what I was asking."

"Shit." Leone said under his breath.

Troy and Chase exchanged a look, then glanced to their mates.

Rafael came toward me, coffee cup in one hand and a glass of chocolate milk in the other. "Told you guys, I watched your disasters and wasn't going down *that* path."

Quinton grinned and shook his head, then turned to look at Michael. "Little brother made you all look bad," he gave Troy a long stare.

Chase waved his hand around. "Impossible. I never look bad."

Rafael set the glass on the table, then pulled out the chair and turned to me. He gave me a heated look.

I went over and sat down in the chair.

Daxx smacked Troy, who jolted, then he pulled out the chair for her.

Victor stood, his arms crossed over his chest, chuckling. He pulled out his phone and looked at it. "Prince Bastian will be here momentarily."

We had all barely gotten seated when Ira brought the prince into the room.

"Well, well, back in the palace." He looked at the thrones at the end of the room. "I haven't been here since I was a child and your," he looked at Troy, "grandfather sat on that gilded throne." He looked at each person in the room, I figured he was doing whatever he did with souls. When he reached me, he cocked his head to the side and smiled at me, "I see your soul is very thoroughly bonded with your mate's, princess."

Putting his arm over the back of my chair, Rafael motioned to the empty chairs. "Grab a seat."

Bowing his head, Bastian sat down. "I'll get right to the point then." He ran his hand through his already messy hair. "It's been one of those days." He looked at Troy, "Your Willis Hubert is a tricky one to track." He sat back and crossed his arms over his chest. "I found him a few times, then lost him—" he shook his head slowly, "mostly due to incidents that are out of my control."

"How do you know it's his soul?" Leone sat forward, resting his arms on the table.

Bastian looked at him for a moment. "Its hard to explain, but souls have a color," He motioned to Quinton and Emil, "Prince Quinton's is pure Alterealm, so its grey and silvery." He nodded, then motioned to Emil again, "Prince Emil's has that same color, but there's human's white brilliance mixed in." Looking down the table, back to Leone, "age changes the color somewhat, older souls and all that, as well as…" he motioned in the air, "I don't know how to describe it, people of bad heart and intention are different…"

"Aura's have colors too." Crissy blurted out. "Yours is," she bit her lip, "interesting. I wonder if it's different because of where you're from or…"

Bastian smirked, "that's very intriguing."

"Perhaps you could discuss aura colors at a later date, Crissy." Daxx suggested.

Crissy nodded. "Yes. Sorry, it's just fascinating that souls have a color." She looked back to Bastian. "What color are souls from your realm?"

"Clear," he gave a slight shrug, "mostly."

"So, you'll be able to find Willis again?" Michael asked, a no-nonsense look on his face.

Bastian nodded, "yes. I need to set up a quick way to reach you, because as I said he's a tricky one, I may not have a long enough window to draw a map or wait."

Troy looked to Victor. Victor nodded, "we could set up a group call, then you would reach all of us and which ever one of us is able to react the fastest could get there."

Bastian nodded. "That would be best. I'm on my off schedule for the next day, so I have time to do a little hunting," he grinned, "between other things." Turning he looked at Rafael, then to me, "of course if we leave off the newlyweds, I'm sure no one will balk at it." He winked at me.

Victor cleared his throat and then looked at Paisley, "could you set up another..."

Paisley nodded as she did something on her phone, "working on it now," she glanced up at Bastian, "I'll need your phone."

Bastian stood up and walked down the table, he handed her his phone. "Have at it, Princess." He tucked his hands in his pockets, "if you could figure out how to block my brothers while you're there, I'd be eternally grateful."

Paisley smirked and shook her head, "I don't get involved in sibling issues." She glanced down the table, "or I'd be too busy."

"Ah, fair enough." He turned and looked around the room, "I like your style, Whitham Royals, no stuffy thrones and constant ceremony." He turned to Chase, "I might have to acquire vacation property here." Paisley handed back his phone. He looked at it. "Whitham group." He shrugged, "good enough." Saluting, he turned toward the door. "Talk soon."

I looked around the room again.

"It's huge isn't it?" Bethany said across from me.

I nodded.

We were having our first dinner in the dining hall. It was four times the size of the dinning room in the chambers, with carved arches above our heads, matching the window frames.

There wasn't a lot of decoration, but the room was still elegant and fancy.

"Dare you to come in here and set dirty swords on this table, Raf," Leone said grinning.

Rafael shook his head, "I'm pretty sure I wouldn't survive if I came in here in battle garb covered in," he waved his fork around, "stuff."

Chase laughed, "I think we should dress for dinner from now on."

Daxx glared at him.

Michael shook his head, "you're the only one out of all of us that loved that era."

Chase shrugged, "could be worse I could love the seventies."

Alona laughed, "no one loved the seventies, not even the people living the seventies, they were just too stoned to know it."

All of our phones rang at once.

Daxx held up hers and then set it on the table and hit the button.

I hit the red button on mine.

"Bastian?" Troy leaned forward and looked at the phone.

"Yes." There were some sirens in the background that faded. "I need you to get here now. I-I don't know what I'm seeing."

"What do you mean?" Victor stood up, leaning on the table.

"I've found one of yours, who is up to no good with one of mine." There was noise in the background, "but that's not what I'm concerned with, there's a mixed soul here—staying hidden, that I've never seen before—ever." He hissed out a breath, "oh and there's humans, mostly, in some sort of dangerous predicament and need aid."

"How many are we against?" Michael stood up.

"Fifteen, roughly. Just…how is that possible? It shouldn't be possible…"

"Bastian," Daxx stood up, "where are you?"

"Oh, this soul is definitely not for me—"

"Bastian? Where?" Quinton wasn't quiet.

Rafael took my hand and stood up, he nodded to Leone, who was taking Beth's and standing up as well.

"Can I ping it on here? Damn technology, I love it. Ah, yes, I can. Incoming. I'm on the top level. See you soon." The line went dead.

I didn't know what was going on, just that I was going to need my bow.

KEEP READING FOR AN EXCERPT OF

The Healer

Alterealm Series

Book 8

By J. Risk

Prologue

She stood in the shadow of the trees, blood dripping from her hand. With cautious steps, she moved into the light toward the small, silent shack. Even though there hadn't been trouble in years, she was taking no chances. She looked around once more before opening the door and stepping inside.

"Rea?"

Rea rushed over and helped her mother sit up. "Slowly, Momma." Keeping a hand on her shoulder, she knelt in front of her.

Her mother reached out to lay a gentle hand on her face. "I was worried, you were gone a long while."

Rea motioned to the table where she'd dropped her kill. "Rabbits are getting scarce here." She pulled the blanket up and tucked it around her mother's shoulders. "We may have to move to a new area soon." Rea moved over to stir the coals in the fireplace. "It's getting too populated here." Her mother's cough had her turning back. It was getting worse by the day. Quickly she moved to ladle out a cup of water from the bucket and bring it to her mother.

Sipping the water, her mother took a few breaths, waiting for the spasm to clear before speaking. "I'm not going to be making any more moves, love."

Rea looked at the tattered gloves on her hands. "We could go into town with people—or, or I could go into town and get an elixir. If you'd let me help…"

"No, Rea. You've been doing that for too many years now." She shook her head. "I'm tired. I've lived lifetimes more than most."

Unwilling to let her mother see the tears in her eyes, Rea turned away. "Do you regret it?" She glanced over to see her mother sitting on the cot, that faraway look on her face again. She sat down at the table.

"Staying?' Her voice was shaky, "no, not for a second."

Her mother's health had been declining for the last ten years. When she was young, before her ability developed, they'd stayed around people so her mother could feed. Once they realized Rea couldn't touch people… their lives became a blur, always on the move, never staying anywhere too long. She paused skinning the rabbit to look around the small shack. As dismal as it was, they'd lived in worse places. "Tell me about it again, Momma." She knew the story by heart, but it always lifted her mother's spirit to tell her about where she came from, and how she met her father.

"I'd never been to this side before." She exhaled a loud breath, "we were advised to delay coming over until after the war. We knew we shouldn't come, but then we would have forfeited our turn and would have to wait for the selection, hoping that our names were drawn again."

Rea didn't interrupt when her mother paused, she knew she was reliving the emotions of the past.

"They made certain we'd come out in a safe area…" she made a noise of exasperation, "or as safe as any place could be. Kin fighting kin, it was madness. You know all of this, Rea…"

Rea pulled off her blood-soaked gloves and pulled on clean cotton ones, then got up to add some wood to the fire. "I know it, but I could hear it every day and never tire of it, Momma." She straightened up and looked at her. "Do you think your friends went back over?" Her mother's memory didn't always work lately, so anything Rea could do to help, she did.

Her mother blew out a breath. "I imagine they did." She shook her head. "I cursed myself for a week when we were separated."

Rea went back to the table and began to slice the flesh from her kill. "Would you truly have been arrested if someone had seen your devices?"

"Our porters? Yes. The light bulb didn't exist over here, not for fifteen years after we came over. Technology like our porters would have created chaos and worries of conspiracy..."

"I heard talk they have electricity in the city now."

Her mother smiled. "*That* is something I have missed."

"I hope to see it someday." Rea admitted.

"You will, daughter. You're going to live long enough to see many amazing changes in this world. Rea—I want you to do what you have to in order to survive and keep going. *Never look back.*"

Rea picked up the pan, full of cleaned rabbit, and placed it on the fire to brown the meat. She couldn't listen to her mother speak of when she was no longer there. "Do you think I'll live as long as you have?"

"You could live *much* longer than I. Your father was quite a relic when we met." She chuckled softly, "his words, not mine. I'm not sure how old he was, precisely."

The sizzling of the meat was the only sound in the small space for a few moments.

"All three of us gave our porters to Synova to keep in her clutch. I hadn't thought to bring one, or you wouldn't exist." She made a soft noise, "I'm glad I forgot." Another pause. "My only regret was I never did get to see the new kings. Your grandmother said they were blond and beautiful. The whole realm was alight with the promise of the prophecy being realized."

Using a cloth, Rea took the pan off the heat and set it on the table. Opening the cupboard, she hoped there were enough potatoes to turn the meal into a stew. "Do you think my father is still alive?" Rea knew anything was possible.

Her mother made a soft sound. "I don't know. Our love was forbidden since time began. When they found out we were together, they took him away. He would have loved you with all of his heart."

Rea looked over to see her mother laying back down.

"Don't go near any with eyes as dark as coal, Rea, you are the result of a love that shouldn't have been." Her mother closed her eyes. "I don't know what would happen to you if they found out."

Rea watched her breathing settle. "I won't, Momma." She whispered.

Waiting a few more minutes, until her breathing was the steady rhythm of sleep, Rea pulled the gloves from her hands and went over to her mother. Kneeling down, she placed her hand on her mothers' neck, as she did each time she slept. Rea knew it wasn't what her mother wanted, but she wasn't ready to face the world without her. "I'm sorry, Momma," she whispered under her breath, "I need you too much to let you go."

Chapter One

Hugging the bag gently against my chest, I ran up the last few stairs and pulled the door open. Loud voices had me crouching down behind the steel barrier. Why were they up here? No one came up here anymore.

With my chin hovering close to the dirty cement, I looked around to see if I could see where they were. This parking garage was rarely used. Maybe the first level once in a while, not the top two. People in this neighborhood couldn't afford cars. It was barricaded off for a reason.

Taking off my backpack, I opened it and worked the bag into it. My bread was going to be smushed now, and if the juice carton was punctured, I'd have a backpack of soggy fruit punch flavored bread. Doing up the zip, I put the backpack on, making sure the straps were tight. I wasn't impressed. At all. It had taken me two days of helping at the clinic to make the money to buy this food and a new pair of gloves. I looked at my new leather gloves. They were almost as important as food to me.

Sighing, I peeked around the barrier again. There was a group of men, a trace of black all around them, so bad men. They were herding six others into the corner of the garage. The same corner I needed to use to get where I lived. The six people were scared, rightly so, judging by the size of a few of those men. Three women, a young girl, a little boy, and a man stood in the corner huddled together. What kind of shake-down was this? Over a dozen douche bags against a few scared people.

I looked the men over, they weren't from any gang I recognized. There were no colors, logos or symbols showing, and they were carrying barbaric weapons. Seriously, carrying swords in this day and age? It was like a role play group gone wrong. I looked back at the door wondering if I could get out without being spotted? I could just wait it out in the stairwell and sit at the top until they left.

I closed my eyes berated myself—because turning the other cheek and pretending life was sweetly full of roses and pretty rainbows was *so* not in my D.N.A. I moved to the other end of the barrier and tried to find somewhere better to hide without being seen. I had no idea of what I could do against that many men, but I hadn't done anything stupidly heroic in a few months, so why not think about it? YOLO, right? You only live once. As far as I knew, that was true.

If I could move without making a sound, I could get to the large pillar and move into the dark corner behind the stairwell. *If*, was the key negative word pretending to be hopeful. It always led to thinking things were possible. Rolling my eyes at my own ridiculousness, I held the small pouch at my side, so the chain didn't jingle. As long as they kept griping at each other, I shouldn't be heard.

I watched and waited for the best opportunity, mentally psyching myself up to succeed. When the focus turned to the big guy in the middle, I hunched down and hurried toward the pillar. I probably looked like a waddling duck, but I was going to pretend I was moving gracefully and undetected across the floor.

Reaching the pillar, I braced against it before bending down to look around it. No one was looking at me. Good job, Rea. I touched my shoulder and gave it a pat. Another quick look and I made a split-second decision to rush to the dark corner.

As soon as I reached the dark, I ducked down, just about to lean back against the wall before I remembered my bread in my pack. I rested my arm against the wall instead.

A very unhappy looking man waved his hands around.

"Why here?" He demanded.

"In case it has escaped your notice, we're running out of concealed locations." The man in the middle replied tersely. "This place is hidden in plain sight."

The first man snorted, "well, if it's going to be a regular drop off location, we need to have chairs while we wait."

"Yes, your comfort will be our top priority. I'll bring it up at the next meeting." Was the sarcastic response.

"I think we should call, Nathas, they're late." Another man said while holding up his phone.

Nathas, the man in the middle, nodded, "message them first, it might be poor timing for a call." He turned to a man leaning against a pillar, his arms crossed over his chest. "You're sure about this bunch?"

The man nodded, then turned and looked over the scared people in the corner. "It's faint, but they have the right genes somewhere in their history."

Nathas smiled briefly. "Good."

I looked back at the man watching their captives. His eyes were as dark as coal. I debated about getting out of here, Momma's warning in my mind. Even if it put me at risk, I knew I couldn't do it. My shoulders slumped as I sighed silently.

I didn't know what genes had to do with anything. I did know I was outnumbered, more bad dudes were on the way, and I could see no way I could get all six people away from these men. I didn't *know* if they were a family, but there was no harm in romanticizing that it was a family huddled together—the family were about three feet away from my bungee. If I could get through the large men to them, I could grab one child, get over the railing and bungee down to my place. Probably. Hopefully. That half-baked plan left the other five with them and the role-playing failures would know where I lived.

Time for a new plan I shook my head. I had no other plan. I pulled out a chain from my pack, slowly to let it pool soundlessly beside me. My wannabe surujin wasn't going to be enough to get through all six men. I could probably trip up two, maybe three, but then what? Aside from cussing and sticking out my tongue. I had no other skills. I was purely a defensive 'run away' type of person, entirely self-taught.

I clenched my teeth together, growling inside my head. All I wanted was a jam sandwich and a glass of juice. Now, I going to be eating squished, misshapen bread and had to skulk around in this corner until they left as I watched them abduct the family/nonfamily they held captive.

The little girl was crying. Dammit.

Noise from loud footfalls coming up the ramp jerked my head around to watch. Their friends had arrived. A blonde woman charged at one of them, growling out a battle cry. Okay. Not friends. I watched for a moment as several more people appeared. They were also carrying barbaric weapons, but they were using them against the original creeps, so I decided that was a better option.

"Nathas Roan, you're a traitorous bastard." A large redheaded man bellowed.

Two of the women skidded to a stop and turned to see who the redhead was looking at. The one with the black hair rushed toward him. "I've got his feet." She told the other woman. She stopped a few feet from him and held out her hand toward him.

The blonde woman beside her snarled. "I've got his face." She did this little jump in the air and spun around and kicked him in the face. He went down, just catching himself before his face hit the floor.

"*What the hell...*" I whispered, in awe of what she'd done. I needed to learn *that*.

A tiny redheaded woman came out of the shadows, with bright orange sparks coming off her hands. I looked at my gloved hand, deciding I was in no place to judge. I watched her toss a flaming ball at the one they called Nathas, and he hit the floor.

"Leone." The tiny redhead said.

"Trying." One of the new arrivals grunted as he blocked the swing of a sword with his own much larger sword.

"I got him." The blonde woman that had rushed into the group ran toward Nathas, still being beat on. She slid toward him holding a box in her hand. I thought she was going to shock him, but instead he vanished.

Vanished.

Gone without a trace.

I swallowed. Okay that was a bit freakier than I was comfortable with, and freaky was my very existence.

The women spun toward those fighting.

I noticed two women standing in front of the abducted family. One was flicking nun-chucks back and forth, the other squatted down with a large blade in her hand. A man rushed for them, sword in hand when an arrow came out of nowhere and hit him. He crumpled to the floor.

I leaned around the corner and looked up. Standing up and leaning over the railing was a woman with a bow. Swords, bows, knives, nun-chucks and flying balls of fire. *What* the actual *F* was going on? Usually I was the only oddity in the room.

"Quinton!"

I turned back to see one of the good barbarians crumple to the floor. He was holding his side.

"I'm fine." He growled. "Get that bastard."

The man with black hair, nodded and turned to the man holding a blood-soaked sword.

I bit my lip and told myself absolutely not. They had this. It was probably just a small flesh wound. I moved out of the dark to one of the pillars, I saw a man running across the cement toward the one laying on the ground. The injured man shifted, trying to pick up his sword as he held his side.

Without debate, I ran out from my cover, swinging the surujin as I went. When I was close enough, I flung it toward the attacker that was about to impale the injured man. It wrapped around his ankle, I jerked and he fell face-first onto the hard surface. Letting go of the chain's handle, I ran past him to the injured man.

Jerking my gloves off, I grabbed the leather and tried to pull it away from his bloodied body. "You'll be fine." I told him, pulling the knife from its sheath at his side using it to ripping the leather of his vest apart.

He had a large slice in his side. I put both hands on it and pushed. "You'll be fine." I told him again, then glanced to his face. Brown eyes stared at me, with fear. "It's okay." I nodded. The brown hair hanging in my face started to turn to grey, I jerked my head, flipping it out of the way. I felt the draw, it was strong. Maybe I'd underestimated how bad his injury was. It must have been life-threatening to take this much energy for me to heal it.

"Stop." He told me, terror in his eyes.

I offered him a brief look, I didn't want him to see my eyes turning black. The blood stopped flowing out between my fingers. "It's slowing, you'll be fine."

"Stop." He growled and grabbed my wrists, trying to pull my hands free of him.

"Rafael, blueish-grey hair." Someone screeched.

"Victor, no." A blond man slid beside me and put his arm in front of me. "I had a vision of her."

A pain went through my chest. I couldn't heal him further. Pulling my hands away, I grabbed my gloves and stood up. I stumbled a few steps. I'd used far too much energy on him. Brushing past the woman kneeling down beside the injured man, I ran for the corner, hoping I had enough energy to get there.

"Stop her!" Someone yelled.

I grabbed the bungee and swung my leg over the railing. Holding on with all I had, I jumped over the edge. I misjudged and released too soon, then fell to my back on the roof below. So much for my bread and juice surviving.

"Where did she go?" I could hear them above me.

Opening my eyes, I saw a few of them looking down over the railing.

I rolled to my knees and stood, my head was spinning. I looked at the small shack at the back of the roof and stumbled toward it. Once I got inside, they wouldn't be able to follow me.

I was almost there when a man with messy black hair appeared in front of me. His eyes were as dark as coal...

He smiled. "I have so many questions for you."

I tried to stand without swaying. "Please, just..."

He held up a hand and looked behind me. "Leave her unharmed. I need to know how she came to be."

"We're not going to harm her, Bastian, we're getting her to medical."

I turned to see the man I'd healed standing there. He was on his feet, leaning against another man, but I'd helped him. He would be fine. They blurred, I took a deep breath trying to stay conscious, but my hair was now white and covered my eyes.

Damn, was my last thought, I wasn't getting that sandwich.

Everything went black.

KEEP READING FOR AN EXCERPT OF

Heart

Animal Senses Series

Book 1

By Jacqueline Paige

Chapter One

Blinking, Rayne glanced around. She was in the underground parking space in her apartment building and didn't even remember the drive. Her chest hurt, hands were vibrating and reality felt far away. Three times, she tried to extract the keys from the ignition, finally after fumbling she managed. *Come on, Rayne, get it together. Think!*

Her mind didn't want to accept the words that had come from Aiden's mouth, her fiancé. In all the years she'd known him, never had he used that tone. Scared her enough to send chills through her spine. She believed he meant every word. *I am not an idiot, I've always known he was a hard man, but the words turned my blood to ice and a part of me knows I'll never feel the same for him again.*

Taking a shaky breath, she groped around for her purse, feeling like she was moving through mud. Somehow, she managed to move and get out of the car. Her legs still felt like rubber, but she couldn't stay in the parking garage all day. Turning, she forced herself to move to the door.

What am I going to do? I can't marry a man like that. I'm not even sure if I can look at him now.

Stopping, she looked at the elevator door. Just the thought of stepping inside left her feeling suffocated and trapped. Hugging the purse again, she turned toward the stairwell. *Keep moving*—she had to.

Trapped, I am, aren't I? Trapped in a relationship. Just that one word showed her the next move. She had to get out of this relationship. Aiden was not her dream man, if such a thing existed, but he had been comfortable. Admitting that, she now accepted that the relationship was too comfortable to be real.

When she reached her third-floor apartment, she wasn't out of breath. But, as numb as she felt, she wasn't sure if she *was* breathing. Maybe this was just a dream and she'd wake up any second now. Giving herself a small reprieve, she let that thought marinate for a few seconds before reality came crashing back.

It took her two tries to get the key into the lock. *What had his associate said just before my world darkened? "We haven't found a body or any sign of him, Aiden."* Him, who? A body? *A body!*

As Rayne stepped inside her apartment the dreamlike veil lifted away, revealing reality. *A reality I'm not sure how I can live with.* She quickly locked the door, all three locks. Not it would protect her, Aiden had keys. Leaning back against the door she tried to calm down and think.

Aiden was some sort of mob, mafia...*whatever?* Standing there she waited to feel her doubts were unsubstantiated, but it didn't happen. Her fear *was* the truth. This explained the dangerous looking misfits he had in his employ. They had never quite *fit* she thought. Aiden wasn't a boy scout—she knew that. He was a powerful man, as his father had been, but what kind of power was now very clear to her. Closing her eyes, Rayne held a trembling hand over her heart, it was still beating too heavily. *I can't look at him again. Ever.* This only meant one thing...

She looked around the pretty apartment for a moment, taking two steps towards the kitchen before stopping. She had to leave, now. Everything was *his*. *He* paid for everything in this apartment, she worked in *his* gallery. Her whole world was controlled by *him*…

Moving in a slow circle, Rayne studied everything in sight.

Every. Single. Thing.

Bought by him, in one way or another. Taking a deep breath, she tried to exhale slowly. Failing, her breath huffed out in one loud whoosh. There was no alternative, she had to get out of here.

Today.

Right now.

Kicking off her shoes, she bent down, scooped them up, and headed towards the bedroom.

Faster than she ever changed before, the skirt was stripped off and tossed on the bed. Barely having both legs in her jeans, Rayne began pulling open drawers and cabinets, dumping the contests all over the bed. All she really owned were clothes, her beloved camera, laptop and a few mementos to remind her of her parents. All of it was going in her car. A thought made her freeze as she held the empty drawer over the bed— her car was in *his* name. Dropping the drawer on the pile, Rayne sat on the bed, defeated. In the mirror, a frightened woman stared back. Seeing herself was enough to jolt her back into action. Giving the frail looking reflection a determined nod, she made a solid decision. To hell with him. She was taking the car. He hated it, called it girlie, and complained it wasn't comfortable. *The car is now mine.*

Forty-five minutes later Rayne surveyed the bedroom. There was nothing left that she wanted. Leaning down and picking up the last bag, she went to set it with the rest. "This is pathetic, Rayne Andrews. Your entire life fits in six cases and a couple of purses."

She walked through the apartment for the last time, working out how to get all of the cases downstairs to the car without causing suspicion, when the ring of her cell phone pierced the silence. She looked over at her purse, the ringtone was Aiden's. A few seconds after it stopped, the phone on the table began to ring. *Can I do this?* Taking a deep breath, "Buy some time," she whispered aloud just before answering it.

"Hello?"

"There you are. You didn't answer your cell."

He may be using that soft tone, but she now *knew* what he was. "Oh, I was taking the garbage to the garbage room." Her hand shook as she held the phone and prayed that her voice didn't give anything away.

"Where the hell is that girl I pay to do that?"

Just the way he said it made her tremble. "I-it's Wednesday, Aiden. She doesn't come in today."

"Right. Listen baby, I may be here awhile. Could be most of the night..."

"That's—fine. I was heading to the spa shortly." Closing her eyes, she waited to see if he questioned that.

"Do you want me to come by in the morning to pick you up?"

For what? "Pick me up?"

He chuckled. "We have a brunch with Donny and his wife."

Letting out the silent breath she'd been holding. "Oh, yes please." *Please let me sound normal.*

"Okay baby. You go get all beautiful for me and I'll see you in the morning. Ten o'clock."

"Okay, Aiden."

"Love ya, baby."

"Me too." She hung up quickly. Suddenly gasping for air, Rayne tried to settle her nerves again. *Ten o'clock.* Looking over at the clock and doing the math, she had seventeen hours to disappear.

It took almost as long to get all the bags down as it had for her to pack them. Of course, if you're planning to pack your whole life up and vanishing, it would probably be easier if you didn't drive a *Cabriolet*. Fitting everything into the micro-sized car had taken more than one attempt. In the time it took to finish, she was much calmer about her decision to leave. Not that she had a choice, but she could always have a mini breakdown and cry her heart out, later. Right now, she needed a plan to figure out the next step.

The first stop was the gas station. Getting out of the car, she looked around, checking for Aiden or one of his men. *Great, paranoia already.* After she assured herself that he couldn't possibly know yet, Rayne walked over to the pump. As she lifted the card up to the slot, she realized that he could track her cards. As if the machine was going to grab it, she jerked her hand back and turned to get her purse. She'd need all the cash she had available. Looking over her shoulder again, she walked to the cash machine. This location was close enough to the apartment to not point in any direction— when she finally decided on which direction. Her hands weren't the steadiest as she punched in the numbers and requested the limit the machine would allow, the shaking increased when she grabbed the cash and stuffed it in her wallet.

Glancing around, she walked back to the pump, inserting a card to pay for the gas. It only took her a few minutes to decide she would hit a few more cash machines in the area to bypass withdrawal limits. Aiden might not drive by, but now she suspected he had people everywhere that would recognize her.

After the gas was pumped, she thought that a map would be a good thing, unless she planned to drive around Chicago endlessly—because that's the only place she'd ever driven. Reaching down, Rayne pulled out the nearest one, only to put it right back, it was a map of the one place she knew. Bending down, she studied the title of each map before spotting an oversized atlas with Canada in it. She grabbed that one. Before she could second guess the decision, she set it on the counter and waited for the clerk to ring it in.

With the receipt and atlas clutched in her vibrating hand, she went back to the car, hoping she could get through the next few moments without questioning what she was going to do next.

An hour later, she sat in an empty parking lot, trying to force a bagel down her throat. The atlas she'd purchased was propped against the steering wheel, endless lines of varying colors stared back at her. So many places and no idea where to go. She looked over at the glove box where she'd put her money–in a make-up bag no less. It had taken five different bank machines to empty her accounts of every cent she had. Her cards were now at their limits, accounts were empty and on a whim, Rayne had taken out a cash advance on the card Aiden had given her for emergencies. If this wasn't considered an emergency, she didn't know what was.

Focus, Rayne. Looking back at the map, she tried to wash down a bite with the lukewarm coffee. She knew making maps took a lot of work and was complicated in a way she didn't really care to understand, but they really weren't telling her anything. She needed her laptop and the internet to make a decision that the squiggly color co-ordinated lines weren't telling her. Sighing, she glanced around the parking lot. A hotel was at the far end. She reached down to pull the laptop case off the floor. Setting it on the passenger's seat, she opened it and hit the power button, praying for it to pick up a signal as she flipped through another few pages. There was a signal, not a strong one, but it would do. Bringing up a mapping site, she entered Chicago as the starting point. *Now what?* A starting point generally meant you needed a destination and that she didn't have. Flipping a few more pages, Rayne picked the first name that jumped off the page. Destination? Timmins, Ontario, Canada. Her heart was pounding as she hit enter.

Strangely, she felt relieved knowing she had decided on a location. Her resolve only faltered for a few seconds when she discovered there was a fourteen-hour drive to get there. Biting her lip, she looked out the windshield, not really focusing on anything. Was she ready for a fourteen-hour drive that would take her far away from Aiden? If she had translated the map correctly, where she was heading was right in the middle of nowhere. That meant there was less chance of her being found. Yes, she was ready. Picking up the notebook that was waiting for the details of *the* game plan, she started to jot down the directions, deciding after a few lines that she'd only write down the first five hours and then reassess her route from that point. She had no idea what it was going to be like driving this far.

Closing the laptop, she put it back on the floor and just sat there. Was she crazy for doing this? Yes, but she couldn't stay here and that left few options. She was alone, just like when her parents died. This time all the decisions to be made were going to be her own.

~

Her eyes felt completely dried out. Was such a thing even possible? She didn't know, but at the first drug store, she was getting some eye drops. Glancing at the time—again, Rayne squinted back at the road. *How long have I been driving now?* Four hours? No, closer to five, she needed to stop soon. A few hours ago, she had foolishly thought she would be across the border before planning a stop, but that wasn't going to happen. Driving at this speed meant she still had at least an hour and a half to go before reaching Mackinaw City and then another hour to the border. Considering the longest she'd ever driven passed an hour back, Rayne knew she wasn't going to make it. She had a newfound respect for people that drove for a living. The quick bathroom stop a few hours before hadn't been long enough. If she didn't stop soon, she was going to make mistakes and end up lost, or worse. Stopping would be for the best.

Blinking quickly, she tried to make her eyes not feel as dry and then focused on the sign she was coming to. A motel was thirty miles from here. Looking at the speedometer, Rayne attempted to do the math and calculate how long that would take, less than a minute later she gave up and decided it wasn't important. As long as she arrived at the motel before falling asleep. A few hours of rest, something to eat and a shower became the new goal.

After what felt like ten hours she could see the hotel's sign not too far ahead. Elation and a bit of pride filled her as she realized she'd made it to here without help. She was slowing down when she noticed two police cars sitting at the motel. All the hair on the back of her neck stood up. Aiden couldn't know she was gone already, could he? Would he involve police? Biting down on her lip, she thought he probably wouldn't, but she wasn't going to take any chances. Gripping the steering wheel tighter, her heart was crashing against her ribs at the thought that Aiden might find her. There would be more motels further away, and another chance to take a break.

It took several seconds for the sign she'd just passed to register. *I've done it!* She was almost to Mackinaw, at least that's what the sign had said. Taking a deep breath and fighting the grogginess that had been closing in for hours, she forced herself to keep going. Maybe a little air would help, not that it had a half hour ago, but it couldn't hurt. She rolled the window down, hoping it would help. Seven hours of driving, minus two very brief bathroom breaks and a stop for gas, and she'd managed to keep going. If she wasn't ready to pass out, she would be pretty impressed with what she'd managed.

After a few minutes of taking deep breaths she groaned, the open window wasn't working. Reaching for the radio, she fumbled with the buttons and flicked through the few stations that were clear, anything to sing to or even pretending to sing might work. She scowled at the radio. Turning it off, she stared at the road once again. "Okay," she tried to ignore how slurred her voice sounded. "Use your brain, get the blood pumping and drive." Wiggling a bit, she tried to sit straighter. "Great, my brain is already sleeping," she yawned while trying to see the sign that was getting closer. "Oh. Interstate one twenty-seven. I've been looking at that for what seems like forever," she mumbled to the eyes in the mirror. "And before that it was I31." She bobbed her head and tried to recall the roads before that. "One ninety...something, not that it matters really—It's not like I'm going to be going on the return trip," Rayne snorted and then laughed, not sure if it was delirium or exhaustion that had her talking to herself. "And what are you going to do when you reach your middle of nowhere in Canada, Ms. Andrews?" She glanced at the speedometer, even though she had no idea what it had said on the Mackinaw sign she'd just driven past. Clearing her throat, she looked at the reflection again. "I have no idea what I'm going to do. I didn't sit down and plot out a course of action before fleeing," she giggled quietly this time and then squealed as she drove by another sign. "What–ah, miles..." biting her lip a couple of times, she looked at the time. "Oh! A half hour!" Gripping the steering wheel with the very last of her energy, she focused on the road. "You did it. And the reward?" She attempted to smile, but yawned and erased what would have been the smile. "The reward is sleep."

Rayne stood, clutching the room key in her hand and looking at the car, deciding. With the way she'd stuffed the cases into the car, there was no easy way to get to the one that had the clothes she wanted, without taking everything out of the car. Did she care if she slept in something fresh? At this point, no, she would come back out later and sort out what to change into. As she started to head for the room, her brain flashed a warning. She wasn't feeling very trusting now. Turning back, she unlocked the car and reached in to grab her purse, money, camera and laptop. If anyone decided to pick up the tiny car and carry it away, she could get by with just this.

Stumbling into the dark room, she kicked the door closed. Her shoes were off in two steps, it felt glorious. Her leg smacked into the bed. Setting the precious items down on it, she shoved them to the other side and flopped down, face first. Had she asked for a wakeup call? The chances of a yes were high, but there was no way she could summon the energy to find out.

About the Author

J. Risk is a pseudonym used by Jacqueline Paige

I wanted to write a story that would fit into new adult levels as well as adult. Something that was serious with fun elements-- paranormal / fantasy that everyone could read and enjoy.

I've decided to use J. Risk as the pen name for this to separate this series from my other writing which is definitely adult reading material.

Jacqueline Paige lives in Ontario in a small town that's part of the popular Georgian Triangle area.

She began her writing career in 2006 and since her first published works in 2009 she hasn't stopped. Jacqueline describes her writing as *all things paranormal*, which she has proven is her niche with stories of witches, ghosts, psychics and shifters now on the shelves.

When Jacqueline isn't lost in her writing, she spends time with her five children, most of whom are finally able to look after her instead of the other way around. Together they do random road trips, that usually end up with them lost, shopping trips where they push every button in the toy aisle, hiking when there's enough time to escape and bizarre things like creating new daring recipes in the kitchen. She's a grandmother to eight (so far) and looks forward to corrupting many more in the years to come.

Jacqueline loves to hear from her readers, you can find her at

http://jacquelinepaige.com/
Twitter
Facebook

Author note:

Did you enjoy reading one of my books?

If so, PLEASE help spread the word on social media. You can help by sharing on Facebook, tweet about it, post something on Instagram, Pinterest. Posting a review on your favorite book sites go a long way to help authors. With your help in keeping my books "out there", I can continue writing to keep those stories coming.

Writing and promoting can be very time consuming. I love talking to readers, but the hours spent on keeping so many social media outlets current can become overwhelming and time for writing pays the price. If you can take a few minutes to help, that would be awesome. Thank you!

www.ingramcontent.com/pod-product-compliance
Lightning Source LLC
Chambersburg PA
CBHW051558100726
47898CB00001B/140